A Royal FAMILY

A Royal FAMILY

The Lion and the Butterfly
BOOK TWO

LINDA FERGERSON

A Royal Family

©2018 by Linda Fergerson

Published by Carpenter's Son Publishing, Franklin, Tennessee.

Published in association with Larry Carpenter of Christian Book Services, LLC.
www.christianbookservices.com

Cover illustrated by Rachelle Williams

Book production by Adept Content Solutions

Printed in the United States of America

978-1-946889-28-7

Dedication

Samuel, Stephen, and Joshua:

You are my treasured gifts from Father God.
I wouldn't trade you for any other sons in this world.

Forever,
Your Mother

Contents

Acknowledgments

I want to acknowledge Royalene Doyle, my first editor on this project. Without her early encouragement, I would have run away from this project. It seemed so impossible.

I also want to acknowledge Hope Flinchbaugh and her editing team at Hope Editors. Without Hope's vision to see this writing project as a novel, her selfless time and patience in training me, along with her content editing expertise and that of her copy editor, Pamela Brossman, this novel would never have happened.

Finally, I want to acknowledge my best friend, confidant, and prayer warrior, Judy Ackerman. She always believed in God's call on my life to write and never gave up on encouraging me forward. Her journalistic expertise was invaluable.

The present Jerusalem…
is in slavery with her children.
But Jerusalem above is free, she is our mother.

Galatians 4:25b,26

Prologue

"Kill her! Her children too! They sicken me! I want this family stopped! The earth belongs to me!" The serpent's poisonous words echoed through the darkened hall as his underlings cowered before him. The hall was deep within the castle, and was being guarded by a host of contorted nephilim descendants, part angel and part man.

The cryptic creatures gathered in a semicircle, and bowed before their bejeweled ruler. Claw-like shadows passed over dragon reliefs etched deep into the stone walls. The hooded eyes of the watchers, now awakened, blinked; their amber globes and squinted into the darkness.

A guttural rumble stirred the dank air as they came to attention. They trembled at the serpent's demand to annihilate the kingdom family, for it was not an easy task. They understood that if they failed, retaliation was certain and their fate sealed.

Light flashed from below and slashed through the darkness. The serpent pulled his black hood over his scaly head and recoiled.

"How dare she invade my realm? I hate her!" Through the dark mist, the reverberations of her song shook him to his core.

"Arise, Lord!" she sang, "Let your enemies be scattered. Let all who hate you flee before you!"

The evil hoard cringed at the power and authority in her words, and slunk backward into darkened corners.

She continued her melodious chords. "Your kingdom come. Your will be done on earth as it is in heaven."

The reptilian creatures covered their ears with their spindly claws.

"Eek!" one screamed, tormented by the power of the love-filled song. "How do we fight against such power?" Paralyzed, the evil host clung to the clammy walls.

From high above, the Lion of Judah heard his little butterfly's song and shook the second realm with a loud roar. A fire fell upon the cruel commanders and they slumped face down, parched and burned.

"Cowards!" their leader cried. "Why are you afraid of him? Fear me! Get up! We still have time to destroy his kingdom." They scrambled to the gates, and awaited the order to descend upon Jerusalem.

"Go! Attack with lies and death!"

Chapter 1

Jerusalem AD 35

A shrill scream echoed in the cool October air. High on Mt. Zion, Jerusha shivered in the twilight. She peered out from beneath a jujube tree outside her villa, and scanned the sukkah booths atop the limestone dwellings of the lower city. The last feast day of Sukkot was not a joyous occasion this year. The child's cry below signaled yet another innocent one being torn from his parents' arms, the price they paid for following the way of Yeshua. Imprisonment, floggings, and possible death awaited them. Poor souls. Even more excruciating would be wondering what happened to their child. Three years of Saul's persecution had taught most children of Yeshua followers where to run. Hopefully, this one knew to flee to her villa for safety.

Jerusha glanced back at the Roman decree nailed to the door. The wax from her grandfather's lion and butterfly seal a little faded, his connections with Rome keeping all who lived under his roof safe. Standing next to her, he towered above her petite five-foot frame.

Jerusha craned her neck so she could look up into his eyes. "How much longer, Grandfather, will Rome protect us?" The question had been haunting her for days.

The gentle giant's thick graying brows peaked, and he gently tapped her nose. "Call me Yogli in public, remember? No one must know I'm your grandfather."

A Roman soldier with Hebrew lineage, he stood guard at his own villa. Trained to hide his emotions, his blue eyes revealed little. The scar on his right cheek twitched though, and signaled his discomfort with her question.

Jerusha cringed at the thought of the temple guards ignoring the decree and tearing Sarah from her arms. How would the six-year-old orphan, who called her mother, survive? Where would she go?

Sucking in the cool evening air, she gritted her teeth and clenched her fists at her side, as anger threatened to override her fragile peace. Memories of the high priest and his son's mocking stares and abuse from the past tormented her. She closed her eyes and drew strength from Ruach Ha-Kodesh, who dwelled inside her heart.

"Holy Ghost help me bring my thoughts captive to obey Yeshua's teachings to love my enemies" she whispered into the wind. A tingling warmth spread through her whole body relaxing every muscle. Her breathing slowed and she opened her eyes. On Grandfather's arm, the sign she needed flittered its purple wings, a rarity at this time of year. Another butterfly joined it. She scooped them both in her hands, released them into the air, and smiled as they fluttered away.

"You do have a way with butterflies." Her grandfather's deep voice echoed the same words as the one who taught her about the chrysalis and butterfly.

My little lioness, never forget who you are. You are royalty. You are from the tribe of Judah.

"Father," she whispered. How she longed to fly away and find him, find a safe place to raise her family, if there was such a place.

"Grandfather," she cleared her throat, "I mean Yogli, I fight hatred every day. Saul conspires with the high priest and they scour the hills and villages outside the city for so-called "blasphemers", and drag them here to stand trial. I do not understand why the Sanhedrin hates Yeshua. What has he done to them? Why do they hate us?"

He ignored her questions, his hand on his sword and strode down the hill to find the child who screamed. She followed, doubling her steps to keep up.

"After sukkot, Timon takes another group out," he abruptly interjected.

The thought of her husband taking another dangerous excursion with orphans and widows to a safer place, stopped her in her tracks.

Yogli kept going, dust swirls kicking up with every step, his Roman sword clicking against his side. "Go back and get him. I might need his help," he added glancing over his shoulder. "And the children will need you."

He disappeared around the corner into the maze of limestone dwellings that led to the marketplace.

Exasperated that he had ignored her questions, she stomped her foot. His chuckle echoed back to her. Jerusha knew her grandfather understood her need for answers. Many times, he had repeated the exact same thing her father had said when she was little: "You ask too many questions." How uncanny. Although he had never lived with them, her grandfather sounded just like her father.

"This is not the time for talk." She jumped, startled by her grandfather's voice coming from behind her.

"How did you sneak up on me like that?" she hissed.

"My secret. I checked an alcove, a special hiding place for orphans and slipped through the back way. I'm going to need Timon. Two sets of eyes are better than one, especially now that my eyes grow a little dim and the city's filled with a multitude of outsiders for the feast. Tell Timon to look for me by the temple gate," he said and trotted down the hill.

Jerusha looked back up the hill at the boarded windows and locked gates. So many families gone. Interspersed among the silent, ghost-like homes, other families celebrated upon their roofs in makeshift booths, waving their palm lulavs.

In the middle of the cobblestone pathway, a donkey loaded with wineskins, pottery, and baskets of bread sat on his haunches. An old man tugged on its rope and slipped. Timon moved swiftly and caught him before he hit the ground. Her husband always seemed to be where Yeshua needed him most.

"Timon!" she waved and ran toward him, admiring his broad shoulders, his robe unable to hide the bulging muscles of his medium-sized frame.

"Jerusha, my little butterfly," he said and winked with thick, black lashes, a twinkle in his dark eyes. His mouth tipped up at the corner and made that endearing lopsided grin she loved, except of course when she was in an embarrassing situation. Then it was just plain infuriating.

"Where have you been?" he asked and lifted the older man upon his feet. Ten years her elder, Timon was loved by many people in the city, and especially in the lower city where he grew up. His thick black beard, blue and white cloak with the corded tizits that hung over a white linen tunic, was in stark contrast to the poorer man's tattered, yellowed outer garment. Timon himself used to dress similarly before her father's inheritance came to him.

"Thank you." The man expressed his gratitude and trotted after the donkey that decided to take off down the hill. Timon threw his head back and laughed from deep in his belly at the man's words as he berated the beast. Jerusha laughed, too. It felt good, like medicine easing her fears of what lie ahead.

"We heard another orphan's cry. Yogli needs your help to find him." She hesitated. "He said you're leaving soon to take another group out of the city. I heard the tradesmen talking in the market. They say they have seen small villages that have been pillaged by marauding Roman soldiers. It's hard enough not to worry about you being attacked by wild animals or thieves. Now this." She threw her hands out and flopped them at her sides. "Why do these zealots antagonize the Romans? Don't they know they can't win? Don't these rebels know they cause innocent Jews to be killed? If you are a Jew who has another King, like us, and won't pledge your allegiance to Caesar, it's worse. We have enough trouble with religious priests who hate us. We don't need to add the Romans to the mix. I asked Grandfather how much longer we will be safe and he ignored me."

Timon pulled her close and cupped her chin in his hand. "There you go again with all your questions. It doesn't matter, Jerusha; our destiny is in Yeshua's hands. I must go. Be sure to lock the gate. I can climb over and unlock it." He grasped her shoulders and kissed her forehead, his rough beard brushing her cheek, then ran to find Yogli.

"Look for him at the temple," she yelled, then turned toward home. The steps up the steep hill took more energy than usual. She slowed as she approached the top, sighed and rubbed her abdomen. *I must tell him soon. Not a good time to bring a son into the world. What will he think? With so many others to take care of, how will he feel?* It had only been eight weeks. She crinkled her brows together and squelched the giddiness of carrying his child. After promising him a quiver full, all she produced was one disappointment after another. Five times in the last three years.

During those months, when she came to see Timon in her father's carpenter shop, she noticed the older women wag their heads and whisper. Sometimes she overheard their sympathy for him that she hadn't given him a son. At night, she wondered the same as she lay beside him and listened to his dreams of teaching his son the same trade secrets her father taught him. Now, the fear of yet another disappointment crept into her thoughts.

Has YHWH cursed me? Am I not pure enough to carry a son for Timon? Is it the touches of the high priest and his son when I was little? Is that what's wrong?" she whispered, then remembered Yeshua's quiet words in her thoughts the last time she lost a baby.

"Delight in me and I will give you the desires of your heart."

The silver olive leaves overhead fluttered their response in the wind. *This time will be different.*

Chapter 2

S tanding outside her villa on Mt. Zion, she looked down at the holy city, a cool breeze caressing her face. In the darkening street, she straightened her radiyd, the beautiful head covering the widows wove from purple and blue wool, and admired the glistening white walls of the temple in the setting sun. The gaiety of the celebration below rose to a high pitch, the laughter and music abounding in joyful glee. She listened again for the faint scream of a child, her ears trained to hear the cries of abandoned ones. She hoped Yogli and Timon found him.

"Yeshua, when will this end? When will your judgment come?" she whispered. The iron gate clanged and beckoned her inside. The widows and orphans waited for her under their sukkah. The children loved this feast when they slept and ate outside under the makeshift booths, the palm fronds, myrtle and willow branches making a roof above their heads. The quietness inside the villa alarmed her, and she wondered if they heard the child's cry, too.

They understood more than anyone did what it was like scavenging for food in dark streets. They knew what it meant to be alone and hungry, hiding from ravenous wild dogs that preyed on the small and weak. Jerusha understood abandonment as well and recognized in them the vacant stare that signaled a protective wall around their emotions. She, too, was once the same, when she had been a child slave in Herod's palace.

Father, where are you? Are you alive? She thought of him so often these days, grateful for the inheritance he left, the large villa, the treasure box, and pendant.

They say you're dead, but I don't believe them.

She was disturbed from her musings by the sound of a bleating lamb on the path. She smiled and remembered making trips to the temple with her father, a lamb tagging along and led by a rope in her hand.

Before answering the gate's call to lock herself safely inside, she crossed the cobblestoned street, leaned on the waist high, grapevine-covered wall and searched again for Yogli and Timon. If the orphan was out there, they would find him.

"Moses, come here!" she yelled, uncomfortable that her words sounded a bit sharp. The gate banged and a youngster skidded to a stop in front of her, his breathing heavy. "I'm sorry, I didn't mean to scare you," she said.

"I-I-It's o-o-okay," the orphan stuttered, his slender frame towering over her. Especially tall for a twelve-year-old, he stood at attention, admiration in his eyes. She softened her words.

"Will you please light the lamps in the garden?" she asked. The eager boy nodded, ran along the outside wall that surrounded the estate, and disappeared around the back corner.

Jerusha crossed the cobblestone road, closed and locked the ornate gate. She wound her way along the pomegranate-lined path that led to the sukkah in the garden, the fragrant blossoms a welcome relief from the smell of sewage that drifted up from the lower city where Yogli and Timon searched for the child. She glanced at the wide-eyed orphans and widows gathered in the shadowy olive trees. Some of the children were playing hide-and-seek with her from behind the pomegranate bushes. Their playfulness reminded her of when she used to play with butterflies and dance for her father while he whittled on acacia wood and told stories. She had felt safe back then.

The wind carried another faint cry, or was it her imagination? Probably not. She was alert and protective, like a lioness, and it served her well. However, she found herself resisting the desire to cover her ears and run. What a quandary. One moment she longed for freedom to fly away, like a butterfly. The next moment, she stood ready to fight like a lioness from the tribe of Judah.

Many times during the previous two years, the children's simple trust in Yeshua's protection had encouraged her not to give up, and to stand strong against the evil forces that sought to destroy them. In those dark times, she coveted how easily the eye of a child could see Yeshua's love and majesty. However, lately she overheard them talking of death, killing, and jail. Way too serious topics for ones so young.

She felt a tug on her robe and looked down into the big, dark eyes of a young boy. She squatted before him with her hands on her knees , ever ready to give each orphan the individual attention he needed. His eyes blinked back tears. She took a deep breath and released it slowly, closed her eyes, and attempted to prepare herself for another painful conversation.

"When will my parents come and get me? he asked, "Will they be out of jail soon? Moriah's parents came and got him yesterday. I rejoiced with him like you asked me. You know, you said, 'Rejoice with those who rejoice.'"

"Yes, Hosea, I saw how hard it was for you and yet, you rejoiced with him anyway, even though you wished it was your parents coming to get you. I'm very proud of you."

Do you think my parents will come? Maybe tomorrow? After the feast is over? I'm packed and ready. I miss them. Can we pray for them tonight?"

Jerusha ruffled his hair, sat on a nearby rock and lifted him onto her lap.

"Oh, Hosea, you remind me of myself. So many questions."

"My parents won't die on the cross like Isaiah's parents, will they?" he whispered in her ear, then stared straight into her eyes, his palm on her cheek.

Jerusha's heart sank..

"Will they?" He pressed for an answer.

The pain Jerusha felt for the boy was almost unbearable. Almost daily, she had witnessed the unfairness and cruelty the little ones had to endure and it knotted her stomach. She wanted to scream.

Why? Why Yeshua?

She looked up at Chaya, Timon's mother, who closed her eyes and nodded, an indicator that Hosea's parents most likely would not be coming to get him. Jerusha figured he might be one of those who would go with Timon. After she checked with her husband, she must find time alone to talk to Hosea like she had so many orphans whose parents died for following Yeshua.

"Well, Hosea, I know you miss them. They miss you, too. As we do every night, I'll pray with you when we bed down. I think there's enough space between the branches overhead that you will be able to see the stars." She stood, straddled him on her hip, and motioned for the others to gather round as she sat him next to her on a bench.

"Are we still going to be safe here, *ami*?" Sarah asked as she climbed onto the bench and snuggled close, her tiny feet dangling. Jerusha loved her with a mother's heart ever since her cherished guardian, Stephen, passed from this life to live with King Yeshua. She loved all the children, but Sarah felt like her own. The tiny boned six-year-old never left her side.

Jerusha put her hand on her stomach, a slight nausea threatened. *How will Sarah receive this new baby? Will she be jealous?*

"Are they going to stone us like they stoned my uncle?" Sarah asked. Jerusha brushed her long black hair from her face.

Before he was killed, Stephen had taken care of all the widows and orphans, including Jerusha and her mother, Abigail. Now the responsibility fell to her and Timon. She looked over at her mother who stood beside the fountain, the water cascading into the blue-and-purple tiled bowl. Abigail's face shone with an inner meekness that enhanced the natural beauty that turned every man's eye in the marketplace, even at her age. The few wrinkles around her eyes were evidence of a joyful countenance, even after all she had endured as a slave in Herod's palace. Jerusha drew strength from the love in her eyes and glanced back at Sarah.

"Such a question for you to ask? Where's your trust in Yeshua?"

"Stephen trusted Yeshua and he was stoned."

"Did he fear death?"

"No."

"Did he love those who stoned him?"

"Yes."

"Did he want us to dance and celebrate Yeshua's kingdom rule on earth as it is in heaven?"

"Yes."

Jerusha pulled out the pendant tucked inside her tunic and rubbed her fingers over the lion's face carved out of acacia wood. The lamplight sparkled on the golden crown in the mane. The purple jewel on the lion's nose cast bouncing light beams on Sarah's face. They recited in unison the words engraved in gold on the back.

"Arise, Lord. Let your enemies be scattered. Let all who hate you flee before you."

Jerusha turned her gaze toward a deaf boy named Joseph and made sure he saw her hand signals and lips as she talked.

"My father made this for me. It's made from the same wood as the Ark of the Covenant that carried YHWH's presence." Joseph smiled. She pointed to the pendant's back. "The words I just quoted from the pendant's back are what the priests said every time they moved the ark. My father told me many stories about it. His favorite one was how dagon, the idol, fell before it." She held up her hands and wiggled them back and forth and fell to the ground. Joseph and the other children laughed. Jerusha stood and continued with her stories.

"Father also told me how the Jordan waters parted before it," she said and put her hands together and spread them wide. "And my favorite was how King David danced before it when it came into Jerusalem." She raised her hands and twirled around and around down the path.

"Jerusha!" all the children screamed at once. It was too late. She hit the pole that held up the sukkah roof and tumbled to the ground. The pole fell in her lap and that end of the roof landed square on her head, the myrtle branches and palm fronds covering her face and body. She heard a man's deep chuckle and felt the branches part in front of her eyes. There it was. That infuriating, lopsided grin.

"Timon, how is it that you always find me at the most embarrassing moments?" She heard the children's giggles ripple across the garden. She couldn't blame them. It must have been a hilarious sight. Timon removed the branches and helped her up. He put the pole back in place, and motioned for some of the older boys to fix the roof.

While brushing herself off, Jerusha heard a baby's cry and looked up. Standing next to a lamp on the wall was a beautiful young girl, the light from the lamp surrounding her with a soft glow. She looked to be about the same age as Jerusha, and she was holding an infant in her arms. She was smiling, and like the others, seemed to be enjoying Jerusha's humiliating situation. A young boy about two years old stood next to her. He must be the child she heard screaming in the lower city, obviously not an orphan because he called the woman ima.

What bothered Jerusha more than her humiliating situation was the way the young widow stared at Timon, her seductive eyes framed with long curly lashes. She touched the ugly black mole on her cheek and glanced at her husband, relieved to see his smiling eyes on her, not the beautiful newcomer.

Chapter 3

Hosea pointed a small finger at the newcomers. "Who are they?" He asked, his tone piqued with interest. Timon lifted up Hosea, and gave directions to the older boys about how to fix the sukkah. The young woman stood with Yogli just inside the garden gate, comforting her son who whimpered and stuck his face into her robe. Yogli's size and sword had frightened the boy. Jerusha watched this intruder, a slight curve on her lips, nestle the baby against her chest, her eyes on Timon, who gave instructions to the boys. Hosea continued his prodding.

"Are they coming to live with us?"

Sarah marched past Jerusha, her chin lifted in superiority, and stopped in front of Timon, her eyes lifted to Hosea, her hands on her hips.

"You're being rude. It's not polite to point."

Hosea stuck out his tongue. Jerusha choked back a chuckle. Her inner child wanted to do the same to the woman who gawked at her

13

husband, but wisdom constrained the childish impulse. Instead, she displayed her ownership by placing her hand on Timon's forearm.

"Don't tell me what to do. You're not my mother!" Hosea spouted.

Timon glanced at Jerusha, a twinkle in his eye, then interrupted their childish discourse.

"That's enough, you two!" Sarah turned around and plopped on the ground, her arms crossed over her chest, her lips pursed in a pout. While Timon placed Hosea down, he leaned into Jerusha and whispered in her ear.

"Does Sarah remind you of someone?"

"Oh, Timon, I'm not a child anymore." A little exasperated at his comparison, she tried to pull away, but he caught her arm and led her around the corner behind a large pomegranate bush.

"Excuse us," he said as he peeked around a branch.

"What are you doing?" she asked as he pulled her close.

"Is a husband not allowed to engage in conversation with his wife?" he said and raised her face to stare into her eyes. She felt his passion in their nearness. "I'm quite aware you are no longer a child," he whispered and gently brushed his finger across the lion pendant that lay on her chest. "I cannot forget the gift you offer when alone in our bed," he teased lovingly. "The lips and caresses are those of a mature woman." His finger traced her chin. A flush rose in her face, and she spontaneously tried to cover her black mole and glanced behind him.

"Timon, someone might see—or hear."

"Let them. Let the whole world know that I love my wife. Is there any wrong in that?"

Jerusha snuggled against his chest, his male fragrance filling her senses.

"Did you sense my insecurities? Is that why this display of affection at this moment?" she asked. The bulge of his muscular arms surrounding her made her feel as safe as a butterfly in a chrysalis.

"If you must know, I saw that look in your eye. You never have been able to hide your emotions. Let's settle this now. I love you. No other woman will ever capture my passion and desire. I'm yours, forever." She heard the rhythms in his chest increase and looked up into his eyes, serious and unmoving.

"It's not you I doubt," she said, "We've never had a widow so young among us. Most have families that provide for them. Is she going to be living here?"

"These are perilous times. Many families have allowed their beliefs to divide them. Remember what happened last week, when our neighbor's daughter thought she did YHWH's bidding by turning in her parents to the Sanhedrin. She believed if they spent time in jail they would renounce their belief in Yeshua. Sadly, love for Yeshua and his kingdom have torn many families apart. Of all people, you should understand that."

Jerusha stepped away and sat on a nearby bench. Her thoughts drifted back to when she was living in Herod's palace. While still a slave, she had forgiven her mother for not believing in Yeshua, and for not going with her father when he wanted to leave Jerusalem. Somehow, it had all worked together for their good. Her mother found faith while attending the secret meetings about Yeshua, and they both found eventual freedom from slavery. Still, what good would come of this? There was no problem with the older widows staying. They were like mothers to her. This one, with her youth and seductive eyes, was different.

"She has no where to go, much like you and your mother when Stephen bought your freedom and took you under his roof," Timon sat next to her and took her hand.

She rubbed her fingers over his knuckles and contemplated how much she missed the guardian her father placed over her before he left Jerusalem. Even the stoning of Stephen had worked to her good. She remembered well how the love of Yeshua radiated from his eyes as they pummeled him with stones. It had melted her cold hatred of the high priest, and his son for their abuse. Through his death, she found life.

"I miss Stephen, and Father," she whispered.

"I know you do. I miss them, too, especially working with your father in the carpenter's shop. We enjoyed so much laughter together. He was a father figure this orphan will never forget. His example taught me how to love these orphans."

"Well," she said as she shrugged her shoulders to her ears and exhaled a deep breath, "I guess you're right. I'm sure father would want it no other way." She turned and looked at him, a wide grin on her face. "After all, he took you in, and you turned out all right."

Jerusha stood, and peeked through the branches and watched as Yogli conversed with the newcomer.

"I don't trust her. Where did she come from? Is her son the one who was screaming?"

"No. We couldn't find that child. Devorah found us."

"Devorah? Her name is Devorah?"

"Hmmm, Devorah the bee. I think we better watch out for her sting. Is she a Yeshua follower?"

"I'm not sure."

"You're not sure? Timon, why bring her here, if you didn't know she was a believer in Yeshua's way? You risk the safety of everyone in this house. And what did you mean that she found you? How did she know who you were? And why did she come to you? And—"

Timon touched Jerusha's lips with his finger. "Stop with the questions," he said with a chuckle. "First, I honored Yogli's discernment. If he thought it was okay, then who was I to question his judgment. He has an ability to see in people's hearts and know their motives. Secondly, a watchman at the city gate pointed us out, and she approached us in the market. She has an incredible story. She told us Roman soldiers killed her husband and family. She escaped and hid in a cave. One of the soldiers found her and told her to wait until the legionnaires broke camp. He gave her some bread and a wineskin full of water. He told her to come to Jerusalem, and that she'd be safe in our home."

"Is our villa so well known that even the Roman soldiers see it as a refuge?"

"It's a strange story, I admit. I questioned its validity, but your grandfather overrode my concerns and invited her to stay."

"That's not like grandfather to trust a stranger. I must question him more about this tomorrow. When do you leave with the orphans and widows?"

"Probably in the next few days. I want to mix in with those leaving after the feast. It won't look so conspicuous."

"Are you taking Hosea?"

"Yes, a letter came yesterday that his parents died in prison. There's a home in Bethany that will take him. The others are going to family members in other villages. If it wasn't so unsafe here in Jerusalem we could keep him with us."

"Timon, I hate it when this happens. He was just asking about his parents tonight. He wanted to know when they were coming to get him. It makes me sick to have to tell him that he will never see them again. I told him we'd pray for them tonight when we bedded down. He's so sure they'll come for him. He's packed and ready to go and confident Yeshua has answered his prayers."

"It's going to be hard for him to understand, but like the others, Yeshua's Father will comfort him and eventually heal his wounded heart." He wrapped his arm around her shoulders and pulled her close. "I know it has been hard on you staying here in Jerusalem and watching the devastation and destruction of families when you want a family of your own. Our heavenly father, YHWH, is watching over us. He knows your desires. It will happen, Jerusha. Until then, we have his children to watch over. As far as Hosea is concerned, Yeshua said his Father will not leave his children orphans. He loves Hosea more than us. He has a plan and it is a good plan. If I had not been an orphan, I would have never known your father or married you. I'd say he had a good plan for this orphan boy and he will provide for Hosea."

"What about Joseph?"

"I haven't found a home for him, yet. His deafness presents a problem. I'm not sure why Yeshua doesn't answer our prayers about that. He must have some greater purpose, or maybe it's the timing we don't understand. I'm finding more and more that his ways are not our ways."

"How much longer will we be safe here, Timon?"

"I don't know. We just have to trust Yeshua."

"Yes, we must trust Yeshua," she whispered, then stood and moved away from Timon her thoughts on the new life growing inside. *I'll not tell him tonight.* The longer she waited, the more confident she became that it would not be another disappointment. Maybe she would be sure enough to tell him tomorrow. She needed to tell him before he left with the orphans.

Chapter 4

Jerusha awoke before dawn and peeked between the branches over head at the stars twinkling above. She could not stop thinking about the newcomer. She rolled over, snuggled into Timon's back, and pulled her cloak high around her shoulders. The dew soaked into her tunic, and a cold shiver moved up her spine as a slight breeze rippled underneath her garment from toes to shoulders. She pulled her knees to her chest, maneuvered the cloak with her feet, and tucked it beneath her legs.

The soft breathing of the sleeping children and widows in contrast to Timon's raucous snoring put a smile on her face, which soon disappeared when Devorah's baby whimpered and made suckling noises. Their presence in her special garden, where Timon offered his betrothal four years earlier, troubled her. For the longest time she lay there and tried to go back to sleep.

Finally, she rose, slipped her arms into her cloak, and pulled the colorful radiyd over her long black hair. She wrapped it around her neck to protect against the cool breeze. Tears threatened to overflow as she looked down at Hosea snuggled beneath Timon's arm. In the light of the full moon, she could see the tear-carved paths on his dust-covered cheeks. The news of his parents' death had been a terrible blow, and she ached for his loss. It was a grim reminder of how alone she felt as a little girl.

While straightening Hosea's cloak around his shoulders, she glanced around at the other children, most of whom had kicked their cloaks off in the night. She stepped over sprawled legs and arms and covered the sleeping children as she made her way to the garden gate. The citrus scent of the etrog branches on the sukkot permeated the air.

Her mother quietly prepared the morning meal with Chaya. She was so grateful for Timon's surrogate mother. Not only did she help with her miraculous birth, she raised Timon as her own when his mother died and his father abandoned him. Her teaching and example made Timon into the man she loved.

Jerusha moved to the crackling fire beneath the lamb and rubbed her hands over the rising heat from the flames. Her heart warmed in the presence of these two women of faith, who showed her the way to Yeshua.

The aroma of roasted meat sparked a sudden wave of nausea and she rushed to hang her head over a garbage bowl set off the tiled path. She inhaled a deep breath and exhaled very slowly as she held the few strands of hair back that hung outside her radiyd. She waited, hoping not to lose her stomach contents in front of others and give away her secret before she told Timon. She hated this part of being with child, but it did signal the certainty of conception. And son, because Yeshua promised.

All Jewish men desired a son. She often wondered if her father regretted that she was a girl, especially since mother never conceived again. He seemed to adore her, taught her the Torah as if he she had been his son, and encouraged her to dance like David danced. He called her his lioness from the tribe of Judah. Nevertheless, she wanted to give Timon a son.

Finally, the nausea passed. She stretched her arms above her head, then held her hands on her abdomen while she rolled her shoulders back to ease the tension in her neck. Naturally, she had been under a lot of stress. Persecutions threatened without, and fear of rejection loomed within. Stephen had taught her to dance during such times and especially during this most joyful of feasts.

She caught her mother looking at her with raised eyebrows, which meant she suspected her pregnancy. Jerusha watched as her mother whispered in Chaya's ear. The two older women began to giggle but abruptly stopped when they noticed Jerusha's eyes were on them.

She tucked her hair inside her radyid, opened the garden gate, and made her way to the large bronze gate that guarded the entrance. She touched the mezuzah on the gatepost and whispered what father taught her, "Hear O Israel! The Lord is our God. The Lord is one. You shall love the Lord your God with all your heart, and with all your soul, and with all your might. And these words, which I am commanding you today, shall be on your heart; and you shall teach them diligently to your sons and shall talk of them when you sit in your house and when you lie down and when your rise up, and you shall write them on the doorposts and on your gates." She yearned for her own son to teach. She imagined him sitting between her and Timon while they opened the law and showed him how Yeshua fulfilled it and then sent the Holy Ghost to give them power to love even their enemies. She needed that power now to overcome her fears and love Devorah. It mattered not whether she was a threat to their safety. Yeshua loved her. Inwardly, Jerusha struggled with this truth. Why? Why love someone who might destroy everything and everyone she loved?

A shofar blew in the distance and silenced the song thrush in the olive tree. She unlocked the bronze gate, crossed the cobblestone street, and looked at the city below. Her stomach rumbled, so she picked a few grapes from the vines that covered the limestone wall and plopped them in her mouth. An orange globe cast morning light on the top of the temple in the distance and the reflecting light sparkled like diamonds. She closed her eyes and listened. A dove cooed overhead in the jujube tree, and a cricket chirped at her feet. These were the familiar sounds of childhood and a reminder of safer times when Romans soldiers and religious priests lived together in peace.

"What are you doing out here?" Her grandfather's words startled her. She turned and almost laughed. The giant stood with bare feet shoulder-width apart, just outside the gate, this time not dressed in a full soldier's attire, but in his white linen under tunic with a sword strapped to his side.

"Don't you know it's not safe to be out here alone at this hour?" He gave her a half-smile, unusual for him when concerned for her welfare. "Come back inside." His words softened and he motioned with his hand and held the gate open.

"Grandfather, can we talk about Devorah?" she asked as she followed him inside. "I don't understand why you let her come here." After fiddling with the gate, he turned and studied her for a minute before responding. She noticed the graying at his temples and eyebrows that framed his deep, blue eyes—subtle cues to honor his wisdom.

"It's not the woman and her story that intrigued me, but the Roman soldier who told her to come to our villa. I asked myself why he would do that. Why would he send her to us? So, I questioned her about this man. She described a typical soldier in size and strength. There was nothing unusual about him, she said, except his eyes. She said she had never seen any like them, green with a deep blue rim. That's when I suspected it might be him."

"Who?"

He stopped walking and took her hands. "Jerusha, the only people I know that have eyes like that are you and your father."

Jerusha felt the breath leave her chest. She closed her eyes and tried to see her father's face. What did his eyes look like? She wanted to remember, but ten years is a long time. She loved him and remembered his jovial laughter, his nimble fingers carving wood, his stories.

"Are you saying this soldier is my father?"

"He could be. I'm not sure. I don't want to give you false hope, but I'm leaving as soon as I can, to see if I can find that Roman legion. I accepted Devorah because I thought the soldier might be your father. If it was, I knew he wouldn't send someone to us that would bring harm to you and your mother. Be kind to Devorah, Jerusha. She needs us, and I think your father sent her."

"I'm not sure about that," Jerusha said, and yanked her hands from his and turned away. "Nevertheless, I know Yeshua wants me to love her," then, turning back she asked, "Have you told Timon about this?"

"Yes."

"How about mother and Chaya?"

"No, not yet. I want more evidence before I raise your mother's hopes. She won't question my judgment about taking in Devorah. I only tell you because you asked. You've had issues with trust," she saw the compassion in his eyes, "but you've grown tremendously in your faith in Yeshua. Your Father would be pleased."

"Father," she whispered, her eyes on the gentle giant's battle-worn fingers that would swallow her tiny hands. Overcome with emotion, she stepped closer. She needed his strength. He took her hands again. One single tear rolled down her cheek and plopped on his rough knuckles. "Oh, Grandfather, I hope you're right. It's strange to think of my father as a Roman soldier. He always hated them." Her eyes fell on grandfather's gladius in the scabbard on his hip, his Roman name Regulus carved into the pommel. "I'm sorry. I didn't mean to insult you by what I said. I'm very grateful for your Roman connections that keep us safe."

"No offense taken." He brushed away another tear that ran down her cheek and wrapped his arm around her shoulders. She laid her head against his strong midsection as they walked toward the garden. "There's one more thing I must tell you. I am going to Rome. With Tiberias's death and Caligula's rise to power, I may not have the same influence in Jerusalem to keep you safe. I hear rumors of his insanity and his need to be a god."

"Oh, Grandfather, what's going to happen to us? Will we be leaving Jerusalem like the others?"

"For now, we stay with Peter and the other apostles."

"Grandfather, I love Peter as a spiritual father, and he's taught me so much, but Jerusalem is a treacherous place to live."

"As I've told you many times, our safety is in Yeshua's hands. We'll know when we are to leave. Until then, we spread the gospel of the kingdom in this city among the Jews even if it costs us our lives."

"I'm tired of watching Yeshua followers die. If our people don't want the truth, then let them die in their foolish ignorance. I'm not ready to give my life for them." She touched her womb. "Or those I love."

"YHWH gave his son for you and made a way for you to become his child."

"I'm not ready to give up my son."

"Your son?"

"Oh! Well, you know, when I have one." His wide grin showed a missing tooth, another evidence of a battle-worn soldier. A flustered red flush crept up her neck and she walked away without looking back, determined to tell Timon before she let it slip again. No more delay. She would tell him that night.

"Jerusha!" She stopped at the garden gate and looked back. "In prayer this morning," he continued, "I was impressed by Holy Ghost to give you a scripture from the great prophet, Isaiah. YHWH said to tell you, 'The children you will have, after you have lost the other, will say again in your ear … give place to me that I may dwell.'"

She stared deep into his eyes for the longest moment.

"What does it mean?"

"Only you know the answer to that. When the time is right, he will reveal it." She ran to him and hugged him with all her might, her head barely above the giant's waist.

"Pray for me, Grandfather, that I can be strong like you," in a voice soft and tremulous.

"Jerusha, your faith is much stronger than you know. The many trials you have endured serve only to make you stronger. Comfort others with the comfort that you received from YHWH. Like Queen Esther, you live for such a time as this. Little lioness, arise and be strong."

Jerusha loosened her grip and wiped her runny nose with her sleeve. Vulnerable and childlike, she lay back against him, his large hands on her back and head.

"I'll try, Grandfather." She felt vibrations against her ear, heard his chuckle and looked up.

"Little lioness, be yourself. You're made to roar and roar you will in the coming days." Jerusha laughed at his analogy.

"Grandfather, I wish Father was here. You remind me so much of him." His smile faded and he rubbed his fingers through his full beard, and then directed her toward the garden.

"Go along, Jerusha. There's much to do. Timon leaves tomorrow." An urgent excitement rose in Jerusha's belly.

Tonight's the night he finds out about his son.

Chapter 5

Jerusha rounded the sparkling fountain in the garden, a bounce in her step. Moses and the other children worked at taking down the sukkot, their laughter and giggles contagious. Her slight nausea and tender breasts added to the overwhelming joy and certainty that this was her appointed time by YHWH. Like the old matriarch Sarah, she waited for sons who would impact the nations. Yeshua promised. It was their secret.

One plan after another splashed through her thoughts. Sarah must sleep with mother tonight to allow for a meal alone with Timon. She would serve roasted lamb his favorite pomegranates, and fresh bread. She would take Sarah to the market with her to help pick out a special cup for their wine. This was a once-in-a-lifetime occasion, the announcement of the conception of their first son. She would also find time to dip in the mikvah bath and use her mother's special frankincense oil, given by father. Everything must be perfect!

She heard Timon's laughter and hurried to the end of the path and turned the corner. His curly, dark brown hair hung to his shoulders and shone in the morning sun. He sat on the bench, his back to Jerusha. Seated beside him was Devorah.

He did not see her slip back behind the pomegranate bush and peek through the branches. This was twice, since last night, she found herself looking through bushes at a woman she had not met yet. She did not care to meet her either. Devorah's son wiggled around on Timon's lap, and he sat him down.

"Tell me more about this soldier," he said. Jerusha leaned into the bush, her head turned and ear cupped. Would Devorah's story be the same as grandfather's? Suddenly, she felt a tug on her robe and looked down at Joseph, the deaf orphan. She lifted him up on her hip, putting her fingers to her lips to shush him. He nodded, his eyes big, and round, then looked over her shoulder. Devorah's son chased a butterfly around the bush and stopped in front of Jerusha.

"Who's dat?" he asked and pointed to her and Joseph. Jerusha sighed, put Joseph down and squatted before the intruding youngster, exasperated that he interrupted her spying mission. Timon and Devorah came around the bush.

Jerusha wondered why she had not seen the baby in her arms earlier. Probably the shock of seeing Timon with *her* was enough. That woman! She had better not get in the way of her special evening with Timon.

"Jerusha, you're just in time to meet Devorah," Timon took her arm and led her up the path, the newcomer on his other side. "Devorah, this is my beautiful wife," he stopped and bowed slightly, as always a perfect gentleman, then picked up the three-year old, who tagged along behind. "And this is little Joseph, one of our orphans. He's deaf so won't be able to speak clearly to you, but if you let him see your lips while talking to him, he understands everything. He's quite smart."

Devorah slowed to wait on her two-year-old and smiled at Jerusha. "And this is Elias," Timon pointed to the baby, "and Micah." He squatted before the little boy and rubbed his hair and made sure Joseph understood what he said by mouthing the words again silently, pointing again to each person.

It was a good thing grandfather told Jerusha to be kind or she would have acted the fool and just walked away. Instead, she greeted Devorah with a kiss on the cheek.

"Shalom," she said. "I'm going to the market today. Would you like to come along? I may even go to the springs to get fresh water."

"Thank you, but I must stay here and make sure my children get naps. Maybe another time?"

"Sure," Jerusha answered, a little relieved, but disappointed at the missed opportunity to ask about the soldier.

"Please, excuse us, Devorah. I need to talk to my wife alone." Timon bowed and took Jerusha's arm. They watched Joseph run up the path ahead of them, anxious to join the older boys in their building venture, a make-believe palace from the removed sukkot branches.

"I'm leaving in the morning with Hosea and the others who have families waiting for them," he said. "Will you help him pack?" He dug in the inner pocket of his robe. "Here are a few denarius. "When you go to market, buy a special gift for him. Make sure it will fit in the box I made that's like yours. We'll put a letter in it, too, like your father did for you. I want him to know that we will always love him."

Jerusha thought about her conversation with her grandfather. She wanted to believe that the Roman soldier was her father but wondered if he would still love her. It had been a long time. If it was true, she wondered why he had not found a way to come to her.

Timon interrupted her thoughts. "He's so young, but I think he's beginning to understand who Yeshua is. His new parents are believers, so they will continue to show him the way. I'm going to help the boys with their building projects. I think you'll find Hosea in the stable. He wanted to see the horses again before he leaves."

***

On the way to the stables, Jerusha passed the gardener, who was spreading fresh manure around the spice and herb plants. She held her nose as she passed his dung cart and quickened her pace, being careful where she stepped. Water flowed from a fresh spring under her path into canals that kept the plants well watered. She lifted her face and let the sun overhead warm her cheeks, her thoughts on her special announcement.

Outside the stable, another servant scooped dried dung into a cart. Some of it would go to the kitchen and be fuel for the fires beneath the baking ovens. The rest would go to the braziers for heat in the rooms. She would need to remember to ask Moses bring some to her room before nightfall and stoke the brazier. She wanted to have a warm and cozy atmosphere for her time with Timon.

When she rounded the corner, she patted the nose of her favorite stallion, his white coat shining in the noon sun. He neighed, lifted his head and stamped his hoof. She quieted the horse and listened. She thought she had heard a child crying. It sounded like Hosea. She paused, staying quiet, and heard it again, along with a soft, feminine voice. She moved methodically, from one stall to another, looking for them. Two stalls down from the white stallion she found them. Sarah sat with her arm around Hosea, atop a large pile of hay.

"It will be all right," she said, her head tipped to the side and a little forward so she could look at his face. "When my uncle couldn't find my parents, he took me in as his own. When he died, I thought I would never be happy again. Then Jerusha and Timon said I could call them ima and aba. You'll see, Hosea. Your new family will love you like Timon and Jerusha love me."

"I don't want to live with anyone else. I want to stay here with you."

"I know," she said. "Sometimes we don't get what we want. Sometimes it's better," she added, quite an insightful statement for a six-year old. Pretending she had not heard their conversation, Jerusha opened the stall and plopped on her stomach in the hay, her chin in her palms.

"What are you two horses doing?" she asked, their giggles a sign she had accomplished her mission to make them laugh.

"Neigh," Sarah responded to the game.

"Neigh," Jerusha answered back.

Hosea rubbed his eyes and neighed, too. Sarah threw handfuls of hay in the air. Jerusha joined her, while Hosea burrowed into the pile like a little mouse.

"Follow me," he said, his joyful words muffled by the deep tunnel. They followed and came out the other end covered with hay, Jerusha's radiyd hanging sideways.

"You look funny," Sarah said, "Hay is sticking out of your hair like a porcupine."

"Oh, yeah, well, you look the same way," Jerusha said and tickled her ribs.

"Stop, stop," Sarah begged. Jerusha reached behind Sarah and tickled Hosea. They all rolled on their backs and laughed and laughed. When she could breathe again, she stared quietly at the rafters above, one child on each side. Jerusha reached for their hands and squeezed them lightly.

"Hosea, when I was little, I had to go away with my mother and live with a mean man. I couldn't understand why. It was hard. Yeshua knew my pain. He understood and sent my grandfather to watch over me. YHWH is always watching you. Don't be afraid. He's got a good plan for you. You'll be safe and loved by this family. I promise. Would I lie to you?

"No,"

"Then let's get you packed and ready to go. You leave bright and early tomorrow morning. My mother always said, 'every day is a new beginning.' Tomorrow's adventure will be a new beginning for you. How exciting! A new family! A new town to live in! A new house, too! Timon tells me they have a son your age.

"Really?

"Yes, you'll have a new playmate, too!" That seemed to please him, and he and Sarah giggled and rolled in the hay. Jerusha's thoughts wandered from Hosea's departure to her secret.

She placed both hands on her abdomen and pictured Timon's surprise and her mother's joyful expression in the garden's morning sunlight upon hearing the happy announcement.

"A new beginning for all of us," she added.

**

A cool night breeze blew through the opened white-latticed shutters. Jerusha leaned out and inhaled the familiar scent of the late-blooming pomegranate blossoms, their red and orange blooms scattered throughout the garden outside her bedroom window. She felt like the butterflies that normally flittered in the bushes found their resting place in her stomach. She had waited long enough to be sure of her announcement. Timon would be so happy.

Giddy, she twirled across the room in her white bejeweled robe and light blue linen tunic, a melody in her heart, a dance in her feet. Dipping and swaying her way to the royal-blue tiled table, she hummed a sweet tune and straightened the red pomegranates letting the green grapes flow over the bowl's edge, a nice touch against the yellow tiles.

She thanked YHWH for the new life she carried, a son, she believed, for Timon's sake. A girl would be wonderful, too. Either would silence the barrenness curse the whispering women in the marketplace put upon her.

She cast aside those thoughts. She noticed the aroma of roasted lamb was more pleasant than had been to her that morning. Her stomach growled a reminder of how hungry she got these days. While nibbling on a piece of bread, she examined the golden cup she bought for Timon that afternoon. His mother knew of her plans and promised to send him when he returned from watering the horses.

In the lamplight, the cup cast dancing sparkles on her face. The words engraved by the goldsmith around its lip spoke of her secret. Ben, Abba, Ben, Abba, Son, Father, Son, Father. It held new wine pressed from the crop's best grapes, a sign of Yeshua's abundant blessings. When the door creaked, she placed the cup on the table beside the bread and looked up at Timon. His lopsided grin spread wide showing perfect white teeth against his full black beard.

"Shalom." She moved toward him with a queen's grace and dignity, even though a childlike glee threatened to erupt.

"You are beautiful." He swept her in his arms and kissed her. She yielded to the pleasure of his caresses and then rested her head on his chest, thankful for his love.

"What's the special occasion that you greet me with such honor?" He waved his hand toward the table. "A feast fit for a king."

She picked up the golden goblet, took a sip and gave it to him.

"A king should have a son to rule with him and share in the inheritance, would you not agree?"

They locked eyes for a moment. As he lifted the cup, his eyes fell on the Hebrew words on the lip.

"Ben, Abba. Jerusha, are you trying to tell me something?" His eyes twinkled. She contained her childlike glee and turned around with a flirty aloofness.

"Maybe."

"Maybe?" He placed the cup on the table and come up behind. His muscular embrace enclosed her in a safe cocoon. She looked down and fiddled with her hair, the long black strands hung free, no radiyd in her husband's bed chamber. She felt his breath against her neck.

"What is it, my love? What secret are you unveiling tonight? Could it be we're having a son? "That soon I'll be a father?"

"Oh, yes, Timon, I'm sure it will be a son. Yeshua told me."

"Oh, he did, did he?"

"Don't mock me. He did tell me that we will have sons, and daughters, too. After our many attempts, I doubted it, and thought I heard wrong, or that maybe I was cursed. This time is different. I just know it." She turned in his arms and looked up. "Are you happy?" He drew her into his chest. She heard his heart beat.

"I've told you many times that your love is more than enough for me. A son? Well, that will be a welcome addition. I'm concerned for you, though. What if this is another disappointment?" Jerusha stiffened, the old feeling crept over her body. Her stomach knotted.

"Do not talk to me of your doubts. This is the longest I've gone past my time. Our time has come to have a son. I know it. I just know it."

"Then let us partake of this elaborate meal you prepared and celebrate." He motioned toward the table. Jerusha moved with grace around his extended arm and curtsied.

"Sir, may this humble mother serve the father of our son?" Timon played the part.

"Why, yes, of course my son's royal mother may serve his royal father." He bowed at the waist and before she moved away, he swooped her in his arms. She felt his passion arise in his loins.

"Later, my love, later." She smiled and broke from his embrace. "Come, partake of the new wine." She lifted the cup. "Abba, father."

***

Later, Jerusha snuggled close and listened to Timon's snoring, her thoughts racing. Seven months seemed like an eternity to wait to hold her son. She had picked out yarn in the marketplace that afternoon to make the baby's swaddling cloths and special blanket with Judah markings. First thing tomorrow, after she sent Timon and Hosea on their way, she would tell both mothers and begin weaving.

Too excited to sleep, she crept from the mittah, the soft lambs fleece wrapped around her shoulders and opened the shutters. The cloudless night allowed her to see each star in the constellations. She remembered trying to count each one, only to have father tell her a story about Abraham, one she must tell her son. He said, "Because Abraham obeyed, YHWH promised to multiply his offspring as the stars of heaven. They would possess the gate of their enemies and in them all the nations of the earth would be blessed."

As usual, her questioning mind went to work in a one sided conversation with Yeshua. *"How will my son, an offspring of Abraham, bless the Romans? Or other nations? Or possess their gates?"*

Not waiting for Yeshua's response, she began to form her own answers. Fingering the lion pendant her father made, she vowed to tell her son about the ark, and how the priests declared, "Arises Lord. Let your enemies be scattered. Let all who hate you flee before you." Surely my son will need to know that declaration, if he's going to possess the gates of his enemies. But how will he bless the nations? A shofar blew in the distance.

In that moment, Jerusha noticed an especially bright star and recalled another of her father's stories. It was the story of Yeshua's birth, and of a star that guided the wise men from the east to Bethlehem and gave Him gold, frankincense, and myrrh. Yeshua, the king of kings, her father's friend, her friend, came that he might restore YHWH's family and manifest his kingdom on earth. That's what her father had told her. That's how her son will bless the nations.

A baby's hungry cry drifted in the air. It was probably Devorah's son, and an interruption to her joyful revelation that brought more questions. Why had they come? What trouble would they bring upon her household? Upon her son?

Jerusha shook her head, closed the shutters and climbed back in the mittah next to Timon, being sure to warm her cold toes between his legs. Tomorrow would be a new day and a new beginning. Even with Devorah living in their villa, she intended to enjoy this season of her life. Her eyelids grew heavy and she drifted into a deep slumber.

In the early dawn hours, she awoke. An uncomfortable sticky substance penetrated her thin tunic and caused the skin on her inner thighs to pull as she tried to turn over. Stunned, she raised up and pulled back the lambskin cover. In the faint moon light, she saw blood everywhere.

"No! she screamed, "Not again! No!"

Chapter 6

"Jerusha, you're shivering." Timon rolled over, jumped out of bed and fumbled with the shutters. "This needs to be fixed before winter." He grabbed his robe on a nearby hook.

"It hurts so much!" She curled her knees to chest and wiped the beads of perspiration from her forehead. How was it possible to be so cold, but still have sweat running down her face? The pain eased a little.

"Timon, get mother. Please hurry. Get your mother, too. They'll know what to do."

He tucked his soft robe under her chin and around her shoulders. The warmth soaked into her wet tunic. She sucked in her breath and gritted her teeth. Another groan erupted into a high-pitched cry.

Timon stumbled and rushed past the mittah and banged the cedar door against the limestone wall as he left the room. After a few minutes, Jerusha heard scuffles and the murmuring of voices outside the door.

"Hurry," The whimper turned to another loud cry. Both hands gripped her womb. *My son*. She squeezed her eyes closed and pinched her lips together. *Yeshua. You promised*. Curled on her side, she felt more warm liquid ooze out. *No!*

Timon smoothed back the hair on her forehead.

"Our mothers are here, Jerusha." She looked up into his gentle eyes and blinked back tears.

"It's too late. Timon. Why? Why has Yeshua let this happen? What's wrong with me?" He scooped her up and held her tight, her uncontrollable sobs muffled in his chest. It felt as if she might never stop crying. Finally, she hiccupped short gasps and stared at the bloodied bed cover.

***

She opened her eyes. The lamplight cast a soft glow in the room. Numb to her surroundings, the same protective wall she used as a child encompassed her heart, the emotional pain to difficult to bear. In her greatest hour of need, Yeshua abandoned her, just like her father. The familiar sense of worthlessness washed over her soul.

Covered in a clean lambskin, she rolled onto her back and stared at the pomegranates Timon had carved in the ceiling beams when he refurbished her father's house. A thick cloud darkened her vision for the future. There would be no royal sons or bloodline, their royal heritage in doubt.

"I see you're awake." Timon stirred the embers in the brazier.

"I'm cursed." Her words came from another world, weak and lifeless. She continued to stare at the beams. "We'll never have heirs. It's useless. I'm a woman abandoned even by Yeshua." She heard Timon hang the brazier tongs on the side and move across the room. Emotionless, she continued staring at the ceiling, even though she felt his presence near.

"I have no answers as to why you continue to be barren, but you are not cursed. Yeshua became cursed so that you may be free from the curse. As your grandfather has said so many times, 'his ways are not our ways.'" He bent over and forced her to look into his eyes. "Is not my love enough?"

"No." Even though his eyes reflected a deep love, she saw the hurt in his countenance as he stood and walked away. She turned on her side and watched. "I'm sorry, I didn't mean to hurt you." Suddenly, she propped up on one elbow.

"Why do you have on your travel clothes?"

"I'm leaving with Hosea and the others this morning. Remember?"

"Oh, I forgot. Do you have to go?"

"Under the circumstances I hate to leave, but I must. Hosea's new family is leaving the area. For safety purposes, they will travel out of Judea with a caravan of pilgrims that will pass through Bethany where they live. That caravan leaves Jerusalem today, and we travel with it. Is Hosea ready?"

Jerusha slipped from the mittah and opened a chest in the corner. Her eyes fell on the cloth she had purchased for her son, and hesitated only a moment before kneeling and continued rummaging through her things to find the special box Timon made for Hosea.

"I bought the gift you wanted for him. It's in here somewhere with the box," Her voice trembled. Timon squatted beside her and lifted her chin.

"You're trying so hard to be brave and selfless. Come here," He lifted her to her feet. "I have a gift for you. Remember this while I'm gone," He kissed her and stared into her eyes for the longest time. "I love you, Jerusha. Every night, when the moon first shows in the night sky, know I'm thinking about you and asking Yeshua to bless you."

"I'll remember."

***

Jerusha walked hand in hand with Timon down the cobblestone path toward the Eastern Gate, the fuchsia sunrise broadening across the length of the city's limestone wall.

"This is the day the Lord has made. I will rejoice and be glad in it," Sarah sang loudly, her young voice filled with joy..

Heavy hearted, Jerusha glanced at her mother and Chaya. They walked beside Sarah, who was riding a donkey loaded with goods for Timon's trip. They knew how much she wanted a son. Moved by their compassionate eyes, a brim of tears threatened to overflow. She rubbed them away with her fist. Timon squeezed her other hand and she looked up to catch his wink. Sarah hung tight to the donkey's neck and giggled.

"It's hair tickles my nose." Jerusha smiled.

A goatskin water bottle and leather bags filled with dried lamb and challah bread for Sabbath, bounced in time with the clip, clop of the beast's hooves on the stones. Several other donkeys, led by the widows who were leaving with Timon, carried personal items, cooking pots, and lentil stew in pottery. Along with Timon and Hosea, three other orphans and two widows were leaving for safer homes.

Jerusha feared no place was safe. She would stay in Jerusalem with both their mothers, as well as Moses, Joseph, and Devorah and her two sons. The holy city had been a refuge for Jews in the past. Now, the Sanhedrin turned Jew against Jew, and with a new Caesar in Rome, even the decree on her door may not protect them against the high priest's threats. Why did Timon have to leave now?

Jerusha and Timon passed the temple and meshed with pilgrims who were leaving Jerusalem. After celebrating Sukkot, they were headed back to their homes. Their noisy chatter and banter with Timon was a bit too cheerful for Jerusha. She tugged on his arm.

"Be careful, Timon. I don't have a good feeling about this trip. Don't take any unnecessary chances. I don't know what I would do without you." She stopped, but Sarah's donkey nudged her back and caused her to stumble forward.

Children waved from rooftops at their friends and relatives who were leaving and yelled, "See you at Pesach."

"When will you be back?

Promise you'll be back before Pesach in the spring."

Jerusha noticed Timon's serious expression. "Timon, what is it?"

Timon releaed a long sigh. "This trip will be longer than usual. I'm traveling across the Jordan into Decapolis."

"Timon, why must you take this trip now? I need you," she pleaded.

"Halt!" The Roman soldier above the gate shouted an annoying interruption. Below him, the hated publicans collected taxes. Timon waved at their group to move to a small opening under the shade of an olive tree. The flow of people passed.

"Let's rest here and say our good-byes. We'll catch up later." He spoke loudly so to be heard over the mewling camels and traders, who waited their turn at the tax booth. He lifted Sarah off the donkey and replaced her with Hosea.

"Your turn to ride." Timon patted his head." Sarah arched her head back and smiled up at Hosea.

"Thank you, for sharing the donkey with me before you leave." She pulled on Timon's robe.

"Halt! Another soldier shouted at the gate.

Jerusha watched the legionnaire block a boy from running past. She cringed. The Roman's black stallion reared up and stomped the ground, a narrow miss for the boy.

"I am so tired of Roman intrusion in our lives."

"It's their decree on our door that Yeshua uses to keep us safe. For that I am grateful."

"Oh! Where *is* grandfather? I have not seen him all morning."

"I've been wondering how to break this to you, but he left after sundown last night to look for the soldier that spoke to Devorah."

"What? Why didn't he tell me?"

"Because he knew you would want to go. He couldn't risk taking you, since he goes to Rome, too. I've asked Peter and his wife to stay with you, until one of us gets back."

A sick feeling swept over Jerusha. She heard sniffles and looked over at Sarah, who patted Hosea's leg, then smothered her face in Jerusha's cloak and choked back sobs. Suddenly, her concern fell on these little ones saying good-bye. She glanced around at the other whimpering orphans saying good-bye to Moses and Joseph. Widows wiped tears on tunic sleeves and said good-bye to her mother and Chaya.

For the moment, she forgot about her fears and questions. She removed Hosea from the donkey and hugged him along with each child and widow, then she and Timon placed their hands on each head and released Abraham's blessing, the same blessing she wanted to proclaim over her own son or daughter. Her father had taught her the power of YHWH's word, and her grandfather helped her memorize much of it. Suddenly, her grandfather's words from Isaiah burst into her thoughts: "The children you shall have after you have lost the other, will say again in your ear, make a place for me to dwell."

What could it mean? Grandfather said YHWH will reveal it.

"Oh, why did he have to leave, too," she spoke out loud.

"Are you talking to me or the wind?" Timon teased.

"It might as well be the wind. I have no control of either." He pulled her close and whispered.

"You have more control of my heart than you will ever know." Flustered, she pushed him away and addressed the group.

"Form a circle everyone. Let's end our time together in praise to our Father YHWH. The Lord reigns, forever and ever." The children repeated.

"The Lord reigns forever and ever."

They clasped arms and moved left, step across, dip behind, step, dip, step, dip, all the way around, then changed directions and went to the right. The children's laughter lifted her spirit, and she began to sing the old song given while in captivity at Herod's palace.

"I am the Lion of Judah. Deep within my inner most being dwells the Holy God of all Israel. I am the Lion of Judah." After awhile the children caught on and sang with her. Timon tapped her shoulder, and she let him in next to her. Their eyes locked as they circled danced round one more time.

When the circle broke, Timon got in line to pay the taxes, while those staying behind helped those leaving gather their things. When he returned, he hugged her one last time.

"I'll miss you so much."

"And I you. Don't forget to give Hosea his gift."

"I won't." He kissed her cheek. "Shalom, my beautiful wife. Let's go, everyone." He flung Hosea onto the donkey's back and yanked the rope. "Get going, you stubborn beast."

"Bye, Hosea. Bye, everyone," Sarah stood at her side and waved.

"Bye, my love," Jerusha kept her eye on Timon, until he disappeared in the crowd, then turned to go home. That's when she saw Devorah. She talked and laughed with a soldier and trader at a shop. Baby Elias snuggled close to her chest, and Micah stood at attention and gripped her cloak. *What's she up to? And why is she blessed with two sons? What have I done wrong to be cursed?* Jerusha took Sarah's hand, the one who called her mother.

If I never have a son, at least I have Sarah.

Chapter 7

The Roman centurion pulled at the locked front gate and pivoted to face Jerusha and those in her care. His soldiers pounded in unison up the hill and surrounded the tired women and children who were huddled in the street, the cobblestones reflecting the heat of the scorching sun. Jerusha pulled Sarah close to her side and glanced at her mother and Chaya as Moses pick up Joseph. The frightened three-year-old hid his face in Moses's muscular shoulder. They all looked to her. She read the fearful questions in their eyes, the same questions running through her own mind.

The centurion motioned to the soldiers to make a pathway between him and her. She watched closely the gruff leader and leaned over to Devorah.

"Is this the soldier you conversed with in the market place?"

"No, I do not know this man."

Jerusha's eyes lingered a few seconds. "It's strange the soldiers come the day after you showed up."

Rows of soldiers lined the street behind them. Devorah covered Elias who suckled beneath her cloak and comforted the two-year old Micah who clung to her leg and fussed.

"I know what it looks like, but you are mistaken if you think I had anything to do with this." The fear in her eyes revealed she told the truth.

Without Timon and Yogli's presence to boost her confidence, Jerusha felt like running away, but if she ran, she feared what would happen to the others. Besides, there was no way she could get past the soldiers. She ruled the house now, and it was her the responsibility to stand firm. Something new and different began to rise up within her. A fire burned inside of her, and she knew she had to muster the strength to defend those she loved. The time for her to be the lioness of the tribe of Judah, as her grandfather talked about, had come. With trepidation, Jerusha drew close to the surly soldier. The stench of his foul breath made her cover her nose with her radiyd.

"What are you doing?" she asked with trepidation, strength draining from her knees.

Hand on his sword, feet shoulder width apart, he eyed her carefully, then reached for the decree on the gatepost. She clenched her trembling fingers and pressed closer. His apparent dismissal annoyed her. Her lion pendant rubbed against her tunic, and she remembered the golden words on its back. *Arise Lord. Let your enemies be scattered. Let all who hate you flee before you.*

"This property belongs to my husband." She tried to calm the returning fear that knotted her stomach. The soldier paid her no attention and continued his efforts to remove the secured parchment. The pounding in her ears grew louder. Her safe haven for the last three years was in jeopardy. Without thinking of the consequences, she slapped her hand on the parchment.

"Don't touch that!" She spoke with more authority than she felt. He stared down, his eyes riveted on her hand, and then reached for his sword. Jerusha froze. Her heart thudded in her chest. The sword's glint flashed. With one quick swoop, he unfastened the decree and jerked it loose, leaving her hand against the rough cedar.

She swirled around and glared at his back, a bold anger threatening to erupt in a tirade. Devorah's baby whimpered again, and she glanced at the innocent company who depended on her. Even little Joseph, deaf and mute, gaped at the soldier, aware of the danger. The soldier whipped around and pointed to the lion and butterfly seal.

"The Roman, who owns the signet ring that made this seal will be arrested for treason. Would that be your husband?"

"No, We are not Roman." The anger subsided a little.

"We are from the tribe of Judah. We are royalty," she said, echoing her father's words.

"The one royalty in this empire is Caesar Caligula," he spat in her face.

Numbly, she wiped the slime from her cheek. A sick feeling washed over her as she watched him roll the parchment and stuff it behind his breast plate, then untie a pouch on his belt.

"Where is he? The traitor who goes by Regulus?" he demanded. She froze and contemplated what to say next. She could never forgive herself if grandfather died because of her. He paid a dear price once for helping, the scar on his cheek the evidence of his flogging. He would not suffer again.

The soldier jangled coins in her face. "We pay well," then enclosed the pouch in his fist and stared. The darkness in his eyes sent a tingle up Jerusha's spine.

"He's done nothing wrong." She stood a little taller.

"Herod reported otherwise. This Regulus claims allegiance to another king." His evil gaze now lingered on Devorah with the same devouring stare Jerusha saw in Caiphas's eyes when she was still a slave.

"You're a beauty. Too bad you have those two brats, or I might take my pleasure with you tonight." He stepped in close and rubbed his finger across her face. "What do you know of this Regulus?" Devorah backed away.

"Sir, I just came here. I don't know a Regulus," she said, a slight tremor in her tone.

"Ha! I bet you don't!" he cackled and turned swiftly and glowered at Jerusha.

"No more delay. Where is he?"

"I don't know."

The centurion motioned to the soldiers behind the women.

"Search the property." He propped his hobnailed sandal on the bottom edge of the bronze gate. "Unlock it, or we'll break it open!" Jerusha hurried to the ornate structure and dug in her girdle for the key, then fumbled it at his foot. Reaching to pick it up, she noticed a man duck behind a cart in the street. The man looked like the trader she saw with Devorah in the marketplace. The ends of his linen turban crisscrossed around his face and neck. Only his eyes showed. At that moment, Devorah gasped. The alert centurion grabbed Jerusha, dragged her to Devorah and grasped her arm, too. The women trembled before his immense stature. His helmet's red plume blew in the wind, and he spoke slow and distinct.

"Where is he?" The centurion waited, then inched closer, his sour breath in their faces. "If we do not find him, we will be back," and ripped the key from Jerusha. She gulped and lifted her chin.

"I told you. I don't know." Acutely aware of YHWH's providence, she almost smiled, grateful that Yogli had left the city. Her grandfather's words lingered in her thoughts. *His ways are not our ways.*

The centurion threw the key to a soldier near the gate.

Within minutes, Jerusha heard the banging of doors and the crash of pottery inside the villa. It awakened an old memory of Caiaphas searching for her father on her wedding day. The centurion rubbed his beard, deep in thought. Suddenly, he pivoted and swooped his arms out.

"Why does a Roman soldier protect this beautiful place? And those who live here?" His eyes narrowed. "Why not take it for himself, make them his slaves?" She must be careful. Her answer could put them all in danger. The centurion waited. The soldiers marched from inside her villa and aligned with those waiting orders in the street. One wrong word from her and they would all be arrested.

Yeshua, please help me. She closed her eyes, and then the words came.

"As a favor to my father."

"Who is your father?"

"Jacob ben Judah. He's dead." She hoped it was not true, but he must think otherwise.

"Why would a Roman soldier do a favor for a Jew?" She smiled inwardly at the remembrance of Yogli's confession to being her grandfather and living with her father in Tarsus.

"They knew each other years ago in Tarsus," she answered.

"Where is your husband? What does he know of this Regulus?" Jerusha hesitated.

"The house is empty. He's not here," a soldier reported. The welcome interruption distracted the centurion, and Jerusha breathed a sigh of relief. He must not know her husband was gone, too, but she would not lie. How vulnerable she felt without male support. A wind gust whipped the gate, and it slammed against the limestone wall. The centurion waved at the soldiers to leave.

"Like I said, if we don't find him, we will be back," and tapped his breastplate with his fist. "You no longer have Rome's protection." Jerusha stood high on Zion and watched the soldiers tromp down the hill, their hobnailed sandals echoing in unison.

Jerusha noticed that several of her neighbors had been watching and whispering amongst themselves. She wondered if one of them had turned them in to the high priest. Embarrassed and afraid, she called to Sarah and motioned to the others to come inside. When she turned to lock the gate, she caught another glimpse of the trader hiding behind the cart.

Who is he, and why does he hide and watch?

Chapter 8

The villa was quiet, and it unnerved her. For now, they were safe, but she knew the soldier would be back. She paused at the gurgling fountain and let the cool waters wash over her fingers. She bent over and splashed water on her face, removing all residue of the soldier's spit.

The filthy pig!

She looked around their home and the damage left behind by the Roman soldiers. "Look at this mess. Mother, will you take Sarah and Joseph inside? Maybe she can hold him while you and Chaya clean up. Moses, please pick up the broken pottery out here. You'll need the small cart from the garden." Already she gave orders like Timon.

"W-w-will the soldiers c-c-c-come back?" Moses stared at her with wide eyes.

"If they do, you will be safe. You've done nothing wrong. Now, hurry along before Joseph comes back outside. We don't want him to get cut on these shards. When you finish, please find Peter. Tell him what happened and ask him to come as soon as possible. Devorah, would you stay?"

After the others left the courtyard, Jerusha watched while Devorah nursed the babe. Each cry and coo of the infant pounded at the hardened wall she had erected around her emotions following her miscarriage. Preparations for Timon's departure had kept her too busy to think about it. She had not yet allowed herself to grieve for her lost child. Only her mother, Chaya, and Timon knew.

I failed again. My little one's life snuffed out. Why? She listened to Devorah sing softly to her baby. *Why does she receive the blessing? What's wrong with me?* She turned her back to the woman she envied, her pent-up emotions threatening to erupt. *Get control, Jerusha! You can't think about that now.*

"Jerusha, are you all right?" Devorah's voice sounded sweet, sympathetic. *What is it with this woman? One minute she seems devious and seductive. The next minute she comes across kind and caring.*

"Yes, I'm all right. We've had quite a scare, that's all. And this heat." She dabbed her face with her cloak. "I wanted to ask you why you gasped at the man behind the cart. Did you know him?"

"I'm not sure. He reminded me of the soldier that told me to find you. It was his eyes. He had the same eyes, like yours."

"Oh! Well, thank you. You can go now. I know you're tired."

Devorah grabbed her little son's hand and looked at Jerusha, who stared for the longest moment.

"I'm not sure how safe you'll be here now," Jerusha confessed.

"I have no where else to go."

"You are welcome to stay, but I can not promise your safety."

"Thank you," Devorah said. As she watched the young widow and her child walk down the tiled path, Jerusha felt a heavy weight on her chest. She couldn't even keep her own child from dying. How will she keep these safe? She wondered what Timon would do? Or her grandfather? Or—?

Suddenly, she remembered father's cloak.

She rushed past Devorah and ran down the portico to her room. It had been several years since she had seen it. She flung open the old chest and began digging. She threw the tattered tunic and robe she wore as a slave to the floor, along with those of her mother. There, at the bottom of the chest, she saw it. She pulled out the cloak and held it up so she could see the tribe of Judah markings. She hugged it to her chest, its fragrant smell still strong after all those years.

Father.

***

A cool breeze rustled the leaves in the big olive tree that shaded her father's bench in the garden. A darkness crept over Jerusha's soul as the sun quickened its descent below the horizon to the west. She tightened her radiyd, flipped its ends over her shoulders and fingered the tzizit of the cloak laid over her arm. When her father gave it to her, he told her to trust him, that he loved her, and that they would see each other again. That had been ten years ago.

The tzitzit in her hand was frayed from the numerous times she had sat holding the cloak, begging YWH to bring her father home and take her away from Herod's abuse. When word came that he had died in an earthquake on Crete, a slave who rowed for a Roman ship, she refused to believe it. Now grandfather told her he might be alive. But a Roman soldier? None of it made sense.

What will happen to grandfather? She loved and respected the gentle giant like a father. Since the death of Stephen, her grandfather was the only father figure in her life. She must get word to him before he arrives in Rome.

I'll talk to Peter. He'll know what to do.

She separated the blue cord from the other strands and remembered her father's childhood instructions. When you are confused, look to YHWH, your Father in heaven. At the time, she was only seven years old. She cherished every word he spoke. Her eyes were on him, rather than an invisible Father in heaven. Later, her grandfather said that if she knew Yeshua, then she knew his Father. They were one and the same.

"I trusted you. You said I'd have a son. You lied! Just like my father lied. Month after month, I have waited. He never came. Month after month, I've waited for your blessing. It never came. Why? Why do you curse me?" She gripped the tzitzit so tight her nails dug into her flesh. An angry flush rose up her neck. "The old women whisper in the market place and point their fingers. I bring shame to my husband and my family. How will anyone be safe living with me? Why do you curse me? Why? I have loved you. I believed in you. I trusted you." Her whispered words were now a loud verbal assault. "And I know, like my father always said," she mocked, "I ask too many questions, but I'm so angry."

A deep yearning for Timon's, touch overwhelmed her. She had seen Devorah's desire for him. Why not? She was alone with two small children. No child could replace a husband. No child could replace Timon, either. She saw that now.

Timon, I'm so sorry.

A dark shadow moved over her toes, and she looked up at the cloud that drifted across the full moon.

A knowing deep within her began to surface. Somewhere, he watched the same moon and thought of her and prayed to Yeshua. She fell to her knees and wept, convinced no one under her roof would be safe, not only because the decree was removed, but because of her. She was cursed, forgotten, and abandoned by YHWH. She wiped the tears from her face, listened to the crickets and reflected on the many nights she spent with Timon in that garden. His words drifted into her thoughts.

Jerusha, our times and purpose are in Yeshua's hands.

Was he right? Maybe Yeshua had not lied. Maybe it was not time for the words he spoke to come to pass.

"I'm sorry, Yeshua. Take this anger from my heart. I want to trust again. I don't want to sink into that deep pit again like I did when I was little. Please help me." She wrapped her father's cloak around her shoulders to protect against the cool evening mist. *His ways are not our ways.* It sounded as if grandfather stood behind her. She turned to see. Her disappointment fanned the building anger, and she struck at the invisible giant.

"Are His ways to curse me?" She felt the anger rise again and wanted to scream.

The children you will have after you have lost the other, will say again in your ear, "make room for me to dwell."

Oh, grandfather, what does all of this mean? She squeezed her eyes shut and lifted her face to heaven. For the longest time she waited, the pomegranate fragrance strong in the damp air that hung over the garden.

"Yeshua, I surrender to your ways, whatever that means. Help me. I need your strength to work this out." She heard footsteps and raised her tired and achy body from the ground.

"Ima?" Sarah called from the gate. "Are you in the garden?"

"Yes, Sarah, I'm at father's bench." Jerusha heard the gate bang and the clip-clop of sandals increase in speed down the tiled path, a slight slide at the corner, and a giggle. When she rounded the corner, Sarah ran full speed at Jerusha and hugged with all her might, as though she would never let go.

'I love you, Ima," she said and released her grip, "Since Timon's gone, can I sleep with you?"

"Of course." Sarah tugged her hand.

"Come here. I found a chrysalis. I want you to see." She stuck her head in the pomegranate bush, her little behind sticking out. "Here it is." She parted the branches. "See?" The moonlight shone on the dark oblong structure. "Remember what you said about this. Remember when Stephen died, you told me not to be afraid, that Yeshua keeps us safe, just like the butterfly inside the chrysalis. When the soldier was at the gate, I closed my eyes and remembered if Yeshua protects the butterfly, he will protect me. It made me stop shaking."

"Sarah, what a big girl you are becoming. Wait until Timon gets home and I tell him how brave you were. I only hope I can be as brave as you."

"You are brave, Jerusha. I saw how you talked to that soldier. I'm glad Yogli was gone. I hope they don't find him. I don't want him to die like Stephen did." Jerusha listened all the way to her room, aware that Sara's constant chatter served to ease the fears they both felt about their future.

Chapter 9

"J-J-Jerusha," Moses yelled, "someone's at the gate." His long spindly legs jumped row to row over the plants. She adjusted the basket with the fresh mint she had picked and chuckled at his awkwardness. The rising sun twinkled off the morning dew covering the garden.

It was easy to slip from bed without waking the overly tired Sarah. Jerusha came to the garden to enjoy the fragrances and have time to think before she talked with Peter. She was happy that he had arrived the night before. His presence brought comfort to all, except her. She stayed away, hidden in her room and grieved.

"P-P-Peter wants you to come."

"Are the soldiers back?" She covered her head with her radiyd.

"No, a man and a woman are here. Let me help you with that." He took the basket. They both stepped carefully around the manure piles as they made their way to the kitchen door.

"What do they want?"

"To talk to you." Jerusha wondered if it had something to do with grandfather. Maybe he had found her father. The thought excited her and made her heart skip. Not only in anticipation of seeing her father, but knowing that her grandfather was safe.

"You can lay that basket on the table." She snatched a piece of fresh baked bread and gave it to him with goat's milk. "Stay here until I call for you and watch for Sarah. Give her some of your bread and milk when she wakes up." She poured water from a pitcher over each hand and dried them.

On the way to the front gate, she stopped at the vestibule, tucked her hair in the radiyd, and stared at her image in the shiny bronze mirror that lay next to the water pitcher on the table. Devorah had compared her eyes to the eyes of the trader. Jerusha never thought of her eyes as that different from anyone else. She looked closer.

They are different. Why had she not noticed his before today? And who was this trader that had eyes like hers?

Her thoughts were interrupted by Peter's boisterous laughter, drawing her attention back to the strangers at the gate. She felt much better since her complete surrender to YHWH. The joyous sounds of laughter infused new strength and confidence in her. Whatever lay ahead, her times and purpose were in his hands, the one who loved her enough to give His Son's life.

"If His power can raise him from the dead, then His power can handle any problem I face." She spoke the declaration with renewed faith.

Early morning rays shone through the olive trees that lined the path to the gate and warmed Jerusha's face. She stopped and peered through the branches at the two strangers. They were dressed in tattered and dirty cloaks, the apparel of beggars, and they conversed with Peter as though he knew them. Of course, many poor and needy people sought his wisdom and power. Even his shadow healed those who believed. What could they want with her?

"Well, let's find out who they are and why they're here." She threw the radiyd tighter over her shoulder.

"Jerusha." Peter took her hand. "I want you to meet Benjamin and his wife, Mariana."

"Shalom." They each kissed the customary greeting. A gnawing in Jerusha's stomach warned to be careful of these two. She eyed them carefully.

"I met Benjamin and Mariana when your uncle was alive. They are Sarah's parents."

Jerusha sucked in a short breath, her stomach hardening against the wave of nausea that swept over her whole body.

"I was telling them how Stephen found Sarah wandering the streets five years ago, and for months we tried to find them, thinking they'd been killed. Couldn't find jailer reports anywhere of what happened to them."

Dazed, she stood motionless and listened. "They tell me after their arrest by Caiaphas, they were shipped to Caesarea, and just released a month ago. Came to Jerusalem looking for her. Someone told them of Stephen's stoning and that Sarah now lived here." Eyes fixed on the couple, Jerusha saw their eyes dart between each other like thieves caught in a lie. "I was telling them you and Timon took good care of her, treated her as your own daughter these last four years."

Compassion for Jerusha showed in Peter's dark eyes. She felt woozy and placed her hand on his arm. "They have come to take her home." His words swirled around like a whirlwind in her thoughts.

Take her. They've come to take her.

In the past, she never let herself get too attached to the orphans, knowing it would make the good byes more difficult when the parents came back for them. Sarah was different. She belonged to her. Her parents were dead, gone forever, or so she had thought. Now, like ghosts out of the grave, they stood before her.

"Could we see Sarah?" The skinny apparition dressed in beggar's apparel with eyes sunk deep in darkened eye sockets approached. "We've missed her." Jerusha's fingers dug into Peter's arm.

"May I talk to Peter alone?"

"Of course," the woman nodded, "I-I can see you are disturbed."

"Follow me and I'll get my servant to bring fresh water to wash your feet." Jerusha played the part of hostess and led the guests past the fountain to the garden gate. "You may wait in here."

***

Jerusha squinted against the morning sun and stepped into the shadowy veranda. "Peter, I cannot bare to lose Sarah. She's like my own daughter. Are you sure these are her parents?"

"Yes, Jerusha, I am sure." He motioned for her to sit on a bench beside a potted hyssop. Its pungent smell was cleansing to Jerusha's senses. She picked a sprig of blue flowers and twirled it for a few minute before sitting. Peter's shadow moved across her face as he moved around the marble column and sat on bench across from her.

"I do not trust them." She bit her lip. "They act like thieves, their eyes darting back and forth between them, eyeing this place like preying vultures. How can they be Sarah's parents?"

"They are, Jerusha. As much as you do not want to admit it. You must let them have Sarah. They showed me a parchment that gave them legal rights to her."

"Peter, what if she does not want to go?"

"I am sure she will want to stay with you, but you must help her with this transition. It will not be easy on her. YHWH's ways are not our ways." Jerusha rolled her eyes. There it was again.

"I am so tired of people saying that. Just when I think I have surrendered it all, something else happens that I don't understand, and I have to give that to Yeshua, too." The angry, hurt little girl from the past wanted to take control again. "Why can't he do things my way just once? Why does it always have to be his way?"

In the silence, she knew he probably prayed. Why else would grandfather's deep voice echo in her thoughts. *YHWH said to tell you, "The children you will have, after you have lost the other, will say again in your ear, give place to me that I may dwell."* Frustrated at the mysterious message, she flopped her hands in her lap. Peter seemed to know her thoughts.

"Trust his ways, Jerusha. They are always better. One day you will understand what YHWH is saying to you through all this." She calmed down a little, and then suddenly she thought of Timon.

"What will Timon think if I let Sarah go with them?"

"He will know you had no other choice."

"Oh, Peter, so much has happened these last few days. You know they want to arrest grandfather if they find him."

"Yes, I heard."

"We need to get word to him."

"I have already sent some one to look for him."

"And they removed the decree form the door. I don't know how much longer we will be safe here," Again she flopped her hands in her lap. "Maybe Sarah would be better off with her parents. Maybe she will be safer with them." She rubbed the watery rim building in her eyes. "But I love her so much. Peter, I don't know if I can do this," Her voice trembled and she buried her face and muffled sobs in her hands. After a few minutes, Peter touched her arm.

"You can. You have more strength than you know."

Chapter 10

Jerusha laughed at Sarah, who sat on a milking stool in the lean-to off the kitchen, and was squirting goat's milk at Moses. The adeptness and strength of her tiny fingers against the udder was surprising for one so tiny. Her giggles echoed against Moses's pleas for her to stop.

She waited before interrupting their playfulness, desiring to soak in every detail of Sarah's facial expressions, her wide-eyed surprise at Moses's retaliation squirt, her wrinkled up nose at the goat's release of gas, and her thin-lipped stare at Moses when he teasingly threatened to turn her over his knee.

"Sarah, what will I do without you?" Jerusha whispered. She called out, a slight catch in her throat, "Sarah, you need to leave the milking to Moses and come with me. I have someone I want you to meet."

Sarah chattered all the way down the tiled veranda, around the corner and past the fountain. Before they entered the garden gate Jerusha picked her up and hugged her tight for the longest moment.

"What's wrong, Ima?" Jerusha closed her eyes and breathed in the straw smell in Sarah's hair, then leaned back and separated hay from hair and tossed the prickly sticks aside, ignoring her question.

"I want you to look pretty for our guests."

"Who are they?"

Jerusha sat Sarah's feet on the ground, straightened her radiyd, tucked in her hair, and brushed hay off her cloak.

"Now let me look at you." Sarah twirled around, arms extended in her butterfly dance position and Jerusha groaned inwardly and grabbed her again and squeezed tight. "I love you, Sarah," she whispered. "I will always love you."

"I love you, too. What's the matter?" Not yet ready to enter the garden, Jerusha sat on a rock next to a pomegranate bush and helped Sarah up.

"A man and woman came this morning," she pointed between the branches behind them. "See those two standing next to Peter. Do you remember them?"

Sarah crinkled her brow and cocked her head.

"Maybe."

"They are your parents." Sarah's eyes grew bigger than usual, and she looked again.

"My parents?"

"They came to take you home."

"No! You and Timon are my parents."

"They have been in jail in Caesarea and have missed you. They came all the way to Jerusalem to find you." She took Sarah's long thin fingers and clasped them in hers. "Timon and I will always love you and be here for you. But you must go with them."

"I don't want to!"

"And I don't want you to go either, but they love you and are your real parents. Besides, without the decree on our door, you will probably be safer with them anyway." She pulled Sarah into her chest and stroked the shiny black hair that shone in the sun where her radiyd had fallen off. "You will always be my Sarah, but I can't keep you from your parents. If they stay in Jerusalem, maybe we can see each other sometimes. Maybe they will bring you to Peter's meetings at our villa.

He's having one tonight, so we can pray for you and your new family. We invited them to stay tonight so you can get acquainted. In the morning you will go with them to your new home."

"Don't make me go," she pleaded. An inward battle raged in Jerusha's mind.

I can't make her go.

You have to.

No, I love her too much.

If you love her, you'll let her go.

She'll hate me if I make her go.

Do unto others what you would want done to you.

If I was Sara, I'd want to stay.

If you were her parents, you'd want her to go. Sarah's sobs soaked into her cloak, and Jerusha wiped tears from her face.

"Don't you love me?" the distraught youngster asked.

"Oh, Sarah. Of course I love you, but I can't keep your parents from enjoying their little girl. You belong to them." *Yeshua help me be strong. Show me the way.*

"Sarah, remember when Hosea didn't want to go with his new family? Do you remember what you said? You said 'sometimes we don't get what we want. Sometimes it's better.'"

"Yes, I remember," she whimpered.

"Sarah, give your parents a chance. They came all the way from Caesarea to find you." She lifted Sarah's chin and looked into her dark eyes. "Promise me you will try." Tears rimmed Sarah's eyes, but she nodded.

"All right, I'll try. For you, Jerusha, I will try."

***

Jerusha nudged Sarah toward the couple in the lamp-lit courtyard, their arms open to greet her. The tiny girl eased her way to the woman whose smile showed crooked yellow teeth. She looked back at Jerusha who motioned her forward. The woman reached inside her cloak and retrieved a dirty rag doll from its folds, and beckoned by bouncing it up and down.

"Hi Sarah. It's been a long time. Do you remember this?"

Sarah ran and grabbed it and held it tight to her chest. "That's mine!" The woman enveloped her in hugs and kisses.

"I've missed you so much. I was afraid I'd never see you again."

"What's your name?

"Mariana, but call me ima."

"I call Jerusha ima."

"Well, maybe for a while you can call me Mariana, at least, until you are more comfortable with being home. I am your mother. Do you remember me?"

"No, but I remember my doll. Did you give it to me?" Jerusha saw the woman's disappointment.

"Yes, I made it. When the soldiers took you from my arms, the doll fell to the ground. I quickly hid it in my garment before they took your father and me away. I've kept it for you. I asked YHWH nightly to keep you safe."

Sarah raised the doll and showed Jerusha, who blinked back tears and nodded.

"It's beautiful, Sarah, just like you."

Sarah pointed to the man behind the woman.

"Who's he?"

"Your aba." The new father knelt before Sarah.

"Timon's my aba. He's married to Jerusha. He's gone. He's taking orphans to a safe place. I love him."

"Well, for now, call me Benjamin." Sarah looked like her father, the same big round eyes with long lashes. His thin muscular build, decimated by starvation, spoke of a man who at one time carried himself like a king, the same aloofness Jerusha saw in Sarah's stride. Sarah looked at him and cocked her head.

"I think I remember you. You carried me on your shoulders so I could see over the people in the marketplace."

"Yes, yes, I'm surprised you remember. You were so young." Sarah took his hand and pulled.

"Come with me. I want to show you my chrysalis." He let her lead him up the path with the woman following. One glance over her shoulder at Jerusha and Sarah turned the corner out of sight. Jerusha rushed past her mother, who stood beside the gate. This couldn't be happening. Wasn't the miscarriage enough? Why Sarah, too?

***

That evening the voices hummed like a buzz in her ears, indistinct and unclear. Nothing mattered now. An empty void in her stomach, Jerusha watched Sarah interact with her mother, while Peter and James, another Yeshua leader of the Way, disputed the kingdom with Sarah's father. Shadows danced on Jerusha's face from the lamp on the wall behind her.

"Why not fight Rome?" Benjamin argued. "YHWH will defend his holy city."

"Yeshua tells us to love our enemies," James countered, "His kingdom is not of this world."

"Love?" the scrawny fighter yelled, "We must destroy the pagan beasts!" Jerusha cared not for their dispute. Her eyes were on Sarah, and her heart felt numb.

A loud commotion at the front gate startled Jerusha from her stupor, and she watched the other Yeshua followers scatter, most running to the kitchen where they could escape if need be. The whole scene unfolded in slow motion before her eyes as Mariana grabbed Sarah and followed Abigail and Devorah, whose children slept in her room. Jerusha moved, like a sleepwalker, toward the gate.

"The soldiers are back," Moses yelled.

When Sarah's father swished past Jerusha, Peter grabbed his arm and abruptly pulled the smaller man to a stop.

"Do not challenge them. We will not fight," he warned, his eyes steady, unmoving.

Sarah's father glowered, then covered the dagger he had tucked in his belt with his cloak and reluctantly nodded agreement.

"Be careful in the days ahead, my friend," he spoke to Peter through narrow eyes. "If you do not fight with us, you fight against us. Many like you have been left with a slit throat, even in a crowed place."

His threats against Peter added to the building confusion that clouded her thoughts.

"Like James said, Yeshua's kingdom is not of this world, Benjamin." Peter spoke with calm authority.

"We came for Sarah, not a fight with Rome, so I yield to your will in this matter, but like I said, be careful in days ahead."

Once at the gate, Peter addressed the soldiers.

"What is it that you want?"

"Where's that woman?" the soldier demanded. "She knows what we want." Jerusha stepped between Peter and James, a numb haze still hovering.

"Regulus is not here." Her words sounded lifeless.

"Where is he?" he yelled.

"I don't know." Again she sounded void of life or power.

"Open the gate!" he demanded. "If he's not here, we return to Rome. It's rumored he's gone to ask the new Caesar for favor. A tortuous death on a cross is the only favor he'll receive."

Jerusha wondered where he learned that her grandfather had gone to Rome. Who told him? No one but Timon and Peter knew, and maybe her mother. Perhaps Devorah had overheard Timon's conversation with her grandfather.

"You may search, but you will not find him," she stated flatly, and then unlocked the gate. A cohort of soldiers crashed through the opening, pushing her aside. Peter helped her up, and they waited as the soldiers rummaged through the villa.

Benjamin looked like a cat ready to pounce. She saw the same hatred in his eyes she had seen in Timon's before he forgave those who stoned Stephen. A sick feeling swept over her. How could she let Sarah live with a man filled with such hatred? Moments later, she locked the gate and listened as the soldiers marched back down the hill.

***

After they left, Peter gathered everyone in the garden. Jerusha separated herself from the others and found her father's bench. A short distance away, the others whispered prayers over Sarah, Benjamin, and Mariana.

"YHWH Father, we thank you for your protection. Their lives are in your hands." James prayed. Jerusha felt a tap on her shoulder and looked up. It was Peter.

"May I join you?" He pointed to the empty space on the bench. She nodded. They sat in silence for a while before Jerusha broke the quiet with a deep plea.

"Am I cursed?" Her words sounded hollow. Staring at the fisherman's giant weatherworn hands triggered a forgotten memory of her father's hands whittling intricate details into wood. She remembered his tender question: 'What has taken the dance from your feet?'

It had been awhile since she danced alone in the garden with Yeshua. Something held her back, and her will to dance was gone. Barren and fearful of her unworthiness, she ran from that kind of intimacy, much like she had done with Timon when she hid from him the shame of her past abuse.

"You are not cursed."

"I feel cursed."

"Jerusha, your father's blood flows through your veins. You are royalty. If he's alive, wherever he is, he's praying for you, just like you will continue to pray for Sarah. The Psalm says, 'Joy comes in the morning.'"

"I can't rejoice in all of this." She threw her arms out in a circle.

Peter sat still and silent as a statue, staring into the darkness. Finally, he spoke.

"These trials will strengthen your faith and trust. When you come through it, you will comfort others. Like Stephen taught you, dance, Jerusha, dance on the injustices you suffer."

That night, after everyone left the garden, she tried to dance, but stumbled in despair. "Yeshua, are you there?" She looked up at the cloudless night, the stars shining bright. Deep within, the old melody rose to her conscious mind. "I am the lion of Judah. Deep within your innermost being dwells the Holy God of all Israel. I am the Lion of Judah. She clasped the lion pendant in her hand.

I am within you, Jerusha.

***

The next morning, Jerusha looked down at Sarah, who clutched her waist and burrowed her head in her chest. Slivers of dawn shone through the olive leaves on the little one's shiny black hair.

"Don't make me go," she groaned. "I want to stay with you."

Benjamin and Mariana waited by the gate, the doll in her mother's hand. Peter stood behind Jerusha, his strength a calming presence.

Jerusha peeled Sarah off her waist, took her hand and led her around the pomegranate bush, its blossoms a refreshing fragrance against the smelly clothes of the parents.

She felt the pendant beneath her tunic and remembered the day father gave it to her. *"This is for you from the one who loves you more than you know. Jerusha, you are royalty from the tribe of Judah. The acacia represents YHWH's presence. The words on its back represent his promise to come one day, destroy our enemies and set up His kingdom. Never forget who you are."* She lifted the pendant and stared at the words engraved in gold on the back. *Arise Lord. Let your enemies be scattered. Let all who hate you flee before you.* She removed it and placed it over Sarah's head and straightened the lion face, like her father had done for her.

"I'm giving you my pendant. Sarah blinked.

"For me?"

"Like my father told me, I'm telling you. Never forget who you are. You are royalty. If you get afraid, remember Yeshua is always with you." She hid the pendant beneath Sarah's tunic, patted it and noticed a glistening rim forming in Sarah's eyes. "I love you more than you know." A single tear broke lose and ran down Sarah's face. Jerusha swept her up in her arms and they clung to each other for the longest moment. Peter peeled Sarah's arms loose and carried her to her parents while Jerusha stared, a darkness enveloping her soul. The father held the crying girl in his arms as Peter let them out the gate, Mariana following behind. She looked back at Jerusha and mouthed the words, thank you.

"Will she be safe?" she asked Peter as she watched their backs disappear down the hill.

"She's in YHWH's hands. You will see her again one day soon." Jerusha saw the grim look in his eyes and wondered why she wasn't comforted by his words.

Chapter 11

Darkness enveloped the city. Jerusha snuck away from the villa unnoticed and crept along the wall that overlooked the temple below. Her shadow was the only movement in the early predawn hours, and her sandaled feet on stone were the only sound. She had get to her father's workshop in the lower city before the sun rose. The note had said, "Come alone before sunup."

She wondered if it was a trap, but why would her enemy wait in her father's workshop? Of course, if they arrested her, there no one would know what had happened until it was too late. She shrugged off the ominous thoughts and continued walking, the light of the full moon illuminating her way. She had to hurry. She only had a few hours before the sun would rise over the horizon.

Down deep, she believed her grandfather had sent the note.

It must be him, but why not come to the villa? Why meet her alone?

She stopped. The wind picked up and rustled the olive trees overhead. *What if it's not him?* She searched the ground for a stone—

one large enough to use as a weapon if it came to that. She spotted the perfect one laying next to the olive tree's root. She dug with her fingers until it was loose and lifted it up. It was heavy, but not too heavy.

With her other hand, she tightened her radiyd and moved swiftly down the bazaar steps. A dog growled in a dark alcove. She backed away and took a different route. She had to make it past the temple guards without being seen.. They would recognize her and would certainly inform the high priest, or worse, arrest her. She crouched low to the ground, watching the guards and waiting for her chance. The guards paced back and forth, alert for any threat. When they were not looking in her direction, she scampered to the nearest dark shadow and stood motionless, her heart pounding in her chest. She waited to make next her move until the guards had reached the end of their route and turned to walk in the other direction. She moved like a ghost into the narrow passage that wound between the limestone dwellings in the lower city. Thick smoke spiraled from windows. She raised her radiyd over her nose, turned left, then right, and then left again. In the dark, every path looked the same.

I think I might be going in circles.

She froze. A slight movement to her right caught her attention. She held her breath and waited, then looked over her shoulder and squeezed the stone tight. The full moon shed enough light to see in the dark alleyway. No movement. Why had she not paid better attention?

She knew most of Jerusalem pretty well. This looked like the part her father had warned her about because it was not safe for little girls. From the looks of things, Jerusha was not certain it was safe for big girls either. Surveying her options, she concluded there was only one way out. Raising her cloak above her feet, she ran as fast as she could down the steep hill, afraid at any moment she'd be grabbed by a stranger. Her feet flew so fast she almost stumbled, but she came to a skidding stop at the bottom. She scanned the open market place and breathed a sigh of relief to see her father's workshop at the far end.

An increased urgency to get there arose, not only to beat the sunrise, but because someone followed. His shadow darted between the dwellings, a growling dog confirming it. Her heart thudded in her chest. She eyed the open space. A few traders slept on the ground, their heads propped on sleeping camels. If she could get to her grandfather, she would be safe. She smiled at the thought of his giant frame towering above any thief who threatened to rob her, and then she remembered he had told her to come alone. Somehow, she must find a way to ditch whoever was following her.

She scampered across the open space and ducked behind a wooden cart. She waited and watched for movement. Nothing. She carefully backed away from the cart, keeping her eyes on the open area and alert for any movement. She stepped between the metal smith's shop and the baker's city oven and then maneuvered herself behind other shops that were nestled along the city wall. Only a few more shops to go before she stood behind her father's tent. Before proceeding, she peeked around the silversmith's wall for signs of movement. She saw nothing, save for a sheep who suckled her newborn lamb and bleated at the donkey tied to the corral gate. Maybe she gave them the slip. Clouds drifted between earth and moon and gave better cover. She relaxed and felt her way in the shadowy darkness.

Only one shop remained before the carpenter's tent, the place where Yeshua and her father shared trade secrets, and where Timon learned to whittle designs on beautiful boxes, bowls, and cups as her father's apprentice.

It was mindboggling. Yeshua, YHWH's Son and Mashiach, was her father's friend, and hers as a little girl. Now, He was her King. *Never forget who you are. You are royalty.* Shadows moved across her feet, and she looked up and searched the sky. The lion sign her father had shown her as a little girl twinkled brightly. The star in its chest, called Regulus, shown brighter than ever. Regulus meant little king or prince and was her grandfather's nickname, or cognomen. She often wondered how he had gotten that name, but whenever she asked, he grew quiet and changed the subject.

Gripping the back flap of the tent, she checked one more time to see if she was followed. Seeing nothing, she ducked inside. The flap closed behind her, enveloping her in total darkness. A large hand covered her mouth, and pulled hard into a muscular body. She could not scream, and she could not move.

"Do not scream and I'll let you go," a gruff, but familiar voice whispered. Terrified, she kicked his shin and wrestled against his strength to get loose.

"My little lioness, don't be afraid." Her eyes popped open.

Father?

Her heart raced, but she stopped fighting. His grip relaxed. Nestled against his chest, her senses took in a fragrance familiar to the little girl of years gone by. It was the same fragrance of the robe she had cuddled while in captivity while dreaming of her father's return. The man removed his hand from her mouth.

"Father?" Her voice was barely audible.

"Yes, it is me." Her body slumped and he cradled her in his arms as they both slipped to the floor. Nestled against his chest, she took comfort in the familiar fragrance of his robe. How long she had waited and hoped for this day. It seemed unreal, like a dream.

"Father!"

"Yes, Jerusha, my little lioness." It had been a long time, but she knew that voice.

"Father." She clung to his neck as he swooped his arms beneath her legs and stood. For the next few minutes, her sobs soaked into his tunic, and he stroked her hair.

"My Jerusha. My little butterfly. How I have missed you."

Chapter 12

The soft light of dawn filtered through the flaps onto Jerusha's face. She squinted and shifted her weight on the wooden stool. She could not help but stare at her father, who sat across from her at a small unfinished table. He looked at home with the mallets, bowdrills, and saws that hung on the back wall behind him. Sawdust covered the apron that held chisels, hones, and bradawls. The man in front of her was not the young man she remembered as her father. His short hair had streaks of silver at the temples. She reached up and touched a deep scar on his chin. Had it always been there? It would have been beneath his full beard, which she had never seen him without, until today. She cocked her head.

"You look different. I almost don't recognize you. I've never seen you without your beard. The pe'ots are gone that I used to twirl around my finger. And your hair is short, like the Roman soldiers that you hated."

He ran his fingers through the short dark strands and rubbed his chin.

"Yes, I have become one of them. YHWH's plan, not mine."

"YHWH's plan? To rip families apart and kill those who love Him? What's happened to you?" Her voice trembled with sad anger.

Jacob stood and turned to face the wall. He seemed shorter than she remembered. Of course she had grown, and not only in height, but in other ways. Her love for Yeshua compelled her to love her enemies, the least of which were the Roman soldiers. This inner struggle was a daily battle. She glanced at his broad shoulders and rubbed her temples. Her father a Roman soldier? An enemy?

"You must believe me when I tell you YHWH miraculously protected me from ever having to do those things." His voice grew softer with every word. "Many a night I spent in darkness throwing up my stomach contents because of the atrocities I watched against YHWH's people. I begged Him to take my life, to let me be killed." He grabbed a chisel from the wall. "I would have ended it, had it not been for a slave boy, a Yeshua follower, who stopped me. That night I looked toward the lion sign in the stars and begged YHWH for relief. A calm settled my thoughts, and a week later, a bright light appeared in my tent. His voice penetrated a deep darkness in my soul. "Son, you are called for this purpose. Many Romans will enter my kingdom because of your station in this army." I have wrestled with the idea of Gentiles in His kingdom. Seemed absurd. Although I believed it would happen, all I wanted was to come home to Jerusalem. Come home to you and your mother." Jerusha rose and stepped close. The deep pain in his eyes tore at her heart.

"Father, I'm sorry I accused you." She touched his arm. "Grandfather says His ways are not our ways," A smile spread across her face. "After his campaign, he came to Jerusalem looking for you, but you were gone. Somehow he found out mother and I were slaves in Herod's palace." She noticed a slight twitch in his brow. "It was only after Saul began persecuting Yeshua followers that he revealed he was my grandfather. He was instrumental in keeping us safe."

"W-wait!" Jacob put his hand up and stopped her. "You said slaves. You were slaves? I thought—"

Jerusha interrupted.

"You thought the high priest loved mother? No, Father, he betrayed her and made us his slaves. Years later, Stephen and the others bought our freedom."

"I must repay Stephen."

Jerusha turned away.

"He's dead, Father. Saul convinced Caiaphas to stone him. You should have seen him. He boldly stood before the Sanhedrin and spoke of Yeshua's kingdom. He loved his enemies, even as they pummeled him with stones."

"I only met Stephen for a short time the night before I was arrested. He promised to watch over you until I returned." After a long silence, Jerusha walked to the tool apron and rubbed her finger across the worn edge.

"Why didn't you come for me, Father?"

"I intended to. I wanted to. My plan was to prepare a safe place, then come for you. I hoped your mother would change her mind and we could be together as a family. But the night you and your mother left, the Sanhedrin arrested me and turned me over to the Romans who forced me into slavery. I survived, only by becoming one of them. At times I hated myself. Had it not been for YHWH's intervention, I would be dead."

"Oh, Father, I'm sorry. I should have listened to Mother. She tried to tell me that you had to leave and that she wouldn't go with you, that she was afraid living with you would get us killed."

"If I thought she loved me, I would have stayed."

"She's changed. She believes in Yeshua's way now. I think she's always loved you."

He swallowed hard, and squeezed his eyes shut. When he opened them, a single tear rolled down his cheek. Unashamed, he wiped it away.

"I still love your mother. She looked as beautiful as ever this morning at the gate."

"That was you? You were the trader who watched from behind the cart?"

Jacob smacked his fist into his palm. "When that centurion spit on you, he about got his face bashed in."

Jerusha chuckled. "Oh, father, I love you." she ran to him and snuggled in his warm embrace, her cheek against the soft tunic. "I was furious when you didn't come. Sometimes I wondered if it was because of what Efah did."

"Argh! I never liked that boy. No offspring of that infidel, Chaiphas, could be any good. The way he used his priestly powers to destroy our family burned at my soul for a long time. What has his son done?" He tenderly lifted Jerusha's chin and stared into her eyes. "Is this what put a wall around my little lioness's heart?"

She nodded.

"Tell me, Jerusha, what happened." No longer that shamed little girl, she opened her heart and told him how they touched her. How she endured by holding the pendant he made and quoting the words on its back: *Arise Lord. Let your enemies be scattered. Let all who hate you flee before you.* She told how she felt dirty, ashamed, and ruined for any husband. How dancing with Yeshua set her free to love and accept Timon as her husband. When she stopped, he waited in silence and stroked her hair.

"I see the wall has come down, but I sense there's something else. What is it, Jerusha? What is wrong?"

Her father had always had the ability to see into her soul. Trying to hide anything from him was foolish. Somehow, he knew her innermost thoughts. He might as well know now that she would not bare him grandsons to carry on the royal lineage. Tears welled up and overflowed down her cheeks.

"Oh, Father, I am cursed." Her voice trembled. "I have not been able to bear sons for Timon." The words sounded flat. "What's wrong with me that YHWH has not opened my womb?" She closed her eyes and tried to compose herself while she waited for his response. Her head hung down in the silence. She heard the squeak of an old hinge and turned to look. He knelt over an open trunk and held a small object wrapped in purple cloth.

"Jerusha, come here." He patted his knee. "I want you to have something." She straightened her cloak and slowly lowered herself onto his leg. The strength in his thigh supported her weight with no trouble and he wrapped one arm around her waist and held the gift in purple cloth in front of her. "Open it."

Her fingers tremble as she unfolded the cloth. A round piece of acacia wood and a gold ring lay in his palm. She felt drawn to the less sparkly one and picked it up.

"Yeshua gave me that at your miraculous birth. At that time, I didn't know he was the Mashiach, our Messiah, our King. He was just a carpenter, a friend, who visited during the feasts." She rubbed her finger over the butterfly shape in the middle, surrounded by decorative pomegranates and remembered the times Yeshua chased butterflies with her in the garden. "He said, you were my special treasure from heaven." Her father pick up the golden ring and showed her the butterfly indention on the nose of the lion face. "Your grandfather gave me this signet ring when I was a boy. Because he was a Roman soldier, I was ashamed of it and hid it. When Yeshua gave me that wooden butterfly ornament, I understood, for the first time, what a wonderful inheritance my father had given me, but it was too late. I thought he was dead. I want, more than anything, to see him again and tell him I love him. When I heard yesterday that he was alive and that the Romans were looking for him, I sent a courier to stop him on the Roman road. I pray the courier gets there in time." He laid the gold signet ring in her hand. "I'm telling you this because, Jerusha, there is nothing wrong with you. You are my special treasure from heaven. Never forget who you are. You are royalty. YHWH has an inheritance for you, special sons and daughters from heaven. I tell you what Yeshua told me: 'Whatever happens, Jerusha, YHWH makes all things beautiful in its time.' She threw her arms around his neck.

"Oh, Father, thank you."

"I love you, my little lioness, my little butterfly," His words were soft in her ear as he patted her back. She never wanted to let go. "And Timon? Is he well?"

"Yes. He left yesterday with the orphans and widows. I'm not sure when he'll return. I already miss him, and he's only been gone for a day. At least I have you back." She sniffled and rubbed her nose.

Jacob pulled her arms from around his neck and lifted her up. He picked up a piece of acacia wood that lay on the floor and savored its fragrance, while he peered around the tent.

"I see he's been at work. That's good." Her father lay the acacia scrap on a table and rubbed his finger on pomegranates carved on the edge. He stared for a long moment at his tools, a far away look in his eyes.

"I hear the soldiers in the distance." He enveloped her in a tight hug. "I must go."

"No, please don't go." Her sniffles turned to sobs in his chest.

"I must, Jerusha, but I'll send letters when I can. Did you get my other letters?"

"No." She hiccupped and wiped her eyes.

"I sent many letters." One eyebrow raised a little and his forehead crinkled. "That tells me there is betrayal in the ranks. Hopefully not the courier I sent to your grandfather." Jerusha's heart fluttered like butterfly wings. "I will try to be in touch somehow. I cannot reveal my identity, yet. I have been preparing a place for us."

"Here's where you belong. In Jerusalem with me." She pouted and crossed her arms.

"Oh, Jerusha, how I wish I could do that, but troubled times lay ahead. We must be wise." He lifted her chin.

"When the time is right, all of us will flee Jerusalem, like Yeshua told us." He paused for a moment. "Tell your mother I love her and will come for her when I can." Then he grabbed her shoulders. "But, Jerusha, this new Caesar is dangerous. Be careful. I'll warn you if I hear anything." She watched him wrap the cloth turban around his head and cover everything but his eyes. "I'm not sure I can trust a courier to come to you." When he lifted the sword, it seemed as light as the pendant around her neck. Such strength. He slipped it in its scabbard and attached it to his belt beneath his cloak.

Suddenly, she remembered Devorah.

"Oh, Father, why did you send that woman to us? I'm trying to be kind, but she annoys me."

"What woman?"

"Devorah."

"I do not know a Devorah, and I most certainly did not send her."

"She said you found her in a cave and sent her to us for safety." He took Jerusha by the shoulders.

"Be wary of her, Jerusha. There is betrayal in both our camps."

"Father, don't leave." Tears came unhindered again. "I need you."
He gave a quick hug and looked back.

"I'll be in touch." He blinked back the tears that threatened to
flow, and then ducked outside. Jerusha collapsed to the floor and
muffled her sobs in the purple cloth. The two treasures rolled off her
lap, and butterfly sparkles bounced on the faded black walls. She was
alone again.

Chapter 13

By the time Jerusha left the carpenter's tent, the market was bustling with activity. She lingered among the crowd, looking for her father. High on the rampart a Roman soldier's red plume waved in the breeze. Light reflected off the helmet. She shielded her eyes to get a better look.

It's him.

Her heart jumped to her throat. She raised her hand but then lowered it. How could he see her among all these people? She watched him descend the steps, and her eyes followed the red plume as it moved among the crowd. She hoped he would come her way, but she lost sight of him. He was probably with the other legionnaires, who were assembling behind the standard. Outside the gate, the aquilifer held the gold eagle high for all to see.

Romans. Her heart sunk to her stomach. *Why? Why a Roman soldier? And why does he have to leave again?* A camel plopped its haunches down and grunted his displeasure. *My sentiments exactly.*

Jostled by the crowd, she bumped against the trader who was busy urging the stubborn beast to his feet. Suddenly, the animal leapt to its feet, knocking her to the ground. She threw out her hands as she fell and hit the ground with a thud. Her breath exploded from her chest, and her head whipped forward. She squeezed her eyes shut just in time, as her face landed in a pile of fresh manure. She blinked and saw the hoof of the camel just six inches from her head. Her stomach lurched and bile came up in her throat.

Don't do it. Don't throw up. Don't make it worse.

She raised herself up on her elbows. The camel's annoyed grunts grew louder, and the shoppers pointed and laughed. Then, she felt strong hands from behind grab her and lift her to her feet.

"Steady, little lioness."

"Grandfather?" Her radyid flopped in the wind. She shoved back the hair that covered her eyes and looked up.

"It *is* you!" She hugged him tight.

"Careful, little one. Others are watching." He removed her arms.

She glanced around. Most had returned to shopping, but a few stared. She could not blame them. She rubbed her mouth with the back of her hand.

"Yuck! I got it all over you." She brushed his cloak.

"Never mind that," he chuckled. "Are you hurt?" He untied a clay jug from the pack on the camel's back and pretended to show it to her. "We are still being watched." Only his blue eyes showed above the turban wrapped around his face.

Playing along, Jerusha took the jug, looked it over, and shook her head. Pretending to be uninterested, she turned away. Regulus put the jug back on the pack and removed a small rug, insisting she examine it.

"Father's alive. I saw him." Her fingers combed through the soft fur of the rug. A knot welled up in her throat. She swallowed. No crying here.

"Yes, I know. I found him or rather, he found me." He glanced around. "We must be careful." He took the rug from her and continued. "Wait here for a while, and then meet me in the garden up the hill. The one where your father gave you the pendant."

She grabbed for it, the empty spot around her neck a cruel reminder.

"Sarah. They took Sarah." She gazed up at him.

"Who? He seemed preoccupied with the camel.

"Her parents." She grabbed his arm. He stopped and glanced down. She looked through a watery film. "They came and took her." Her fingers dug deep into his skin.

"I'm sorry, Jerusha." He sniffed and rubbed his nose.

"I am afraid, Grandfather. For her. For us."

"Be brave. Remember who you are." He pulled the camel around.

A cursed woman, that's who I am. She swallowed and dipped her chin. Grandfather's home. The camel snorted, and she looked into his brown eyes.

"Do not blink those lashes at me." She tapped his nose and turned away.

***

Jerusha knelt by a stream, dipped her radyid in the cool water and dabbed at the manure on her face. Phew. She smelled horrid. What would Timon think? She flipped loose hair to one side and began braiding it, but then stopped. He liked her hair to hang free. She began braiding again. It can hang free when he gets back. Today she needed it off her neck. When her grandfather arrived she would tell him about Devorah.

"Shalom," her grandfather's voice thundered across the garden. Her heart danced. Oh, how she loved that giant and depended on his wisdom. Timon, too. Both men's discernment and insight had guided and protected them for some time. She jumped to her feet and ran to greet him.

"Shalom. Come. Sit on my favorite rock." Her hand swept toward a large, smooth stone beside the stream in the shade.

I'm so glad you're home." She threw her arms around his waist and hugged tight. It did not matter that he smelled like manure; after all, so did she. He was home, and she never wanted to let go.

"Jerusha, my little lioness. If you only knew the authority you carry." When she was around her grandfather, she felt strong and courageous. She finally released her arms from his waist and sat beside him on the rock, her toes touching the stream below. She could hear the silver green olive leaves that rustled overhead.

"What's going to happen to us?" She scratched her wrinkled brow. "I fear for Father's safety. He's in the Roman army. What could be worse than that?

"He could be dead." His words landed flat on her ears. She ignored the comment.

"And Timon. Who knows where he is? If he is safe? She wiggled her toes. The coolness felt good. The late afternoon sun filtered through the branches, their scraggly form casting shadows like spindly fingers. "The high priest hates us. Sarah's gone. Rome wants to arrest you. And I'm barren."

"Do you have any more good news?" He chuckled.

"Oh, I almost forgot." Water splashed as she jumped down and spun around. "Father did not send Devorah." The smelly radyid flopped her nose, and she flicked it away. "She lied." Jerusha rested her hands on his knees. "I never trusted her," She straightened up. "Who sent her? Why is she here? What does she want?"

"There you go again with the questions."

"I mean it, Grandfather. We need to watch her. She's trouble," Jerusha shrugged her shoulders back. As if we needed any more trouble." She spun around again." Maybe she's the cause of all this. The Romans pulling down the decree and seeking your arrest. Do you suppose she told Sarah's parents where we live?"

Both elbows on his knees, grandfather leaned his chin on clenched fists. His stare across the horizon told Jerusha to be still. She had seen him like this before. Contemplative. Quiet. Listening for YHWH's voice. Maybe that's what she should do, too. Wrapping her radyid around her head and shoulders, she scooted next to him, comforted by his presence. Could the soft wisps across her face be angels' wings? King Yeshua must be watching. A calm settled over her thoughts. She closed her eyes and listened for His still, small voice.

"J-J-Jerusha," Moses called. "Where have you been? Your m-m-mother has been worried." She flinched, his voice not the one she expected, but one who loved her just the same. Scanning the garden, she found him next to the gate.

"Oh, no," she groaned, "I forgot Mother didn't know I left," she jumped up. "Moses, quick, run tell her I'm all right." She glanced at grandfather. "But Moses do *not* tell her you saw grandfather. I'll explain, later.

"Don't worry, Jerusha. You can trust me. I w-w-won't tell. Your s-s-secret's safe with me." Dust flew from his sandals as he wound down the path. Grandfather stood.

"You must go. It's not safe to be caught with me." He gathered his things. "Tell Peter I will meet him in the stable at midnight. I have some things to discuss with him."

"But, Grandfather, they might be watching for you to come back. Devorah may be their spy."

"You forget that this villa was built by me. I have secret passages you don't know about." He tapped her nose. "Don't worry, and remember to tell Peter—midnight. And tell him to come alone."

"Where are you going now?"

"There's a tomb, not far from here. James arranged it. I will be safe there.

"Be careful. The priest's guards know you well, and they will be looking for you. A blond, blue-eyed giant will stand out. She considered her words, tilting her head in curiosity. She had always wondered about her grandfather's appearance.

Tribe of Judah? He certainly doesn't look like a Hebrew.

"Take the camel with you, but bring it back at the early morning watch." He handed her the rope. Just pull. He will follow."

"Bring him where?" The camel lowered his head as if to say, "You again?" She rubbed his nose.

"Look for me among the other caravans outside the city gate. I will be leaving with them."

"Don't leave, Grandfather. I need you. Timon's gone. Father's gone. What will I do without you?"

"Trust Yeshua. Be strong, like the lioness you are."

"Why do I have to be the strong one? Why can't you just stay with me? She hung on his arm. "When will this all end?"

"Our times are in YHWH's hands. You're not alone, Jerusha. Your Father in heaven watches over you. His thoughts toward you are more than the sands of the sea." He wrapped the turban high around his face. "Peter will stay until Timon returns." He prodded the camel. "Now go, Jerusha. I'll see you in the morning."

Chapter 14

"Where have you been?" Abigail held the gate open. Jerusha dropped the rope and ran up the last incline, her cloak raised high over her sandaled feet.

"Mother, I have so much to tell you." She unwrapped her radyid.

"Phew. You smell. And where did you get the camel?" She motioned to Moses. "Take the beast to the stable."

Dust flew in the air as he grabbed the rope. He slapped the beast on its rump and then moseyed down the path that led to the stable. Jerusha stared at the animal's rump and pondered her grandfather's words. *What secret entrance does he know about?* She shook her head. A man of many surprises.

"Stop daydreaming. I'm not too happy with you." Her mother locked the gate. "You may be married, but in times like these, until Yogli or Timon come back, you need to tell me when you're leaving. I talked to Yeshua all night. He seemed unconcerned, but it made for a long night for me. It's difficult for a mother not to worry, even when Yeshua says, 'Peace. Be still.'"

"I am sorry. I should have told you, but I was afraid you'd try to stop me." Jerusha looked around. "Mother, please, can we find a quiet place to talk alone? How about your room?"

"Yes, I want to hear all about your night. I will meet you there after I check on Devorah."

Jerusha's eyebrows raised. "How is Devorah?" She tried not to mock, but her insides boiled. She intended to do a lot of checking on Devorah.

***

Clean clothes and a washed face did wonders for Jerusha's morale. She hid the treasures her father had given her in her favorite hiding place. The long stroll down the hallway gave her time to think what to say. Lamps flickered fingers of light on the wall. Devorah's door squeaked, and Jerusha stopped. She slipped back and peeked around the corner. Devorah stuck her head out and looked both ways before stepping into the hallway. Suspicious behavior. Maybe she should follow. Jerusha ducked into the shadows, unseen by Devorah, as she past the corner. A strong fragrance lingered.

Jerusha started to follow, but quickly changed her mind. *Mother's waiting and I have so much to tell her.*

As Jerusha approached her mother's room, she could hear her humming a joyful melody. Jerusha wondered how her mother would feel about her father's return. *Maybe she doesn't need to know everything tonight. She definitely needs to know about Devorah, but if I tell her about Devorah, I will have to tell her about Father.* Her thoughts were interrupted by Abigail's voice.

"Come in. Sit. I have water ready for your feet." Her mother waved a welcome. Jerusha sat on the mittah and let her mother remove her sandals and dip her feet in the cool water.

"Now, tell me about last night. Why did you leave, and where did you go?"

"Well, Moses brought me a note. A stranger left it. The note said to come to father's workshop before dawn, and to come alone."

"Jerusha! You met a stranger alone? You are right. I would not have wanted you to go."

"I thought it was a note from grandfather. I knew he would be arrested if he came here. I know they are watching our villa for his return.

"If it was him, he would have told you who he was."

"I didn't think of that."

"Well, next time, maybe, you should think before you act."

"Mother, please, look at me." Her mother looked up. "It was Father." The water stopped pouring on her feet. Abigail's mouth fell open.

"Your Father's alive?" She placed the pitcher down.

Jerusha took her feet out of the water and dried them herself. "Yes. He's a Roman soldier."

"What?"

"I know it's hard to believe. He looked so different. His hair is short. He has no beard."

"Why didn't he send for me, too?"

"He wasn't sure if you would want to see him. Mother, he still loves you."

"He said he still loved me?" She straightened her hair and gazed out the window. Even in the shadows she glowed; her beauty hadn't faded over the years. Still the prettiest woman in Jerusalem.

"Mother? Are you all right?

"Yes, I'm sorry. My thoughts were far away, many years ago, when your father and I first fell in love."

"Wouldn't it be wonderful to be a family again?" Jerusha jumped up and twirled around.

"Yes, Jerusha, I never stopped praying for that until they told me your father was dead. After that, all hope died."

"I never gave up." Jerusha knelt before her mother. "But, Mother, he's a Roman soldier. Nothing's more dangerous."

"A Roman soldier? He despised the Roman soldiers."

"I know. He said YHWH called him in His service there. He said there are some, who will follow Yeshua. He stays until YHWH releases him, even if he dies as one of them."

"A Gentile in His kingdom? How can that be?"

"He questioned it, too, but is convinced he heard from YHWH." Jerusha's heart raced. "We have just found him, and I am afraid that we will lose him again."

Abigail took Jerusha's hands. "Yeshua kept him alive this long. He can keep him alive until we can be together. We must pray." She pulled her shawl over her head and closed her eyes. Jerusha marveled at her mother's faith.

"YHWH, Father God, keep Jacob safe until he can come back to us." Her mother continued praying softy, her words indistinguishable. Jerusha sniffed and wiped her nose. Her heart ached. Her mother deserved a husband who stayed and protected her. She deserved a father. A few minutes later, Abigail finished her prayers and looked up at her daughter.

"Now, where did you get the camel?" She patted the sheepskin cover on the mittah. "Tell me everything. Did your father give you the camel?"

"No, but I'll get to that. First, I want to tell you another thing he told me. Father doesn't know a woman named Devorah. He did not send her. She's lying. She's not who she says she is. I want to know who she is and why she is here"

"I like Devorah. Although she has been secretive. Doesn't talk much about her husband. I am not sure if she's a Yeshua follower."

"So why is she here?"

"Yeshua knows. Maybe he sent her."

"Oh, Mother. Why would he send someone here who is not a follower? There are too many who hate us."

"Maybe, he wants to reveal his love through us."

"And get us all killed? I do not trust her. Be careful, Mother. Do not tell her anything about father or grandfather."

"Yes, I suppose you are right. I wonder if your grandfather is alright?"

"I saw grandfather, too. After father left, I was returning through the market place and I bumped into grandfather. Or rather, I bumped into his camel. That's why I smelled so bad when I got home. I fell in its manure.

Abigail shook her head, but before she could speak, Jerusha continued.

"Grandfather arrived with the trade caravans, and he's hiding in the city. He wants to meet Peter in the stable at midnight." She checked the door to see if anyone was listening, and then continued talking in a whisper. "Says he has a secret passage in and out of the villa. I've never seen it, but he says it's there."

"What a day! Your father's return. Yogli's return. Have you seen Timon, too?"

"No, but I wish I had." Jerusha stood to leave. "One more thing. In the morning, you must keep Devorah occupied. I'm taking the camel to grandfather outside the city where the caravans are camped. I don't want to take a chance on Devorah following me. Is Peter here?"

"No, but he should be back soon. I'll have Moses watch for him and give him the message from Yogli."

"Okay. Be sure to tell him about Devorah." She gave her mother a quick hug and left.

***

Jerusha wrapped an extra shawl around her shoulders and walked the familiar path to father's bench. It was an unusually cool October evening, and the pomegranate bushes rustled in the slight breeze. Overhead, in an Acacia tree, a shrike shrieked. She jumped and looked above her head at the bird. Her nerves were on edge. Hard to believe the tiny bird could be so vicious, and it reminder her of Devorah.

I will not allow her to swoop in and destroy my family.

Lightening flashed and lit up the night sky. Jerusha inhaled deeply. She loved the smell of rain on the wind. In the distance, she heard the entrance gate creak. Someone was entering the villa. Her breath caught in her throat, and she froze. The crescent moon, partially obscured by clouds, gave only enough light to see a few feet away. Enveloped in darkness, she moved off the path and ducked down behind a bush. Light footsteps approached her hiding place, and she could barely make out a shadowy figure. It was Devorah.

Of course. It would be her. She's out rather late isn't she?

When Devorah had gone, Jerusha slipped out of her hiding place. A chill crept up her spine as she looked up at the moon. It was almost midnight.

She sighed. *I wonder where Timon is tonight?* She longed for his embrace and closed her eyes and envisioned his lopsided grin. *When will he return?* There had been no time to think about the miscarriage or deal with the whirlwind of emotions brought on with Sarah's departure. She had a sick feeling, deep in the pit of her stomach, but she would not allow it to overcome her. She had to stay focused. A spy lived in the house.

***

Jerusha felt guilty for hiding in the stable. Grandfather told Peter to come alone, but her curiosity got the best of her. A loud clap of thunder rattled the rafters. She buried herself deeper in the hay.

"Little Lioness, what are you doing here?" Her grandfather towered above her in the darkness. She could tell by the tone of his voice that he was not happy with her.

"Well, I—," she sighed in surrender. "Grandfather, you know how curious I am. Besides, I'm watching out for Devorah."

"I'm not sure how good a guard you will be buried in hay. Sentinels normally guard the outside perimeter. Now, back to the villa. We'll be safe enough." He helped her up.

Jerusha felt like a scolded child. When will her grandfather see her as a grown woman? Peter appeared out of the shadows.

"Shalom." His eyes smiled. "Are you joining us tonight?"

Jerusha brushed hay from her sleeve. "Shalom. No, I was just leaving." She hoped Peter had not overheard her grandfather's scolding

"Excuse us." Grandfather ignored Jerusha and motioned to Peter. They stepped into the next stall, and began talking in hushed tones. Jerusha strained to hear what they were saying, but could not. She felt her way through the stable in the darkness, following the wooden railings. She reached the stall where she had put the camel, where the beast stood waiting. She rubbed his nose, and he snorted his pleasure as she started out the door.

"See you in the morning," she whispered.

"Wait," her grandfather called after her. "We have decided you need to hear this. Come back inside." He shoved a couple benches together.

The tone of her grandfather's voice troubled her. He seemed serious, and concerned. She was not sure if she wanted to hear what they had to say.

"What I'm about to tell you could open some old wounds, but you will hear this soon enough from others. I want you to hear it from me." He hesitated. "I met Saul on my journey."

"Did he try to arrest you?"

"No. Yeshua appeared to him on his way to Damascus. He's now a follower of the way."

"I don't believe it." Her grandfather was right. Old wounds were opening, and out of them came a burning anger. She thought she had forgiven Saul for what he had done to her uncle Stephen. Now, she was not so sure. Her stomach churned.

"Soon, Saul will be coming to Jerusalem to meet with Peter." A loud thunderbolt cracked and more rumbled in the distance. She closed her eyes.

"Yeshua," Just saying his name brought comfort. "Yeshua, I know you love Saul. Help me to love as you do." Peter and her grandfather raised their voices in prayer. Even the thunder could not drown out their pleas.

"Almighty YHWH, the one and only true God, reach out and save your people. Open their ears. Open their eyes. We want none of our brethren to perish when your judgment comes."

The rain pounded against the roof. Regulus and Peter continued in their prayers, but Jerusha felt compelled to leave. Peter and her grandfather suggested she wait until the rain stopped, but she could not wait. Lightening lit the sky as she stepped out of the stables. Out of the corner of her eye, she saw a figure move in the shadows a short distance away.

Devorah. Why am I not surprised?

She raised her radiyd over head and ran through the downpour. As she rounded the herb garden, she lost her footing and landed in a huge mud puddle. She tried to get up, but slid again. One of her sandals got stuck in the thick mud and came off her foot. She yanked it free, removed her other sandal, and crawled out of the puddle. Finally, she got to her feet and made it to the kitchen. By the time she stepped inside the kitchen door, she was soaked and covered with mud.

Devorah stood by the fire dropping herbs into lentil stew, the morning meal.

"Jerusha, you're shivering." As Jerusha removed her wet cloak, Devorah removed hers and wrapped it around Jerusha's shivering body.

"I see you're seasoning the stew. Were you in the herb garden tonight?" Jerusha was suspicious and did not try to mask her tone.

"Why, yes, I just came inside. Nearly got soaked. There's my wet cloak over there. It's always good to have an extra cloak in the kitchen. Accidents do happen." She poured warm water in a bowl.

"Yes, accidents do happen." *And they always happen to me.* Once again, the word forced its way into her thoughts. *Cursed.*

"If you'll sit over there, I'll wash your feet." The last thing Jerusha wanted was for Devorah to wash her feet, but how does one refuse such a gesture with tact?

"Jerusha?" Abigail walked into the room holding Devorah's baby. "What happened to you?"

"She came in here drenched and shivering like a wet cat." Devorah sat the water on the floor in front of Jerusha, picked up one foot, and placed it in the warm water. It felt good, but to have Devorah wash her feet was humiliating.

"This child needs his mother's milk. Here, let me do that." Abigail handed the baby to Devorah and took her place on the stool. Devorah exposed her breast to the child, and then covered up and sat in the shadows. Tears formed in Jerusha's eyes. For so long she yearned to hear suckling noises at her breast.

Tiny hands pulled on Jerusha's arm. It was Joseph.

"Joseph, what are you doing up so late?" He shrugged, then stood motionless, his brown eyes widened as big as a camel's. She lifted him onto her lap. "He's shaking."

"The storm. He saw the lightening and wanted you. He misses Timon." Chaya stood at the kitchen entrance. What would she have done without Timon's mother? She had been a companion and mother to the all of the orphans. Chaya's eyes flashed from Devorah to

Jerusha. Such compassion. She understood. Jerusha's tears threatened to flow unhindered and she snuggled Joseph close, burying her face in his long curly hair.

"He can sleep with me tonight. I am grateful you brought him to me." Thunder boomed. Joseph grabbed her tighter, his little fingers digging into her arms.

"He feels the vibrations of the storm. In his deafness he's more sensitive to touch. Jerusha could feel vibrations too. Warnings of a coming storm.

Chapter 15

Jerusha arose early, opened the latticed shutters, and breathed deep.

Ah, fresh rain and pomegranates blossoms.

She looked at Joseph curled up in a ball under the lambskin and thought of Sarah. "YHWY, your children need you. I need you." She missed Timon. He was her rock and strength. How would she make it until he returned, especially without her grandfather? The soft breeze blew against the shutters. Their movement, like butterfly wings, awakened an old memory her of sitting on her father's lap. She could hear his words.

Never forget who you are.

You're from the tribe of Judah. You are royalty.

She remembered him placing the pendant over her neck and reading the words on the back.

Arise, Lord. Let your enemies be scattered. Let all who hate you flee before you.

She wondered if her father would he be upset that she gave the pendant to Sarah? *What would Timon think? The butterfly jewel was his betrothal gift.* Jerusha gasped as another memory surfaced. *The other gifts! I almost forgot.*

She closed the shutter and dug at a crack in the wall with her fingernails. It was her secret hiding place. If she had learned anything while being a captive, it was how to hide things. The limestone square loosened and flopped out into her hand. Her two newest treasures lay inside the opening. Her father's signet ring and the round wooden object Yeshua gave him when she was born. She stood for a moment and stared at the ring.

Her grandfather had one just like it. It was the same design as her pendant. What did it mean? A lion face and a butterfly. She picked up the wooden object made by Yeshua, rubbed her fingers around the pomegranates carved into the edge, and stared at the butterfly relief in the middle. A single tear escaper her eye and ran down her cheek.

Like the butterfly, you may not look like you know where you are going, but you always arrive at YHWH's destination.

Her father had spoken those words to her. He told her that YHWH makes all things beautiful in its time. Is he making his little butterfly's life beautiful? A woman cursed with a barren womb?

A light rap at the door disturbed her thoughts. Jerusha unlocked the door, and her mother peeked in.

"Umm. I can see you are busy. I will come back." She turned to leave.

"Wait." Jerusha opened the door wide. "Please, I have something to ask you." She pulled a chair over and motioned to her mother to sit. "Father gave this to me. Do you know what the design represents?"

Her mother picked up the wooden object and smiled. "I haven't seen this in years. Did your father tell you who made it?"

"Yeshua."

Abigail stared at the wooden piece. "It was the day of your birth. Yeshua knew the difficult times that lay ahead. He told us, 'No matter what happens, YHWH makes all things beautiful in its time.'"

"Even a woman with a barren womb? Am I beautiful?" Jerusha swallowed and looked away.

Abigail cupped Jerusha's chin, turned her face, and gazed into her eyes. "Let me tell you, my precious daughter, what I see. I see a beautiful, dancing butterfly, who does not look like she knows where she's going but always gets to YHWH's appointed destination. I see a beautiful, royal lioness whose words carry power to scatter the enemy."

Jerusha jerked her face free. "I tell you who I see. I see an ugly, cursed woman, a danger to all who touch her life. That's who I see." Tears flowed unhindered.

Joseph slipped quietly from the bed and walked over to Jerusha, leaning his head over against her arm. Jerusha helped him up on her lap. He touched the watery flow down her cheek, then snuggled his face in her chest.

Abigail smiled tenderly. "I see a beautiful woman who loves children. I am sure Timon and Yeshua see it, too." Her mother turned and left the room, closing the door behind her.

***

Jerusha took Moses with her to meet her grandfather at the caravan campsite. The camp spread across the side of a hill one mile outside of the city. She finally found him and weaved her way through the throngs of people and animals, leading Moses by the hand.

Her grandfather greeted her as if she was his slave girl. She understood why it was necessary, but she longed to hug him good-bye. The look in his eyes, and stern expression disturbed her. Her stomach was in knots.

"Were you followed?" He took the rope from Moses and slipped a small piece of parchment in his hand.

"No."

"I love you." She mouthed the words and wondered if she would ever see him again. He mouthed the same words in return, and she felt the tears well up in her eyes. If she did not leave soon, she would burst into tears in front of everyone. Her humpbacked friend lowered his head and nudged her shoulder. She stroked his nose and hugged his neck instead.

She whispered into the camel's ear. "Take good care of my grandfather." She looked up at the gentle giant who had protected and nurtured her from the day she had been set free from Herod's palace. She never knew how he could be a Hebrew, yet have blond hair and blue eyes, but it did not matter. All that mattered to her at that moment was that he might never return.

"Shalom, my little lioness." He pulled on the camel harness, turned his back and walked away. Overcome with emotion, Jerusha took off running down the hill, dust flying in the air with every footfall.

Moses called after her. "W-w-wait, J-J-Jerusha."

She could not wait. If she stopped running, she knew she would run back, throw her arms around her grandfather, and never let go. Moses would catch up. He was a strong young lad.

She had stopped sobbing by the time Moses found her at the Gihon Spring. She stared at the cave above and waited for the water to flow, as she had done hundreds of times as a little girl. She would love to be that little girl again, talking with her father and following him wherever he went.

"I am sorry, Moses. I could not wait for you." She stood and dipped her hands into the water, and splashed some on her eyes. She sat down in the shade of a palm tree.

"Y-y-you will see him again." Moses's sensitivity touched her heart.

"I hope you are right, Moses. I love him so much. He always had a way of being there when I needed him, even when I was a slave. Yeshua's love flows through the big giant. He's so kind and gentle with the orphans and widows. He was even accepting of Devorah."

"I th-th-think this is for you." Moses handed her a small piece of parchment. "Your grandfather dropped it in my hand when I took the camel's rope."

Jerusha stared at the Hebrew words. "Never forget who you are."

A lion and a butterfly had been drawn on the other side. Somehow, she would find a way to make her grandfather proud. She would be who YHWH created her to be, whoever that was. A royal mother of children? Probably not.

"On my way here I saw Devorah." Moses shuffled his feet.

"Do you think she followed us?" Jerusha tucked the parchment inside her girdle.

"I don't know. She talked with one of the p-p-priests' servants."

"You know this servant?"

"Yes, he serves in Herod's palace."

"I wonder if she saw grandfather with us?"

"She might h-h-have. They were talking just outside the city gate."

"We must warn my grandfather. But how?"

"I h-h-heard one of the traders talking to Yogli. They may not leave until tomorrow. It would be easier go unnoticed into their camp, if we go in the darkness."

"We will leave after everyone's asleep. Meet me at the gate at midnight. And Moses, you cannot tell anyone. Not Mother. Not Chaya, and especially not Devorah."

Chapter 16

Jerusha and Moses stood at the night entrance under the east gate and peered through its bars. The moonlight lit up the hillside.

"They're gone." Jerusha's heart sunk to her stomach. "We are too late." Tears ran down her cheeks. *Grandfather, I love you.* She sighed and closed her eyes. *May YHWH guard and keep you.*

"He w-w-will be all right, J-J-Jerusha." Moses's words sounded far away. She was in a different world. Her heart was with her grandfather. For years she had wanted to leave Jerusalem and fly away like a butterfly to some unknown destination. She longed to ride on her grandfather's camel to other places.

"What are you doing?" The guard grabbed Moses and Jerusha. "Get away from this gate. This is the second time someone has been at this gate since the third watch began." His grip dug into Jerusha's flesh.

"Was the other one a woman?" Her words sounded like the rhythm of a drum as he jerked and dragged her and Moses away from the gate.

"I do not owe you an explanation." In the darkness, she was unable to see his eyes. She pressed for an answer. "Please. It is most important."

He grinned. "What's it worth to you? My watch ends at three. A pretty lady like you could be of assistance to me." He ran his finger down her chin.

"Do not touch me!" She tried to pull loose. Moses yanked on his arm. The annoyed guard swung around and slapped Moses. He moaned and rolled on the ground. The guard's long spindly fingers grasped hair and radiyd and flung Jerusha into the dark alcove. She scrambled to get up and caught her feet in her robe. His knees straddled her chest. Wrists pinned to the stone, she looked up at Moses, who clung to the guard's back, his eyes wide with terror.

"What's going on over there?" another guard shouted from the rampart.

The brusque soldier bent near her face, his foul breath making her nauseous. "If you ever come to my gate at night, I will finish what I started," then spit in her face and jumped to his feet.

"The other harlot went that way." He pointed west. "I've seen her at Herod's palace. Would have had my way with her, if she hadn't been so sly. She's experienced and knows the ways of the world."

Jerusha wiped the spit on her sleeve and stared at the soldier's back. A sick feeling crept over her whole body. She clenched her trembling hands and ran to a nearby watering trough. The soldier's laughter roared in her ears. After drying her face and hands, she motioned to Moses.

"Let's go. Mother will be worried if she finds out we are gone."

"Look!" Moses ducked behind the trough. "Get down. I think I see her." They both squatted and peeked over the edge.

"Where?" she whispered.

"Watch over there, by Gate Beautiful." His finger pointed straight in front of her nose. "I saw her duck into the shadows and move along the temple wall."

"Are you sure it's her?" The slender figure stepped into the moonlight and a gust of wind blew her radiyd off.

"Devorah." Jerusha watched her move up the hill and around the corner. "Quick, we don't want to lose her." They ran across the opening and reached the wall. They kept moving, staying near the wall, until they reached the corner. Spotting her again, they watched her run up the hill.

"D-d-did the soldier say he saw her at Herod's palace?"

"Yes." Jerusha shuddered.

"It looks like that's where she's headed. What do you want to do, Jerusha?"

"I know the perfect shortcut." Her heart thudded. She missed her grandfather. He made her feel safe, even when she had been a slave.

Be brave. Never forget who you are.

"Come with me." She stepped past Moses and ran across the opening into the yellowed limestone maze, pausing long enough to be sure he followed. The air was more pungent than usual, and it stirred up old memories.

"Stay with me," she instructed. She gathered her tunic and cloak up over her feet and zigzagged through several passageways and up a steep hill. Her pace slowed as she neared the palace.

Out of breath, she stopped for a moment and listened. She could hear the waterfall, a sound she had not heard since leaving Herod's palace. Remembering what had happened with the high priest and his son made her blood boil. She hated what they did to her, and the guard's behavior back at the gate had torn open that old wound.

She could smell the fresh water ahead. They were close. She looked over her shoulder at Moses, who gave her a quick nod. She took off again. The water gurgled deep in the bushes along the path. She moved swiftly and ducked under a branch to wait for Moses. When he reached her side, she took his hand and stepped behind the waterfall. She reached out and let the water run through her fingers. She splashed some on her face; she needed to be alert.

She dried her face with the edge of her cloak, looked at Moses, and put her finger to her lips. "Somewhere behind us is the secret opening to the palace," she whispered. "We must be very quiet."

Moses nodded he understood.

She searched the bushes until she came to a wall and followed it until she found the opening that led into the palace kitchen. Bending low, she squeezed into the opening and disappeared into the darkness. Moses followed close behind. When her eyes had adjusted to the darkness, she took Moses's hand and placed it on the wall, indicating to him to use it as a guide in the darkness.

Her toe stubbed against the first step, and she leaned close to Moses and whispered very low.

"If you count them, there will be twenty-four steps to the top." A creature scampered across her toes. She remembered well her first trip down these stairs. There had been cobwebs, scaly lizards, and rats. She would have done anything back then to get away from the palace long enough for a Yeshua meeting. Now, she would do anything to spy on Devorah. She would do whatever it took to protect those in her care.

A sliver of light pierced the darkness near the top of the steps, but not enough to illuminate the creepy stairway. She slid her hand along the slimy wall and counted the steps, stopping only once to swipe away a web.

What if I am doing all of this for nothing? What if Devorah used the night entrance at the front gate?

It was too late now. She had committed to this path, and there was no turning back now. Besides, someone had opened the heavy limestone door or there would not be light showing through. Someone had gone through that door, and she was convinced it was Devorah.

As she drew near the top of the steps, she heard voices. She reached the top step and peered through the opening. *Devorah.* Just as she had expected.

Devorah had her arms around a handsome man. Not as handsome as Timon, but still handsome.

Jerusha leaned close to Moses, careful to whisper softly. "Is that the servant you saw talking with Devorah?" Moses leaned over and looked through the opening. He saw the man and nodded. It was indeed the same man. Devorah kissed the man on the lips, and Moses quickly looked away. *So, that's where Devorah went the other night smelling so good. Could the man be the father of her children?*

The cold, damp air soaked into Jerusha's bones. She wrapped her cloak tighter around her shoulders and pulled her radiyd higher around her face. Maybe it was only a secret romance, but why had she come to them and then lie about it? Something was not right.

Watching their embrace made her long for Timon. She waved her hand at Moses to go back down and felt for the first step in the darkness. She had no desire to listen to their romantic interchange.

"Regulus."

Jerusha froze. She clearly heard them mention her grandfather. She swiveled back toward the door and cupped her ear.

"What did you find out?" the handsome servant spoke with urgency. A shadow moved across the opening. *They're coming!*

Fingers wrapped around the edge of the door. Jerusha waved Moses down the steps, flipping her hand like a fan. Her heart raced. If Devorah found her, it would be more than embarrassing; it would be dangerous.

Moses impressed Jerusha with how swiftly he moved. She held her tunic above her ankles with one hand and kept her other hand on the wall for balance. At the bottom, she followed Moses behind a large pomegranate bush just in time to see Devorah step outside, straighten her radiyd, and swish past, that familiar fragrance lingering behind. Jerusha and Moses came out of hiding and went the other way.

***

Jerusha shook her mother's shoulders. "Wake up! I have something to tell you."

"What's this about? Why are you waking me in the middle of the night?" Her mother rolled over and sat on the mittah.

Jerusha moved to the brazier that warmed the dark room and rubbed her hands above the orange coals. Her insides tumbled. *Calm down, Jerusha. Yeshua knows all. He will work this out. Be brave like Grandfather said.* Her silent chiding did little to settle her stomach.

"Moses and I caught Devorah at Herod's palace tonight."

"You went out again? Jerusha when will you learn to listen to my wisdom?"

"I'm sorry, but Moses saw Devorah at the gate this morning talking to one of the priest's servants. I wanted to warn Grandfather that she might have given him away. We thought it would be better to go at night when they were sleeping. Less conspicuous."

"What were you thinking? Entering the traders' camp at night is extremely dangerous, especially for a beautiful young woman like yourself. In these perilous times, we must not react to circumstances without hearing from our Father above. His plan is perfect. Did you wait for Him to reveal His plan?

"No, but—"

Abigail cut her off with a raised hand. "I am concerned for your safety." She stood up and placed her hands on her hips. Mother had reason to be concerned. YWHW's ways are not our ways. Grandfather's words. Her way almost got her raped. No tidbit of information about Devorah is worth that.

"Now, what is so important that you woke me at this hour?"

"Moses and I followed Devorah to Herod's palace. Remember the secret passage we took to meet with Yeshua followers?"

Yes, I remember" Abigail's brow arched.

"Well, Moses and I went there. We hid in the stairway. The door was cracked open, so we listened and watched Devorah and the high priest's servant being romantic. I thought that was all it was, a romantic encounter, until I turned to leave. I heard him mention the name, 'Regulus' and 'what did you find out?'"

"Hmm, I wonder what she's looking for?"

"I'm worried about Grandfather. I wonder if she told him that he travels with the caravan. That information might be worth a fancy sum to the Roman centurion. Maybe this is the high priest's way of getting rid of Grandfather. You know he wants our villa for himself. Ever since Father's fight with him, he has hated our family."

"I deeply regret causing division between your father and Caiaphas. They had been such good friends until-well you know what happened. I pray your father has forgiven me."

"Caiaphas wants revenge. It would give him great delight to destroy the family Father has fought so hard to keep—the family he was forced to walk away from. What will happen to us now that Grandfather and Father are gone?"

"If YHWH's purpose for our lives is not complete, we will be safe. It's not just revenge Caiaphas seeks. He fears us and the kingdom power we carry within us."

"Grandfather told me I didn't know the authority I carried. What does that mean?"

"Power to love, even your enemies, and the authority to release the kingdom within you, especially through your words. Most religious leaders are looking for a different kingdom, one that will crush the Romans."

"Father believes YHWH wants to save some of the Romans."

"I have heard Peter say that Saul is now Yeshua's instrument, and carries his name before the Gentiles. Maybe your father is right."

"Grandfather also told me Saul was converted to Yeshua's way. It's hard to believe the man who instigated Stephen's stoning is now a believer."

"Now, about Devorah. Whatever her purpose is here with us, we must love her."

"I do not trust her."

"Jerusha, I have watched her. She admires you. She even seems to want to be like you. You may be just the one to reveal how much Yeshua loves her."

"Not me. I will be kind, but I will be on guard. She's up to no good, of that I am sure." She yawned. "I am tired. I will see you in the morning. I am going to bed."

Jerusha opened the door and paused before stepping into the hallway "I just saw a shadow. I hope Devorah wasn't listening."

Abigail leaned out and looked. "I don't see anything. Jerusha, you are so obsessed with Devorah, I think you are imagining things. Go to bed." She closed the door.

Jerusha stood motionless in the hall. There it was again. She was not imagining it. A door creaked shut, confirming her suspicions. No, she definitely was not imagining it.

Chapter 17
Three Weeks Later

Devorah walked beside Jerusha through the crowded bazaar in the agora of the upper city. With its mosaic designs and Greek architecture, the market was a beautiful place. Abigail had insisted that Devorah accompany Jerusha on her outing. Jerusha cringed at the thought of spending the entire day with the woman she most distrusted. However, she would honor her mother, even if she was convinced her mother was deceived about Devorah.

She stopped for a moment and examined some silk garments. They were purple and she loved that color, especially after her father had given her treasures wrapped in a purple cloth.

"A good color for you." the merchant handed her another cloth of the same color. "Your Yogli would like, eh? Do you like?" He handed Devorah a beautiful silk piece with gold woven throughout.

"Shalom, Jerusha," a woman called from another shop. "How is your mother?" She dodged the shoppers and crossed the mosaic path. "I have been meaning to visit."

"Mother is well." Ever since being a slave in Herod's palace, Jerusha felt uncomfortable in this part of the city. Their gawking stares as she had served them, their whispers, and demeaning laughter while they had played with corrupt politicians and Romans had sickened her. She only came today because of Devorah. They paid attention to her only because the villa she lives in is the largest in the upper city. *Hypocrites.* She nodded and turned away.

"The people favor you." Devorah smiled and wrapped the silk around her head. "What do you think? My color, too? Her admiration sickened Jerusha as well. For weeks now, she followed her everywhere. Compliments flowed from her mouth like fake jewels that sparkled without worth. *What's with this woman? Why won't she leave me alone? She can't get any information, so she torments by her presence.* As much as she missed Timon, she was glad he was not home, or he would take Mother's side in this issue. That would be big trouble.

They strolled beneath the portico, the late morning sun gleaming off the temple's golden gates in the distance. So many memories of going there with her father as a child. Jerusha found her way down the terraced steps and stood beneath the decorative archway remembering the lambs she took for sacrifices. No need for lambs any longer. Yeshua, the lamb of YHWH was sacrificed once, and for all. Her heart ached for His children who had not recognized Mashiach Yeshua as their resurrected King. She looked at Devorah, who looked out over the valley. He died for her, too. Maybe she could give her a chance.

"Devorah, tell me about your life. You're a widow. Tell me about your deceased husband. Did you love him?" Jerusha was aware many arranged marriages lacked love.

"No." Devorah dropped her head.

"A marriage without love. I am sorry for you." She continued down the pathway toward the temple.

"It is apparent that you and Timon love each other." Devorah's voice sounded almost sweet.

"Yes, we love each other very much. He was so patient with me. He didn't force himself on me. Waited for me to fall in love with him before we—well, you know what I mean." A flush warmed Jerusha's face. She opened up and shared a delicate part of her life with a woman she did not trust at all. *What was I thinking?*

"It was not that way with me." Devorah wiped a tear from her cheek. "If you don't mind, I would rather not talk about it." Several giggling children ran past. She perked up. "Do you and Timon want children?"

Children. Now that was a topic Jerusha did not want to talk about. A love relationship without children felt more like a curse.

"Look, there's Sarah." Devorah pointed to a crowd several yards away.

Jerusha scanned the open area in front of the temple. Soldiers eyed the men in the group surrounding Sarah. Her stomach churned as they walked under the last archway. Sarah's father argued with a Roman official while the little girl stood beside him and stared up. The vacant stare in her eyes troubled Jerusha. *What has become of my little girl?*

Jerusha tried to meander away from Devorah. Maybe she understood because she stayed back. Jerusha did not want Sarah to see her because if they embraced, she may not have the courage to let go of her again. She just wanted to get close enough to be sure Sarah had been properly cared for. She did not know what she would do if she looked unkempt and thin. As she moved closer, her worst fears unfolded before her eyes. Sarah's thin arms wrapped around the sacrificial lamb, and she rubbed her smudged cheek against the lamb's face. Jerusha could not bare to watch it. She turned to leave.

"Jerusha!" Sarah's voice squealed above the crowd. Jerusha turned back and squatted. Sarah ran straight into her arms. Oh, the feel of her precious little girl in her arms again. She never wanted to let go. She picked her up and straddled her spindly legs around her waist.

"Oh, Sarah. How I have missed you." She enjoyed Sarah's snuggle against her cheek and tight hold around her neck.

"That's my lamb," Sarah spoke over Jerusha's shoulder. "I remember what you taught me about Yeshua being our sacrificial lamb. I told my father we don't need to kill my lamb because Yeshua already died for our sins. He didn't listen." She snuggled again against Jerusha's cheek. "He slapped me. I want to live with you and Timon." The little one whimpered and clung tight.

"I am sorry, Sarah. I am sorry your father treated you that way. Remember what Stephen taught us. We must forgive and pray for those who mistreat us. When your father gives his life to Yeshua's control, things will be different. We will keep praying."

"Jerusha, I want to be brave like you. You are brave. Your grandfather told me how brave you are."

A knot formed in Jerusha's throat. She swallowed.

"I'm brave only when Grandfather is here, or Timon. I am learning to trust Yeshua, just like you."

"Sarah! Get over here!" her father yelled. "You sniveling little brat. Get over here! You left your lamb to wander away." He grabbed the rope and waited.

"Be brave, Sarah. Yeshua is with you." Jerusha whispered in her ear and kissed her cheek. Sarah would not let go. "Sarah, Grandfather also said, 'His ways are not our ways.' If I had my way, I would keep you with me." Sarah's body shook. "I tell you what YHWH told Joshua when Moses died. 'Be strong and courageous! Do not tremble or be dismayed, for the Lord your God is with you wherever you go.'" Sarah's body relaxed. She unwrapped her arms and let Jerusha set her feet on the ground.

"Sarah! Get over her!" Sarah's father yelled again.

"Bye Jerusha. I will be brave like you." Tears glistened in her eyes.

Jerusha refrained from grabbing her and never letting go. "Go, Sarah. I will be praying for you and your father." She watched Sarah as she ran to the lamb and hugged his neck. Her father went back to his argument.

Numb, Jerusha swallowed her tears. There was nowhere to go to release them. There were people all around. As she moved among the crowd toward home, she remembered Devorah. There she was talking to the man again, the priest's servant. It did not matter. Nothing mattered but the empty void she felt in her stomach. A Roman soldier filed past her. Then another. And still another. She came to her senses and glanced around. More and more soldiers were beginning to mingle among the worshippers who waited to enter the temple. In the distance, she saw Sarah squished between the soldier and her father. Sarah squeezed the lamb's neck, her eyes closed, and her lips moving. She was probably praying for him.

Without warning, her father pulled a knife from his belt and lunged at the soldier.

"Pig!" he screamed.

Sarah's eyes popped open. Other zealots attacked. There were screams and chaos throughout the market. Jerusha pushed against the people running away. She had get to Sarah. Someone stepped on her foot, and she tumbled to the ground. Her face smashed on the cold stone street as one foot after another trampled her body. She curled into a ball. When the crowd past, she looked up in time to see Sarah jump in front of the soldier as he thrust his sword at her father.

"No!"

Sarah lay motionless, blood pouring from her wound. Jerusha stumbled to her feet and watched as Sarah's father escape unharmed. She glared at his back as he ran away. How could he leave his daughter?

The skirmish was over as quick as it started. There were dead zealots everywhere. Blood covered the ground. Soldiers laughed and mocked the weakness of the attack. Of course there were two soldiers to every zealot.

Arrogant pigs.

Sarah moaned. Jerusha gently brushed hair from the little one's face. She held pressure on the wound with her hand, blood oozing from between her fingers. *She's barely breathing.*

Sarah's eyes fluttered, and her lips began to move. Jerusha tilted her head, bringing her ear close to Sarah's mouth.

"Was-I-brave?" her words came in short gasps. Sarah's hand clutched the pendant Jerusha had given her. Blood covered the lion's mane.

"Yes, Sarah. You were very brave. Grandfather would be proud. Yeshua would be proud."

"I see him. I see Yeshua." Her eyes widened. "And Stephen." Blood gurgled from her mouth. "Tell-tell-my-father." Jerusha marveled at how she was able to speak. Such love she had for her father. Yeshua's love. "I-love-you-Ju—" Her head fell to the side and her body slumped.

"No!" Jerusha screamed as she hugged Sarah's limp body. "It's my fault. It's all my fault." She sobbed heavily. "I shouldn't have let you go with him." She sat for the longest time and rocked back and forth with her baby. The sun peaked from behind the temple and then disappeared. Darkness within. Darkness without. Jerusha managed to stand with

Sarah's body draped over her arms. She stumbled in the shadows toward home. In the distance, she saw a light that moved toward her. It was a lantern, and in its dim light, she could see Moses, Chaya, Devorah, and her mother. They were carrying a stretcher.

"I'll take her." Moses reached under Jerusha's arms, and carefully scooped the child up and placed her on the stretcher. "Devorah told us what happened. We came as soon as we could. I'm sorry, Jerusha." He started to cry. They were all crying, even Devorah. Jerusha thought she could cry no more, but when she found herself wrapped in her mother's embrace, the tears flowed freely. In that moment, she wondered if she would ever stop crying. How could her pain ever be healed?

Chapter 18

The round stone that sealed Stephen's tomb, where they buried Sarah, shone in the moonlight. Jerusha fought to keep her eyes open. After the burial procession, she had collapsed and refused to go home. No one would be hurt again because of her. She wanted to die with Sarah. What purpose did her life have? Motherhood elluded her, and those she did love, like Sarah, suffered because of her.

"J-J-Jerusha, you must go home," Moses coaxed. "Your m-m-mother is worried. It has been th-three days. It is time to come b-back to those who love you."

"I can't. I won't put anyone else in danger because of me."

"It is n-not your fault." It was the first time she had noticed the deeper sound in his voice. Almost a man. He had grown so much since that first night when Yogli found him hiding outside the window in the rain. "If you r-refuse, she sends w-water and bread." He plopped the goatskin next to her, unwrapped the bread, and put it in her lap.

"And I am st-staying with you." He perched himself, slingshot in hand, on the rock above. "N-no one w-will get p-past me."

Jerusha sniffed the air. A faint whiff of frankincense on the light breeze caught her attention. She lifted her head and sniffed again, trying to pinpoint its source. They hadn't used frankincense oil in Sarah's burial, so she was mystified.

The grass rustled. Moses heard it, too, and stood ready with his slingshot. Someone was near. Moses released his first shot. The rock flew past Jerusha's head and into the tall grass. It hit something—or someone. Moses reloaded, and was about to fire again when a voice spoke into the night air.

"Whoa, Moses. I have enough dents in my armor." Jacob stepped out of the grass carrying his helmet under his arm.

"Father! What are you doing here?" Jerusha sat up straight.

"I could ask you the same thing. Does my daughter not know how dangerous it is to be out here? A single bandit could strip you naked and take everything you own."

"I have nothing to take but my clothes and my life, which would be a welcome relief."

"J-J-Jerusha, do not s-say that." Moses zigzagged down from his post.

"My sentiments exactly. Climb the hill and keep watch while I talk with my daughter. That slingshot is quite the weapon. Keep it ready." Moses's grin widened as he scampered up the incline. Jacob set his helmet beside Jerusha and lifted himself onto the short cliff. She scooted back to give him room and leaned against the steep limestone wall.

As happy as she was to see him, it felt strange to be in his presence. She refrained from giving him a hug. Maybe she was angry with him for leaving her again. She had lived half of her life without him. In some ways, he felt like a stranger, but she still loved him. Her memories of the garden, dancing with the butterflies and watching her father in his workshop were some of the best times of her life. Family meant everything to her yet always seemed out of reach.

His silhouette under the moon reminded her of her grandfather. Same square chin and high cheekbones. Both men were handsome with their light colored eyes and strong physiques. He and her mother made a perfect couple.

"I'm sorry for your loss. My soldiers caught Sarah's father. They wanted to crucify him. I used my authority to get him jailed instead." He kept his head down.

"He deserves crucifixion, leaving his daughter like that. She gave her life for his. What kind of father does that?" She felt uncomfortable. Her anger seemed as much directed to her own father as to Sarah's. Had he noticed? She had no desire to hurt him.

"I was able to talk to him alone." Jacob's facial expression never changed. He appeared undisturbed by her animosity. "Sarah's father professed faith in Yeshua at the jail. He said Sarah's love convinced him. He wept, admitted he had beaten Sarah, and that there was no reason for her to love him. He understands now that Sarah's love for Yeshua is the reason he is still alive. Jerusha, her death was not in vain." Her father looked up, his eyes glassy. "As Yeshua told me at your birth, no matter what happens, YHWH makes all things beautiful in its time. I pray, when it's time, we will be together again." The lines around his eyes revealed a man worn and tired. He stayed alive. He came back. He was not so different from her. He survived.

"Father, forgive me for being angry at you. It's not just you. I'm angry with Sarah's father. I am angry with myself for letting her go. I am even angry with Yeshua. For three days I've looked for answers." She choked back the tears. "Why did I have to give Sarah back? Why am I still barren? Why was my father called to serve the Romans?"

"Remember, Jerusha, He makes all things beautiful in its time." Her father stared straight ahead.

"Even me?" She sniffed.

"Especially you." He scooted back and wrapped his arm around her shoulders.

"Then why hasn't he blessed me with children?" She leaned her head into his chest. "I'm doomed. I cannot ask the high priest for the blessing like Hannah, the matriarch of old. Caiaphas hates me, and he hates our family. He would rather kill me than bless me."

"Your mother and I, along with Yeshua, laid hands on you at birth and released the blessing."

"Then why? Why have I not conceived?"

"Jacob," Moses's immature voice squeaked, then dropped in pitch, "s-s-someone's coming."

Jerusha yanked the end of her tunic up and tucked it into her girdle, then scurried down.

"There's a cave over the hill. Hurry. Hide. I will stay and see who it is." Her father gave orders with authority, like the Roman soldier he was.

"But Father—"

"Go! Now! Moses, you too. Take care of her."

Moses held her elbow down the steep slope. He directed her to the left. The moonlight sliced through the dark cloud that drifted overhead. Moses helped her slip through a narrow opening into total darkness.

"What is this place?" She shivered and pulled her radiyd over her head. "Keep your hand on my elbow so I know where you are. I can't see anything."

"I w-w-will not let go." Moses's voice quivered. "I think we are in a burial cave."

"What? Father sent us to a burial cave?"

"W-w-well, n-no one will l-look for us in here."

"I am not staying in here." The silence inside the cave unnerved her.

"Your father said to take care of you." Moses held her arm tight. "You stay put."

"Moses, that's the first time I have ever heard you speak without stuttering."

"Stay put, until your father calls us." He spoke with a new confidence. A short while later, a shadow crossed the entrance. Jerusha froze and held her breath.

"You can come out now." Her father's body blocked the light. "Let me help you." His hand extended toward her. She had a notion to slap it for sending her to hide into a burial cave. Reason overruled the thought, and she grabbed his hand. *Get me out of this death pit.* She felt the strength in his grip. The sharp limestone edge rubbed against her chest. *How did Moses get through?* She burst through the opening and fell into Father, the armor cold against her cheek. He swooped his arms beneath her legs and carried her to the top of the hill. She felt like a little girl again, protected and safe. Tears started to flow.

"Don't leave me, Father. I need you now more than ever."

"Jerusha, you are stronger than you think." He placed her in the soft grass.

"No, Father, I am not strong. I need you."

"You will not be alone. Yeshua will strengthen you."

"No! No, Father. You must stay." The little girl inside of her was hurting and demanded her way. She noticed the pain in her father's eyes and suddenly realized that he was hurting too.

"I am sorry, Father. I can see it's hard for you, too. I am a grown woman now. I will be strong."

"I have missed out on so much of your life. It grieves me to leave again. I've had many talks with Yeshua about this. He assures me that in the near future, I will be here for you and your children." He tapped her nose and winked.

"I am s-sorry to interrupt." Moses cleared his throat. His stutter was back. "B-but who came to the tomb?"

"It was Devorah. She came looking for you."

"Devorah? You told me not to trust her, and that she had lied. You didn't reveal who you are, did you? She's Caiaphas's spy. You would be in danger."

"I didn't tell her I was your father. I told her I was a friend." He cocked his head sideways. "Partially true. Is it not good that your father is also your friend?"

"And she believed you? She believed that we have a Roman soldier for a friend, who came to Sarah's tomb? That is even hard for me to believe."

"You forget that it's your grandfather's connection with Rome that kept you safe these last few years. I've met many Roman soldiers who are sympathetic toward, and even admire, followers of Yeshua. They don't say it openly for fear of retaliation. Cornelius at Caesarea is one such example. Is Devorah a follower of the way?"

"Mother doubts she believes in Yeshua but is praying for her. I'm finding it difficult to pray for her. She's being so deceptive. I have asked Yeshua to give me YHWH's heart for her and to see her through his eyes. Not that she deserves such love."

"Jerusha, none of us deserve such love. Would it help you to see her differently if you knew she told me the high priest knows your grandfather is with a caravan, and intends to have it attacked?

"No. It doesn't make me feel better, and why did you say 'your grandfather' and not 'father'?" Jerusha's questioned surprised even herself.

"When I came to Jerusalem, as a young boy about Moses's age, I disowned my father. I hated that he was a Roman soldier. The boys in the synagogue beat me and mocked me because of it. It was only after I gave my life to Yeshua that I desired to know him again. As I told you the other day, by that time, it was too late. I feel I don't deserve to call him father, but I love him."

"He loves you, too. He went looking for you."

"Only through Yeshua can our relationship be restored." He closed his eyes and took a deep breath. "I saw the caravan Devorah mentioned. Our legion passed it coming here. It took the path of our patriarchs, heading north toward Shiloh. I must find a way to warn him."

"Don't trust her, Father. It may be a trap for you both. I overheard her talking to the high priest's servant. I heard them say 'Regulus', and the servant asked Devorah what she knew It must be a trap. Why would she help us?"

"I don't know, but I can't risk doing nothing. There is a chance he will be killed. Surely you can understand that I must go." His eyes begged.

"I understand, but I am afraid I will lose both of you. Please be careful."

Chapter 19

Jerusha tightened the saddle on Boaz, the white stallion. He pawed the hay, restless to go.

"Whoa, boy, we will leave soon enough." His silky nose nuzzled against her cheek. She stepped under his head, took the lantern from the post, and walked out the back entrance. Despite having lived in the villa for years, she had never seen anything that looked like a secret passage. The full moon lit up the countryside. She followed a well-worn path down the hill to the limestone wall that surrounded the villa. She looked back up hill for anything that could indicate an opening. Nothing. *It wouldn't be on this path anyway.*

The wind rippled her radiyd. She tightened it around her face, and cupped her hand over the lantern. A sudden gust of wind extinguished the flickering flame and left her staring at the moonlit path. She set the lantern down, turned around, and felt her way along the limestone wall.

Suddenly, she lost her footing and fell six feet down a hidden shaft. She landed on her back with a thud. The wind was knocked out of her, and she gasped to refill her lungs. She looked toward the opening and could see the moonlight, just before a large stone fell over the opening. She was left in total darkness. She hoped it was not another burial cave. Her heart pounded.

Even though I walk through the valley of the shadow of death, I will fear no evil—for you are with me.

She sat for a minute on the cold stone and let her eyes adjust to the darkness. In the distance, she could barely make out a speck of light. She stood and felt for the sides of the tunnel. She kept her hands on the wall to guide her, and moved toward the faint light. It grew large the further she walked. Her heartbeat slowed a little.

Maybe I will find my way out of this place, yet.

She came to the end of the wall and stepped into a large opening. Moonlight streamed through small openings overhead and allowed some light into the small room. She felt all around the walls for something, anything to help her get out. Panic threatened to override her reason. *Think, Jerusha, think.* "Yeshua, I know you're with me. Help me calm down." Her words echoed off of the stone walls.

"J-J-Jerusha." Moses's voice came from the other side of the wall.

"Moses!" she yelled. No response. "Moses!" she yelled louder.

"Boaz, where's J-J-Jerusha? Moses sounded distraught.

"Moses!" she yelled and ran her trembling fingers over every crack in the wall. "There has to be a door somewhere. Why doesn't he answer? Can't he hear me?" she mumbled.

"Oh, what's that?"

Her fingers touched a curved line, and as she followed it with both hands, it seemed to form the shape of a lion head like her pendant. A chain hung from the middle with something dangling at the end. She pulled on it. Nothing moved. The object at the end felt smooth. A butterfly jewel like her pendant. She felt an indention in the middle of the lion face, placed the jewel in the indention, and pushed hard with both hands. The wall opened a little. She pushed with her shoulder, and it opened a little more. Finally, she opened it enough to squeeze through. There was Moses, staring at her with wide eyes. She collapsed in the hay.

**

"Moses, did you slip the note I gave you under Mother's door?" Jerusha straightened the supplies on the donkey, untied Boaz, and led them both out of the stalls.

"Yes, j-just like you told me." He took the donkey's rope from Jerusha.

"Did anyone see you?" She led Boaz to the secret opening and looked back at Moses.

"No. I w-w-was very careful." He carried the lantern with one hand and led the donkey with the other.

"I'll go first, but hold that lantern up so I can see what's ahead. The part of the tunnel I came through is large enough for our animals. I don't know what's ahead, but I know that Grandfather got in and out through a secret passage. This has to be it." Once inside, Jerusha tied Boaz to an iron post that stuck out of the wall and looked for a way to close the door. She pulled on the chain, and the butterfly came off the lion. The door crept shut. The lantern flickered but stayed lit.

"Follow me." She tugged on Boaz's harness. He whinnied, and she rubbed his nose and quieted him.

"Will your mother be angry at me for going with you to Shiloh?" Moses sounded scared. She was a little scared, too.

"She may be angry with me, but not you." She held the harness and kept Boaz's head down. "That's a good boy, Boaz."

The musty tunnel wound up and down for what seemed like a mile. She worried a bit that they might not get out. It seemed like the most logical way to get away unseen by anyone. Her grandfather did it, and she would do it too.

Shiloh. What better place to go for answers to being barren? Hannah's cries produced one of the greatest prophets of old. Maybe YHWH will hear her cries for a child too. Besides, she may run into her grandfather's caravan. Her father said it headed in that direction.

Guilt pierced Jerusha's thoughts for leaving her mother a note. She most certainly would not have approved of the journey to Shiloh and would have tried to stop her.

At last, they reached the end of the tunnel. Moonlight shone around a crack in the opening. Jerusha and Moses grabbed the two-foot handle and put all their weight on it to turn the stone until it moved out of the way. They ducked under a low limestone ridge, guided the animals underneath, and stepped outside. Boaz stamped his hoofs, ready to go. The donkey brayed and kicked a little. Moses held him tight. Jerusha led Boaz out of the dense bushes, then returned to help Moses roll the stone back in place. How appropriate. A secret passage disguised as a tomb. *Only Grandfather would think of that.*

"Be careful, Moses. The bushes are thorny." She remembered the jujube thorns on the tree in front of her villa. She heard that's what they had used to make Yeshua's crown with. She shivered. The mighty YHWH's son being humiliated and tortured for her and all of mankind. She sighed. *Even Devorah.*

"There's the Emmaus road." Moses held branches back with one hand. The donkey sauntered past untouched.

"We need to find the king's highway and go north." Jerusha mounted sidesaddle and gave Moses a hand. "Hop on behind. If you hold the rope, the donkey will follow."

After Moses was situated behind her, she squeezed the horse's flanks. He reared and took off in a gallop. Her cloak tightened around her neck as Moses hung on and let out a squeal. The donkey moved faster than she had ever seen a donkey run. Her deep belly laugh echoed in the ravine, and she reined in Boaz to a slow trot.

"Moses, I remember the days when my father and I rode under the full moon. Timon and I have done it a few times, too."

"I hope you don't mind me saying so Jerusha, but we need to be paying attention to our surroundings, not jawing about the past. There could be robbers out."

"You're right. I'll move Boaz off the road and into the grass. It should help to muffle his hoofs a bit. We should be in Shiloh by the end of the fourth watch, unless we see the caravan."

***

"Moses, wake up." His head bobbed on her shoulder. Her eyelids felt heavy, too. She veered left off the road, up a slight incline, and reined Boaz in under a grove of almond trees. "Let's rest here." Moses slid off and helped Jerusha down. She stretched her achy arms and legs. "The moon has moved. It will be dawn soon." She tied Boaz to a limb, and stood still for a minute taking in her surroundings. "We're at the bottom of Mount Ephraim. Shiloh's not far. The creek should be over there somewhere." She untied Boaz and led him toward a gurgling sound. Moses followed with the donkey. After the animals had drunk, Jerusha and Moses knelt by the stream, cupped their hands and partook of the fresh, cool water. She removed the saddle from Boaz and propped it against a tree trunk. She lay down and used the saddle for a pillow.

"Moses, can you stand watch? I need to rest." She wrapped her cloak tight and rolled over. She was too tired to care that, in the distance, lightening streaked the western sky. Before she heard Moses's answer, she had nodded off. *A man's face. Gentle eyes. Long white beard.* "I've seen you before," she mumbled. A clap of thunder startled her awake. She sat straight up, her heart racing. It took all of her strength to stand against the wind gusts that buffeted her body. She tucked her head low, and inched her way toward Boaz. As she lifted the saddle, the gale switched directions and drove her into his side. He whinnied and reared.

"Whoa, boy." She held the reins tight while he stamped his hooves. With Moses's help, she saddled and mounted. She reached down a hand to Moses and helped him into the saddle. "Hold tight, and whatever you do, don't let go of the donkey's rope. We must get to Shiloh before it starts raining." She kicked Boaz in his flanks. "Let's go, boy. You can do it." He stumbled a bit and took off.

Instead of riding straight up the mountain, she zigzagged up the slope. It was easier on the donkey. Crack! Thunder roared, and Boaz started to rear. "Whoa, boy." She stroked his face, and looked over her shoulder at Moses. "Still have the donkey?" Moses nodded.

Jerusha shielded her eyes against the wind. "I see the city gate. It's not far." She squeezed Boaz's flanks. "Let's go."

As Jerusha crested the last ridge, the rain slashed against her face, and the wind's gale roared against Boaz so hard it stopped his forward progress. She urged him on. He reared, lost his footing, and started to topple. "Moses! Jump!" She flung herself from the saddle, and hit the ground rolling.

***

"Who are you?" Jerusha lay beneath a lambskin cover and peered up at a stranger. Gentle eyes. Long gray beard. His face hovered near. "I think I've seen you before."

"Yes. We have met. Do you remember? At your betrothal celebration. I knew your father. I brought you the gift, the jasper stone your father asked me to give you if he didn't return. I never saw him again." He rose and stirred the brazier coals.

"He's alive." She raised herself up on one elbow, lips quivering. Moses dipped bread in a pot over a fire. He smiled and shrugged.

"Yes, I have been told that is true. I have also been told by YHWH that you would be coming to Shiloh." He squatted by the fire and warmed his hands. "Come, warm yourself. If you would like, I can give you a fresh tunic and cloak to wear while yours dry. It would be too large, but at least you would not be shivering in wet garments." He laid out a set of dry garments for her and motioned for Moses to come with him.

Alone, she shed the soaked garments but kept the girdle with her father's signet ring and the acacia butterfly piece that Yeshua made. The old man was right. The cloak hung way past her feet. She gathered it above her ankles, positioned herself close to the fire on a soft leather pallet, and gripped the lion and the butterfly-jeweled pendant that hung around her neck. "Arise, Lord. Let your enemies be scattered. Let all who hate you flee before you." She hoped her grandfather's enemies were scattered and that her father found him in time to save him. No sign of the caravan. It could have gone on to Shechem or veered west to Caesarea on the coast.

The stranger seemed harmless enough. Why would YHWH tell him she was coming? She was exhausted. Her eyelids fluttered, and her chin dipped to her chest. *A little nap would be good, and then find the tabernacle ruins. Maybe this evening.* The warmth of the fire soothed her achy bones. She rolled on to her side, pulled her knees to her chest, and let herself doze off.

Chapter 20

The setting sun warmed Jerusha's face as she peered down at the olive groves that dotted the slopes surrounding Shiloh. She stood on sacred holy ground. For more than 300 years the tabernacle of old rested on the soil beneath her feet. She imagined YHWH's glory. A cloud by day, and a fire by night, as He hovered over the Ark of the Covenant.

Father had explained the power of His holy presence. She grasped her pendant, made from the same type of wood as the ark, and quoted Moses's words. "Arise Lord. Let your enemies be scattered. Let all who hate you flee before you." Her words pierced the air and echoed in the valley. A gentle breeze caressed her face like angel's wings. A soft mist engulfed the mountain top.

She glanced at Moses and the stranger who sat on the wall of the tabernacle ruins. She unwrapped her radiyd, held it out like butterfly wings, and spun around several times, her wavy hair blowing in the cool air. With her eyes closed and chin lifted, she breathed deep, then whirled and dipped as she danced. Guided by an invisible presence, she never stumbled or tripped. One tear escaped and ran down her cheek, then another. Finally, she could hold it back no longer, and an uncontrollable sob erupted from her soul. She folded in her wings and collapsed to her knees. Worthless. Cursed. Surrounded by a misty shroud.

Her cries echoed across the valley like a captured mourning dove. On and on it rang; a gut-wrenching sob that would not stop. Finally, Jerusha had no more tears to give, and her sobbing subsided. The sun dipped over the horizon and left the valley in a rosy glow.

"Jerusha." The stranger's words came from inside the fog. "You are like Hannah to this generation, a prophetess, and a mother of nations." A covering fell over her head and shoulders. Not her radiyd. It lay in her lap. In the twilight, she glanced left. Nothing there, then right. She felt its weight, like a shawl, but saw nothing. Something supernatural.

"How can this be? I am barren and worthless." She searched for his face in the mist.

"Your worth is not in being a mother, but in being YHWH's royal daughter, through Yeshua's bloodline. Your sons will come from afar, and your daughters will be nursed at your side." The sound of his voice came from a shimmering light in the fog. His words vibrated with life. A fire burned in her belly and Hannah's words, memorized as a child, sprung forth from her mouth.

"My heart exults in the Lord;
My horn is exalted in the Lord,
My mouth speaks boldly against my enemies,
Because I rejoice in thy salvation.
There is no one holy like the Lord,
Indeed, there is no one besides you,
Nor is there any rock like our God.
Boast no more so very proudly,
Do not let arrogance come out of your mouth;
For the Lord is a God of knowledge,
And with him actions are weighed.
The bows of the mighty are shattered,
But the feeble gird on strength.

Those who were full hire themselves out for bread,
But those who were hungry will cease to hunger.
Even the barren gives birth to seven,
But she who has many children languishes.
The Lord kills and makes alive;
He brings down to Sheol and raises up,
The Lord makes poor and rich;
He brings low, He also exalts,
He raises the poor from the dust,
He lifts the needy from the ash heap
To make them sit with nobles,
And inherit a seat of honor;
For the pillars of the earth are the Lord's,
And he sets the world on them.
He keeps the feet of His godly ones,
But the wicked ones are silenced in darkness;
For not by might shall a man prevail.
Those who contend with the Lord will be scattered;
Against them He will thunder in the heavens,
The Lord will judge the ends of the earth;
And He will give strength to His king,
And will exalt the horn of His anointed."

She rose to her feet. "Sons of Jacob, come forth. Sons of Jacob, come forth. Sons of Jacob, come forth." Like arrows in the darkness, her words reverberated across the valley.

Jerusha understood not the power of what happened in that declaration, nor did she understood why she felt compelled to speak with such boldness. She also did not understood the tingly sensation that ran through her body.

The fog lifted. She turned to ask the stranger to explain. Moses lay prostrate on the ground. The stranger nowhere to be found. She covered her head with her radiyd and closed her eyes. She basked in YHWH's holy presence, consumed by a peace like she had never known. Nothing mattered, except basking in her Father's loving arms, a daughter not cursed. Her identity now ingrained in her consciousness by His all-powerful words. She heard from her Father above, the one who created her, the one who gave her life. She would return to Jerusalem with a new purpose, unafraid to face the future. She would tell her grandfather, if she ever saw him again.

Low in the night sky, Regulus outshined the distant stars. Jerusha smiled. Her grandfather's story entered her thoughts. His deep, rich voice echoed in her memory as he had pointed to the bright star: "In Hebrew, arye, the lion, treads under foot his enemies. Regulus, the Roman name, means prince or little king. Never forget who you are. You are royalty from the tribe of Judah."

***

The early morning sun peeked over the horizon. Its rays filtered through the low-hanging clouds and fanned across the hillside where numerous flocks grazed, their shepherds standing watch. A few women ground grain, their millstones turning in rhythmic cadence.

Jerusha plopped the last bite of bread in her mouth. It was the last of the bread they had brought with them. She would be home by nightfall. She had so much news to tell her mother and Chaya. Maybe her father would be back with her grandfather.

"Moses, what happened to the man who sheltered us? He just disappeared. Did he tell you where he went? I would like to thank him for his hospitality, and ask him some questions before we leave." She straightened Boaz's saddle, and turned with her hands on her hips.

"No." He shrugged. "One moment he was there. The next moment he was gone." His bewildered eyes made her smile.

"What's this?" He pulled an elongated object from the donkey's backpack and handed it to Jerusha. She unrolled the soft camel leather.

"A scepter?" Her eyes widened. "Where did this come from?"

"It was not there when we left." Moses shook his head.

"It must be from the stranger. But why?" She admired the golden staff covered with twelve jewels and read the Hebrew letters engraved around the top. "The scepter shall not depart from Judah until Shiloh comes."

"Do not tell anyone about this," she instructed Moses as she wrapped it in the leather and replaced it in its hiding place. "We must go." She mounted Boaz and reached for Moses.

"I will ride the donkey, Jerusha. Going downhill will be easier than coming up." He climbed on the stubborn beast and kicked his sides. "We cannot lose this old guy. He carries a treasure." Moses sat tall like a little prince on a stallion. Jerusha chuckled, the laughter a welcome release. She followed Moses out of the city gate. The guard nodded as they passed.

When they had rounded the first almond grove, Jerusha looked back for the stranger. In the distance, she could see another traveler followed, which was not unusual. Many travelers on the king's highway.

When they got to the spring, they rested awhile and gave the animals a drink. Jerusha sat in the grass beside the creek and pondered the happenings of the trip. Moses waded up stream. Boaz pawed the ground and raised his head, his ears up.

"What is it, Boaz? What's got you so restless?" Jerusha rose and stood before the horse and whispered in his ear. "It's all right. Calm …" A hand smothered her mouth and nose. A sharp point pierced her back and she slumped to the ground. "Moses!" Hands all over her body. Pain seared through her back. She groaned. Her head jerked up as someone ripped her tunic. Cool air blew over her chest. She opened her eyes. Someone grabbed her pendant. *Fight him. Fight, Jerusha, fight.* Her vision faded to black. She could hear a voice in the distance. Could it be? Her eyes fluttered open. Through blurry eyes, she could make out a hand holding an orange glowing object.

"I am sorry, Jerusha, I must sear your wound or you will bleed to death. Forgive me." It was Timon.

Jerusha tried to speak, then came the white-hot pain in her back. Her scream echoed, then she succumbed to the blackness.

A cool, wet cloth dabbed at her face and neck. She opened her eyes.

"If I had gotten here any later, you and Moses would be dead." There was no twinkle in Timon's eyes this time.

"Moses?" She raised her brow.

"He's fine. He managed to escape. I found him running on the road. When I returned to Jerusalem, your mother showed me your note." He helped her sit up.

Moses patted her hand. "I'm sorry I ran, Jerusha. I did not know what else to do." The men didn't get the scepter or your pendant. I hit one with my slingshot. Timon smacked the other one and caused him to drop your pendant. They both took off running, empty handed."

"You were foolish to come here without a male escort." Timon dabbed the wound with fresh herbs. "You will be all right. It's a surface wound." He wrapped torn linen strips around her body, being careful to keep her chest covered with her cloak. "Somehow your girdle acted as a shield. YHWH was with you." He looked into her eyes, tears hovering at the edges. "I almost lost you."

"Timon, I missed you." She reached up and winced, then dropped her arms. "I have so much to tell you." She longed to embrace him. She could tell he wanted the same. Now was not the time. He folded a lamb's skin cover into a pillow, helped her lay on her side on the soft grass, and covered her with his cloak.

"Rest. We will stay here until you can travel." His lips lingered on her cheek.

"I love you." She nuzzled her nose in his cloak. His fragrance filled her nostrils. The fire crackled near where she lay.

"I love you, too." He curled around her body being careful not to touch her wound. Jerusha rested inside the cocoon of his protection. Her husband was back.

Chapter 21

One week later

Timon rode his smoky cream stallion next to Jerusha and Boaz. Her husband was at her side again. She thought of what her grandfather had said before he left to find her father. *The children you shall have, after you have lost the other, will say again in your ear, "make place for me to dwell."* The stranger said she would be a mother of nations. She no longer felt cursed. Still there were many questions only YHWH, her heavenly Father could answer.

Her heart swelled with a new confidence in His love. Her destiny wasin His hands. He had supernaturally laid an invisible covering over her head and shoulders. His royal daughter returned to Jerusalem, a city torn with conflict, ready to embrace the purpose for which she was created. A mother to the nations. What could this mean? Timon would have a son. Of this she was sure. *His ways are not our ways.* She smiled at her grandfather's wisdom.

The villagers gathered around chattering and pointing at the horses. Timon dismounted, led both horses to the watering trough, and helped Jerusha dismount. They were in Bethel. Ten more miles and she would be back in Jerusalem. Maybe her father would have come with word of her grandfather's caravan. Jerusha chuckled at the children's delight in seeing the horses. Their wide-eyed innocence brought back good memories of riding with her father and playing with butterflies. She had not felt this content in a long time.

A group of young boys had gathered, admiring the horses. They shoved the smallest boy forward.

The little boy looked up at Timon. "Can we ride?" He put his head down and shuffled his feet. Timon swooped him up and sat him on Boaz.

"Who else wants to ride?" He grinned at the many hands that flew up.

"Well, I think we can all take a turn. Who's first?" He glanced from smiling face to smiling face. "How about you?" He chose a little girl that reminded Jerusha of Sarah. Her long dark eyelashes blinked bashfully. He picked her up and carried her to his horse. Not surprised he had chosen her, Jerusha choked back tears. Timon had sat by the creek, mostly silent, for three days after she told him what happened to Sarah. When he spoke about it, he blamed himself. He believed he could have talked her parents out of taking her. Jerusha understood the guilt he felt. She cried herself to sleep three nights at Sarah's tomb. Only at Shiloh did she find peace.

The other children waited while he led the two horses around in a large circle. His interaction with the children gripped Jerusha. A good father he would be. Moses stood beside the donkey, acting so grown up. He was guarding the donkey. No one would steal the scepter from him.

Jerusha looked around the small village where the old patriarch, her father's namesake, Jacob, had encountered YHWH. YHWH's house lay in ruins. How much longer before her father's house lay in ruins? She walked toward a group of women who kept their heads down, busy grinding grain.

"Shalom." She tried to engage the women. They ignored her greeting. One glanced up. *Fear?*

"The Roman soldiers passed through a few days ago." An older woman spoke from the doorway, her radiyd wrapped high around her face. "They did this to me." She unwrapped her shawl and revealed a slash on her cheek. "I would not tell them where they could find the giant."

"What giant? Did the giant have blue eyes?" Jerusha's heart pounded.

"Yes. He was gentle and kind. He gave us bread and lentils. I would not betray such a man."

"Did the soldiers catch him?"

The woman nodded. "A few hours later, they came back through. Stopped to water their horses. He had been beaten." Her eyes filled with tears. "He received no water, his lips cracked and swollen. Even with them, he showed love and talked of Yeshua. I could not stand to watch. They mocked and beat him. Why would he care if some Gentile knew of Yeshua's love? She shook her head. "Only YHWH knows."

Jerusha turned away. Grandfather had told her to love her enemies. It must be him. Her ears rang, and spots swirled before her eyes. She staggered toward Timon. He caught her and swooped her up. Her head flopped against his chest as he walked.

Grandfather.

"Is there somewhere I can lay her?" Timon asked.

"Over there on the pallet." A shaky hand stroked her head.

"Jerusha." Timon's voice sounded far away. "Jerusha." He held her against his chest and patted her face. She blinked, and opened her eyes.

"They have Grandfather."

"Who?" He looked at the old woman and helped Jerusha sit up.

"The Romans. Pigs! One beat and raped my daughter. She also refused to tell where the giant had gone. After they left us, she died with her son in her arms." The old woman wiped her eyes, squatted and lifted a small bundle from a pile of rags. "Her baby son needs a mother and father." She swallowed and continued. "Would you raise her son? You appear to have more means to raise him than I. We have no nursing mother here. If you do not take him, he will starve." She placed the infant in Jerusha's arms. "Maybe you can find a wet nurse where you are going, eh?"

Your sons shall come from afar. The stranger's words at Shiloh echoed. Jerusha ran her finger across the tiny cheek and looked up at Timon. "We will find a wet nurse for him." He nodded. *You're like*

Hannah to this generation. She looked at the whimpering child. "This is our son. YHWH's gift." Timon knelt beside her.

"Samuel. We will call him Samuel Jacob." He took the bundle from her hands and stood. "My son, the prophet." Her husband's twinkle was back. "My mother can get him a wet nurse. Perhaps Devorah can nurse him, until she finds someone else."

Jerusha had not thought of Devorah for days. Her enemy and the enemy of her grandfather. Devorah a nurse for her son? She decided it would be all right, if it was the only way to keep the child alive. She reached up for her son. Timon squatted and placed him in her arms. He whimpered and nuzzled his head against her arm, his mouth open.

"How long since he has been fed?" Jerusha looked at the old woman. The pain in her eyes grieved Jerusha's heart. The frail soul had lost her daughter, and the baby was the last link to her child, and she was losing him too. All because they had protected her grandfather. Unlike Devorah, the traitor. *How do you love someone like Devorah?*

"May I?" The grieving grandmother reached for the child. Timon helped Jerusha to her feet, and she placed the infant in the old woman's shaking arms. "I tried to dribble goats milk into his mouth." She stared at Jerusha with vacant eyes. "He rejected it, and it made him sick." She held him tight against her chest and rocked back and forth. "My daughter would want him to live, even if it means giving him away."

"I am sorry for the loss of your daughter." Jerusha choked back the lump in her throat. "Thank you for what you did for the giant. He could be my grandfather."

"We would have nothing, if it wasn't for his kindness." The old woman's eyes brightened. "We would not know that Yeshua is the Mashiach, and that his kingdom is not of this world. Because of him, my daughter is with Yeshua in his kingdom, instead of in Sheol." She closed her eyes and breathed deep, then stared straight into Jerusha's eyes. "I will see her again one day, in His kingdom." She handed the baby back to Jerusha. "You will be a good mother to my grandson, eh?" She looked at Timon, who had his arm around Jerusha. "And you will be a good father." She shook her head, sat by the fire and stirred the lentil soup. "Go. The baby needs milk."

***

The sun was setting by the time they reached the outskirts of Jerusalem. Samuel squirmed and fussed in her arms, his cries growing weaker as the hours passed. He needed nourishment.

A crowd had gathered outside of the city wall, which was unusual at that time of day. A sense of foreboding swept over Jerusha. It was the same feeling she felt in Herod's palace as a little girl.

Timon's expression was sober, the twinkle in his eyes gone. As they drew nearer, the people parted and let them pass, their voices lowering to a murmur. Then she saw it. A cross. She held her son tighter to her chest. They moved closer and the figure became clear. It could not be. Jail, maybe, but not this!

Blood ran down his feet and dripped from his toes. Jerusha watched in horror as her grandfather lifted himself and gasped for air. His eyes locked on hers.

"Grandfather!" She spoke the word without shame for everyone to hear. He had been Yogli to her in Herod's palace. He had been Yogli, the Roman soldier whose decree had protected her home. Now, he was Grandfather. He deserved to be known for the wonderful man he was, a giant in heart, not only in body. She held the baby up for him to see.

"My son, Samuel." She wanted to scream to those who watched and ask them why this was happening, but she had only a little time to say good bye. She would not waste it screaming questions to others. This time she cared nothing about asking questions. She only cared that her grandfather took his last breaths.

"He refused to vow allegiance to Caesar. Let this be an example to you of what happens when there is an uprising against Rome. You will be crushed." The threat came from behind Jerusha. She turned as the people scattered. A Roman soldier rode up, leaned over, and talked with one of the Sanhedrin, his black robe and phylactery a repugnant sight to Jerusha. In the distance, another soldier followed, dismounted, and led his horse through the bystanders.

One by one, they parted to let him pass. It was her father.

How could he let this happen? She wanted to run to him, beg for her grandfather's life. The serious glare in his eyes stopped her. He handed the reigns to the soldier attending him and walked past Jerusha without acknowledging her. Doing so would be his demise. Somehow, she felt that did not matter to him. His Roman helmet under his arm, red plume waving in the breeze, he knelt on one knee before the cross. He squeezed shut his eyes and swallowed hard. He raised his head and looked up at his father.

Jerusha grimaced. She felt anger, guilt, and pain all at once. She watched as her father stared up at her grandfather. The seconds passed, feeling like hours.

"Father! I am sorry. Forgive me." He dropped his head and wept. The sound of his sobs echoed in the darkness that had descended upon the crowd. He kept his head down for several minutes. His attendant stood guard beside him with the horse's reigns in one hand and a sword in the other.

"Son," Grandfather gasped. Jacob lifted his head and their eyes met. "I love you." Her grandfather's words were barely a whisper. Her father's jaw tightened and he swallowed hard. He rose to his feet and slapped his fist across his chest in salute. He grabbed the reigns from the attendant and mounted his horse.

"Stay. Give the body to the family." Her father addressed the soldier, his eyes locked on Jerusha. *I am sorry.* His lips moved in a silent apology, and his eyes begged for forgiveness. He galloped past them and up the hill, disappearing in a swirl of dust.

Jerusha tried to soothe the crying infant and looked again at her grandfather. His brow was bloodied and his cheekbones bruised. He was barely breathing. She could not tear her eyes away, even though she felt as though she would be sick. She tightened her stomach muscles and forced the bile back down her throat. Tears formed in her eyes, but this was not the time to cry. She must be strong.

"I'll be brave, Grandfather." Her words sounded stronger than she felt. His words echoed in her mind. *His ways are not our ways.* She half smiled. He was still teaching her, even from the cross. *Love your enemies. Forgive those who persecute you. Never forget who you are.*

"I won't forget, Grandfather." Her whispered words seemed to give him strength. He lifted himself up again and gasped for air. Timon was at her side and helped her down.

Her grandfather breathed his last words, "I love you." His head dropped forward, and his whole body slumped lifeless.

Jerusha buried her face in Timon's chest, the baby between them. Tears flowed like a torrent. Timon held her close and stroked her head.

"He's with Sarah and Stephen in Yeshua's kingdom. You will see them again." The baby nuzzled against her chest. Her son fought for his life. She could not help her grandfather, but she could help Samuel.

"Moses, take her and the baby home." Timon sensed the urgency. "I will take Yogi down and place his body in the tomb. We can prepare it with spices in the morning."

Jerusha wanted to stay and hug her grandfather's body, but she knew she must take care of her son. *That's what Grandfather would want.* Samuel whimpered as Timon took him from her arms. Moses helped her mount Boaz.

This cannot be happening. Grandfather's dead. Timon placed their son back in her arms.

"YHWH allowed Yogli to see his great-grandson before he died. I saw the pleasure in his eyes." He tried to smile at Jerusha. A single tear slipped from his eyes and ran down his cheek. "I will be home soon. Take care of our Samuel."

Chapter 22

"Grandfather's dead." Jerusha handed Samuel to Moses and dismounted Boaz. "They crucified him."

Abigail unlocked the gate. "We heard. We stayed here with Joseph. I could not watch it." Tears filled her eyes. "I have been so worried about you." She swung the gate wide and rushed out. Jerusha welcomed her hug. There was nothing like a mother's embrace.

"It was terrible. He suffered so much. Father was there." Abigail broke the hug and searched her daughter's face.

"Jacob?" Her mother's eyes lit up. "Is he—"

"—is he coming home?" Jerusha finished the question. "No. He asked Grandfather to forgive him, and then he left. His attendant stayed and is helping Timon with Grandfather's body. They are taking Grandfather to the tomb."

"So Timon found you."

"Mother, I have so much to tell you."

"What do we have here? Another orphan?" Abigail glanced at Moses's bundle.

"This is my son, Samuel." Jerusha smiled and uncovered his face, then glanced at Moses, who grinned ear to ear. In the midst of all the suffering, her little Samuel brought joy beyond words. "He needs a wet nurse. Would Chaya know of someone?"

"Maybe Devorah could help." Abigail cleared her throat and touched Jerusha's arm. "Until another wet nurse is found."

Devorah came from around the pomegranate bush and walked up the tiled path. Jerusha took Samuel from Moses and snuggled him close to her chest. Handing her son to her enemy would take more courage than she thought she had. She pulled the swaddling cloth back. So pale. Almost lifeless. She nudged his chin and placed her finger to his lips. No response.

"You must live." Tears formed in her eyes. *I shall not die, but live and declare the works of the Lord.* That was part of the Psalm that Grandfather loved. "You will not die. Grandfather died, but you will not die. You will declare the works of the Lord." The corner of his mouth curled up. "Chaya said that look on a baby's face was gas. Maybe. I believe you agree with my declaration, but you need nourishment. Of that I am certain." She looked up at Devorah. "This is my son."

"Timon will be pleased." The young widow's words pierced Jerusha's heart.

"He is pleased. That is true." She glared at Devorah.

"He found you. He was quite distraught when he came back and you were gone. I did not know you left. Your mother did not tell me. Only when Timon stormed into the kitchen looking for you did I know. We searched everywhere until Abigail came back from the market. Later, I heard them talking in the garden."

"I am sure you did." Jerusha hugged Samuel tighter. "My son needs nourishment. Will you nurse him until Chaya can find another wet nurse?"

"Of course." She reached out for the child. Jerusha pulled back. Samuel rode in her arms only a few short hours. She looked at him, the son promised by Yeshua. Four long years she waited for this day. She sighed, then emptied her arms and placed her Samuel in

Devorah's care. It felt like a part of her soul had been torn away. She so wanted to nurse him herself, bond with him. Poor little thing. She stroked his brow with her finger. Even though it had to be, she would not watch her son suckle at another woman's breast, especially Devorah's.

"After you nurse, bring him to the garden." She looked at her mother, a heavy weight in her chest, tears running down her cheeks. She ran to the place where she felt safe and secure in YHWH's presence. Her Father's bench.

***

Jerusha felt someone's presence. Wiping her nose on her sleeve, she peered into the darkness at the shadowy silhouette by the gate. Abigail stepped into the moonlight.

"I waited for you to finish crying." Her soft, tender voice carried a mother's concern and love. "Jerusha, you have grown so much in your faith." She sat next to Jerusha. "Your selfless love for Samuel and allowing a woman you loath to nurse him. Come. Lay your head right here." She drew Jerusha to herself. Frankincense. Mother wore the oil everyday in remembrance of Father. Several swifts twittered and swooped past to their nest in the garden wall. Jerusha closed her eyes, rested in her mother's embrace and listened to the crickets.

"Do you think Devorah betrayed Grandfather?"

"I do not know. Your grandfather liked her. And she told Jacob about the attack on the caravan."

"Was there really an attack, or was that a lie, too. We don't know for sure what happened to Grandfather. Why couldn't Father have stayed and told us?"

"Your father could be in danger, too. The high priest looked for him at your wedding. He may still be on the lookout for him. I have heard some of the religious leaders are working with Rome."

"Jerusalem is not a safe place to raise a son. Timon feels Yeshua has not released us to leave, yet. I am beginning to feel the same way. There are many in Jerusalem that do not believe Yeshua is the Mashiach." Jerusha looked up at her mother. "While I was at Shiloh, I had an encounter with YHWH. He put an invisible covering over my head and spoke to me through the old man who came to my betrothal. Do you remember him? He had a long white beard. He said he knew Father and gave me the jasper jewel."

"Yes. I remember. What was he doing in Shiloh?"

"He said YHWH sent him, and he knew I was coming. It was a good thing, too. Boaz slipped and fell in the rain. He provided a refuge from the storm, dry clothes, and food. Even more important, he spoke YHWH's words. 'You are like Hannah to this generation, a prophetess, and a mother of nations.' Imagine, Mother, me a mother of nations. When I argued that I was cursed, He said my worth was in being YHWH's royal daughter. His words carried such power. They shattered my self-doubts and filled me with purpose and destiny. The strangest thing, though: he just disappeared."

"He did that at your betrothal feast, too. One minute he was there. The next he was gone. Not even a shalom. Just disappeared."

"Could he be an angel?"

"Maybe."

"Oh," Jerusha sat up. "Before we left Shiloh, Moses found a gold scepter in a bag on the donkey. It had words engraved on it. 'The scepter will not depart from Judah, until Shiloh comes.' I have heard them talk about Shiloh coming in the synagogue. They believe Shiloh is the Mashiach. That's Yeshua. Didn't he already come and set up his kingdom? Why was I given this scepter?"

"I fed your son." Devorah stood at the gate, the infant snuggled in her arms. Jerusha's heartbeat increased. How much of their conversation did she hear? "He will survive." Devorah appeared calm. "At first he turned away." She smiled. "But I kept placing it before him until he attached. He suckled gently at first, then with more vigor. Chaya said a wet nurse will be here for his next feeding." She handed Samuel to Jerusha and turned to leave, then turned back. "I am honored that you allowed me to help."

What choice did I have? The words stuck in her throat. Devorah appeared sincere. *Be kind to Devorah.* Grandfather's words echoed in her thoughts. She swallowed and pursed her lips. "Thank you, for being willing to help." Her words sounded tart. Grandfather would have given Jerusha that stare, but it was the closest thing to kindness she could offer tonight. A tinge of guilt clawed in her gut.

"We'll leave you to enjoy your new son." Her mother took Devorah's arm, and they walked under the portico toward their rooms.

Jerusha looked up at the stars., Regulus shined bright as always. *Yeshua, cleanse my heart so I can love my enemies.* Samuel squirmed. She laid him in her lap and rewrapped the swaddling cloth. "Tomorrow we both need to dip in the mikvah." He stretched one foot out of the cloth. She giggled. "You will be strong like your father and grandfather. Look at those tiny toes. You have a long way to go, to be as big as your great-grandfather. What a sight it would have been to see that giant holding you." She snuggled him close. *Be kind to Devorah.* Grandfather's words again. The stars shone brightly above. "And, Yeshua, tell Grandfather I will do better tomorrow."

"Tell him yourself." Timon opened the gate.

"You scared me. After everything that has happened these last days, I am a little jumpy. Do not sneak up on me like that again."

"I did not sneak up on you." His eyes twinkled. "Come with me to the stable. I told Moses to bring Abigail and Chaya. "We need some help."

"Who needs help?"

"The soldier and me."

"You are not making any sense. What's going on? What did you mean when you said 'tell him yourself?' You know grandfather's dead. What kind of a cruel statement is that?"

"No more questions. Be still and come with me." He smiled at Samuel and took her arm.

"Where are we going?"

"You just had to ask one more question." He teased and winked.

***

In the darkness, Timon guided Jerusha and little Samuel along the path toward the stable making sure she avoided the stones that could cause her to trip. She enjoyed his protective care. A contentment filled her soul. They were not just man and wife. They were a family. She wondered why they walked in darkness without a lantern. Somehow, it didn't matter. She was with the man she loved, and she carried his son in her arms.

The stable smelled of fresh hay. Boaz neighed and raised his ears when she passed. Why were they sneaking around in the dark? She glanced up at his face. He almost smiled. At the end of the stable she saw a faint light. It looked as if it came from the secret tunnel. She stopped.

"How did you know about this?" She stared at the sliver of light coming through the opening. Timon grinned like a little boy and pulled the stone open. Light shined in Jerusha's face, and she was momentarily blinded. Timon took her arm and helped her duck under the opening. She gasped.

"Grandfather? Why did you bring his body here?" She froze. The soldier stood at attention at his head. She wanted to run to him, hug him, and speak life into him the way Yeshua did with Lazarus. She turned away. His lifeless, battered face was too much to endure.

"Your grandfather is alive. He's near death, but still breathing. Your father gave the soldier orders to take him down before he took his last breath and bring him here." Timon reached for Samuel. "Talk to him, Jerusha. He can hear you."

Jerusha rushed to his side and knelt. She touched his cheek, being ever so gentle. "Grandfather. Can you hear me? I love you." She looked up at Timon. "Are you sure he is breathing? He looks so lifeless. His cheek is so cold."

Timon squatted and felt the side of his neck. "There is a faint beat."

"Grandfather, you can't die." Her voice quivered. She laid her face on his chest, the lambskin cover soft against her cheek, and wept. "Don't die. Please don't die." The words sputtered forth between her sobs.

Chapter 23
Several Days Later

Jerusha peeked through the shadowy opening. Boaz lifted his head, snorted, and stamped his hoof. She smiled at his alertness to her scent. Timon stroked his nose and listened to Luke, the physician.

"He is slipping away fast. He may be with Yeshua in his kingdom before morning." A dark cloud descended. Her stomach knotted. She stepped back inside the tunnel. Her father's Roman attendant rose from grandfather's side and dipped a cloth in the herbs that soaked in the healing waters.

"It's not working, Marcus." She closed her eyes.

"Yeshua, you surely didn't save Grandfather just to have him die." She and Marcus had kept vigil since Timon first brought her to him. Not even Mother and Chaya could get her to leave his side. It was partly because of Marcus. How could she leave Grandfather with a Roman soldier, a Gentile, and as far as she knew, someone who did not believe in Yeshua's way. He loved her father and said he saved his life many times in battle. Loyal to him, he intended to keep the orders her father gave: "See that my father does not die." He would not leave either, until he could give her father good news.

"Jacob, your father, is praying to his god. I have seen the power of his prayers. Many soldiers healed." He applied the poultice.

Samuel stirred on his mat, and she picked him up. The same words she had spoken over him two days earlier came to her mind. Why hadn't she thought of them sooner? She bent over the pale giant.

"Grandfather, you will not die but live and declare the works of the Lord. Remember? It's one of your favorites from the Psalms. 'I will not die, but live and declare the works of the Lord.' She stood and walked back and forth. The words from Psalm 118 flowed without effort.

'O give thanks unto the LORD; for he is good: because his mercy endures for ever.' She turned and faced the lifeless body.

"Hear that, Grandfather. Let Israel now say, that his mercy endures forever. Let the house of Aaron now say, that his mercy endures for ever. Let them now that fear the LORD say—" Her eyes fell on Marcus. "—that his mercy endures for ever." Marcus's head bowed. She sat beside the lifeless form. "Speak it, Grandfather. Speak it in your heart. His mercy endures forever. I speak it for you, for me, for Samuel." Marcus swiped a tear away. "His mercy endures forever." She continued pacing.

'I called upon the LORD in distress: the LORD answered me, and set me in a large place. The LORD is on my side; I will not fear: what can man do unto me?' Hear that, Grandfather. What can man do unto us? Nothing. Our lives are in YHWH's hands. Live, Grandfather. Live." A new strength rose in her body. She shifted Samuel to the other arm. 'The LORD takes my part with them that help me: therefore shall I see my desire upon them that hate me. It is better to trust in the LORD than to put confidence in man. It is better to trust in the LORD than to put confidence in princes. All nations compassed me about: but in the name of the LORD will I destroy them.' Marcus did not flinch. His eyes showed compassion. 'They compassed me about; yea, they compassed me about: but in the name of the LORD I will destroy them.' Treasonous words to a Roman. She watched him, but his gaze was steady, unmoved. 'They compassed me about like bees.'

She stopped. *Devorah, the bee.* She hadn't thought of her in days. She no doubt caused this. 'They are quenched as the fire of thorns: for in the name of the LORD I will destroy them.' *Destroy Devorah. Out of my life. Yes. Destroy? How could she destroy the woman that nursed her son?* 'You have thrust sore at me that I might fall: but the LORD helped me.' *Could this be love? YHWH's love? Not wanting her enemy destroyed?*

'The LORD is my strength and song, and is become my salvation. The voice of rejoicing and salvation is in the tabernacles of the righteous: the right hand of the LORD does valiantly. The right hand of the LORD is exalted: the right hand of the LORD does valiantly.

"'I shall not die, but live, and declare the works of the LORD.'" Grandfather's voice mixed with hers. Jerusha swiveled around and stared wide-eyed. His deep blue eyes upon her, and he smiled. She rushed to his side and knelt.

"Grandfather. Oh, Grandfather. You will live."

"Is that not what we just declared?"

"You always liked to sneak up and surprise me." She chuckled and squeezed his arm. Her little bundle wiggled. "I have a surprise for you." She touched his cheek, then with gentle care nestled the infant in the niche of Grandfather's arm. "I present you with prince Samuel. Can you believe it? I have a son."

"Remember what YHWH said to you from Isaiah. 'The children you shall have after you have lost the other, will say again in your ear, make room for me to dwell.' You lost those you never held. You lost Sarah. Make room, Jerusha, in your heart. There will be others."

"I ran to Shiloh where Hannah found her answers. YHWH met me there. He said, like Hannah, I'm a mother to this generation, a prophetess, a mother of nations." Her voice softened. "I'm not cursed. My worth is in being YHWH's royal daughter, even if I never had a child. He gave His Son's life for me. That's what makes me valuable."

"'His mercy endures forever.'" Jerusha twirled and lifted her face toward heaven. "'Your mercy endures forever.'" She twirled and shouted. "'Your mercy endures forever.'" What a joy it was to dance again. "'Your mercy endures forever.' Grandfather lives."

***

Wisps of clouds floated past the moon. A small breeze rustled the thorny jujube trees outside the entrance to the secret tunnel. Jerusha watched as the large limestone rock rolled away to reveal the tunnel's entrance. Standing in the darkness outside of a fake tomb felt creepy. Jerusha pulled her radiyd higher over her face. Her grandfather lay on a stretcher attached to Marcus's horse. She straightened the lambskin cover with one hand while holding Samuel in the other. She laid her hand on Marcus's arm who stood waiting by his horse.

"I know you will take good care of him. I can see why my father trusted you. You are a good man." She felt Timon's hand on her shoulder and squeezed his fingers.

"Where will you take him?"

"Perea. Your father has a place prepared for him in the mountains. No one will be looking for us since they believe he is dead. He will be safe there."

Abigail and Chaya stepped outside of the tunnel.

"We were hoping we were not too late." Her mother looked beautiful in the moonlight. "Give Jacob this note." She handed Marcus a small scroll.

"I will guard it with my life." He bowed and stuffed the parchment behind his breastplate.

"You talk about me as if I cannot hear. I am wounded, not deaf." Grandfather's gruffness was a welcome sound. Jerusha smiled and stood with the others around the stretcher.

"'YHWH, you are my refuge and my fortress, my God, in whom I trust. You delivered me from the snare of the trapper.'" Yogli raised up from the stretcher and raised his hands toward heaven. "Now I ask that you cover my family and hide them under the shadow of your wings. You are our shield and bulwark. We will not be afraid of the terror by night or the arrow that flies by day. No evil will befall us. Nor any plague come near our dwelling. Give your angels charge over my family and guard them in all their ways." Tears flowed down the giant's scarred cheeks.

Jerusha touched the old scar. She recalled the beating he took at Herod's palace for helping her and mother attend Peter's meeting. She knew him then only as Yogli the giant, not Grandfather. She bent close and kissed the scar.

"Thank you, Grandfather. You protected me when I didn't know who you were. You loved me when I was an angry little girl, full of pain and bitterness."

"My little lioness. Never forget who you are. You carry the King's glory within. He has given you the scepter of his authority. His words spoken with your mouth carry power. You are his royal daughter."

"Shalom." Jerusha waved with the others as Grandfather's stretcher moved away in the darkness and disappeared.

"Mother, how did you keep Devorah from finding Grandfather? I have been so busy nursing him, I hadn't thought about the possibility of her finding him. You didn't tell her, did you?"

"Chaya and I took her with us to his burial tomb, along with the other mourning women and flute players. Of course, the high priest watched from afar. Devorah cried. I believe she cared for Yogli. It is a shame we had to be deceptive with her. I am afraid that is what caused her disappearance."

"She's gone?"

"She left in the night while we were sleeping. She took her two sons and fled. I had the servants ask about her in the city. No one has seen her."

"Are you sure she doesn't know Grandfather is alive? Why would she leave now?" Jerusha's old suspicions surfaced. "Her task was complete. Grandfather was dead," she mocked.

"I thought your feelings about Devorah changed."

"I'm glad she is gone. I only hope she doesn't know about Grandfather. It would not bother me if I never saw her again." *Be kind to Devorah.* "I tried to be kind like Grandfather wanted. My heart changed a little toward her. I would not want her life destroyed, but I am happy she is gone." She smiled at Samuel and ran her finger down his cheek. Life without Devorah was a welcome thought. "We are a family now."

Chapter 24
Six Months Later

"Aba, aba." Samuel reached pudgy fingers toward Timon. "Ima wants to go to the market alone my son." Jerusha loved it when Timon referred to her as ima. When the day came that Samuel called her ima, it would be even better. He would learn the Hebrew sounds for mother soon enough.

"Are you going to follow in your father's footsteps and become a carpenter?" She picked him up from under the workbench and brushed wood shavings from the top of his head. "Or maybe you want some hair? She rubbed Samuel's shiny scalp. "Good thing we didn't call you Samson."

"I will teach Samuel the trade while you prepare for Pesach." Timon removed his apron and took his son from Jerusha. "He can be my helper." Timon's grin spread wide; his white teeth gleamed in contrast with his dark beard and peyots. Samuel eyed Timon's longer side hair, giggled, latched on with his tiny fist, and pulled.

Timon burst out laughing. "You found it again, my son." He sat down on the floor of the tent among the pile of different size cubes made especially for his son. "We will build a beautiful surprise for ima."

The large tent made from cilicium, black goat hair from Tarsus, rippled with a strong gust of wind. Jerusha's heart warmed at the sight of her husband playing with their son on the floor of her father's tent. She had many fond memories from her childhood of watching her father work with Timon, who was an apprentice at the time. He trained him well. Many men, even from the upper city, bought from Timon due to his impeccable woodcarving skills.

The wind whistled through the flaps of the tent. The strong breeze on the warm Nisan day made it known that spring had come. Pesach, or Passover, was only a few days away.

"Yeshua came every year during the feasts to visit Father in his carpenter's shop." Jerusha picked up a bowdrill. "Much of what Father taught you, he learned from him."

She searched the row of shops trying to spot her father. It was hard to think of him as a soldier. Her fondest memories were of him in his tunic, cutting and carving acacia, or in the synagogue with his head covered in a white cloth with blue tizits. Seeing him dressed as a Roman soldier just did not fit with how she remembered her father. She was beginning to understand how her father must have felt seeing his own father become a Roman soldier.

"Yeshua taught us both." Timon's words interrupted her memories. "He is the one who recommended that your father apprentice me. They both were like a father to me. A ten-year old boy without a father soaks up the attention of men who love him. Who could not love Yeshua and your father? I hope to be as good a father to our son." Timon noticed that Jerusha was only half-listening. He playfully tossed one of Samuel's blocks at her. "What has you so occupied that you hesitate to respond?"

Jerusha caught the block just in time. "I'm sorry. I was just thinking about Father. So many childhood memories come back to me when I am here." Jerusha cupped her ear. "The lambs are bleating in the marketplace as the people enter the city. I have fond memories of picking out the lamb for Pesach with Father. He was so tender with me when I wanted to keep it instead of sacrifice it." She turned toward Timon and looked at Samuel. "How horrible that YHWH had to sacrifice Yeshua to take away the sin of the world. I'm already so attached to Samuel, so much more than the little lamb. YHWH's love for us is beyond my understanding." Jerusha watched Timon stacking blocks and knocking them down. Samuel giggled every time. Tears filled her eyes. Her father and grandfather would not be a part of the feast celebration this year. She had her own family now.

***

With the bulging wine skin for Pesach slung over his shoulder, Timon carried Samuel on his shoulders. Holding his son's hands, he bounced along side Jerusha as they passed the Temple. The setting sun glared on the golden door and reflected in her eyes. She squinted and shielded her eyes with her hands.

"Is that Devorah?" She yanked on Timon's arm. "Over by the temple, in the shady alcove talking to the high priest's servant." She pointed into the sun.

"In this glare, I can't be sure, but I think it's her." A sinking feeling gripped her stomach. Would that woman ever be completely out of her life? "I think she sticks around to torment me."

"Love your enemies, Jerusha." Timon winked.

"Only by the power of the Holy Spirit can I even love myself. I pray every night that his fruit manifests in my life. Yeshua sent the Holy Spirit to dwell in us and give us the power to follow his law of love. It should be easier."

"I see love in you, my wife. Let is shine. Just be who you are, the divine, royal daughter of Father God. You cannot be anything less than you are. His love lives in you. Let it shine."

"When it comes to Devorah, I don't want it to shine. I never want to see her again. That woman is a thorn in my flesh."

"Tomorrow we celebrate the Pesach meal. Draw strength from his sacrificial meal. He shed his blood to set you free."

***

The next afternoon Jerusha watched the priest kill one lamb after another, the blood running down the temple steps. She leaned into Timon.

"What an abomination. Killing all these lambs when Yeshua has already paid the price. It must grieve Him that they don't recognize Him as the supreme sacrificial lamb of God. I cannot stand here and watch this. I am going back to the villa."

"I will go with you." Timon took her hand. They walked against the flow of people with lambs heading to the temple altar. Little boys and girls cried. Fathers comforted.

"They are like lost sheep without a shepherd." She squeezed his hand.

"Like Devorah." He squeezed back.

"You can be so infuriating. Why do you defend her?" She jerked her hand loose.

"I want you to be free." Timon's eyes pleaded with her.

"I am free as long as she stays away from me." Jerusha stomped uphill, her lungs burning with the effort.

The sun dipped behind the city wall and cast a fuchsia glow across the horizon. Jerusha reached the gate, unlocked it, and made her way across the blue-and-purple tiled path through the courtyard. Timon caught up with her and drew her to himself.

"I love you, little butterfly." He kissed the top of her head. "You will find the path to express love the way YHWH desires for us, and only you can travel that path. I am confident you will get there. You got there for me." He lifted her chin and looked into her eyes. "Remember how you spurned me at first?" The corner of his moth tipped up. That endearing lopsided grin. "In the end, Yeshua's love won out, and you surrendered. You will this time, too. I am confident of that. His love never fails."

"Timon, I can never stay mad at you for very long." She snuggled her head into his chest, then looked up. "Forgive me?"

"I already have." He winked and hugged her close.

"I am sorry to interrupt." Moses's face flushed. "Your mothers have the table ready for the Pesach meal."

"After we change, we will be right there." Jerusha enjoyed Timon's embrace and hesitated to look up. When she did, she saw Moses's hasty retreat. "I think our love embarrassed him."

"If he sensed what my thoughts are right now, he has reason to be embarrassed." He tapped her nose. "That can wait until later."

"I have no idea what you are talking about," she teased, broke from his embrace, and hurried up the path, then looked over her shoulder. "Yes, later."

Timon caught up, and they entered the villa hand in hand. They sat for the foot washing and grinned at each other while servants poured warm water over their tired feet. It felt wonderful. One foot was dried and placed to the side, and then the other.

"Thank you." She pulled her attention away from Timon and looked down at the servant.

"Father?" She would recognize those eyes anywhere. "What are you doing here? Why are you washing my feet?"

"My daughter the inquisitor," he smiled. "Never forget who you are. You are royalty from the tribe of Judah." Then he took her hands and lifted her up. "My lady." He bowed.

She threw her arms around him and hugged tight. She breathed in frankincense. He was dressed in servant's clothing, but he still smelled like a king.

"You saved Grandfather. Aren't you in danger coming to Jerusalem?

"As always, you have so many questions," he chuckled. "Cornelius, a Roman centurion at Caesarea spoke before Caesar and gained favor for me to take a leave."

"How long will you be with us?"

"Until they call me back. YHWH knows the time. It is in His hands. I brought Marcus with me. He tells me you are a roaring lion in prayer. I have been talking to him about Yeshua. His faith is not there yet, but loves to hear about, 'our God', as he puts it."

"Timon, my apprentice." Jacob greeted him with a kiss. "You always were more like a son to me. I hear you do excellent work." He took Jerusha's hands. "And have taken good care of my daughter."

"Does Mother know you are here?"

"Not yet. I've been incognito. Some servants stared questioningly at my clean-shaven face but kept to their duties in solemn trust. Don't tell her I am here just yet. I want to change into more appropriate clothing before I see her."

"She won't care what you are wearing, only that you are here."

"In the message she sent with Marcus, she indicated that she has prayed for my return." A red flush rose in his cheeks. "She said that she still loved me, and wanted my forgiveness. I forgave her a long time ago. That's why I never gave a writ of divorce."

"You are still married?" She giggled.

"It will be just like old times. Our family together again, only now I have Timon and a son." She twirled and stopped. "You don't know about Samuel."

"I saw an infant in your arms at the cross." He drew close and whispered. "Your grandfather filled me in. No one must know that he's alive."

"I am afraid Devorah may know. I do not trust her."

"She told the truth about the caravan. I was too late. They searched and arrested my father before I got there. If she knows, we must pray she keeps it to herself. Now where is that son of yours?"

"He's sleeping. I will bring him to the feast. We must hurry before Mother comes looking for us. She already sent Moses once."

"I met that young man. He has a special future ahead of him. We all have a special future."

***

Jerusha donned her jewel cloak over her light blue silk tunic. She braided her hair but left some on her shoulders in honor of Timon's request. Her radiyd, made of the purple cloth given to her by her father, completed the ensemble.

"My beautiful butterfly." Timon's broad shoulders bulged beneath his striped cloak, made by his wife's own hands. His muscular build was difficult to hide.

"Timon, I love you."

"And I you." He took her hands. "I am happy for you. Your family is back together. Your grandfather is alive, and you have a son." He lifted Samuel from the mittah.

"Do not forget." She slid her arm beneath his. "I have the most wonderful husband in Judea."

"Only in Judea?" he teased.

"In all of the earth." She smiled. "I see that look in your eyes." Her warm cheeks gave away her passion. "Later. Father is waiting to meet our son."

Chapter 25

All eyes turned to Jerusha and Timon when they entered the lamp-lit dining hall. Peter was there, along with his wife. They were reclining around a long table with Chaya, Abigail, James, and Luke the physician. Moses kept vigil on Hosea. After Jerusha reclined beside her mother, Abigail whispered in her ear, "I haven't seen you this content in years." Timon handed a jabbering Samuel to Jerusha. Abigail grinned and continued. "A child does you good. You glow tonight."

"Mother, I could never outshine your beauty." Jerusha touched her black mole and admired her mother's complexion. The few wrinkles around her eyes served only to accent her beauty. She had seen how the men in the market kept their eyes on her as she passed.

Timon reclined across from Jerusha, the twinkle in his eyes causing a flush to rise in her face. She hoped the others had not noticed.

Everyone looked at the empty spot at the head of the table. No Grandfather. No Father. Her mother glanced at Timon and motioned for him to take his place there. He shook his head.

"I thought Timon would serve our meal this year since we don't have your father or grandfather. I guess not." She turned to Peter. "Will you serve our meal tonight?"

"I believe that position belongs to the head of the house." He grinned.

"I don't understand."

Jerusha stifled a giggle.

Abigail shook her head. "Jerusha. That is inappropriate and disrespectful."

"Do not be too hard on our daughter." Jacob's voice boomed from the doorway.

"Jacob?" Abigail's mouth fell open.

"Shalom, my beautiful wife. Your loving husband, at your service." Even with a clean-shaven face, Jerusha had never seen her father look more handsome. He was dressed in his striped Hebrew cloak, with tzitzits at its corners, over a white tunic. Jerusha could see that her mother also approved. Marcus followed Jacob into the room, dressed contrastingly in a roman toga.

For a few moments no one spoke. The love that flowed between Abigail and Jacob was almost tangible. Their eyes locked on each other as if there were no one else in the room. They had not looked at each other that way since before the high priest wooed Abigail with his lies. Theirs was a true love. Jerusha breathed deep and looked away, not wanting to intrude on their intimate moment.

"Would you allow a few moments alone with my wife before we begin?" Jacob barely took his eyes off Abigail as he spoke.

Abigail's eyes beamed. "Wife?"

"I did not give you a divorce." Jacob grinned.

"We will wait." Timon waved to them to exit.

Jerusha's heart was full. Her mother and father were together again. As they walked under the archway that led to the garden, the chatter began among the guests. Timon's eyes softened as he watched his own mother, a widow. He moved to her side and kissed her cheek. His tender respect for his mother warmed Jerusha's heart. He had often expressed his desire for his mother to have a husband. She had him, but that was not the same as a husband. Jerusha hurt for her. Like Timon, Chaya served Yeshua without asking for anything in return. She even loved Devorah.

Jerusha looked around the table. How many others hid their pain? Smiling faces, even in the midst of troubled times. She remembered well Yeshua's words: "If they persecuted me, they will persecute you." Many people had left Jerusalem for that reason. The people around the table with her had stayed to witness to their neighbors and friends. Samuel squirmed in her arms.

"My son, you will live and not die and declare the works of the Lord to this generation." Timon heard and nodded.

"Yes, he will be a mighty man of God."

"Blessed are you, O Lord our God, King of the universe, who has created the fruit of the vine." Jacob entered the hall with Abigail at his side, her arm wrapped around his. "Blessed are you, O Lord our God, who has kept us alive, sustained us, and enabled us to enjoy this season." Jerusha grinned.

"Your father is back, at least for a while," her mother whispered as she reclined beside Jerusha.

"We're a family again." Jerusha juggled Samuel on her lap. She smiled at Marcus who was serving the wine.

"Say therefore to the sons of Israel, I am the Lord, and I will bring you out from under the burdens of the Egyptians and I will deliver from their bondage. I will also redeem you with an outstretched arm and with great judgments. As we drink this Passover wine let us remember what our King said on the night he was betrayed. 'This cup, which is poured out for you, is the new covenant in my blood poured out for many for the remission of sins.'"

"Yeshua, cleanse my heart so that your love flows unhindered in my life." As the wine touched her lips, she closed her eyes. The man, Yeshua, who played with her in the garden as a little girl, suffered, bled, and died. His bloody image on the cross, beaten and bruised beyond recognition, appeared before her closed eyes. "For you, Devorah, and for the world." The words swirled in her thoughts.

"My God and my King." Her declaration formed with each swallow of wine.

Jacob broke the unleavened bread and passed it around. "Blessed are you, O Lord our God, King of the universe, who brings forth bread from the Earth. Blessed are you, O Lord our God, King of the universe, who has sanctified us with your commandments, and commanded us to eat unleavened bread. Let us remember as we eat the bread what Yeshua said that night: 'Take eat, this is my body given for you.'"

Jerusha took the unleavened bread and ate. *I am one with you, my Lord, bone of your bone and flesh of your flesh. I am forever yours. Let not man separate us.* She glanced at Timon. *Marriage is a holy covenant, whether with Timon or my Lord.*

"Not to us, O Lord, not to us but to your name be the glory, because of your love and faithfulness." Jacob began the final hymn, his voice sweet and melodious. "May the LORD make you increase, both you and your children." He paused, his eyes resting on Jerusha and Samuel.

Jerusha smiled softly, her son slept in her arms. *I am blessed beyond measure. Mother of nations. YHWH's words. What could it mean? Sons from afar. Daughters nursed at her side.*

Her father's blessing interrupted her musings. "May you be blessed by the Lord, the Maker of heaven and earth. The highest heavens belong to the Lord, but the earth He has given to man. Your kingdom come, your will be done on earth as it is in heaven." Jerusha and the others joined his declaration as the flutes and timbrels played a joyful melody. "Hallelujah. The Lord reigns forever and ever."

Mother and father clapped. Jerusha swayed with Samuel. Timon's eyes indicated that he had not forgotten her promise for later that evening. She placed one piece of roasted lamb in her mouth and smiled coyly. The festivities continued. There was much laughter, music, and dancing. Yeshua bought their freedom. Freedom to love. Freedom to serve. Freedom to rule over their enemy.

After serving the wine, Marcus stood in the corner and guarded, rarely taking his eyes off father. What was he thinking? He was a Roman. Could he be trusted? Jerusha appreciated what he had done for her grandfather, but Marcus had pledged his allegiance to Rome. Had her father done the same? She must ask him about that sometime.

"Your chuppah awaits." Jacob stood beneath the archway and motioned to Abigail, his hand extended. Abigail's cheeks flushed as she took his hand. "If you would excuse us, we have many years of stories to share." The corners of his mouth tipped up. "And much love to share as well."

Jerusha had not seen her father so jovial. His love for her mother was evident in his eyes. He adored her and had forgiven her. It filled her with joy to see them this way. It was evidence of Yeshua's power to restore a broken relationship.

"Your chuppah awaits as well, my little butterfly." Timon lifted Samuel, who was fast asleep, from her lap. "Mother will take him to the wet nurse and bring him to our room later. He winked, and Jerusha's face flushed. No one seemed to hear his last word or understand its connotation.

"Thank you, Chaya, for your kindness." Jerusha touched her son's cheek. She had waited so long. She cherished every moment with him, but Timon needed her now.

***

A soft breeze rustled the pomegranate bushes outside the window. Their fragrance filtered into the room. Jerusha shivered in her lightweight tunic. Her pendant in hand, she stared at the stars. The moon light reflected off the butterfly jewel.

"I remember when you presented this at my betrothal. I was so rude and trusted no man."

"You were hurting." Timon wrapped the soft lambskin cover around her shoulders.

"And angry," she added.

"When I found out what they did to you, I was angry too. It's only YHWH's grace and mercy that I didn't kill him and his son."

"These are troubled times in Jerusalem." She drew the cover tight around her shoulders. "I am glad father's home, but he's under Rome's scrutiny. We have a Roman soldier under our roof. None of this makes sense. Even what YHWH said about me being a mother of nations." She turned and looked up at Timon. "Who knows how long it will be before Father is called back, and what will happen to Grandfather?

I may never see him again. I want to be brave like he asked, but—"
Her voice quivered.

"Never forget who you are. You are royalty from the tribe of
Judah." He kissed her cheek.

"Oh, that reminds me. I almost forgot." Jerusha slipped away from
the cover and moved across the room. "I never showed you what
Moses found in his bag before we left Shiloh." She unrolled the camel
skin and lifted the scepter. It glittered in the lamp-lit room. "The
stranger must have given it to us, but I have no idea why." She handed
it to Timon. "Look at these engravings."

"'The scepter shall not depart from Judah, until Shiloh comes.'"
Timon rolled it around under the lamp. "That's from the Torah. It is
part of Jacob's blessing to Judah. Your father taught me that blessing."
He closed his eyes and thought a moment. "'Judah, your brothers shall
praise you; Your hand shall be on the neck of your enemies.'"

Jerusha joined him in his recitation. "'Your sons shall bow down
to you. Judah is a lion's whelp; From the prey, my son, you have gone
up. He couches, he lies down as a lion, and as a lion, who dares rouse
him up? The scepter shall not depart from Judah, nor the ruler's staff
from between his feet, until Shiloh comes, and to him shall be the
obedience of the peoples.'"

"Father also taught me that part of the Torah. Why do I have this
scepter, and what am I to do with it?"

"I am not sure." Timon rolled it back in the camel skin. "But we
need to protect it until we do know."

"I know just the place to keep it." Jerusha dug out the limestone
piece in the wall, laid the scepter inside and replaced the stone. It
blended in with the other cut stones in the wall.

"That is quite clever. If I didn't know it was there I'd never find it."
Timon rubbed his hand over the hiding place.

"Being a captive in Herod's palace taught me how to hide things.
He would have taken my pendant, and destroyed it, claiming it was
an idol. Although the corrupt pig would have probably sold it for his
treasury." The bitterness in her voice surprised herself. "I thought I
was healed of what happened while living there. I guess I need more
deliverance."

"You need to embrace and trust in Yeshua's love." He led her to the mittah. "And mine." He snuggled her beneath the lamb's skin and crawled in beside her. She grasped her pendant.

"It is written, 'Arise Lord. Let your enemies be scattered. Let all who hate you flee before you.' I ask for this bitterness go, in Yeshua's name." She sighed deeply. "That is not who I am. I am the beloved daughter of the King."

Timon kissed her neck. "It is also written that a man shall leave his mother and father and cleave to his wife. And they shall become one flesh."

"Timon, I can't think of that now. I am worried about what will happen to us." He rose up on one elbow.

"'Do not be anxious for tomorrow; for tomorrow will care for itself.'" He smoothed the hair back from her face.

Jerusha laughed. "I humbly submit to your wisdom." Her fingers stroked his dark hair. "'Each day has enough trouble of its own.'" She smiled and surrendered to his love.

Chapter 26
AD 39

"Timon, it could be a trap. What would Devorah want after all this time? Why meet in the dead of night? What is she trying to hide? Or better yet, who is she hiding from?" Jerusha threw the parchment on the mittah. She turned toward Timon, hands on her hips. "Or what does she want from you?" She grabbed her radiyd. "If you go to meet her, I'm going with you." She wrapped it around her head and took his arm.

"I can see you will not be persuaded otherwise." He opened the door. "If you would have finished the letter, you would know she ask for both of us to come."

"Oh. Well, good." She glanced up. "Because you would not be going by yourself. I am thankful that Samuel sleeps with Mother and Father tonight. Should we tell them we are going?"

"I have already informed your father. He said he would be praying."

"It is a good thing. I do not trust that woman. Yeshua said love your enemies, but also—" she pulled on his arm and stopped. "—be wise as a serpent, harmless as a dove."

"Has it occurred to you that she may be in danger and needs our help?"

"We are the ones in danger, by meeting with some one as deceptive as her."

"You don't have to go." He grinned that irritating lopsided grin.

"What? And let her get you arrested?"

"And you think you will protect me." He chuckled. "Will you prevent my arrest?"

"Well, I could run for help. Besides, you are too trusting of her. I can see through her conniving ways."

Timon burst out in laughter. Jerusha jerked away and marched ahead of him, his guffaw echoing in the garden. She stopped and hurried back.

"Be quiet. We do not need the whole villa knowing what fools we are, going out in the middle of the night to meet a deceptive, lying Judas."

"If she is a Judas, who is she reporting to?"

"The high priest, of course. He has always hated my family. He wants us destroyed for more than one reason. He hates what we believe, and he covets this villa. Sometimes, I think the only reason anyone is kind to us is because we live in the largest villa in the upper city. At least when I was a slave in Herod's palace, I knew that when someone was kind, it was because they liked me, not my money."

"You may be right about Devorah." Timon sobered. "We will be careful."

"It's so dark. She would choose this night to meet." She clutched his arm. She remembered the night the Roman guard attacked her at the city gate. She shivered. "I am worried. Where are we meeting?" She frowned.

"At a villa not far from Herod's palace. James has secret meetings there." Timon unlocked the gate. It creaked, and he looked around. "As much as I can tell in this black night, I don't think we are being watched."

Jerusha stepped into the street. Outside the lamp-lit courtyard, the night was pitch black. She clung to his arm.

"James needs to be careful," Jerusha whispered. "Devorah never claimed to be a follower of the way. Has she been going to his meetings?"

"James welcomes all who want to hear. He walks in wisdom and discernment. I am sure he would know if there was danger by her presence and would pray for protection." He stopped, took her hand, and stepped down the terraced step. "Be careful. Feel your way. It's so dark you cannot see where it goes down. I'll guide you."

"Even Yeshua had a Judas among his friends." She felt the limestone edge and maneuvered her way to the next landing. One. Two. Three steps and another ledge. She grasped his hand and hopped to the next landing.

"All a part of YHWH's plan." Timon led her down the cobblestone path toward the hippodrome. The massive structure towered above them, and the wind whistled through the high marble portico. "There have not been chariot races in recent days. Herod has been spending more time in his palace in Caesarea."

Suddenly, Timon grabbed Jerusha's arm and yanked her behind a column. "I think someone is following us. I saw a shadow duck behind the fountain." He guided her back into the darkness. Being cautious, they moved against the wall, then edged around the corner and waited. Jerusha's heart raced. She knew this was a bad idea.

Timon checked the hippodrome arched entrance and motioned for her to follow. They increased their pace and crossed the mosaic path to the other side. They walked a short distance and then turned down a dark passageway, stopping at a small villa that had a lamp lit in the window. Timon tapped three times.

The porter slid open a small hatch to see who was at the door. "Yes?"

"We are here to see Devorah." Timon kept Jerusha in front of him and peered up and down the street. The porter shut the hatch. A minute later the lock clicked, and the door swung open, to reveal only darkness. Jerusha looked at Timon and stiffened her knees.

"Let's go back." She stretched her neck to see inside and shook her head. "I am not going in there."

Timon prodded from behind, and she stumbled over the threshold. She turned and glared at him. His soberness brought little comfort.

"Shalom." Jerusha heard Devorah's voice. It came from a darkened corner. A tall shadowy figure stood beside her, his hand on a sword. Was he a soldier or a servant?

Jerusha moved closer to her husband.

"I was not sure if you would come." Devorah sounded weak and tired. "I am sorry I disappeared without warning. I never thanked you for your hospitality. I cannot explain. You must trust me."

"You have a strange way of building trust." Jerusha retorted dryly.

"My plans are not to hurt you."

"My grandfather is dead because of you. You told my father they would attack the caravan, but how did you know he was with the caravan? How did Rome know? Did you tell them?"

"I cannot tell you how I knew about the caravan."

"And we are supposed to trust you?" Jerusha spat.

"I cannot blame you for your lack of trust. I assure you that I am your friend."

Devorah stood and moved into the light, a tiny infant snuggled in her arms. "The mother of this baby died giving birth. The father wants nothing to do with the child. I no longer have milk to nurse. My sons are five and seven. Since Chaya is a midwife, I thought she could find a wet nurse for him."

"Him? It's a boy?" Jerusha drew near, her mothering instincts awakened. "May I?" She reached for the baby. Devorah stared for a moment at the child, then slipped him into Jerusha's arms. She smiled at the child. "Shalom, bright eyes. You are alert for such a little one. He nuzzled his face against her chest. "I am sorry. You will not get nourishment from those breasts." She ached and longed to be able to nurse. *Your daughters will be nursed at your side.* She looked up at Timon. He understood her pain.

"His name is Paul. It means little or humble." Devorah touched his cheek.

"His round eyes and plump face, along with his weight, speaks of a large stature. A giant with a humble heart." She looked back at Timon. He winked. "When I think of humility I think of Stephen. Would it be all right if we added Stephen to his name? Stephen Paul."

"You speak as if he is your own son." Timon spoke gently.

"Timon, could we raise him as our own? Remember, our sons will come from afar." Suddenly, Jerusha forgot about Devorah and the danger. All that mattered was the baby in her arms.

Timon surrounded Jerusha and the babe with his embrace and stared into the little one's face. "You realize, Jerusha , that this child is not a Hebrew." He stared at Devorah, a question in his eyes.

"His mother was an Egyptian slave in Herod's palace. His father is a Hebrew of high esteem in the religious community." Devorah blinked and backed away.

"It will cause much controversy among our neighbors and Jewish friends to take a Gentile as our son, especially in these turbulent times."

"There is much talk in Herod's palace of Saul's new teachings about the Gentiles." Devorah stepped closer.

Jerusha stiffened, alert again to the danger. "What would you know of the talk in Herod's palace?"

"I live there. That's how I knew about this baby." She glanced at the tall guard in the corner.

"How do you have access to the palace? You are a widow without means to care for herself."

"I cannot tell you my connections."

"But you want us to trust you." Jerusha's curt response hung in the air. She stared at the child. Would taking this Gentile as their son bring them even more danger, or imprisonment? A war raged in her thoughts. *It is not the child's fault. He may die.* She cuddled him next to her breasts. *Mother of nations. A son from afar.* If a Jew entered the home of a Gentile or even ate with one, they would be declared unclean. Her father allowed Marcus to serve wine at the Pesach meal and live under their roof. The infant's cries interrupted her thoughts.

"Shhhhh. I know." She rocked him back and forth. "You are hungry." She looked at Timon.

Timon rubbed his finger across the infant's forehead "Our new son needs a wet nurse. We must get back so my mother can find someone to nurse him."

"Thank you. Thank you." Devorah appeared genuine in her appreciation. Maybe she meant no harm after all.

The porter opened the door and Jerusha stepped into the darkness with a new son, husband at her side. Timon looked both directions and guided her back through the passageway that led away from the hippodrome.

"Did you hear that?" He spoke in a whisper. "It sounded like footsteps behind us." He pulled her around the corner and into a dark alcove. "Stay here. I am going to find out who is following us."

"Timon, no. Please don't leave me here." Jerusha's heart raced.

"You will be safe. Keep your back against the wall. No one can see you in the darkness."

"But what if something happens to you?" She grabbed his arm.

In the sliver of light that shone on his face, she saw him smile. "Remember? You will protect me and run for help."

"Oh, you are impossible sometimes." She jerked her hand away.

"Don't worry; I'll be back." His grin widened, and he slipped into the passageway. Jerusha heard nothing for several minutes, but then she heard a scuffle. Paralyzed, she held her breath and listened. Silence. *Be brave, Jerusha.* Her grandfather's words echoed in her mind. She moved with her back to the wall until she could peer around the corner. She could see nothing.

"Where is he?" she whispered to herself.

"Jerusha." The voice came from behind her. She jumped, barely stifling a scream. The baby was startled and let out a small whimper.

"Why did you sneak up on me like that?" she scolded.

"If you would have stayed against the wall in the dark, you would have seen me coming." He started to laugh until he saw her glare. "I am sorry. I didn't mean to scare you."

"Did you find anyone?"

"It was Marcus. Your father sent him to follow us and make sure we were safe. He was to report to your father if anything went wrong. He's waiting at the fountain and will accompany us home."

"A Roman soldier living in our home. Now an Egyptian son. I fear trouble lies ahead."

"May I quote you the words of our King? 'In this world we will have tribulations. But be of good cheer. I have overcome the world.'"

Chapter 27

Jerusha held Stephen in the crook of her arm. She gently rocked him back and forth as she listened to her father tell Samuel stories. They were seated together on her father's favorite bench. She laughed because as soon as her father finished one story, Samuel would say, "Another one." His inquisitive mind soaked up every word. Every morning Timon taught him Hebrew. Her grandfather taught the Torah in the afternoon. Samuel never tired of learning YHWH's ways. Abigail and Chaya gathered grapes from the vines on the back wall.

Memories flooded Jerusha's mind as she watched her family. She remembered her father's goodbye when she was sent away with mother to Herod's palace. She remembered Timon's betrothal and catching butterflies with Sarah. Most of all, she remembered dancing before her God and King. *Dance, Jerusha, dance.* Her guardian's admonition during difficult times proved to be true. The chains had fallen off as she adored her King in dance. She stood and twirled around with Stephen Paul in her arms.

"I love you YHWH, the great I Am, the Father of all creation."
She hummed and twirled again. "I love you Yeshua, King of Kings, my
Deliverer and Redeemer."

Stephen opened his eyes, and she bent down near his face. "It
matters not that you are Egyptian. Your frame was not hidden from
YHWH when you were made in secret, and skillfully wrought in the
depths of the earth." Her finger rubbed his tiny brow. "His eyes saw
your unformed substance, and in your book were written all the days
that were ordained for you, when as yet there was not one of them."
Her father had taught her well. The Psalm flowed without effort off
her tongue "It was ordained, little Stephen, for you to be a part of this
family, a royal son. One day you will see and enter the kingdom that
is as near as your breath." She closed her eyes and took a deep breath.
"My God and my King, I love you."

"Ima," Samuel came running toward her. "I want to see." He
pulled on her arm and she bent low to show him his brother. "He's
kinda black."

"Does that matter?"

"No. Can I hold my brother?"

"Come, sit on the bench." She sat beside her father. He helped
Samuel up. His legs dangled, and he clapped his hands. Jerusha smiled.
The excitement of another family member filled her with joy too.

"Be careful with him." She laid the baby in his arms, keeping her
hand beneath just in case. "I think he's smiling at you. Look at those
big round eyes. I think we should call him, bright eyes." Samuel felt
the top of his head.

"His hair is fuzzy. Fuzz." He giggled. "Call him Fuzz."

"His name is Stephen." Timon clanged the gate and approached.
"We will call him Stephen. How would you like to be called, fuzz?" He
ruffled Samuel's hair. "When you were a baby we could have called you
baldy. You had no hair."

Samuel felt his own head. "Baldy?"

"Your mother called you precious. She was so excited to have a
son." Timon helped Jerusha up. "It is time to go to the synagogue."

***

As they entered the oblong room, Timon took Samuel's hand and followed Jacob to the men's side. Marcus stood guard outside. Jerusha held Stephen close and followed her mother and Chaya to the women's side. Old women pointed at her and whispered. Jerusha's stomach knotted.

"I heard that you have an Egyptian son. Is that true?" A woman whispered and tried to get a look. A part of Jerusha wanted to hide her son from judgmental stares. She sat up straight. She would not cowl down. His blood was the same color as theirs. They have no right to think so highly of themselves.

She nodded and uncovered Stephen's face for the woman to see. "Isn't he beautiful? He's named after Stephen the deacon who helped the widows and orphans."

"Crowned one." She smirked and moved away, being sure not to touch the child.

Jerusha tipped her chin up and smiled at father, who stood on the platform at the end of the room, every eye on him. Five-year-old Samuel looked on with admiration. He loved his grandfather. He already recited much of the Torah. Jacob wore his striped robe with the tizits on the corners. She remembered as a child holding the blue-knotted one while she listened to her father's stories in the garden. Her father's beard had grown back, and Jerusha thought he looked handsome. The scribe handed him a scroll. He studied it, looked up at Jerusha, and smiled.

"I read from Isaiah the prophet. 'Shout for joy, O barren one, you who have borne no child; Break forth into joyful shouting and cry aloud, you who have not travailed. For the sons of the desolate one will be more numerous than the sons of the married woman.'" He caught her eye before continuing. "'Enlarge the place of your tent; stretch out the place of your dwellings, spare not, lengthen your cords, and strengthen your pegs. For you will spread abroad to the right and to the left. And your descendants will possess nations, and they will resettle the desolate cities.'"

Mother of nations. The stranger's words echoed in Jerusha's thoughts.

"Fear not, for you will not be put to shame; neither feel humiliated, for you will not be disgraced; But you will forget the shame of your youth."

Jerusha wondered if she would ever forget the horrible days at Herod's palace. The unholy touches and humiliation? The disgrace had faded since receiving Samuel and Stephen. They were special gifts from YHWH and sure signs of His blessings. Her eyes found Timon on the other side. His eyes twinkled, and he winked.

"'I hid my face from you for a moment: but with everlasting lovingkindness I will have compassion on you,' says the Lord your Redeemer."

"Thank you, YHWH, for your mercy," she whispered.

"'If anyone fiercely assails you it will not be from Me. Whoever assails you will fall because of you,'" her father continued. Jerusha glanced at the woman who sat next to her. *Love your enemies*. Her contempt for the woman softened as she yielded to YHWH.

"'No weapon that is formed against you shall prosper, and every tongue that accuses you in judgment you will condemn. This is the heritage of the servants of the Lord.'" Jacob's face glowed as he glanced around the synagogue and finished quoting the prophet, most of it by memory. When he had finished, he replaced the scroll in its designated place in the carved box on the platform. "Men and brethren, Yeshua fulfilled the law and the prophets."

"Yeshua broke the law and is dead for it." A Pharisee shouted from across the room, his face red, fire in his eyes. "When he lived he dined with Gentiles." He scoffed. "What kind of kingdom can you set up from the grave?" His mocking Yeshua, who gave his life for him, burned red hot in Jerusha's belly. "He was not our Mashiach. Rome still rules our nation."

"His kingdom is not of this world. It comes not with observation. It is within you." Her father stood strong against his attacks. The argument between her father and the Pharisee awakened the old memory of Stephen before the Sanhedrin. *Be careful, Father.*

Another scribe arose. "What has happened to you, Jacob? You once taught the scripture with the wisdom of Gamalial. You now sound like the fisherman, Peter."

"Do not mock my friend from Tarsus." A voice boomed from the doorway. "He studied harder and learned quicker than I. A Pharisee of Pharisees." Jerusha gasped at the sight of Saul, the persecutor of Yeshua followers. For a short time, the crowd went silent as he strode down the middle of the synagogue and stood beside Jacob. Her father stared at him, his mouth open.

"Shalom, my friend." He greeted him with a kiss. "It has been many years since we studied together in Tarsus. We were mere boys when I left to come to Jerusalem." Her father's gracious response sickened her. She almost choked. She had heard about Saul's conversion. It had been difficult to erase the picture of his pompous actions against Stephen. He did look different. He had a softness in his eyes that was not there before.

"I have heard you changed your position on this subject," the angered Pharisee chided. "Tell us why we should believe you."

"I have come to present my case to Peter and James."

"You surely do not approve of Jacob's Gentile grandson. You know the law. We are not allowed to eat with Gentiles, or go into their homes, without purification. Why take one as your own son?"

"Has not the Torah said that in Abraham all the families of the earth shall be blessed? And Isaiah says, "'It is too small a thing that You should be My servant to raise up the tribes of Jacob, and to restore the preserved ones of Israel; I will also make You a light to the nations so that My salvation may reach to the end of the earth.'"

"This cannot be the same man that stoned Stephen. He speaks like him," Jerusha whispered to her mother. Her mother shrugged.

"Yeshua, our Mashiach, came to destroy the works of the enemy and restore all families of the earth back to His Father." Saul spoke with power but had peace in his eyes.

"Blasphemy! One man yelled.

"You speak blasphemy!" another disgruntled listener yelled. The women, who surrounded Jerusha, murmured and pointed.

"Mother, I fear for Father. These men sound like the men who stoned Stephen."

"Pray, Jerusha." Her mother whispered between quiet indistinct utterances.

You have more authority than you know when you speak his word.

"'Arise, Lord. Let your enemies be scattered. Let all who hate you flee before you." Jerusha whispered the words written on the back of her pendant, Moses's words when the ark of His presence moved. She grasped her pendant that lay beneath her tunic.

The men swarmed the platform. "'Arise, Lord. Let your enemies be scattered. Let all who hate you flee before you.'" She spoke a little louder.

One grabbed her father. Another grabbed Saul.

"Release them." Timon yelled and picked up Samuel. The mob surrounded him. Samuel's lip quivered, and he began to cry.

Jerusha's heart pounded in her ears. *No! Not another stoning!* "'Arise, Lord. Let your enemies be scattered.'" She stood. "'Let all who hate you flee before you.'" Her words rang loud and clear. The women's attention turned to her. Most glared, while others shook their heads in disgust. *What have I done?* Stephen whimpered. She cuddled him closer. Shh, my little one." She jiggled him. "Do not be afraid." She spoke as much for her own comfort as his.

Two shadows moved in the doorway. Jerusha turned to see Peter and James standing in the entrance with Marcus next to them, his sword drawn. A mysterious presence saturated the atmosphere. Hair stood up on her arms. The angry men released her father and Saul, grumbled among themselves, and dispersed. The women continued to stare at Jerusha and filed out behind the angry men.

Her father grasped Saul's arms. "My friend, come to my home. I want to hear about your encounter with Yeshua."

She leaned into her mother. "What is Father doing? I do not trust Saul."

"If I would have listened to him instead of Caiaphas, we would never have served as slaves in Herod's palace," Abigail spoke, her eyes locked on Jacob, her voice soft and loving. "I will not dispute his wisdom this time."

"Ima," Samuel ran across the synagogue and nestled his face in her cloak. Timon rushed to her side.

"Are you hurt?" His eyes betrayed the calm in his voice.

"We are fine," she answered. "At least physically." She would not talk to him about her concerns in front of Samuel.

The immediate danger had passed. She glance up at Peter and James and watched the beloved apostles turn and leave.

Chapter 28

Jerusha yawned and lay her head on Timon's shoulder. The pomegranate bushes rustled in the soft breeze and stirred the butterflies from their nighttime resting places. Stephen slept in her arms, and Samuel's head lay in Timon's lap. The lamplight danced on their face's.

"Father and Saul talked nonstop about childhood memories. It was good so see him laugh again. He has been so sober of late. I see it in his eyes. Something is bothering him."

"It's a serious time we live in." Timon smoothed the sweaty hair away from Samuel's forehead.

"Not the best time to be raising children." Jerusha admired Stephen's long lashes.

"We must prepare this generation for Yeshua's coming judgment on Jerusalem."

Jerusha raised her head up. "Timon, do we need to go to James's meeting tonight?" She doubted anything good would come from going to a place where Saul and Devorah may be. If Timon had to go he would not go alone, but she wanted to talk him out of it.

"I want to hear what Saul will say to Peter. Many are afraid of him."

"Rightly so. He arrested and killed many of their family members. I thought I had forgiven him until I saw him again. The memories came flooding back. Then I remembered Stephen's last words. 'Hold not this sin against them,' I knew I could not do otherwise. Still, I struggle to trust. I pray our little Stephen never faces a stoning."

"We can trust Yeshua. He took the bitterness from my heart and the dagger from my hand. I would have killed Caiaphas for what he did to you and most likely have been killed myself."

"In some ways, you had died. I saw the hate in your eyes. The man I fell in love with was gone. I am so grateful Yeshua captured your heart again." Jerusha listened to the shofar in the distance. A new watch. She looked down at Stephen, his sleep undisturbed. What would his future hold in these troubled times?

"Our Stephen may suffer persecution, too, because he's a Gentile son in a Hebrew family. I often wondered why Grandfather eyes were blue. Mine and Father's are green, and mother's are brown. Grandfather is tall, and most Hebrew men are short. Now, with Stephen, we have a different skin color in the family. What difference does skin or eye color make anyway? All are created by YHWH." She shook her head. "Already people wag their tongues against Stephen and us." Tears filled her eyes. "How did YHWH watch His son suffer and die? I cannot grasp the pain He must have felt. Such love is hard to understand."

"We will teach our sons how to forgive with our example, by forgiving those who speak against them and us."

Forgive us our sins as we forgive those who sin against us. "Yes, we must forgive," Jerusha whispered. "But how?"

"Yeshua said to pray for those who persecute us."

"Pray he rains fire down and destroys them. That is what I would want, if someone hurt my baby." She smiled up at Timon. "Or the love of my life."

Jacob appeared at the gate, Saul by his side. "I am sorry to intrude on your family time, but Saul wanted to talk with you." Timon glanced at Jerusha, who nodded her consent.

"Come. Let us reason together." He answered and waved them inside the gate. "Please excuse me for not getting up." He pointed to sleeping Samuel in his lap. "But join us. Hearing from our elders is a good thing." He pointed to the bench across from them.

Jerusha smiled at his graciousness. She would listen. Be respectful. She owed him that much. Her father had been trained by the most respected teacher in Jerusalem, as had Saul. If Timon wanted to hear what they had to say, then so did she.

Saul sat with his head down for a while before he spoke. During the uncomfortable silence, Jerusha rubbed her finger along the pomegranate carvings on the edge of the bench. It reminded her of something her father had once told her. *Much like the tough skin of the pomegranate, you seem to be protecting yourself.* Jerusha thought her heart had softened after Stephen's death. It had, but only enough to let Timon in. He proved his love. Total trust was difficult, and she guarded herself against being hurt by those who had not proven their love. Like Saul and Devorah.

Finally, Saul spoke. "I thought I was doing YHWH's will by arresting those who belonged to the Way."

"I am sure you did." Jerusha glared at Saul.

"I knew the scriptures as well as anyone. I don't know how I could have been so blind. It is hard to understand." Saul's voice cracked.

"Yes. It is hard to understand." Jerusha wanted to be respectful, for her father's sake, but could not hide her anger. She smiled weakly at her father and mouthed the words, "I am sorry."

"On the road to Damascus, my blindness became literal when a bright light struck my eyes, and I fell to the ground. I heard a voice say, 'Saul, Saul, why are you persecuting me?' And I said, "Who are you, Lord? And He said, 'I am Yeshua whom you are persecuting.'" Saul swallowed.

Pressure rose in Jerusha's chest. It felt like the pomegranate-like protective shell was being ripped apart. She grabbed her chest.

"He instructed me to arise, enter the city, and that I would be told what I must do." She wanted to tell him to stop. She choked back the words.

"After three days, Yeshua sent Ananias to lay hands on me that I may regain my sight, and I was filled with the Holy Spirit."

Jerusha looked at Timon. His eyes were glassy and fixed on the man who had killed his beloved teacher and friend. A strange sensation ripped at her heart. It was sharp and piercing. For some reason it had never occurred to her that Timon had suffered as much as she had. How could she have been so selfish?

"He told me Yeshua revealed to him that I was his chosen instrument to bear his name before the Gentiles, kings and the sons of Israel, for he would show me how much I must suffer for His name's sake." Silence. Even the song thrush stopped singing.

Jerusha was overcome by remorse. She squeezed Timon's hand.

"Nothing I could suffer physically can compare to the pain in here." Saul pointed to his chest. "I caused innocent children of YHWH to suffer because of my actions."

He stood and bowed slightly to Timon and Jerusha. "I cannot bring Stephen back to life, nor can I heal the pain you have suffered because of me. Only Yeshua can do that, but I ask your forgiveness. I pray that it will help bring healing to you and to me. Will you forgive me?" Tears flowed down his face.

"I forgive you." Timon wept. Never had Jerusha seen such emotion in him. She stared at Saul, realizing that she was not much different than him.

"I forgive you." her voice quivered. "Will you forgive me for holding this against you all these years? I did not know how selfish I had been."

"I forgive you." Saul's voice rang with the song thrush and crickets. "Yeshua forgives you."

"Timon," she said as she took his hand, "forgive me for never thinking of your pain but only my own. Forgive me. I am so sorry." She could hardly get the words out without crying. "You have always been there for me, encouraging me to love my enemies and to forgive." Jerusha's protective shell shattered and years of deep-seated bitterness poured out. A waterfall of tears flowed unhindered. Her tears fell on Stephen's face, who still slept in her arms. She wiped his face and held him close to her chest.

"Why are you crying, Ima? Samuel sat up next to his father. "Why are you crying, Aba?

"My son, we are being washed by Yeshua's living water, and cleansed from within. Our old dirty thinking being washed away."

**

Marcus stood at attention inside the door, his eyes on Jacob. Jerusha admired his loyalty. The others in the dimly lit room stared. She sat with Timon against the wall, Stephen in her lap. Samuel slept on Timon's shoulder. They waited, along with the others, for Peter and James. After their conversation with Saul, they wanted to come and support him when he spoke to Peter.

"What's he doing here?" a man asked, his lip snarled in disgust. "Is it not enough we have to deal with Romans in the marketplace and outside the temple court? Do they have to guard our secret meetings, too?"

"This is an abomination," another man yelled. "Get him out of here! Who brought him?" "He is my attendant and friend." Jacob stepped to Marcus's side.

"And why are you a part of Rome's military, Jacob? You have changed."

"Has not Yeshua taught us to love even our enemies?" Jacob spoke with calm authority. The men quieted. "This man has been more loyal than some of our own priests. I trust him with my life. He will not betray us. And this man is my friend, too." He motioned to Saul, who stepped from the shadows. The men gasped. Some moved toward them.

"Fear not. He comes in peace." Jacob put his hand up. Marcus placed his hand on his sword. "Barnabas spoke in his favor in the other meetings in the city. He told how he proclaimed Yeshua to be the son of YHWH. I came tonight as his witness, along with Timon. We saw him speak boldly about Yeshua in the synagogue today."

"What do James and Peter say about him?" one man asked.

"I saw him speak today in the synagogue, too." Peter stepped over the threshold. James followed. "And you are?" James stared at Marcus.

"This is my attendant, Marcus," Jacob intervened. "He is my loyal servant." The men started grumbling again.

"Be still and be seated," Peter's spoke with both love and authority, which Jerusha admired. "I have just returned from Caesarea. I have been with Cornelius, a Roman centurion of the Roman cohort."

The men grumbled among each other again. Peter raised his hand. "Men and brethren, hear me out before you pass judgment on me or on Marcus." He waited until they quieted before continuing. "While I was in Joppa, at about the sixth hour, I was on the rooftop to pray. I became hungry. I was in a trance and I saw the sky open and a great sheet came down to the ground and there were all kinds of four-footed animals, crawling creatures of the earth and birds of the air. A voice said, 'Arise, Peter, kill and eat!' I said, 'By no means, Lord, for I have never eaten anything unclean or unholy.' Three times this happened. While I thought on this, three men from Joppa came to the door looking for me. An angel had appeared to their master, Cornelius, and said his prayers had been heard and to send for a man named Peter in Joppa. The Spirit told me to go with them, so I went. Cornelius had gathered many at his house and waited for me to come. While I was speaking with them about Yeshua, the Holy Spirit fell on them, just as he did for us. I now understand that YHWH is not one to show partiality, but in every nation the man who fears Him and does what is right is welcome." He turned to Marcus. "You are welcome in our meetings anytime." Marcus nodded. His expression was sober and he glanced at Jacob.

If Father and Peter trusted Marcus, Jerusha trusted him. After everything this Roman attendant had done for her grandfather, she owed him some respect, even if he was not yet a follower of the way. She would pray for him. Maybe this Gentile's eyes would open in the same way as Cornelius's. She smiled. YHWH accepted Gentiles into his family. Stephen squirmed in her arms. A Gentile son. *Grandfather was right. YHWH's ways are not our ways.*

Chapter 29

Timon and Jerusha walked in silence, hand in hand under the full moon. Little Stephen was wrapped tight to his mother's chest, his swaddling cloth strapped around her neck. Samuel slept on his father's shoulder. They walked past the fountain in the plaza, its sparkling water a refreshing reminder of Yeshua's living water. A new peace had come upon Jerusha. She was calm and knew that, no matter what the future held, Yeshua had a plan. A good plan for her life, and her family. *Your kingdom come. Your will be done in my family as it is in heaven.* She glanced at Timon, her rock and strength, and leaned her head into his shoulder. What more could she ask of a husband?

They climbed the terraced steps to their villa and looked out over the Temple Mount. She was in awe that a holy God desired intimacy with her, a wounded, fearful little girl. He chose to make his dwelling place within her, instead of the beautiful temple that glittered in the moonlight. It was a privilege and honor to be loved by Him. She sighed and thought of Samuel and Stephen. Like her, they were chosen. How many more sons and daughters would she have the privilege to mother? Only He knew. *I am so grateful YHWH Father for my family. Your family.*

A shadow moved from under the jujube tree. Her heart jumped, and she reached for Timon's arm.

"Did you see movement by the gate?" she whispered.

"I sensed some one has been watching us." Timon's awareness brought instant comfort. She squeezed his arm as the shadow moved into the open. It was Devorah.

"I have been waiting for you." She wrapped her dark cloak higher around her face. Only her eyes showed. "I have come to warn you. I overheard talk in the palace about Saul and your father. The Hellenists came to Herod. They plot to kill Saul. I could not hear what they said about your father, but his name was mentioned." Jerusha was suspicious. Was this an act or genuine concern? Why would she care about her father or Saul? Unless she was trying to impress Timon.

"Why should we believe you?" Jerusha glared.

"I have never lied to you, Jerusha."

"That is disputable."

"Timon, I beg you to listen. Saul's life is in danger. I am not sure about Jacob, but Saul is most definitely in danger. If he does not leave Jerusalem immediately, he will be killed."

"Why do you care about Saul? Who is he to you?" Timon asked.

"I listened to him in the plaza as he and James argued with the Hellenist Jews. His eyes shined with a love that I have only seen in a few men. You, Timon, are one of those men. Peter and James are the same, even when they speak boldly. I cannot let the Hellenists kill a man with that kind of love. One that seems to even love his enemies." She closed her eyes. Her jaw tightened, and she released a deep breath. "I questioned whether you would believe me, but I had to try. I had to do something."

"I believe you." Timon's words sounded soft and tender. Was Devorah working witchcraft on him, or had the Holy Spirit given him understanding? Jerusha wanted to believe the latter. Still a man can be enamored with a woman's wiles. "We will warn Saul." He continued, "Are you alone? Do you need someone to accompany you back to the villa?" Jerusha sucked in her breath. If he took Devorah back, she was going with him. A man stepped out the shadows. Why had she not seen him before?

"I have him to accompany me." Devorah pointed to the same man who had accompanied her when she brought Stephen to them. She stared at Jerusha. "I assure you that I am your friend." Jerusha let out a sigh of relief.

"Friend, indeed," she whispered to Timon as they watched Devorah descend the terraced steps. "Do you really believe her?"

"Jerusha, jealousy does not behoove you." Timon placed her hand into the crook of his arm. "My love is forever with you. I would not have gone with her. I would have sent Moses or someone else. It is not appropriate for a married man to be alone with a single woman." His eyes twinkled in the moon light and he winked.

"I am not jealous. Just cautious," Jerusha stated.

"Protecting me again, huh? What would I do without you?" He flashed her that infuriating lopsided grin.

"Timon, one day, you will see how much you need me."

"Oh, you are wrong about that, Jerusha. I know how much I need you now." He kissed her lips. She surrendered to his argument.

"Are we home?" Samuel's head popped up.

"We will continue this later." Timon whispered in her ear. He rubbed Samuel's head. "Yes, my son. We are home." He set his feet on the tiles. "You will be in your mittah soon. Take your mother's hand. I will be back soon." He kissed her cheek. "I must find your father and Saul. They must know what Devorah has heard."

"Tonight? Can't it wait until morning."

"I am afraid not. I only hope I am not too late."

***

"Jerusha, wake up." Timon's voice startled her. "Wake up!" A light shone in her face. She blinked her eyes open and squinted. Timon was leaning over her.

"You are back. Put that lamp out. You will wake Samuel and Stephen."

"Jerusha, your father is leaving with Saul. He wants some time with you before he leaves. He wants to see Samuel and Stephen, too."

He set the lamp on the table, reached for her cloak on a hook and threw it to her. While she slipped it on, he opened the door.

"Come in." He motioned to Jacob, who waited outside. Jacob stepped over the threshold dressed in his Roman armor. He was clean-shaven and held his helmet under his arm.

"What is this about?" Her voice betrayed her fear. "Why are you in your armor?"

"I am accompanying Saul to Caesarea. He goes on to Tarsus. I go to Rome. Caesar Caligula has summoned me to return."

Rome? Father, please do not go. I have heard Caligula kills anyone who even mentions a goat in his presence, just because he's so hairy. What will he do to you if he knows you won't pledge your allegiance to him?"

"Jerusha, my life is in Yeshua's hands. There are many soldiers, like Cornelius, who must hear about Yeshua. If I don't tell them, who will? You and your mother will be safe here in Jerusalem until I return."

"Who can be safe in this city when Yeshua's judgment looms near? How much longer, Father, before he comes?" Before we can leave?"

"Gamalial taught the scepter shall not depart from Judah until Shiloh comes. Then all nations will gather to him." He placed the helmet on the table.

"Oh, I almost forgot." She felt the wall for her secret hiding place, then dug with her fingers at the edge and lifted off the stone. The scepter sparkled in the lamplight. "The stranger at Shiloh gave me this. I have been meaning to ask you about it." She picked it up and handed it to him.

"Your grandfather showed this to me when I was a boy." Her father examined it. "He never explained why he had it in his possession. Of course, I ran away to Jerusalem before he had a chance to explain." Her father's eyes filled with tears. "I deeply regret that decision. How did this stranger obtain it?"

"I am not sure it was he that placed it in our bag. It just appeared there before we left Shiloh."

"Did you notice the top is like the pendant I made for you?" He rubbed his finger around the lion image. "At the time I made the pendant I didn't fully understand the significance. Let me explain what I have surmised. The lion represents the Lion of Judah. Of course, we know that is our King Yeshua. The butterfly represents you and all those like yourself who want to draw close to Him. Like the butterfly, you don't look like you know where you are going, but you always arrive at the destination he has planned for you.

"But Father, you call me your little lioness, not a butterfly."

"When you rest in his holy presence and look into his eyes, you will be transformed into his image, a lioness with great authority." He took her hands. "Draw strength from Him. He knows you better than I and has written in your book the plans he has for you."

He cupped her chin in one palm. "I will miss you, my little lioness. But you will find your way."

"Father, you talk as if I won't see you again." She hugged him and buried her face in his chest.

"Our lives are in Yeshua's hands. He has not revealed whether I will return from this campaign. If I do not, I will see you in His kingdom." He squeezed her tighter. "I love you, Jerusha."

After a brief silence, he broke their embrace and handed her the scepter. "Remember, all authority belongs to Him." She wiped the tears with the back of her hand, then looking at the glittering scepter, her eyes fell on an empty spot, void of a jewel.

"Father, there's a jewel missing. I never noticed it before today."

"The jasper stone." He grinned. "Your grandfather gave it to me. I gave it to a stranger when I was gone on my first campaign. I asked him to bring it to you at your betrothal, if I did not return. He helped me build a place for you and your mother for when we leave Jerusalem. That is where Marcus took your grandfather. The stranger never told me his name. When I asked, he said it wasn't important. It is a mystery to me why I trusted a man who would not reveal his name."

Jerusha dropped the scepter on the mittah, and ran to her hiding place and pulled out a piece of purple cloth and unfolded it. Is this the jewel?" She held it in her palm for him to see.

"That's it. See if it fits on the scepter." He picked it up and handed it to her.

"It fits perfectly. Father, I think the stranger I met in Shiloh may be the same stranger who gave me this jewel. Who is he?"

"Ima, I want to see." Samuel tugged on her cloak. "I want to see."

"This scepter is your grandfather's inheritance." She held it for him to see.

"The scepter will not depart from Judah until Shiloh comes." Samuel touched the jasper stone and it fell into his hand. The light glittered off it. He stared, his eyes wide, like in a trance. "I see a throne. Whoever sits on it shines bright as this stone."

Jerusha glanced at her father and then at Timon.

"Did he learn those words from the Torah?" she asked.

Timon nodded. "We went over it last week."

She knelt before her son. "Samuel, what are you seeing?" She spoke softly.

"A throne. The person sitting on it shines brighter than this stone. It's gone."

"What is gone?"

The picture I saw. It is gone." He handed the jewel back to her as if it was normal to see things like that.

"Samuel, have you seen pictures like this before tonight?" she asked.

"Sometimes."

"If it happens again, Samuel, you need to tell me or your mother, okay?' Timon took the jewel from his hand, picked him up and put him in Jacob's arms. "Give Grandfather a hug. He will be gone for awhile."

"Why do you wear armor?" Samuel tapped Jacob's breastplate.

"I am a soldier."

"Will you kill people?"

"I am a courier for the centurions. I only fight if I have to defend myself."

"I wondered where you were." Abigail stepped into the room. I should have known you would be with Jerusha and the children." She kissed him on the cheek, then lifted Stephen off the mittah.

"I am telling Jerusha and the family goodbye. Isn't that right, Samuel?"

"You are going on a long journey, but you will come back." Samuel smiled.

Jerusha wanted to believe he spoke the truth. She grabbed Timon's hand. Her faith wavered. Tears formed in her eyes. She lost her father as a child, and now she may lose him again. Her children needed a grandfather. She needed a father.

Everyone followed Jacob as he walked to the gate. He hugged Samuel one last time and handed him to Timon. He pulled Jerusha into his arms.

"My little lioness, you have more authority than you know. Be strong and courageous. You are royalty. Never forget who dwells within you." He released her and stared at her mother; the longing in his eyes tore at Jerusha's heart. His desire to stay was evident and painful to see.

"He took Stephen from Abigail and kissed his cheek. "Stephen, the crowned one. Your bright eyes will see into the kingdom. Your will share with joy what you see." He handed him to Jerusha and turned to her mother.

"My dearest Abigail. You are more beautiful today than the day we made covenant. I will love you forever. As much as is possible I will send word of my well-being." He tenderly wiped the tears from her cheeks and kissed her on the lips, a long passionate kiss. He reached for his helmet from Marcus. After strapping it on, he bowed before Abigail. "Until we meet again," he said, then strode through the gate with Marcus at his side. Timon locked the gate behind them.

Jerusha wrapped her arm around her mother, who held her face in her hands and sobbed. Jerusha choked back tears for her sake. Life without her father would be difficult. She could not imagine living without her husband, and her heart ached for her mother. She glanced at Timon and winced.

"I am sorry, Mother, that Father had to leave again. Yeshua is with us. We will pray he returns soon."

Chapter 30
AD 45

"Look at them, Timon. They flood into the city to celebrate the Feast of Shavuot, and most not do not know where they will get their next meal." Jerusha stood outside the villa leaning against the wall. She watched as the pilgrims approached in the distance. The golden temple glistened below in the morning sun. "They come with their first fruits offerings, and the priests fatten themselves while their sheep starve." Jerusha wiped sweat from her brow. "The famine is spreading across Judea. What are we going to do? Our food supply is dwindling."

"We will trust Yeshua for provision." Timon's sober expression troubled Jerusha. She had not seen the twinkle in his eyes for quite some time. With her grandfather and father gone, the weight of their provision fell on his shoulders. She could not tell him that another child may be on the way. Samuel was almost ten, and Stephen was five. A little sister would be good for them and the fulfillment of Yeshua's promise. She ate less these days to ensure there was enough for the children. If she birthed the child growing in her womb, where would she get the nourishment needed to nurse?

"Aba," Stephen yelled. His arms wide open, he ran at Timon. The gate clanged shut. Timon swooped him up. "Look." The youngster pointed to the stream of people coming down the Mount of Olives and into the city. Dry, dusty air swirled above their heads. An ominous cloud moved across the city. Jerusha wrapped her radyid over her nose and mouth and rubbed her watery eyes with her fist. The boys seemed undisturbed by the dirty air. What boy cared about a little dirt? She smiled and cleaned a smudge from Stephen's cheek.

"Are we working in the shop today?" Samuel walked around the corner with the donkey.

"After we go to the springs to fill the water pots for your mother."

"I am going with you." Jerusha smiled.

"I wanna go." Stephen pulled his father's beard.

"It is settled. We go as a family."

The boys chattered nonstop as they neared the temple court. "Stay close Samuel and hold your brother's hand." Jerusha eyed the women who stared at the boys. Rumors had been rampant about her son Stephen. Where did he come from? Why a Gentile son? He looks nothing like a Hebrew boy. On and on it went, especially in the shops of the upper city bazaar. The owners stared. The other mothers huddled their sons close and moved away. After five years, you would think they would accept him. Jerusha now did most of her shopping in the lower city.

Her sons fired their slingshots with the sons of the shop owner next to Timon's carpenter shop. This owner cared not what color of skin or eyes they had. He was more generous too than the rich in the upper city who hoarded their money. Sure, they could buy the more expensive bread now, but what good would their money do them if there was no bread to buy? She sighed.

"Timon, how much grain is stored in the city?" Jerusha looked deep in his eyes for the truth. He would not want to worry her, of that, she was sure.

"We have enough." He looked away.

Jerusha's stomach tightened. She grabbed his arm. "Timon, look at me. Will we have enough?"

"I am trusting Yeshua to provide. He multiplied the loaves. He can do the same for us." His expression revealed his concern.

"More beggars than usual sit at the temple gate." Jerusha eyed several priests, who scoffed as they passed the hungry children with handsout.

"That makes my stomach churn." Jerusha clenched her jaw.

"I agree. Sometime soon I leave with more orphans and widows. I must get them out of Judea, somewhere safe from the famine. Some of those at the gate will go with me."

"What about us?" Jerusha's troubled mind spun with jealous thoughts. He never had time for her and the boys. She grabbed Stephen's hand. "I asked you to stay close."

"Samuel's not close."

"Where is he?"

"Over there talking to those men."

"I'll get him," Timon interjected and handed the donkey's rope to her. "No doubt he is in a deep discussion about the Torah. He can hold his own with the best teachers."

"He is taught by the best." She smiled, her jealous thoughts melted away by his eagerness to teach his son. "I am sorry, Timon. I know you care about us, too. Enjoy your time with Samuel. Stephen and I will meet you at Gihon Springs."

With so many people in line at the mikvah to bathe before entering the city, Jerusha turned and decided to go another way to the springs. The donkey brayed and sat on his haunches.

"You stubborn beast. Get up." She yanked on the rope and slipped, then caught her balance. "Stephen, pat his rump, and I will pull." She yanked again. He jumped up and trotted into a trader's tent, Stephen running behind him.

Jerusha tucked her hair back in her radiyd and stepped beneath the flap, eyeing the pile of bread in the corner.

"How much for the bread?" She felt the pouch in her girdle. Empty.

"More than what you have to spend by the look of you." She straightened her cloak and dusted her sleeve. Her pendant slipped out of her tunic and shined in the afternoon sun. "Although, I might trade for that pendant."

"That would be robbery." She tucked it back out of sight.

"Where did someone like you get such a beautiful item?"

"What do you mean, 'someone like me?'" Anger burned in her belly.

"Well, anyone who mothers a half-breed like him cannot be too wealthy." He cackled, then grabbed her arm and reached down her tunic for the pendant. "That's a beauty." He stared at it. "Take it off, and I will give you the bread."

"Let me go!" She struggled against his grip. "I would not take your bread if you gave it to me. I most certainly won't take my pendant off and give it to you, you pig! How dare you treat me this way!"

"Let go of my ima." Stephen cried and tugged on his arm. The stranger cast him aside, and he landed against a stool. He covered his bloodied mouth and whimpered. Jerusha's anger flared.

"You are a big man throwing around a five-year-old. Let-go-of-me." When she jerked her arm, he let loose, causing her to fall backward. The man guffawed.

Someone caught her and he slid her into another's arms. Whack. "Don't ever." Whack. "Touch my daughter." Whack. "Again."

Jerusha looked at the man holding her.

"Marcus!" She threw her arms around him; his faced turned red.

"Ima." Stephen buried his face in her tunic.

"Leave the bread and get out of here," her father scolded the trader. "Or I will hand you over to Rome."

The trader ran, but paused to looked back. "You will pay for this."

"Are you all right?" her father asked. She nodded. He squatted before Stephen, who showed him his lip. "How about you? You protected your mother like a man. I am proud to call you my grandson." Stephen smiled, but then winced from the pain

"Father." Jerusha hugged him. "I am so glad you are home. I didn't know if I'd ever see you again. You don't wear your armor. Are you home to stay?"

"Since Claudius rose to power I have obtained favor and believe my misson for Yeshua is fulfilled. Marcus travels with me and reports to the praetorium."

"Does that mean you are finished serving as a Roman soldier?"

"These old bones are ready to play with grandchildren. What do you say, Stephen? Can you teach me how to use that slingshot?" He held his mother's cloak and nodded. He pointed at a man coming up behind Jacob.

"Who's that?"

Jacob turned around.

"Saul," Jacob said as he smiled.

"Jacob, my friend. Shalom." Saul kissed Jacob's cheek. "Jerusha." He bowed. "And Marcus." He gave the Roman salute. "You know Barnabas, my traveling companion. We bring food for the followers from Antioch." He spread is hands toward two donkeys laden with bags filled with grain. They heard of your plight."

"We will meet you at James's meeting tonight for the dispersion. I'll have Timon spread the word."

***

Jerusha, Abigail, and Chaya helped hand out bags of grain. The lamps flickered in the darkened room. There were so many people in need. The crowded room smelled of perspiration. Most of them came from the fields outside the city where they scavenged for any grain they could find. Each kernel was more valuable to them than gold.

The priests would not release the grain gathered into the temple grainery. She grinned at the children, who had begged at the temple gates. They laughed as they hid bags of grain in their cloaks.

"No hungry thief will get my grain."

"Mine, either."

"You two boys are to stay with these widows until they get to their assigned houses. Can you do that for me?" He patted their backs as they nodded. "I know I can depend on you to keep them safe."

Timon decided it was better not to keep all the widows at their house as they had done in the past. If soldiers came to arrest him, the fewer widows there were at the villa, the better. That's why he was gone so much—checking house to house every day to be sure they had everything they needed. After Shavuot, he planned to relocate them outside Judea. How could she be jealous of his time with them? It was his tenderness that attracted her to him in the first place.

Jerusha looked around the crowded room and saw someone she recognized. Devorah. She was in the back of the room in the farthest corner. Her knees were tucked into her chest, and her head was down. She lifted her head and looked around the room. Her once beautiful eyes sunk deep in their sockets, dark circles surrounding them. She stared at the room, her eyes void of life. Tears flowed down her cheeks. She wiped them away and put her head back down. What was she doing here? Did she need grain? How did find out about the meeting? She looked terrible, even worse than the last time she saw her. Apparently she was not fairing so well in Herod's palace.

The door banged against the wall. Soldiers spilled into the room. Amidst the screams, Jerusha frantically searched for Samuel and Stephen.

A soldier stepped forward and put a hand on his sword. "James, the owner of this house. Timon, the widow's caretaker. Come with us. You are under arrest. Herod's orders."

This is Devorah's fault. Judas! No wonder she cries.

The guard kept his hand on his sword. "If you do not comply, we will arrest everyone."

Jerusha's heart throbbed. First James, then Timon stepped through the crowd. *No!*

"Aba, Aba." Samuel and Stephen clung to his cloak. "Don't let the soldiers take you away." Timon peeled them off and squatted. "Whatever happens, remember that I love you." He glanced up at Jerusha, who stood beside them. "Take care of your mother."

"That's enough. Get going." The soldier shoved him against the wall and tied his hands. He looked over his shoulder at Jerusha and mouthed, "I love you." She ran to him. The soldier jerked him around.

"Tell her good-bye. It will be the last words she hears from you."

"Timon. I love you." She hugged him, her tears soaking into his robe. "What shall we do?"

"Pray, Jerusha. Pray His will is done." The soldier yanked him out of her arms and threw her aside. She hit her stomach against the table on the way down.

"Ima! Ima!" Stephen cried next to her on the floor. "Why are they taking aba?"

"They are evil men," Samuel yelled. "Evil!"

Jacob knelt beside Jerusha.

"Grandfather." Stephen clung to his shoulder. "Go. Get my aba away from them. You are a soldier. They will give him to you."

Jerusha locked eyes with her father. He lifted Stephen and extended a hand to Jerusha. Saul gave her his hand too, and they helped her to her feet. The women surrounded her and began praying. Jerusha was in shock, but she composed herself for the sake of her boys. She pushed back her feelings and her tears. She steadied herself on her feet, but suddenly a sharp pain struck her abdomen. "The baby," she whispered to the women so the men would not hear.

Her mother stepped forward and whispered to her father. Jacob nodded, gathered the men together and ushered them out.

"Leave Jerusha with the women." He glanced at his daughter, his face drawn and concern in his eyes. "Samuel and Stephen, come with me."

"I want to stay with Ima." Stephen cried.

"Ima needs her mother." Samuel spoke to his brother.

Jerusha winced. The pain was growing more intense. "Go with your grandfather. I will be all right." She smiled at her sons. "Be brave. Never forget who you are. You are royalty."

"What's going to happen to Aba?" Stephen asked, his lip quivering.

"His life is in Yeshua's hands. Pray for his release." She winced again. "Now, go with your grandfather and Saul. I will be back by morning."

"If the soldiers come to our villa, I will shoot my slingshot at them." Stephen gripped it in his hand and shook it in her face. "Are you sure you want us to leave? Father said to take care of you."

"Come here, you two." She hugged them both to her chest. "I will be safe. Go with your grandfather."

Her father took Stephen's hand and pulled him away. He whimpered. Samuel stood tall, tears in his eyes. A single tear broke free and ran down his cheek. He wiped it off and sniffed.

"We will pray." He sounded so grown up.

They both looked over their shoulders as they walked out the door. Just before her mother closed the door, Devorah slipped past and out into the darkness.

Judas.

Chapter 31

J erusha screamed. She squatted over the pallet holding her abdomen, her tunic tucked high under her breast. "Ooooh, it hurts." She sucked in her breath hoping the pain would stop.

"Breathe," her mother persuaded. "Breathe." Chaya dipped a cloth in cool water and wiped her forehead. Blood dripped from between Jerusha's legs. She knew she would never hold her precious daughter in her arms. Her daughter lay somewhere in the midst of the clots on the pallet. Jerusha moaned and rolled onto her side. The pained subsided, becoming more of a dull ache. Most of the pain she felt was in her heart.

"Yeshua, why?" she sobbed.

Abigail squeezed her daughter's hand, wishing she could ease Jerusha's pain.

Jerusha raised her tear-filled eyes to her mother. "He promised, Mother. He promised to give me a daughter. Am I not worthy?" She felt rejected. "And why take Timon from me? He is my rock and strength. What will I do without him?" From the depths of her soul, she cried out. "Yeshua. YHWH. Deliver my husband from their hands. You did it for Grandfather; please do it for Timon." A light breeze moved through the open window, sending a chill over her body. Her mother held her close as she cried.

Jerusha was exhausted. She closed her eyes, rolled onto her side and wrapped her arms around herself. Abigail pulled Jerusha's tunic down over her body and covered her with the lambskin blanket. Soon, the crying stopped, and Jerusha drifted off into a fitful sleep

***

Jerusha felt the warmth of the sun on her face. As she soaked her weary body in the mikvah waters, she reflected on the scriptures read in the synagogue a few days earlier.

You will pray to him and he will hear you; you will also decree a thing and it will be established; when you are cast down, you will speak with confidence; he will be delivered through the cleanness of your hands.

Jerusha felt hope rising within her. It was a new day, and perhaps Timon would be released. She stepped out of the mikvah, dried herself off and donned the fresh tunic and cloak her mother brought from home. She felt strange. She was experiencing the most difficult days of her life, yet she almost felt like dancing. She must hurry home; her sons would be waiting for her. She wondered if her father could take her to see Timon. He surely had authority with the praetorium. She would ask her mother to stay with the children. She considered the possibility of Timon's release. What could the charges be against him? He had done nothing wrong.

A man yelling outside interrupted her thoughts. "James is on trial."

"Where?" another man yelled.

"The Chamber of Hewn Stone in the Temple. Herod turned him over to the Sanhedrin."

Jerusha held her breath. *Is Timon on trial, too?* She gathered her cloak and ran to the door. The street was crowded with men, women, and children moving toward the temple. She allowed herself to be carried along with them. Moving against the flow to get home would be impossible. Samuel and Stephen were safe with her mother.

When they reached the temple she slipped away from the crowd and entered through a secret entrance that she and Timon had used at Stephen's trial. She looked around to be sure no one had seen her and then hid behind a marble pillar. Her stomach was in knots. Being there brought back too many memories, none of them good. She felt a tap on her shoulder and jumped.

"Marcus. What are you doing in here?"

"I was the one who guarded James through the night. They would not let Roman soldiers accompany him inside the temple. I saw you slip in here and followed."

"Follow me up the stairs." She ran across the marble floor and up the steps. His hobnailed sandals echoed as he climbed. When they reached the top, they looked over the balcony. James stood below, looking up at his would be judges. The seventy-one Sadducees sat in a semi-circle around him glaring. The high priest arose, went to the railing and stared down at James.

"Why do you continue to teach in Yeshua's name and bring this man's blood upon us?" His robe swished as he turned and took a few steps up. "Maybe we need to give you more than a flogging," he smirked.

"My answer is the same now as it was then. I must obey God rather than man." The other Sadducees railed against him. The high priest raised his hand and quieted them.

"I give you another chance to renounce this man, Yeshua. "Or I send you back to Herod. Maybe a beheading will quell this uprising."

"Yeshua," Marcus spoke with respect, "Your father heals in His name."

"Do you renounce this dead carpenter as your king?" the priest yelled, sneering as he awaited James's response.

James peered around at the men, who once had been friends. "God of our fathers raised up Yeshua, whom you had put to death by hanging Him on a cross. He is the one whom God exalted to His right hand as Prince and Savior. I am a witness of these things and so is the Holy Spirit whom God has given to those who obey Him." James's boldness penetrated the atmosphere with truth. "Repent. And you, too, may enter the kingdom."

"I repent," Marcus whispered.

"I have heard enough blasphemy. Take him to Herod." The high priest waved a dismissal and walked up the stairs.

"I must go." Marcus turned to leave. "Along with your father, this is one of the most courageous men I know. I must profess my faith with James."

"Wait." Jerusha held his arm. "Where is Timon? Have you seen him?"

"He was flogged and placed under guard below the eastern tower at the Antonia Fortress. He leaves soon to train in Rome. Because he is a Greek, he will be pitted against a Jew in a fight to the death in the theater at Corinth. He never begged or faltered during the flogging. A peace that transcends my understanding kept him strong."

"Why did they arrest him? He has never preached openly about Yeshua."

"The Jews are afraid of him. The people admire him more than they do the high priest. His love for the widows and orphans shines through him. They cannot fight against such love. They believe if they remove him, the people will scatter and turn away from this teaching."

"How do you know this?"

"I overheard the priests talking at Herod's palace. He cares not if he is innocent. He covets their money and their approval. These religious leaders are corrupt."

"I must go." He ran down the stairs and shoved the large ornate door open. The mob yelled at James as the temple guards passed.

"I fear for your life. Come with me, and I will keep you safe." He ran back and grabbed her arm. "Your father would never forgive me if something were to happen to you."

***

Herod stood on the balcony at his palace as the guards approached with James. Marcus kept Jerusha close to him and searched the faces in the crowd.

"There is your father and Saul." He maneuvered them through the crowd.

"Jerusha." Her father hugged her, and turned to Marcus. "Thank you."

"I pledge allegiance to your God." Marcus saluted with a fist on his chest. "After seeing the courage and peace of these men, I know what you teach is true. Your God is my God. Your kingdom is my kingdom."

Marcus turned away, broke through the crowd and stood beside James.

Jerusha could not hear Marcus speak over the noise of the crowd, but she could read the words on his lips: "If you die, I die."

The peace on both their faces astounded Jerusha. *Just like Stephen.* She looked at Saul, tears streaming down his face.

"I once was blind like them. By God's grace it is not me condemning an innocent man."

"Marcus has been like a son to me." Her father's eyes glistened.

The crowd chanted, "Blasphemer. Blasphemer."

"Father, where are all the Yeshua followers? Why aren't they speaking out on his behalf."

"They are afraid if they speak against the high priest, their families will suffer. Most would give their own lives, but it's not so easy if your loved ones suffer because of you." His eyes revealed his pain and opened Jerusha's eyes to how hard it had been for him to leave her and her mother.

Herod adjusted his cloak and smiled at the crowd. Clearly, he was enjoying himself.

"Remove the head and the body dies. Behead him." The crowd cheered. Marcus raised a fist toward Herod, who raised both hands and waited for the crowd to quiet, then nodded at Marcus.

Marcus removed his helmet. "I renounce Caesar and Rome and pledge my allegiance to Yeshua and his kingdom. I choose to die with this courageous man." The crowd jeered and rushed toward him and James. The Roman soldiers, who stood guard, raised their shields and formed a wall around James and Marcus.

Saul and Jacob placed Jerusha between them and moved through the crowd. They found refuge under an alcove as the mob swarmed forward. A centurion and his legionaries rode past on horseback and broke up the crowd.

"Take these men outside the city wall. Execute them there," the centurion commanded. The mob grumbled, but began to disperse. They knew better than to confront Rome.

Jacob's eyes widened in recognition. He knew the man on horseback.

"Cornelius." He turned to Jerusha. "I know this man. I met him in Caesarea. He's a good man. Stay here with Saul." He glanced at them both. "I love you, Jerusha."

It felt like a good-bye. Jerusha was terrified at her father's words.

"She will be safe with me." Saul took her arm and her father moved through the dwindling crowd. She watched from the alcove, her heart pounding in her chest.

"Wait!" The centurion stopped the soldiers and stared at Marcus for the longest moment, then saluted. "Why do they arrest you?"

"I renounce Caesar as my king and Rome as my kingdom. I pledge allegiance to Yeshua and His kingdom."

Cornelius dismounted. "You would give your life for Yeshua. Would He not be better served if you lived?"

Marcus locked eyes with her father, who stood behind the centurion. "His kingdom is not of this world."

Jacob moved past the centurion, who nodded in respect, and grabbed Marcus's shoulders. "My son." He kissed his cheek. "I have prayed for the day your eyes would be opened to Yeshua. We will die together."

"No." Marcus clenched his jaw. "You have a family. I am single and an orphan. I go to my Father and your Father, who is in heaven. Live Jacob. Many sons will come to you." Jacob waited and peered into Marcus's eyes. Jerusha held her breath.

"As you desire, my son." Her father embraced him.

Jerusha's mind raced. *Is Marcus, a Roman soldier, Father's son? A royal heir through the blood of Yeshua, the Lion of Judah.* Jerusha remembered her words at Shiloh. *Sons of Jacob come forth.* She wiped the tears away with the back of her hand.

Cornelius took off his helmet and knelt. "I cannot kill these men. I, too, renounce Caesar as my king and Rome as my kingdom. I pledge allegiance to Yeshua and his kingdom." He rose and gave the command to the officer behind. "I die with them." He grasped Jacob by the shoulders. "Take care of my family. Until we meet in his kingdom." He saluted and gave his sword to the next in command.

"Fools. Behead all three," Herod ordered.

**

Jerusha slipped away from the women who were mourning in the inner courtyard. She sat down on her father's bench in the garden. She had many wonderful memories in that garden. There, as a little girl, she had played with butterflies and danced before her King. Years later, she had fallen into the arms of Timon when he had asked her to be his wife. Her father told her many stories while sitting in the garden on the very bench she now occupied. She needed the comfort and safety the garden provided.

Timon was in jail, and she could not imagine life without him.

The smell of the burning olive oil from the lamps filled her nostrils; the sound of crickets singing their nighttime song filled her ears. She took off her radiyd and let the breeze blow through her hair and wrapped her cloak tighter around her shoulders.

"May I join you?" Her father stood by the gate. She nodded. The years of war campaigns with Rome had aged her father. She, too, had aged. She was no longer the innocent little girl of yesteryear. She was a grown woman capable of fighting for her loved ones, and she readied herself for the fight of her life. Timon could not die.

"What can I do, Father, to free Timon?"

"Pray. His life is in Yeshua's hands. Nothing is impossible with Him. I prayed Marcus would give his life to Yeshua. I never dreamed he would volunteer to die for Him. Cornelius, too."

"Oh, father, why does anyone have to die? Why couldn't the death angel pass over them, like it did for Moses."

"There is a worse death than physical death, Jerusha. Because of the blood of the Yeshua, Marcus, James, and Cornelius will live forever with Him in His kingdom. Those who kill their them, will die a worse death for they will experience eternal separation from YHWH. Unless they repent before it is too late."

"Excuse me." It was Moses. "Devorah is at the front gate and wants to talk to Jerusha."

"Me?" Jerusha pointed to her chest. "I do not want to talk to that Judas." She saw the look in her father's eye. "I know, love even your enemies." She stood and moved toward the gate.

"Be kind, Jerusha. She may not be the enemy you think she is." He walked along side of her.

Devorah waited in the dark under the jujube tree. When she saw Jerusha, she stood erect.

"I have news of Timon."

"Is he well?" Jerusha asked

"He wants to see you. If you meet me tomorrow at midnight at the Antonia's east gate, I can get you past the guard."

Jerusha's eyes widened and she looked at her father. Could she trust Devorah?

"You must come alone, or I will not be able to get you past the guards."

"How do I know this isn't a trap?"

"I told you before that I am your friend."

Jerusha took a deep breath. The turmoil in her heart battled the fear in her mind. Could she trust Devorah? She glanced again at her father. His slight nod gave her courage. She must see Timon.

"I will be there."

Chapter 32

Jerusha held the hands of Samuel and Stephen as she climbed the narrow path from the Kidron Valley up the Mount of Olives. The sun reflected brightly against the limestone wall behind them. The temple glistened in the distance.

"Where are we going, Ima?" Samuel was much like his mother, questioning everything. He sought the truth of every situation and never accepted a simple answer. When Jerusha gave an explanation, he would ask one why, then another, and kept at it until Jerusha found herself quoting her father by saying, "You ask too many questions."

"We're going to Gethsemane, where Yeshua often prayed. We will pray for your father's release." She slowed her pace for Stephen, since his short legs had trouble keeping up, and he was out of breath. Besides, it was a good excuse to rest her tired body. Timon's arrest and her miscarriage had drained her strength. Her legs felt like heavy stones, and, like Stephen, she was short of breath. She stopped and used her sleeve to mop the sweat from her forehead. She would welcome the shade of the olive trees.

"It's a little further, Stephen, over that ridge and to the left." She pointed ahead. Samuel ran up the hill, the dust swirling beneath his sandals.

"Let's go, Ima. We can make it." Stephen took her hand and pulled as he walked past. She smiled at her gentle giant. Like his namesake, he had a kind way about him. If his body grew into those large hands, his stature would compare to that of her grandfather. She missed her grandfather terribly, as well as his wisdom and insights. Someday, she would like to ask him about the scepter and his Roman cognomen, Regulus. She followed Stephen up the hill and into the garden.

"I want you both to find a place under an olive tree to pray." She glanced around, saddened by the lack of blossoms on the trees. "Ask for rain as well as your father's release." She settled beneath an old tree with long scraggly limbs. She wondered if it was the same place Yeshua had prayed. She closed her eyes and envisioned Him sweating drops of blood. His desire to obey had been greater than His desire to avoid death by crucifixion.

"James and Marcus died. YHWH didn't save them. How do we know he will save Father?" The same tormenting fear she felt in her gut looked at Jerusha through Samuel's eyes. Would they ever see Timon again?

"He will not die, but live and declare the works of the Lord. I prayed this portion of the Psalm over your grandfather, and he lived."

"What about the portion of the Psalm where it says, 'Precious in the sight of God is the death of his saints?'" Samuel's knowledge of the scriptures surprised Jerusha. Timon taught him well. Her heart sank at the thought of her husband. His death was not an option. Timon would live. His death may be precious to God, but it would not be precious to her.

"Your father will not die." She spoke the only words her heart would allow.

"Ima is right. Aba will not die." Stephen ran to Jerusha and crawled onto her lap. Samuel's head dropped.

"I am sorry, Ima. I do not want father to die. I only asked the question." Samuel sniffed back tears.

"You are a wise son. I am surprised how well you remember the scriptures." Jerusha watched him sit up straight. "You will speak truth into many people's lives." She smiled and watched a grin spread across his face. "Let's be quiet and talk to YHWH."

They prayed for a while, and then Jerusha pulled out a small piece of unleavened bread from her girdle, She tore it into three pieces. "This week we celebrate the feast of unleavened bread."

"'Seven days you shall eat unleavened bread.'" Stephen quoted the Torah. "'On the first day you shall remove leaven out of your houses, for if anyone eats what is leavened, from the first day until the seventh day, that person shall be cut off from Israel; you shall observe this day, throughout your generations, as a statute forever.'" Jerusha's heart warmed at how much Timon had taught the boys. Once again, her eyes filled with tears.

How many more tears must I shed?

"You are a good student of the scriptures, Stephen." She tapped his nose and sat him beside her. The sun filtered through the silver green leaves and reflected off his face.

"Before we pray for your father, let us eat this unleavened bread and ask the Holy Spirit to search our hearts for any unclean thought or action. If He shows you something, repent. He lifts up the humble and answers their prayers." She handed the bread pieces to them and settled on a large twisted olive branch.

Jerusha looked out over the city. She saw the tall Antonia tower in the distance, the place where Timon had been flogged. That thought sickened her. Later that night she would go with Devorah, who claimed to be her friend. Jerusha was skeptical, to say the least. It seemed that every time Devorah showed up, something bad happened. She shook her head, trying to clear her mind and closed her eyes. "Help me, Yeshua, to see her through your eyes, and to love her with your love," She sat still, feeling the warmth of the sun on her face.

"Ima." Samuel stood before her. "I saw something again. Father told me to tell you if I saw something."

"What did you see?"

"I saw that same place, the place with a throne. The one who sat on it shined like the jasper stone. Father knelt. There were many others around him. The one on the throne rose extended his scepter and touched his head. Father glowed, then he rose, turned, and touched the heads of those around him and they glowed. Then the picture faded."

"That is wonderful, Samuel. Did you recognize any of the men who were with your father?"

"No. The one on the throne is Yeshua, isn't it?"

Jerusha nodded. "YHWH showed you that for a reason. Ask Him to reveal what it means. Stephen and I will ask too. In time, He will show us."

The sun dipped down in the west, reflecting on the golden temple doors. Jerusha shaded her eyes as she approached the city. How would Yeshua answer her prayers? Whatever way He chose to answer. She cared not, so long as Timon lived. She would meet Devorah that night, though it was possible that she, too, would be arrested.

They stood in the long line to pay Roman taxes before entry into the city. Jerusha brushed the hair from her face and tucked it inside her radiyd. She would dip in the mikvah again before seeing Timon. Excitement stirred in her bosom. She longed to see the familiar twinkle in his eyes and his mischievous lopsided grin, though the flogging may have robbed him of both. She never knew the depth of her love for him, until that moment. His contagious joy had kept her going, even when she questioned their future. She dug in her girdle and retrieved the coins for taxes and dropped them in the treasury.

"Hurry along." The soldiers shoved her in the back. She stumbled, but Samuel caught her arm. Stephen's wide-eyed stare meant he wanted nothing to do with the Roman soldiers. Most pilgrims moved uphill toward the temple mount. Jerusha steered the boys another way to avoid parading her gentile son in front of the priests.

"Come, Stephen, we can make it." She raised her cloak, and trudged up the steep incline. The dry air and dust from fellow travelers made her throat dry. Stephen coughed, no doubt choking on the same dust. At the top of the hill she stopped and handed the goatskin water bottle to Stephen and then to Samuel.

"There is only a little left, Ima. You can have it." Samuel offered the bottle to her.

"No, Samuel. You drink first, but thank you."

"What are the soldiers doing?" Stephen pointed at Herod's palace. The cohort marched past the high terraced wall, their hobnailed sandals tromping in unison. Up ahead, the crowd jeered like hungry dogs. Jerusha drew Samuel and Stephen close. People ran past them toward the mob.

Jerusha caught the arm of one of the women and stopped her.

"What is happening?"

"They are arresting another one of the heretics who follow the Way."

"Who?"

"I don't know."

Jerusha guided the boys around the outskirts in order to bypass any violence that might erupt. Her heart raced. It could not be Timon. He had been arrested already. Maybe it was his trial. A sharp pain shot through her chest. No. Yeshua wouldn't let that happen.

"Keep moving, boys." When they reached the plaza, people rushed in from every direction. Surrounded, Jerusha looked right, then left. No way of escape. The mob jostled them and tried to get close enough to watch the arrest. The soldiers advanced against the crowd, their shields locked together, the accused man enclosed behind them. One by one, the people peeled away and let them pass.

"Who is it?" someone yelled.

Jerusha's heart pounded. *Don't let it be Timon.* Stephen whimpered and clung to her skirt. Samuel, curious like always, peered through the heads.

"It's Peter." Samuel's eyes narrowed. He shielded his mother as the soldiers pushed their way through." Jerusha closed her eyes, afraid to look. If she did, she might fall apart in front of the boys.

"Why arrest Peter?" Samuel questioned.

"The same reason they arrested your father and James. They hate the followers of the Way."

"Who hates us? The Romans?" He glanced over his shoulder.

"And the Sanhedrin. Herod wants their approval, and Rome wants peace. Rome believes we are the cause of the uprising." She took Stephen's hand. The crowd was thinning and it was time for them to move.

"Are they going to arrest us?" Stephen asked, tears in his eyes.

"If they try, I'll use my slingshot against them." Samuel patted his hip.

"That would not be enough. You would need a sword." Stephen jabbed with an imaginary sword.

"Enough of that talk." Jerusha admonished. "Our lives are in Yeshua's hands."

***

The aroma of frankincense hung in the air. Jerusha applied some of the sweet perfume following her mikvah.. She straightened her clean radiyd and flipped it over her shoulder. It was almost midnight. Yeshua's brother, James, had called a meeting to pray. She waited for the others to leave and held the gate as they filed past one by one.

"We want to go with you," Samuel and Stephen begged. "We want to see Aba, too."

"Devorah said to come alone." She kissed their cheeks. "Stay with your grandfather and pray."

"Will you be arrested, too?" Stephen's eyes opened wide.

Jerusha hugged him and patted his back. "Do not worry. I am in Yeshua's hands."

"He let Peter get arrested." He whimpered. "Please don't go."

"Jacob peeled Stephen away and picked him up. "Wipe those tears away, little big man. We have some praying to do." He took Jerusha's hand. "Be careful, my little lioness."

Jerusha blinked back her tears. Her mother's hug felt like a cocoon of safety. After a moment, her mother pulled away and looked her in the eyes.

"My daughter. You are stronger than you know. Go in peace. We will be praying."

She watched as her family joined with other followers of the way who left for the prayer meeting with James. Her father guarded from the back, the last one to turn the corner. Stephen's big eyes staring over his shoulder was the last sight she saw. Then, she was alone.

She looked up at the moon. She must hurry to get to the eastern Antonia tower by midnight. She scampered down the terrace steps. Out of breath, she stopped and listened to the night. Quiet darkness in all directions. She slowed her pace, crossed the bridge, and looked up at the decorative arch as she entered the temple area. Grief gripped her heart as she walked along the western wall. What would happen to those who believe the corrupt religious leaders? The temple no longer housed the presence of YHWH. He came to dwell within each believer. It was a miracle. She hoped He had a miracle for Timon.

As she got closer, she ducked into an alcove. The soldier's red plumes dotted the darkness high on the eastern tower and both sides of the gate below. *Devorah, where are you?* So desperate to see Timon, Jerusha hadn't thought about how Devorah had access. How was she able to get past the guards? *What a fool I have been.*

Several figures stepped out of the darkness into the lamplight and moved toward the gate. Jerusha remained hidden, watching.

One of the soldiers opened the gate. "We thought you were not coming tonight, Devorah."

Devorah motioned the figures inside and looked around. "I will wait here. I am meeting someone."

Jerusha's heart raced. Should she identify herself or run away?

Chapter 33

"Devorah," Jerusha called and ran up the tiled steps. "Come inside." Devorah took her hand and led her through the gate. The soldier's eyes stared at Jerusha's breasts. That old dirty feeling crept up her spine. "Don't pay attention to him. He will leave you alone. Follow me." She pulled a key from her girdle. Jerusha was puzzled. *How is it that she has access to keys, and why do the guards leave her alone?*

She followed Devorah down a narrow spiral stairwell, the air dank and musty. At the bottom, the guard devoured Devorah with his eyes and motioned to an open iron door.

"I will be back." She grabbed a torch from the wall and walked past several closed doors. The grunts and heavy breathing sickened Jerusha. Chills ran up her neck as childhood memories flooded her thoughts. Men touching her, the heavy breathing of the high priest and his son, their rancid breath in her face. She shivered and fought down the urge to run. Panic and icy fear paralyzed her. Her throat constricted, and she could not breathe. *No. I must be brave for Timon.*

Keys jangled as Devorah struggled with the lock. The rusty hinge squeaked, and the door swung wide. Her torch lit up the cell. Seated with his back against the back wall of the cell, was Timon. He squinted and covered his eyes against the light's glare.

"Who's there?" A sliver of moonlight illuminated his face, revealing swollen eyes and a bruised face. His eyes held no twinkle, his mischievous grin replaced by swollen lips.

Stunned, Jerusha stumbled forward and tripped over a smelly bucket. Rats scattered.

"Timon." She sat numbly at his side, oblivious to anything except her husband's pain. He grimaced when she kissed his cheek. "I'm sorry you are going through this. If I could—" The old anger started to rise in her voice.

"That's my Jerusha." He reached for her hand, and the old lopsided grin started to form, then he grimaced.

"I will leave you two alone."

"Devorah?" He sounded confused.

"I have not time to explain." She kept looking down the hall.

"Where's the guard?"

"He is busy. Do not try to leave. Other guards are watching. If you are caught trying to escape, you will be killed on the spot. I will be back for Jerusha. We only have a short time." She carried the torch outside and shut the door. Total darkness.

Jerusha's eyes adjusted to the darkness, and she tried to examine Timon's wounds. When she raised his tunic, it stuck to the blood dried from the slashed skin, the marks too numerous to count. His body shivered violently, and he was unable to hold his hands steady or keep his teeth from chattering. Jerusha felt helpless, and anger was boiling up inside of her. What kind of God lets this happen to a man who loves and serves others? What good purpose would this serve? She removed her cloak and covered him. Perspiration beaded on his forehead, which was hot with fever. The cell smelled of urine and worse.

She snuggled next to him, being careful not to lean too hard against his wounds.

"I am so angry. You do not deserve this."

"Jerusha, no matter what happens never forget how much I love you. Do not waste time or strength blaming YHWH. He warned that through much suffering we enter the kingdom. He did not cause this."

"He could deliver you. He delivered Daniel from the lions' den."

"As I have told you numerous times. Our lives are in Yeshua's hands."

"Yes. Our lives are in Yeshua's hands." She laid her head on his shoulder and gripped her pendant. "Arise, Lord. Let your enemies be scattered. Let all who hate you flee before you."

All too soon, the door hinge creaked, and the cell was filled with light. Devorah poked her head around the door.

"Jerusha. We must go. Please hurry." She stepped back in the hall.

"My little butterfly, I love you," Timon whispered.

"And I you," Jerusha's voice quivered. "I hate leaving you this way."

"We will see each other again." He forced a grin.

Jerusha followed Devorah up the winding stairway, each step taking her farther away from the one she loved. With each step she took, her legs grew heavier. The guard at the top sneered and opened the gate. The three figures who came with Devorah waited in the shadows.

"Thank you, Devorah." Jerusha smiled and blinked back tears. The three figures stepped into the moonlight. Jerusha gasped.

"They are girls, not much older than Sarah when she died. Why bring them to a horrible place like this?"

"I have no time to explain." Devorah motioned the girls to keep moving. "Just know it's not by my choice. We must get back to Herod's palace before sunrise. I will try to explain at another time." She ran to catch up with the girls.

***

The stars twinkled bright against the black sky. Jerusha stared and tried to count them all. It was impossible, of course, but it was something she had done with her father when she was a little girl. She turned the corner and looked over the city. Timon loved this city. He stayed to save its widows and orphans from destruction as well as the deceived lost sheep who believed the religious leaders. He may end up giving his life for them. His love astounded Jerusha. He was a perfect father to his sons and to all the children YHWH sent. Could she be as good of a mother?

She was almost back to the villa when a psalm she learned with her grandfather came to mind. *The Lord builds up Jerusalem. He gathers the outcasts.* He surely gathered her into his loving arms, an angry outcast. *He heals the broken hearted. And binds up their wounds.* "YWHW, I couldn't be more broken over Timon's arrest. I don't want to become bitter and blame you. Holy Spirit help me." *He counts the number of the stars. He gives names to all of them.* She looked up at the stars. There were millions, each one named. She watched as a dark cloud moved across the sky. The air smelled of rain. *Sing to the Lord with thanksgiving, who covers the heavens with clouds, who provides rain for the earth.* By the time she reached the street where her villa stood, only a few stars remained visible. A man stepped out of the darkness under the Jujube tree. She jumped and grabbed her chest.

"Peter! What are you doing here? I thought you were arrested."

"Tell your father and the others, YHWH delivered me tonight. I went to Mary's house first. They thought I was a ghost." The lightening lit up the horizon. He smiled. "A storm is coming. Nothing like the smell of fresh rain."

"Is Timon delivered, too?" Jerusha pulled her radiyd tighter around her face and spread it further down around her shoulders. Large drops plopped to the ground. A cool wind stirred the branches, and her tunic whipped at her legs. She had forgotten her cloak in Timon's cell. She rubbed her arms for warmth and hid in the shadows from Peter's sight.

"I have not seen Timon. The angel appeared in my cell. He told me to gird myself. We walked past the guards unnoticed. I thought I was having a vision. When I came to myself, I was outside. Tell all who prayed, their prayers have been answered." He stepped closer to Jerusha. "I can see you are concerned about Timon."

"Why have my prayers not been answered?" She did not wait for Peter's response. "He told me not to blame YHWH for his arrest. How do I reconcile your release, with him suffering in a cell, still a captive? He may die in Corinth, that is, if he does not die of his wounds before." Jerusha shivered in the wind, puddles of rain formed at her feet.

"Our times are in His hands. Yeshua once told me, 'What did it matter what happened to another disciple. Follow me'. All who live godly in Yeshua shall suffer persecution. If you are reviled for the name of Christ, you are blessed because the Spirit of glory and of YHWH rests upon you. If you suffer, be not ashamed, only that his name be glorified." Peter's words penetrated her heart like the rain that soaked her garment.. The filth from Timon's cell washed away with the rain. A soothing acceptance replaced the bitterness and anger.

"Thank you," Jerusha opened the gate. "Would you like to come out of the rain?"

"No. I must go. Peace be with you, Jerusha." Peter's quiet presence disappeared down the hill, the thunder masking his footsteps.

An hour later, Jerusha heard the gate clanging. She arose from her mittah, slipped on her cloak and lit a lamp. The noise grew louder. Her heart pounded in fear. She shined the lantern on Samuel and Stephen's pallets. Empty. Her father and mother were not yet home. She was alone in the villa. She thought of hiding and waiting for whomever it was to leave. *What if it is Timon? What if the angel came for him?* She hurried down the veranda. The rain had stopped, and the stars shone bright again. Her sandals splashed in the small puddles on the path.

"Help! Please help!" Devorah yelled. The gate clanged, and Jerusha heard other voices.

"What is it, Devorah. Is it Timon?" Jerusha unlocked the gate.

"No. We are in trouble." Devorah rushed past and hid in the garden. The others followed. The foursome shivered in the cool air. Jerusha checked outside the gate and saw no one.

"What is wrong? Why are you afraid?" she asked and relocked the gate.

"Come into the kitchen where it's warmer." Jeruha tried to comfort the three girls, who cried uncontrollably. "You will be safe here." She eyed Devorah. *Once again, Devorah arrives and so does trouble.*

She led them into the kitchen where the fire burned beneath the lentil stew for the morning meal. Oil lamps flickered on the wall.

Jerusha turned and gasped. The faces of the girls were bloody and swollen.

"What happened?" She reached for a soft rag and dipped it in the cool water on the table. "Sit here and let me attend to your wounds." She arranged wooden chairs around the table.

"How did you get these cuts and bruises on your faces?" She dabbed at the blood on one girl's face. She winced and looked at Devorah, her eyes empty and void of emotion.

"I am sorry to bring them to you. I had no where else to go." Devorah's face looked bruised, too, an old bruise. She paced back and forth. "I do not know what we are going to do."

Jerusha motioned to a chair. "Sit, Devorah. Start at the beginning. Tell me everything."

"Will we be safe if they come for us?" Her eyes darted around the room.

"You will be safe. No one knows you are here. If they do come, I have someplace to hide you. First, I need to know the truth, Devorah. Tell me the truth. No lying."

Devorah sat down. "I was born a slave in Herod's palace. My mother died at my birth, and my father was sold to another owner when I was six. I learned at a young age to obey everything Herod and the high priest asked of me. As soon as I matured, they forced themselves on me. After awhile, I became numb. I shut off all emotion. I earned a certain respect from them, and they charged me with taking care of the other slave girls. Then they learned they could earn money by selling us to the soldiers who stayed in the Antonia."

"If you had freedom to come and go, why didn't you run away?"

"I had two sons by Herod. He called them bastards."

"The two boys you brought to our villa? Micah and Elias?"

"Yes." Devorah broke down and sobbed. "I hated their father, and he did not claim them, but they were my joy and delight."

"Where are they?"

"He took them away to Caesarea to be his sexual slaves. They will be killed when he's through with them. He will force them to jump off the cliff. I have heard the stories of what happens to the boys that serve him." She held her head in her hands and sobbed again.

Jerusha came near and touched her shoulder. After awhile, Devorah lifted her head and wiped her face.

"That is why I lied when I first came here. You were right not to trust me. Herod and the high priest planted me here to get information about your father, and to find out if he was alive. They threatened to take my sons away if I didn't give them what they wanted. They hate your family. I came here tonight because I overheard them talking about what they did to you when you were a slave at the palace. I figured if anyone would help us, it would be you."

"Why are they coming after you tonight?"

"One of the guards told Herod that we let you see Timon. They beat us and would have killed us if we had not escaped."

"Forgive me for doubting you." Jerusha stopped dabbing at wounds. "I am glad you felt you could come to me." *Your daughters will be nursed at your side.*

"Soldiers are here." Samuel ran breathless into the room. "We found them at the gate when we came home."

"Samuel, take Devorah and these girls to the hiding place in the barn. Shut it so no one can open it or see it."

Chapter 34

"Why do you come to my gate so late at night?" Jerusha stared at the soldiers, her hands on her hips.

"We are looking for a woman, Devorah. We know she lived here with you."

"She is not here." Jerusha felt a tinge of guilt for lying and looked down. What else could she do? She couldn't let these animals get their hands on the girls.

"Open the gate! Now!"

She felt around in her girdle for the key, then fumbled it to the ground. She picked it up and finally unlocked the gate. The soldiers burst through the gate and tromped through the garden, stabbing at the bushes with their swords. Finding the garden empty, they spread out to search the villa. She hoped Samuel had made it to the barn in time. She glanced at her father and Stephen, who stood at the fountain.

"What are the soldiers doing? Are they arresting us?" Stephen asked his grandfather, who held his hand. Her father looked at Jerusha, a slight smile on his lips.

"No, Stephen, they are not arresting us." He picked up the boy. "They will be gone soon." Moses hurried up the tiled path. Joseph tagged along behind with her mother.

"Samuel hid the girls in the barn," he whispered in Jerusha's ear. Abigail bent down so Joseph could see her lips. She mouthed the words, "Do not be afraid. The soldiers will leave soon." Joseph nodded that he understood.

Doors were slammed and pottery shattered as the soldiers' search proved fruitless. One by one the soldiers reported to the centurion and lined up outside the gate. The centurion glared at her father as he walked past, then stopped and looked back. "You look familiar."

"Some centurions treat other's property with respect. Did you find what you came looking for?" Her father's slight smile never wavered. Such confidence.

The centurion rubbed his chin. Jerusha held her breath. What was he thinking?

"I remember you. Your father was Regulus. Too bad he was crucified. Good soldier." He saluted. Her father nodded, his eyes steady. At the gate, the soldier turned and looked at Jerusha. "We take your husband to Corinth this morning. I will see he is not mistreated, in honor of your father." He turned and marched beside his men as they tromped in unison down the terraced steps.

Jacob put Stephen down and closed the gate.

"Run along to the kitchen. You have been up most of the night. Eat some bread and lentil stew, then to bed with you."

"But Grandfather, the sun is coming up." Stephen pointed to the orange globe in the distance. "It's morning." He rubbed his eyes with his fist.

"A little nap for those sleepy eyes is in order. What do you say, Jerusha?"

"Listen to your grandfather." She took her father's arm, and they followed Stephen up the path. "We need to talk," she whispered, "in the garden."

"Our favorite bench?" He patted her hand.

She lay her head against his shoulder. "Of course."

Jerusha dried the bench with her cloak before sitting. "The soldiers were looking for Devorah. She's hiding in the secret tunnel with three slave girls who have been beaten. I was wrong about her. Like me, she suffered at the hands of Herod and the high priest." She looked up at her father. "They are so young. It brings back many memories." Her father's cloak settled over her shoulders. Warmth eased its way into her achy bones. "They need our help. Herod is taking Devorah's sons to Caesarea." She leaned over, propped her elbows on her legs and held her head in her hands. "What am I going to do? It's not safe for them to stay here, and I may never see Timon again." Her shoulders began to shake. She tried to fight the pain in her chest, her body shook as she sobbed. Jacob rested his hand on her back.

"I have a plan." Jacob released Jerusha's hair from the radiyd. "We will take the girls and leave for Corinth tomorrow. I will see what I can do for Timon. I know some officials that owe me favors."

Jerusha closed her eyes, and envisioned Timon in jail. She wondered if he would be alive when they got to Corinth. *Believe, Jerusha, believe.* "He will live and not die, but declare the works of YHWH." She opened her eyes. A purple butterfly flittered on the pomegranate bush. *You will arrive at the destination assigned for you by YHWH.* If anyone could fix this, her father could. She composed herself and began thinking of the journey to Corinth..

"What will we do with Devorah and the girls?"

"I know a tent maker who lives there, a follower of the Way. He will find homes for them. But first, we will stop at Caesarea and get Devorah's sons back."

"How?"

"Leave that to me. Prepare the wagon for the journey. Your mother and Chaya will help. Keep Devorah and the girls in the hiding place until we leave."

Abigail approached the bench where Jacob and Jerusha were talking. "I have been looking for you two."

"Did Samuel tell you about Devorah?" Jerusha asked.

"Yes. We brought bread, a little stew, and some water to the hiding place. She wants to talk with you." Her mother never failed to be hospitable, even in times of distress.

"I will go talk to her as soon as Father and I are finished." She turned to her father. "Do we all go?"

"What do you two have planned?" Abigail raised a suspicious eyebrow.

"We leave in the morning for Caesarea and Corinth." Her father stood and helped Jerusha up.

"Who leaves?" Abigail's expression made Jerusha smile.

"Father, we must take Samuel and Stephen. They will want to see Timon." Jerusha ignored her mother's question.

"I am not sure it's a good idea for them to see him beaten and bruised, and it will be a dangerous trip."

"Could it be any more dangerous than living in Jerusalem? If he is released, we can travel home as a family. They would love the adventure." She tried to convince herself that all would turn for the better. A kingdom family. No worries. On earth as it its in heaven.

Jacob looked at Abigail. His shoulders lifted as he took a deep breath, and then dropped as he exhaled. He reached for Abigail's hand.

"We go as a family." He squeezed her hand and pulled her close. "When I came home, I swore I would never leave this beautiful woman again."

Jerusha backed out of the gate and left them alone. As she approached the stable, her thoughts raced. She would journey with both her father and mother. She had only left Jerusalem once, when she went to Shiloh. Now she would journey to Caesarea and Corinth. How different would the culture be? Would her father's authority be enough to free Timon as well as Devorah's sons from Herod?

She opened the heavy limestone door and entered the secret place. Samuel had lit a lamp, and its flames flickered on the wall. The room smelled of burning olive oil. Devorah sat on the stone floor with the three young girls huddled next to her. They all had lambskin blankets around their shoulders. They dipped bread in a large pot of lentil stew and drank water from goatskin bottles. Their wounds had stopped bleeding.

"Mother said you wanted to see me."

Devorah stood. "Jerusha, thank you. I am sorry about Timon. He's a good man, and he loves you."

Jerusha wanted to hug her but hesitated and looked down. Devorah moved closer. Jerusha looked up and locked eyes with her. She could see the pain. A common bond. Why had she not seen it before today?

"I am sorry for what you have suffered." Jerusha reached out and Devorah ran into her arms. She began to cry, softly at first, but then she broke down into deep sobs. Jerusha remained silent, allowing Devorah to release her pain.

Finally, Jerusha spoke. "In time, if you trust Yeshua, you will be free of the shame." Jerusha looked at the other girls. "You all can be free, not only of the shame, but the physical abuse. Tomorrow, we travel to Caesarea to see if we can find Devorah's sons, then on to Corinth. You can start a new life there."

***

Jerusha kept busy the rest of the day packing. Exhausted, she looked out the window at the garden terrace. The plants flourished again after the rain. One drink and they sprang back to life. The full moon rose in the distance, and she remembered Timon's words when he traveled with the widows. *When you see the moon first come up, remember I am thinking of you.*

"I am thinking of you, too, Timon." Her words drifted across the garden.

A lone purple butterfly fluttered to the wall. "Carry my love to him, little butterfly." It disappeared in the darkness. She breathed deeply the fragrant blossoms and exhaled. Her shoulders relaxed, and she swayed back and forth. A new melody formed in her mind, perfect for Solomon's love song. She hummed the tune. "May he kiss me with the kisses of his mouth; your love is better than wine." *Dance with me.* She extended her arms and twirled, then swayed to the melody in her mind. She paused and gazed out the window into the night. *I love you Timon.*

She turned away from the window, certain he stood in the room with her, stirring the brazier like he did every night before they crawled into bed. She dipped her head to the side, grabbed the tongs from the wall, and stirred the orange coals. Samuel and Stephen slept on their pallets. She chuckled at Stephen's snort as he rolled onto his side.

A light rap at the door disturbed her solitude. She clicked the lock, cracked the door open, and peeked out.

"Father, what are you doing up this late?"

"Get your cloak. You have a visitor waiting in the courtyard." She grabbed her cloak from the hook behind the door.

"Who is it?" she asked as they walked down the hall.

"A young slave girl. She won't talk to anyone but you. She has a baby."

"Another orphan?" Without Timon's help, she wasn't sure she could handle another orphan. Maybe she could send the child to one of the other men assigned to help.

"You and Timon are known in the city for your generosity." Her father looked tired. They rounded the marble column on the veranda and Jerusha's eyes fell on a girl who stood by the fountain, staring into the water. The timid girl raised her eyes and looked at Jerusha. Biting her lip and jiggling the bundle in her arms, she asked, "Are you Jerusha? The woman who takes in orphans."

"My husband and I have helped many orphans and widows."

"I was asked to bring this baby to you. Her mother and father were killed by Herod's soldiers today."

"Why?"

"Because his father guarded Peter, and he escaped. The law is that you receive the same punishment of the criminal who escaped. When they came for him, his wife stepped in front of him and the sword ran through both. Before she died, she begged me to bring the baby to you. She heard you had Gentile sons and wanted you to raise him as your own. She believed her son would be safe with you and taught Yeshua's ways."

"She was a follower of the way?"

"Yes. Her husband, too. He served with your father in Rome's legions. Never told anyone he believed."

"My husband has been arrested." Jerusha's stomach tightened. "I'm not sure he will live to raise another son." Jerusha felt an overwhelming sense of peace as she reached for the child, and pulled back the cloth from his face.

"He smiles at you." The young girl slipped him into Jerusha's waiting arms.

"Hello, Smiley," Jerusha rubbed his chin with her finger. "Your father was a warrior. Your grandfather was a warrior." She thought for a moment. *Joshua Caleb.* She looked up at her father, who leaned against a marble column, then back down at the child. "YHWH calls you Joshua Caleb, a wholehearted warrior that proclaims salvation to the nations." Jerusha's words flowed out like a river, unhindered by her own questions and doubts. *Prophetess, like Hannah.*

"Does that mean you accept him as your son?" The girl's eyes brightened.

Jerusha's thoughts turned to Timon. "As long as you understand he may not have a father to help raise him. We are praying for his release, but," she glanced again at her father, "he will have a grandfather. Of course, he has a heavenly Father as well who knew that you would bring him here tonight." She hoped the child was a sign that Timon would soon be free. She could not raise a son without him.

"May I hold him one last time?" The girl's eyes teared up.

"Of course." Jerusha handed him back. The young girl made clucking noises and kissed his forehead. "She will take good care of you, little one."

"You seem attached to him."

"Sometimes I nursed him for his mother. My baby died at birth last month." Jerusha eyed her for the longest time. Mother to mother.

"Would you want be his mother."

"I could never do that. I have no husband, no means to raise him. He would become a slave like me." She leaned close to the child's face. "We couldn't have you be a slave." She looked back at Jerusha, her eyes rimmed with tears. "My mistress wanted you to be his mother. I would not betray her last request. She was like a mother to me. You are meant to be his mother." She handed the infant back. Jerusha's heart ached for this young girl. If Sarah had not been killed, she would be about her age. She looked like her, big round eyes, and thick eye lashes.

"Would you want to stay and be his wet nurse until he is weaned?" Jerusha waited. The girl stared into the babe's face.

"It would be even more difficult to leave. Watching him call you Ima would tear at my heart. I would have to wean him before that happened." Her eyes never left the child's face.

Jerusha understood the longing to be called Ima. Nursing a child that would not be yours, after losing your own, would be torturous. "You are free to go. Chaya can find another wet nurse." Jerusha felt the woman's longing. "Or you are free to stay for as long as you want. Since your masters are dead, you are no longer bound to slavery."

"That is the only life I have known. I have no where to go." She touched the child. "I will stay and nurse him, if you will let me."

Joshua fussed as he turned his open mouth toward Jerusha's breasts. As much as she wanted to feed him, she handed him to the girl. "Will you feed him? I think he's hungry." She watched as the girl attached him to her breast. He belonged to Jerusha. Her son forever. In time, he would call her Ima. She could allow this girl a few fleeting moments a day to nurse him.

"What is your name?" Jerusha asked.

"Miriam."

"Miriam, tonight you and Joshua can sleep with me. We will be leaving before dawn. You will travel with us." Jerusha's father wrapped an arm around her shoulder. The three walked past the fountain and the white marble pillars. A shofar blew in the distance. A new son. A new day coming. A new confidence in who she was; the mother of nations.

"Miriam, are you a follower of the Way?"

"My masters believed he was the Mashiach. I have many questions."

"I knew him as a child. He played with me in the garden. We chased butterflies together." Jerusha smiled at her father. "He is my friend and my King."

Miriam glanced at Jerusha. "Your face tells me you love him."

"One day soon, you will love him too."

Chapter 35

Jerusha yawned. She held Joshua in a sling tied around her neck. She led Boaz through the cave and looked back at Devorah and the three girls. Their names were Cassia, Helena, and Inez. Jerusha wondered about their Roman and Greek names. Maybe she would learn more about them on the journey. Moses carried a torch, their only light. Their shadows crept along beside them like minions.

"It's so dark," Inez moaned. Jerusha smiled. The young girl reminded her of herself the first time she found her way through Grandfather's secret passage into the villa.

"We will be outside soon. Father will meet us with the wagon."

They wound their way down the narrow passage until they came to the exit. Moses placed the torch in a holder on the wall and rolled open the stone that covered the opening. The fresh morning air rushed in. Boaz snorted, and Jerusha rubbed his nose as she watched Moses help Devorah and the girls duck under the limestone opening. They gathered beneath an olive tree. Jerusha covered Boaz's eyes with her radiyd and coaxed him under the opening and outside. She tied his reins to the tree and helped Devorah and Moses roll the stone back into place.

Cassia's green eyes widened.

"It looks like a burial tomb." Her astonishment brought a smile to Jerusha's face.

"The perfect hiding place. Who would search inside there?" Helena giggled.

The wagon rumbled down the road, the donkey tied to the back. Jacob looked almost majestic on his black stallion. Abigail rode Timon's horse, and Miriam rode beside her. Samuel drove the wagon with Stephen and Joseph bouncing inside holding tight to the side. The donkey, its rope tethered to the back, trailed behind. Their little caravan was quite the spectacle.

Boaz pawed the ground, and Jerusha fed him a handful of grain. She mounted and was careful to keep Joshua snug against her chest. The wagon stopped beside the girls, and Jacob dismounted his stallion.

"Devorah let me help you and the girls into the wagon. We padded it with wool pallets so you all would be more comfortable. Moses and I will cover it so you will not be seen by any soldiers looking to find favor with Herod. Temple guards may be searching this area as well." He bent over, locked his fingers for them to use as a step, and helped Devorah and the three girls into the wagon. Stephen and Joseph climbed over the edge and dropped to the ground.

"Get as comfortable as you can. It will be a bumpy ride. There are piles of fleece to lay your heads on." He waited for them to snuggle down on the thick pallets. "Moses, help me secure this tarp."

He started unrolling a thin flap made of black goat's hair attached at the front of the wagon. Moses hurried to the other side.

"Joseph can ride with you on the donkey," he said as they worked. "Stephen." He looked down at his big round eyes. "You ride with me. We will switch later."

"How long will it take to get to Caesarea?"

It is a two-day journey. We will travel until it's dark, make camp, and leave after a few hours rest. We should arrive in Caesarea by the time the sun rises high in the sky."

Jerusha searched the darkness for movement as they rode northwest on the road to Joppa. Robbers would not catch her unaware again, nor would soldiers looking to gain favor with Herod. Moses hurried the donkey along so they could keep up with Miriam, who was leading the way. The wagon rumbled along behind her, followed by Abigail and Jerusha. Jacob brought up the rear. He wanted to protect them from the rear as well as keep an eye on the small party. Jerusha pulled on Boaz's reins and circled back to join her father.

"How long will it take to get to Corinth from Caesarea?" She was worried about Timon and if they would make it in time. If not, she was putting her children in danger for nothing.

"It depends on the weather. If there are good winds and no storms, it might take ten or twelve days. It could also take weeks. We will pray for fair weather and good wind."

"Will you be able to get Timon released?" she asked, her eyes searching the hillside.

"I'm not sure." He leaned forward and patted his horse's neck. She glanced at him, his expression sober.

"What are you thinking?"

"If I can get him released, he won't be able to come back to Jerusalem. That's one of the reasons I let you bring the boys. Are you prepared to leave Jerusalem?"

She looked at Stephen, whose head lay on her father's back. Her father held tight to his hands so he would not fall off. She looked at Samuel, who was driving the wagon. He was growing up so fast. She looked down at Joshua, the son with the perpetual smile. She sighed. All she had ever wanted was Timon and a family living safely outside of Jerusalem. She thought of Devorah and the girls bouncing in the wagon. Miriam was chatting with her mother. Even in the moonlight, she could see a smile in the young girl's eyes.

"I thought that is what I wanted, but now I am not so sure. Devorah says there are many more young girls being abused and used as sex slaves. Something is stirring in my heart. As much as I want my family together in a safe place, I long to help the other girls in Jerusalem. I want them to know their worth is in being YHWH's daughter, not what they can give to a man. Being a royal daughter is what gives them worth. Like you taught me. Never forget who you are."

He smiled. "I see you have grasped the truth. It is not about you. Never forget the One who made His abode in you. Through Him His Father makes you his royal daughter and gives you authority to spread His kingdom on earth, starting with Jerusalem."

Jerusha thought about his words and glanced again at all her children. Her sons were Hebrew, Egyptian, and Roman, all one royal bloodline in Yeshua. Sons come from afar. She looked at Miriam. Would she become a daughter like Sarah? She certainly needed to be nursed in Yeshua's ways.

"As Timon has told me numerous times, our lives are in Yeshua's hands. His timing in all things is perfect. Wherever and whenever He leads, I will follow. Timon would agree."

Stephen moaned as her father pulled him around in front of him and faced him toward his chest. With one hand on Stephen's back, he took the reins and grinned at Jerusha.

"My daughter has become a wise woman." He kneed the black stallion and galloped to catch up with the wagon. The sun cast a fuchsia glow across the horizon.

"Come on, Boaz, let's catch him." She kneed his flanks. He reared a little, neighed, and took off. Her radiyd slipped from her head, and the cool breeze blew through her hair as she galloped and reined in beside her father and Stephen.

"A wise daughter learns from a wise father."

"My father teaches me." Stephen looked up at his grandfather. Then lay his head back on his chest and closed his eyes, his head bumping to the horse's rhythmic trot.

"He sure does." Jacob glanced at Jerusha. He was somber, and that troubled her.

Several hours later, the sun had risen high overhead. The animals glistened with sweat, and Stephen had asked numerous times when they could stop. Abigail and Miriam had circled around and rode beside Jerusha and Jacob. Though her hair was wet with sweat and clinging to her face, Abigail was as beautiful as ever. Jacob eyed her, his love apparent to Jerusha.

"Abigail, you are a distraction. Searching the dry countryside does not compare with looking at your beauty," he teased. "Maybe you should ride ahead of me." His smile spoke of his adoration. Watching her parents made Jerusha envious for Timon's presence.

"When can we stop?" Stephen held his hand between his legs and wiggled. Jerusha knew what that meant.

"Father, I think we better find a stopping place, or you will have a wet spot on your tunic."

He laughed. "Samuel, stop at that grove of olive trees up ahead. We have gone far enough that it will be safe to remove the tarp from the wagon. I am sure they are ready to get out and stretch their legs."

***

It had been a long day. They had traveled past Joppa. Only a few more hours before they reached Caesarea. The sky was clear, and the moon watched over them from above. Jerusha stood under an olive tree, Joshua fast asleep in her arms. The others slept around the campfire or in the wagon. Jerusha could not sleep. How could she sleep, not knowing if Timon were alive or dead? A branch snapped behind her. She spun around, fearing the worst. It was Devorah.

"I couldn't sleep, either. May I join you?" Jerusha shrugged. The woman showed up at the most inconvenient times.

"I guess." Jerusha hurt for Devorah and what she lived through, but sharing her heart with her about Timon would not happen. She remembered how she looked at him when they first met.

"Do you remember the first time we met?" Devorah stepped closer. Jerusha nodded. That was not a topic she cared to discuss.

"I envied your relationship with Timon. I had never seen that kind of love. He adored you in a way that wasn't just physical. All I had ever seen was lust. I began to search for more. That's when I decided to attend James's secret meetings. I had to know what it was that made Timon so different than Herod and the other men. It was Yeshua. I will forever be grateful for the love I saw between the two of you. It brought me to Yeshua, the One who forgave me. After that, I couldn't respond the same way to forced encounters. I am sorry

Jerusha." Her voice started to quiver. "It's because I could not be what the men wanted me to be any longer that Herod arrested Timon. He wanted revenge. It's my fault your husband is in prison." She crumpled to the ground and wept.

Jerusha was stunned.

Devorah looked up. "And now you risk your life and that of your family for me and my sons."

Jerusha sat next to Devorah and put her arm around her. "It is not your fault. Marcus said he overheard the priests talking. They wanted Timon arrested because the widows and orphans loved and admired him so much. They thought if they arrested him, their food supply would be cut off and they would stop following Yeshua."

"But it was Herod who gave the order, and it was because of me. Had I given him what he wanted, he may have not given the priests what they wanted."

"Devorah, Herod is corrupt, and he wanted the Jews' approval. It's not your fault. The enemy of your soul is tormenting you with this lie. I understand what it's like to blame yourself. I blamed myself when Sarah died. I thought I was cursed."

"Cursed? Why?"

"Because I was barren, and it seemed like everyone who got close to me ended up hurt or dead. In the past, I would have blamed myself for Timon's arrest, too, because I thought I was cursed. Now I know I am blessed, a royal daughter loved unconditionally. Grandfather says it is written that YHWH's ways are not our ways. I take authority over this lie that tells you that you are to blame for Timon's arrest and bind it in Yeshua's name." She lifted Devorah's chin and looked into her eyes. "Believe the truth, Devorah, that you are now a royal daughter. There is no condemnation or blame in YHWH's kingdom." She held her in her arms and stared into the darkness.

Timon would be pleased.

Chapter 36

Jerusha had only been asleep for a few hours when her father woke her. Thankfully, Joshua had slept, cuddled next to her stomach. She rolled over on her back and stared at the stars. She found Regulus in the constellations and wondered if her grandfather looked at the same star. He would be glad she was being kind to Devorah. She groaned as she stood and stretched. Her bones ached. It had been awhile since she had slept on something as hard as the ground. She shook her head. How did her mother and father do it at their age? She hoped she had that kind of stamina when she grew older.

She checked on Joshua again. He slept soundly. The lamb and lentil stew smelled wonderful. She hadn't eaten much over the past few days. Something about resolving her differences with Devorah had awakened her appetite. She joined the others around the campfire. Samuel ladled stew into a bowl and handed it to her.

"Thank you, Samuel." She looked up at his face. In the light of the campfire, she thought she saw a little fuzz around his cheekbone.

Surely not! He is so young. He had a few more years before he grew a beard and became a man.

Stephen gave her a piece of bread. "We let you sleep while we prepared the meal with Grandmother." A smile spread across his face.

"You honor your mother like the Torah commands." Her father came up behind Stephen and ruffed up his hair.

Jerusha dipped a piece of bread in the stew and was about to eat when Joshua started fussing. She rose and picked him up. His open mouth rubbed against her breast. She still longed to nurse. Nothing would fill that void.

She looked at Devorah and remembered their late night talk. Bringing comfort to those who are hungry for love came close, though. Joshua began to whimper.

"Miriam, after you eat, would you mind feeding him?"

"Of course."

Jerusha jiggled him and walked around.

"YHWH says, 'Be still and know that I am God.' Shhh. Peace, be still. 'Man will not live by bread alone, but by every word that proceeds from the mouth of God.'" Joshua began to settle down.

"Look," she showed him to her mother, "He's smiling."

"Are you sure that is not gas?" She chuckled.

Jerusha nestled him close and then held him out and looked at his eyes.

"Oh, no, that is the joy of the Lord." She bounced him in rhythm to her words. "This is the day the Lord has made. I will rejoice and be glad in it." She kissed his cheek and handed him to Miriam. Her stomach growled as she picked up the bowl and moved to the fire. She took a seat beside Inez.

"Girls, tell me about yourselves." Jerusha dipped her bread. "How did you come to be slaves in Herod's palace?" She took a bite, closed her eyes, and savored it. Mmmm. So good.

"We all came with a trader's caravan." Cassia spoke first. "Each of us were sold by our father for food and then sold to Herod." She kept her head down as she spoke, avoiding Jerusha's eyes.

At first Jerusha thought she lied. Then she remembered how shamed she felt when she thought her father had abandoned her. How hard it was to hold her shoulders back, chin up, and look others in the eye. Only when her anger flared up could she stand tall and straight.

Anger had been a tool of survival. It took a long time to rid herself of that defense. It still erupted during vulnerable times. Even at YHWH or Yeshua when she thought she had been betrayed. In recent days, since going to Shiloh, she trusted His love and His ways.

"Were you angry with your fathers?" She took another swipe in the stew with her bread and took another bite.

"I was." Inez's face turned red, clenching her jaw. "I hate him," she snapped.

"I understand." Jerusha looked at her father's eyes. The pain she'd seen in the past was gone. She only saw a peace that radiated contentment. Yeshua had healed it. She was thankful. "I thought my father abandoned me. At the time, anger is what kept me going. I eventually had to forgive and let it go."

Inez mumbled, her eyes focused on the ground. "I cannot forgive."

"Not in your own power." Jerusha stopped eating and lifted Inez's chin. "With Yeshua all things are possible and for your own sake, you need to forgive him."

"I do not want to forgive." Inez jerked her chin away.

Yeshua help her.

"I understood why my father sold me." Helena interrupted. "If he didn't, the whole family would starve. I wondered, why me? Why not my brother or sister? What was wrong with me that he chose me?" Her shoulders shook and she held her face in her hands, the sobs continuing for several minutes.

"Nothing is wrong with you. You are like Yeshua." Jerusha stood, moved to her side and placed her hand on her shoulder. "He could have asked the same question." Jerusha sat crossed legged next to her.

"Why would he ask that question?" Helena dried her eyes.

"He may have wondered why he had to be the one to die so we can live forever with YHWH, His Father.

"Like I had to be sold for my brothers and sisters so they could live and not die of starvation."

"That's a good analogy. And yet, YHWH loved His son, even though He let Him die for us."

"Do you think my father loved me, even though he sold me?"

"He thought he had to choose one to be sold, for all to live. That would have been a hard decision. Whether he loved you or not, YHWH loved you and gave His son for you. That is how valuable you are to him."

"Do you really think He loves me after what I have done with the men in Herod's palace?"

"I know He does. He arranged to get you out of there, and He wants you to enter into his kingdom."

"How do I get into his kingdom?"

"By faith. Believe and you will be saved."

"I believe," Cassia stood up. "I believe, too." Inez looked into Jerusha's eyes. "And I want to forgive."

"I believe, too." Helena stood up.

Jerusha looked at each girl, her heart full and filled with wonder. She glanced at Devorah and her mother and father. No one had a dry eye.

"I believe, too." Miriam stood across from Jerusha with Joshua nursing on her breast. Jerusha felt like singing and dancing. Yeshua said the angels rejoice when one comes into his kingdom. At that moment, she jumped up and twirled around.

"I am dancing with the angels. All heaven is rejoicing now about your decision."

***

"Father, what is that noise?" Jerusha rode beside Jacob through the streets of Caesarea. Jacob led the small caravan down the street. The roar of a cheering crowd echoed off of the buildings.

Caesarea was markedly different than Jerusalem. The architecture was heavily influenced by the Romans. There were even elaborate public bathhouses. They rode past the hippodrome, similar in structure to the one in Jerusalem. This one was larger, more decorative. They were surrounded by beautiful architecture but none as beautiful as the temple in Jerusalem.

Jacob paused at the amphitheater. Roman soldiers, who stood under the arched entrance, laughed and pointed. Jerusha watched them, anger in her eyes. She would have liked to tell them what she thought of their Rome, and their Caesar. She gritted her teeth and forced herself to look away.

"Where are all the people?" She twisted on her horse, baby Joshua in her arms, and glanced around. The few people she saw, besides the Roman soldiers, were Greeks dressed in flowing robes with ornamental clasps at the shoulders. A couple of Roman officials entered the amphitheater wearing togas.

"What is going on?" She halted Boaz and watched as her father dismounted and talked with the Roman soldier at the theater entrance.

"Today is the quinquennial games in honor of Caesar." The soldier's eyes darted between Jerusha and Jacob. "Your King Herod makes himself a god, in his shining silver garment. The people cheer him as he gives his oratory." His stare made Jerusha uncomfortable, and she turned her head.

"More than a man. You are a god." The crowd cheered in unison. "More than a man. You are a god. You are a god. You are a god." The adulation continued and increased in volume. It sickened Jerusha's stomach. Joshua's cries indicated his agreement. Gently, she bounced him up and down, patted his back, and tried to comfort him. Stephen held his hands over his ears.

Suddenly, an unnerving silence fell upon the crowd. Joshua's whimper the only sound. The soldier Jacob had been talking to ran inside the amphitheater. Jacob mounted his horse and motioned for them to turn around. Moses had just gotten the wagon turned when a small unit of soldiers rushed out. Four of the soldiers carried Herod on a stretcher. The others surrounded him for protection.

As the soldiers ran past, Jerusha heard one of them say, "I heard him say the owl that landed on a rope above his head was an ill omen for allowing the people to call him a god."

Another soldier answered. "After that, a severe pain struck his belly, and he crumpled. He's dying. We must get him to the palace."

Good. That is what that pig gets for arresting my husband for nothing. Jerusha refrained from speaking aloud her angry thoughts. She had been so consumed with getting Timon released and keeping Devorah and the girls safe that she had not acknowledged her feelings about

Herod. What she had just witnessed revealed her hate for the man. She glanced at her sons. She could not allow Samuel and Stephen to be poisoned by her bitterness. They were likely thinking the same thing, but she would not encourage them. *Love you enemies. Do good to those who persecute you.* She closed her eyes and took a deep breath. *Only by your power Yeshua.* She released the air slowly. *Your ways are not my ways. Take the bitterness from me.*

They rode in silence until Jacob stopped them at an elaborate Roman villa.

A woman standing at the gate greeted them. "Shalom, Jacob. Welcome to the house of Cornelius. I didn't recognize you at first, with a beard and dressed in Hebrew garments. But I could never forget those eyes." She looked at Jerusha." "Is this your daughter? She has the same eyes."

"Yes, this is my Jerusha. The babe is her son, Joshua." He pointed at Samuel and Stephen. "Those two are her other sons. The older one is Samuel. The younger one, Stephen." He smiled at Abigail. "And this is my beautiful wife, Abigail." His smile spread wide. "The other boys are orphans who live with us. The taller one is Moses. The shorter one, Joseph. He is deaf. Miriam is Jerusha's wet nurse. As you can see, the baby is not Hebrew. He is Roman. Stephen is a Gentile son as well."

The woman smiled softly. "Welcome to you all. I am Floriana." She turned to Jacob. "When my husband called for Peter to come to our villa, I thought he had lost his mind. What Hebrew would set foot in our house? However, YHWH had other plans. You spoke to Cornelius many times, and it bore fruit. I am grateful he served with you Jacob. Our whole household believed, because you served as a Roman legionary." She looked at Abigail and Jerusha. "Thank you for the sacrifice you made as well. Living without a husband and father. I can never repay you."

Jerusha did not know what to say. She bowed her head slightly and nodded.

"Who are these young ladies?" Floriana asked.

"Those young ladies are looking for a new beginning. Devorah, Inez, Cassia, and Helena." He pointed to each one in order.

Jacob dismounted, and laid his hands on Floriana's shoulders. Tears filled his eyes

"Floriana, Cornelius died a brave man. He was full of YHWH's spirit, a glow on his face." He wiped a single tear from her cheek. "We will miss his presence, but his impact on YHWH's kingdom continues. Your face shines brighter today than ever."

"At first bitterness threatened to steal my peace. I hated Herod for what he did." She rubbed her eyes with the back of her fists, and looked up. "Then Yeshua took it away. My heart found His peace."

"Before we came here, we were at the amphitheater. The crowd cheered for Herod and called him a god. He was struck down and is in the palace dying."

"My husband would be grieved that he allowed pride and man's approval to destroy his life. He spent many long nights talking with him about Yeshua." Her gaze fell to the ground. "He would not listen to Cornelius."

"Wide is the gate to destruction. Narrow is the way to life."

While listening to their conversation, the bitterness in Jerusha's heart faded. Replacing it was sadness, because Herod died without knowing Yeshua's way. It overpowered her hatred of him. Whether Timon lived or died, he reigned with Yeshua in his kingdom. The same could not be said of Herod. *Thank you, Yeshua, that Timon belongs to you.*

Floriana motioned for everyone to come inside the gate. Abigail dismounted and took Joshua while Jacob helped Jerusha dismount. Jerusha stretched her arms and shoulders before taking Joshua back. He needed to be fed and nuzzled her breasts. Miriam also dismounted and came to her side. She slipped Joshua into her arms. Her father and Samuel helped Devorah, Inez, Cassia, and Helena out of the wagon. Moses helped Joseph off the donkey. Servants rushed to take the horses, wagon, and donkey to the stable.

They followed Floriana into a lush garden filled with flowering hibiscus, rose of Sharon, fig, olive, and myrtle trees. Grape vines covered the back wall and marble columns of the portico. Servants scurried to get bowls of water and set them in a row below a mosaic bench.

Jerusha waited for the servant to wash the feet of her mother. When they were finished, she sat down. The cool water on her feet felt so refreshing. One slave motioned for Devorah to sit.

Devorah sat down awkwardly. "Are we to have our feet washed, too?"

"I see you are not accustomed to being served." Jerusha smiled. "I was the same way when I came out of captivity. Relax. You are their guests. They serve you with pleasure."

Miriam, Inez, Cassia, and Helena took in their surroundings, whispering and pointing at the ornate structures. Jerusha encouraged them to be seated, too.

"It is uncomfortable to be served when all you know is to serve." Jerusha grinned at the girl's delight as the servant poured water over their feet. Inez kept reaching down and trying to help them.

"Relax, Inez. They know what to do. Enjoy."

Despite the pleasure of being treated so well, Devorah appeared anxious. "Jacob, when can I look for my sons? I cannot enjoy these surroundings knowing they may be suffering or dead. I must find out what has happened to them."

"I will leave immediately to look for them." Jacob answered. "Is Antonius in the palace?" he asked Floriana.

"Yes, he was at Phillip's meeting last night."

"Who is Antonius, Father?" Jerusha asked.

"A Roman legionary who served with me and loves Yeshua. He may be able to help find Micah and Elias." He exited the gate and looked back. "Pray that all goes well."

"Father, will you be safe going into Herod's palace?" Jerusha feared he would not return.

"Do not worry. I have connections here." The gate clanged shut.

Chapter 37

After Jacob left, Floriana showed them to their rooms. Pitchers of water awaited them so they could wash their faces and hands before going to eat in the dining hall.

"This villa is beautiful," Jerusha spoke to her mother as she laid Joshua on the mittah in their room. His cries grew louder. She picked him up and laid him in Miriam's arms, who would be sleeping in the room with her. She glanced out the latticed window at the garden. "It is laid out much like our villa."

"It's Roman architecture." Abigail's eyes narrowed. "Your father never talked about his father's Roman connections and why we lived in a Roman-styed villa, the largest in the upper city. Maybe sometime we can ask him about it."

Jerusha heard scuffles in the next room. The boys would need her father's oversight. It was a good thing they slept with him. Waiting around with nothing to do would not be good for her sons. Their active minds and hands needed something to do. She could not help but worry whether her father would return. She had experienced so much loss already; she could not bear to lose her father too. She took Joshua from Miriam's hands and smiled at his contented face. Gazing at the small boy and feeling her love for him helped her to deal with her fears.

After everyone had the opportunity to wash up, they were summoned to dinner. As they strolled into the dining hall, Jerusha admired the decorative arch over the entrance. Samuel and the other boys sat together on a bench at the table, their grins broad and mischievous. It would be difficult to raise three sons without a father. Surely, YHWH would see that Timon was released.

When everyone had finished eating, Jerusha decided it would be good to take her sons, who were full of energy, out for a while. "Floriana, would you give me directions to the wharf? My sons are restless, and I need to stretch my legs."

"If you do not mind, I would like to go with you. It is not far. There is much to see." Floriana poured water over her hands from a pitcher, then dried them on the linen cloth on the table.

"Would you mind if we went, too?" Devorah waved her hand at the three girls sitting on a bench.

""C-c-could we go?" Moses and Joseph looked up from the table.

Jerusha looked over her shoulder at Miriam, who trailed behind her and mother. "You want to go too?"

She nodded shyly. "Maybe Joshua will get hungry again."

Jerusha could not blame them for wanting to see the ships. Like her, none of them had ever been to the sea. Though they had only been with Floriana for a short time, Devorah and the girls had decided to stay in Caesarea with her while the rest of them sailed to Corinth. The outing would be good for everyone. *These friends might not see each other again.*

Every eye was on her, awaiting her decision. "All right. We all go." Jerusha laughed at their instant chatter. If you are finished eating, get your cloaks. The sun will be setting by the time we get there. I hear the breeze off the water is much cooler."

"I will get Stephen's cloak, Ima." Samuel jumped and ran down the portico.

"He tries so hard to please." She smiled at Floriana. "Thank you. We all need this."

On their way to the wharf, Floriana pointed out the temple, built by Herod, seated on a hill to their right.

"It was dedicated to the goddess Roma and god-king Augustus." Jerusha shielded her eyes against the sun's rays that glistened off the white marble pillars. She hated how it sat high on a foundation overlooking the port. "You are not my god. Nor do I look to you for protection." Jerusha's anger flared. "Rome's idol in the capital of Judea is an abomination."

"You are much like your father." Floriana grinned. Abigail nodded in agreement.

"For not being with him half her life, she is very much like him. Determined. Opinionated. Strong minded. But also tender and kind. She never gives up on those she loves." Her mother hugged her shoulder.

"This Augustus cult is dangerous," Florina continued. "It is spreading Imperial worship across the eastern empire." She shook her fist in the air. "More and more we are not allowed to worship Yeshua. We are being forced to worship this Roma goddess or be killed. In the past, they left us alone to worship how we wanted. Herod is responsible for this."

"Yeshua warned of this persecution." Jerusha's stomach tightened. "Boys, stay close. Do not run too far ahead. There are too many people. I want to be able to see you."

They made it to the wharf, and everyone stared with amazement at the throngs of people and ships. They saw women disembarking from the ships, many wearing flowing robes made of colorful silk wrapped around their bodies and clasped at the shoulder with golden clasps. They were very different from the simple garments most wore in Jerusalem. Jerusha looked down at her linen robe and brushed the dust from her cloak. Numerous Roman soldiers roamed the streets and wharf, many more than in Jerusalem. Some eyed her as they past with a look that made her skin crawl.

"Devorah, you are very quiet. Thinking of your sons?" Jerusha stretched her neck to see between the heads of the women ahead. She smiled at Samuel, who stood and gawked at them as they past.

"I feel so guilty about what happened to them." Devorah tightened her radiyd as a soldier past and looked away from him. "I keep wondering if there were things I could have done to stop it."

"Do not torment yourself with such thoughts. That is a tactic of our enemy." Jerusha looked ahead at the pier. The water lapped against the ships tied to the pier. Servants loaded barrels and crates onto ships. The hustle and bustle intrigued Stephen, who held Samuel's hand and stared, his mouth open.

"Mother, would you help keep an eye on Stephen and the other boys?" Ask Inez, Cassia, and Helena to help too. I need some time alone."

"There is a bench at the end on the dock. Just walk straight ahead. I will stay with your mother and help watch your sons," Floriana offered.

"Are you sure?" Jerusha felt some guilt leaving them.

"Go. Go." Floriana flapped her hands.

"I know what it is like to miss your husband." Abigail gave her a hug. "Now go."

"Thank you." Jerusha's brisk walk to the end of the dock got her heart pumping. She needed that. Not enough exercise these past few days. She breathed deeply and let her heartbeat calm, then sat on the bench.

The still waters reflected the orange glow of the setting sun. The moon, already visible, shone its glory over the rising waters. It was called a tide, according to Floriana. Jerusha had never seen so much water. She had not even seen the Sea of Galilee, much less the Mediterranean Sea.

The deep blue waters extended as far as the eye could see. She closed her eyes and let the salty mist blow in her face. She hoped Timon was not locked away in a dark cell unable to enjoy the beauty of the moon, a constant reminder of their love. She envisioned his arms around her in the moonlit garden back home. *Timon, my love. What would I do without you? What would your sons do?*

"Ima, look." Stephen interrupted her solitude and pointed to a ship tied to the pier. "Are we going to ride on one of those?" His big, dark eyes widened in awe of a small, but impressive ship.

"That is Roman warship. You will sail on a merchant ship like that one." Floriana pointed to a large ship being loaded with barrels and large crates. "The warship is lighter weight and travels much faster." She took his hand and led him back up the wharf, then glanced over her shoulder. "I'm sorry for the interruption." She picked up Stephen and pointed at some sailors furling the sail.

So many new sights. The trip was a grand adventure for them all. She prayed it would be a safe one. She sighed and looked out over the blue waters.

"Are you thinking of Aba?" Samuel came around the end of the bench and sat next to her.

"She wrapped one arm around his shoulders. "Yes. Are you?" She sensed his concern.

He dropped his head, fiddled with his fingers, and then chewed his fingernails.

"When I was separated from my father as a little girl, I never gave up thinking I would see him again, even when everyone thought he was dead. I believe we will see your father again." She removed her arm and cupped his chin in her palm. "Do not give up hope, and try not to chew your nails.

"I pray for him every night." He held his hands in his lap and looked out to sea.

"Me, too. We better head back." She stood and as she turned, she saw Inez with a man. "Why is she talking to a stranger? Inez! "Jerusha tried to get her attention.

"I'll get her." Samuel ran between the people up the wharf.

Jerusha followed at a quickened pace. "Inez!" She called again peaking between the heads of two soldiers. They turned and glared.

By the time she reached her, Samuel, Floriana and her mother stood beside the man.

"Inez, why are you talking to a stranger, a man no less?" Jerusha's words came out sharper than she intended. Inez looked at her, her face covered with tears.

"He loves me, Jerusha."

"What?"

"This man is my father." She grabbed the man's hand. "I found my father, Jerusha.. He loves me just like you said. He's been looking for me. He regrets what he did and asked me to forgive him. I found my father, just like you." Tears streamed down her face,

Jerusha looked at Floriana, who shrugged, obviously bewildered. Jerusha eyed the man, who kept his eyes on Inez, a single tear on each cheek. For Inez's sake, Jerusha hoped he meant it. She would hate to see him take her back, only to sell her again. If they had more time together before going back to him, the truth would be revealed.

"Would it be all right to invite him to your villa?" Jerusha whispered in Floriana's ear.

She nodded approval.

"Inez, that's wonderful." Jerusha looked at Inez's father. "Do you live in Caesarea?"

"No. I just came in on that ship." He pointed behind him. "I had heard Inez lived in Judea and came searching for her. Our family lives in Ephesus."

"Floriana offers her hospitality, if you care to stay with us at her villa for the night." Jerusha examined his facial expressions for any sign of evil intent. One night to discern his intentions may not be enough. *Yeshua reveal the truth. Don't let Inez get pulled into another dangerous situation. If his intentions are not good, show us, show her, before it's too late.*

"I accept your invitation." He took Inez's hand. "I want to hear how you fared these last years."

Inez dropped her eyes and shrugged. Jerusha recognized the cloak of shame. Telling her father about her life in Herod's palace would be difficult.

***

Jerusha watched Inez laugh uncontrollably as her father told story after story of his escapades with people who traded with him on his journeys across the east. The lamps in the courtyard cast bouncing shadows on the grapevine covered wall.

"Every place I went, I asked if anyone had met a young lady named Inez." He tapped Inez's nose and placed a piece of bread in his mouth, then sobered. "After you had left, I locked the pain away behind a thick wall." He swallowed. "Until one day I met a giant of a man, who traveled with another caravan." Jerusha's heart jumped. *Grandfather?* He carried himself like a Roman soldier, but the look in his eyes spoke of something or someone else. Yeshua. Have you heard of him?" He looked around the courtyard.

"Many in Judea have met him. He was born in Bethlehem. Died a horrible death on a cross and was resurrected." He glanced around, face to face. "I can see you have met him. You have the same love in your eyes." He took a drink from the goblet. "I was a drunkard. I drank away the pain of selling my own daughter. What decent father could do such a thing? Yogli listened." Jerusha gasped.

"Grandfather." Jerusha looked at her mother. "It was Grandfather." Stunned, Abigail blinked and sat down.

"I called him a gentle giant. Meeting him changed my life. He convinced me Yeshua had died for me. Can you imagine a perfect man, Son of God, dying for my sin? That's when I started my search for Inez. Yogli said he had searched for his son, too, and found him. It gave me hope."

"Oh, Father, I, too, have found forgiveness for my sin." Inez flung her arms around his neck and kissed his cheek.

Jerusha blinked back tears. Their warm talk reminded her that her father had not returned, and it was late. He should have been back. The familiar fear of abandonment knotted her stomach. She thought she had conquered it, but it still had a hold on her.

"If you will excuse me, I need to put Joshua down. It has been a long day for him. Samuel and Stephen, go to your room and obey Moses until Father gets back. Moses, take Joseph. He fell asleep under the olive tree over by the wall." She stood and bowed to Inez's father.

"I am so pleased you met my grandfather and he introduced you to Yeshua." She hugged Inez to her side. "And I am so happy for you that you have at last discovered that your father loves you."

"Do you think your father has found my sons?" Devorah touched her arm. Jerusha sighed. "I don't know. I hope he will be back soon." She wouldn't add to Devorah's fears by revealing her own fear that he may not come back at all.

Chapter 38

Jerusha heard a light tap on her door. She tried to ignore it. Her concern about her father was too raw and unnerving to deal with anyone else. She wanted to scream, *Go away*. Moses's maturity, at twenty years, could handle Samuel and Stephen for a few hours. He would come only if necessary. Samuel admired Moses and wanted to please him. He rarely caused him trouble. If Samuel behaved, Stephen behaved. The light tap came again. She sighed.

She cracked the door open. It was Cassia and Helena.

Cassia shuffled her feet. Helena kept her head down. "May we talk to you?" Cassia's voice quivered.

Jerusha widened the opening and stepped back. "Come in." She tried to smile. Probably not too convincing. "Sit over there at the table." She cleared her throat. "What is this about?"

"Are we cursed?" Cassia's words surprised Jerusha.

"Why do you ask that?" Jerusha remembered that feeling and could not imagine why they felt that way.

"What have we done wrong that Yeshua does not give us back our fathers like he did for Inez and you?" Helena placed her face in her hands and tried to stop the muffled sobs. Cassia sniffed and rubbed her red nose.

Jerusha tipped her head. She remembered all too well how the two girls felt. *That old, "what's wrong with me?" lie again. What have I done, that I am not blessed like others.* "Lies and doubt." She mumbled to herself. Seeing the enemy use that tactic on someone else awakened the lioness within her. A roar rumbled within her belly. Enough.

"That is a lie." Her words boomed. "From the author of lies. There is nothing wrong with you. The truth is that you are royal daughters of YHWH. He gave His Son's life to buy you back to Himself." She paced back and forth. "He has wonderful plans for your life. Do not let the enemy tell you otherwise." She paused, caught her breath and continued. "When you come through, to the other side of this pain—" she took their hands "—you will speak to that lie in someone else, someone who needs to hear the truth." She looked deep in their eyes.

"You are accepted and loved. Whenever you hear otherwise, speak the truth to that lie, out loud, and tell it to go. Don't listen to it."

"What is the truth?" Cassia mumbled.

"The truth is you have a heavenly Father who will never leave you or forsake you. Trust His plans and when life doesn't go the way you want, rejoice anyway like Habakkuk the prophet.

"Haba who?" Helena asked puzzled. Jerusha forgot the girls were not Hebrew and had not been taught the words of the prophets.

"Habakkuk was a Hebrew prophet, a man who spoke for YHWH. He wrote, 'though the fig tree should not blossom and there be no fruit on the vines, though the yield of the olive should fail, and the field produce no food, and there be no cattle in the stalls—'" she hesitated, "'—and my father never returns.'" she grinned. "What does Habakkuk say to do when these things happen?"

"I don't know." Cassia's eyes questioned. "What do we do?"

"Even though these things happen, Habakkuk says, 'yet, I will exult in the Lord. I will rejoice in the God of my salvation. The Lord is my strength, and He has made my feet like hinds' feet, and makes me walk on my high places.'"

Jerusha took their hands and pulled. "Stand up. Now twirl around and delight in your heavenly Father who loves you and will never forsake you." She extended her arms and twirled around. "Turn that mourning into dancing." She twirled again. They looked at her, obviously not yet convinced.

"Dance and rejoice when things don't go the way we want? I guess I can try it." Helena extended her arms and spun around once. "I rejoice in you, YHWH, Father God," then again, "I rejoice in you're love for me," and again. "I rejoice that you will never forsake me." She started to giggle. Cassia watched. "That seems backwards to how I feel."

"God's ways are not our ways." Jerusha twirled again and looked at her. Cassia slowly extended her arms and turned around. "I rejoice in you, YHWH Father." She spoke, her words slow and steady. "I rejoice in your love. I rejoice that you will not forsake me." They all stopped and looked at each other.

Jerusha felt the joy in her belly bubble up, and she started laughing. Cassia and Helena stared as she laughed. Then Helena started laughing, and Cassia joined in the merriment. Jerusha hugged them both.

"The joy of the Lord is our strength. The old proverb says, laughter does good like medicine. I am so glad you shared with me tonight. You will never know how much I needed this." Jerusha opened the door to let them out.

To her surprise, her father stood outside, his knuckles raised and ready to tap the door.

"Father!" She threw her arms around him. "I was so worried when you didn't come."

"It didn't sound like you were worried." His grin spread wide.

"Did you get Devorah's sons back?"

"Yes. They are with her now. They need YHWH's healing in more than one way. In time, as they get to know His love, the wounds will heal."

"Maybe we can share with them what our heavenly Father is teaching us." Cassia looked at Helena. "We should pray about that."

"The change in you girls from the moment you walked in my door until now is a miracle." Jerusha hugged them.

"We leave tomorrow." Jacob's abrupt change of subject startled Jerusha. "That's why I am so late. I bought supplies and passage on a ship. We leave at sunup. I did not buy passage for Devorah and her sons." He looked at Cassia and Helena. "Or for you girls or Joseph. There was not room on the ship for everyone. I had to choose who went."

"YHWH is working because Devorah, Cassia, and I have decided to stay with Floriana. Inez will be leaving with her father." Helena beamed.

"Her father?" Jacob's puzzled look tickled Jerusha.

"He came looking for her." Cassia's eyes showed acceptance and even joy for Inez. She smiled and nodded.

"He met Grandfather. "Jerusha added. "Oh, there is much to tell you." She hugged him again.

"We are happy for you, Jerusha. Our heavenly Father has not forsaken us. We are his royal daughters." Cassia eyes shined.

Yeshua, the Lion of the tribe of Judah, dwells within us." Helena added.

"That revelation came from heaven." Jacob eyed Jerusha. "Never forget who you are."

"Royal daughters." Jerusha and both girls spoke at the same time. Their eyes grew big, and they started laughing. All the way down the hall, Helena and Cassia chuckled.

Jacob held Jerusha in his arms for a long time. Snuggled against his chest, his heartbeat in her ear, she felt safe and secure.

"Do you think Timon is still alive?" She looked up.

"If he is alive, we will find him." He pinched her chin. "Get some sleep. You will need it. It's a long journey to Corinth."

Jerusha closed the door, stood at the mittah and stared at Joshua. Freed from the swaddling cloths, he stretched and kicked his legs and cooed. "Smiley, in a few weeks you will meet your father." She scooped him up, cuddled him close, and wrapped her cloak around him. She walked to the latticed window, opened it, and gazed into the night.

The moon had moved high overhead. A slight wind rustled the pomegranate bushes, and one lone butterfly fluttered to the window and landed on the ledge. A sign from heaven. Butterflies never flew at night. She watched it open and close its purple wings.

You don't look like you know where you are going, but you always get to YHWH's appointed destination. "Stay alive, Timon. We are on our way." She prayed the wind carried her whispered words across the sea to Corinth. "YHWH, take care of him until we can find him."

***

"Who is he?" Jerusha whispered in her father's ear. The man was tall and stood next to her father. He was outfitted in armor, a red cloak attached at shoulders, the red plume on his helmet waving in the wind. His square jaw and high cheekbones reminded her of Timon. The scowl on his face, however, was nothing like her husband. He stared straight ahead, hands at his sides.

"Antonius, this is my daughter." Her father slapped him on the back. "He will be traveling with us."

Jerusha eyed him out of the corner of her eye. Why would father bring a Roman soldier with them? She would ask him about that later.

Antonius bowed slightly and nodded. She had never seen anyone with dark blue eyes like his. Blond wavy hair hung below the helmet. Nothing like the Hebrew men she was accustomed to seeing. Her grandfather was the only Hebrew she knew who had blond hair. Many times she had wondered why. Humph. Timon was more handsome, and certainly more amiable. She had no use for a Roman soldier, even if her father liked him.

Everyone stood on the wharf. Florian, Devorah, Joseph, and the girls came to see them off. Jerusha and the others waited in line to load the ship.

"Jerusha, we will miss you." Devorah hugged her and stood back. "You and Timon have done so much for me and my sons. Thank you."

"We will pray every day that you find Timon and he gets released." Cassia looked at Helena and she nodded agreement. Tears rimmed her eyes, and she wiped them away. Jerusha felt tears filling her eyes too.

"Shalom." She kissed their cheeks individually and then grabbed them all in a group hug, "Devorah, you started out my enemy, and I wanted to get rid of you. Now, my dear friend, it is hard to leave you." Her voice quivered. She hugged her one last time. She felt a tap on her shoulder and turned around.

"Joseph." She made sure he saw her mouth. "I will miss you, too. You have grown so much since you came to live with us. Thirteen years old. A man any woman would want to marry." She mouthed the words slowly so he could read her lips.

"I would marry him." Helena piped up. Her cheeks flushed instantly. She was about his age, and Joseph was a handsome young man. Jerusha smiled at the thought of them married. Only Yeshua knew what the future held for all of them.

"Floriana, you have been so kind. I am so sorry about Cornelius. Your willingness to forgive Herod helped drain the bitterness I held against him for arresting Timon. Pray for me and I will pray for you that we continue to love our enemies."

"I feel like I have known you all my life." Floriana embraced her, then her mother. "Shalom, until we meet again."

Jerusha took Joshua from Miram's arms. Jacob took Stephen's hand and motioned for Abigail to walk in front of him, next Jerusha, Miriam, Samuel, and Moses. Antonius, the soldier, was the last to board the ship.

Jerusha smiled at Samuel and Stephen, who gawked at the sailors as they scurried to unfurl the sails. Father had said, "The tide and winds were perfect. YHWH's with us."

The ship started to rock and moved forward. Jerusha wobbled and caught the railing. Jacob grabbed Stephen. Moses held Miriam's hand. Jerusha smiled. *Hmmm. When did those two become so friendly? Why not?* She was only thirteen when she married Timon. Jerusha waved to those on the wharf. The shipped moved faster than she expected, carrying her far away from her homeland.

"Shalom, my friends." Tears ran down her cheeks. If Timon was released, she would not be back. She thought that was what she wanted, yet her heart ached.

Chapter 39

Several days later, Jerusha stood on deck with her eyes on the horizon. She had a queasy stomach and a bucket in hand. Her father never told her about that part of the trip. As far as the eye could see in all directions was nothing but water. The ship creaked and rocked. She had given up wearing her radiyd and braided her hair instead. Whenever she hung her head over the bucket, they both got in the way. She wondered if she would ever eat or drink again. Her head throbbed, and every time she closed her eyes, she felt like she danced with the boat. It reminded her of when she was a child and would twirl around in the garden with her eyes closed, then lay on the ground and look up. The clouds would spin circles over head. What she felt now was worse. Much worse.

"Stand on deck. Keep your eyes forward on the horizon." Her father had given instructions to three of them, her mother, Moses, and her. "In a few days you will get your sea legs."

Thankfully, Miriam avoided this plague and could feed Joshua. Jacob showed Stephen around the ship and introduced him to the pilot and the captain. He had strutted around like the king of the sea. Abigail had found some rest below deck with her bucket nearby. Moses stood on the starboard side of the deck with Miriam. Jerusha smiled now that she knew what starboard meant. She stood on the port side. Her father's teaching of sea language kept her mind off Timon.

"Here." Antonius reached over her shoulder with a wooden mug. "Sip this slowly. It should help your stomach."

Jerusha moved away but then hesitantly reached for the mug. His stoic look never waivered. His white toga whipped in the wind, and he held the red cloak over his arm.

"What is it?" She let the steam drift up in her face and sniffed.

"Ginger tea." He took the cloak and offered it. "Are you cold?"

"No." She tugged on her cloak and pulled it higher around her neck. Even if she was cold, she would not accept anything from him. She turned away. The wind blew into her face, and she breathed deeply.

"Your father told me about your husband. He sounds like a good man. I am sorry about his arrest. We will get him released." His voice was deep, like Timon's.

"I love my husband." When she turned back, he was gone. The hot liquid soothed her stomach. With each sip, she thought of Timon and kept her eyes on the horizon. What kind of conditions surrounded him? Had he been beaten again? Was he even alive? Tears welled up.

She looked over at Moses, who hung his head over the bucket. Poor man. Miriam held his forehead and wiped his mouth. A loneliness crept over her soul. No one could take Timon's place. At times like these he had a way of making her laugh, even if she got angry at that infuriating lopsided grin. She looked back at the horizon. How much longer before they reached Corinth?

When she looked back at Moses, Antonius stood beside him with a wooden mug. He stood taller than Moses by half a foot. Broad muscular shoulders, narrow waist. A well-conditioned soldier. Nothing to look at in comparison to Timon. When Jerusha looked away, her eye caught a woman a few feet from Moses.

Other passengers hung their heads over the railing. This woman, a Greek with her fancy jewel clasped robe, eyed Antonius. Her look reminded Jerusha of the first day she met Devorah. Seductive. What did she care? She could have Antonius. Jerusha had a husband. Just the same. She hated it when women preyed on men. The woman moved closer to him and pretended to be sick. That was enough to make Jerusha feel even sicker.

The tea worked, and she felt somewhat better. She walked across the deck to go below when a wave hit. The ship tipped to one side, and she slipped. The tea tumbled overboard, and she rolled toward the railing when a hand grasped her arm and lifted her up. Antonius. He wrapped his cloak around her, picked her up, and carried her below deck.

"Put me down!"

He dropped her on the pallet in her cabin, turned and left without a word.

"What was that about?" Her mother knelt over a bucket. The room wreaked of stomach contents. Jerusha gagged. "Mother, you need to throw that out and wash the bucket."

"A wave hit as I was walking across the deck, and I slipped. As I was rolling toward the edge, Antonius caught my arm, lifted me and brought me below deck. I guess I should be grateful. I am not used to another man holding me that close."

Her mother's eyebrows arched.

"Never mind that. You need some ginger tea. It helped me tremendously."

"Where did you get ginger tea?"

"Antonius." Jerusha sat up straight. Antonius had quietly slipped in the cabin and handed her mother a mug, then turned toward her, another mug in hand.

"You lost yours. Thought you might want another one." He set it on the table and walked out.

"He is so methodical and stoic." Jerusha shook her head. "He does everything with a soldier's precision."

"He is a soldier." Her mother smiled. "This is helping." She sipped another sip and rubber her finger around the rim. "Why do you let him bother so much?"

"He doesn't bother me." Jerusha picked up the mug. "But I wondered why father thought we need him on this trip."

"Your father told me that Antonius has connections in Corinth. Without him, he would not be able to get access to Timon. Antonius fought in the games. That is how he got his freedom and became a Roman soldier."

"That is why he has blue eyes and blond hair." Jerusha thumped her cheek with her finger. "Is that why Grandfather has blond hair and blue eyes?"

"Jerusha, you will have to get that answer from him."

***

By nightfall Jerusha had gained her sea legs. The wind settled down a little, and Jerusha strolled the deck under the moon, thinking of Timon. She had unbraided her hair and let it hang loose. Wisps flicked her face as she looked overboard at the waves. It seemed like a long time since she had been with Timon. So much had happened since his arrest. Devorah ran way from Herod with the girls. Inez's father came back. Timon didn't even know Inez. Her father found Devorah's sons. Most importantly, they had a new son. How could so much happen in such a short time?

"What has you in such deep thought?" Her father placed his hand on her shoulder.

"So much is happening so fast." She leaned into his chest and looked at the stars. "What's going to happen to us? To Timon? There are many in Yeshua's kingdom who are tortured, imprisoned, and killed. I'm not sure I could live without Timon. How do the other widows do it?"

"They depend on Yeshua to be their husband."

"Well, a flesh-and-blood husband would be nice, too."

"Jerusha, you talk as if he is dead. Don't give up hope that we will find him and get him released."

"That is what I told Samuel. Never give up hope."

"The pilot says we are making good time. If the winds hold and we do not encounter storms, we will be at Corinth's port Cenchreae in a few days."

"Regulus." She pointed above her head. "Little prince shines bright. Have you heard from Grandfather?"

"No. He has a way of taking care of himself. I am sure he is fine and we will hear from him soon. Remember, if Timon is released, your family will not be able to go back to Jerusalem."

"I try not to think about it because I am afraid Timon will go back anyway, even if it means his death. He is so committed to helping our people." Jerusha nodded toward Antonius, who was standing starboard side.

"He seems so methodical and stoic."

"Soldiering, training, and fighting are all he knows. He's a good man. Like Marcus, I trust him with my life. He is softening toward the message about Yeshua. We've talked numerous times."

Jerusha chuckled. "Another one of your Roman converts."

"Samuel and Stephen enjoy his company. They are the only ones able to put a smile on his face. His smiles are few and far between. He carries much pain and is in need of much healing."

"Hmm." She eyed Antonius. "I'll try to give him some slack."

"I remember a little girl with a hard covering around her heart once, like the pomegranate. Wouldn't tell her her father the problem." Jacob hugged her a little tighter. "It took Yeshua to rip it away. Be patient with him. He's here to help."

"A pomegranate would taste so good right now." Jerusha hadn't been this hungry since living in Herod's palace. She closed her eyes and imagined the red stains on her fingers as she ripped it open, then slurping the delicious red juice as she chewed the plump seeds. Being patient with Antonius or making him smile was the least of her worries.

"I see you are feeling better." Antonius had a way of sneaking up on her. She opened her eyes. In the shadowy moonlight, she imagined Timon standing in front of her with his infuriating lopsided grin. How she missed him.

"Timon." She closed her eyes. When she opened them, Antonius was gone.

Chapter 40

"Look, Samuel." Jerusha stood starboard and pointed to the same horizon she had been staring at for days, more than half of those days carrying a bucket. "See the land in the distance?" She and Samuel had been talking and scouting for land since the spotter had informed them. "Come here, Stephen." She waved, and he came running, being careful to step over the ships' rigging as her father had told him. They looked like simple ropes to her.

"Ima." Stephen pointed to Antonius. "He told me about a sailor who lost his foot in the tackling when he unfurled the sails." Stephen puffed out his chest, so proud of the new words and story.

Jerusha looked up at Antonius. He looked straight ahead, his wavy blond hair blowing in the morning breeze, his sandaled foot propped on the rigging, his hand on the mast.

"See the land? We will be in port Cenchreae soon." Jerusha's hair was loose. She would cover her head with the radiyd when they got closer to land. She looked at the other passengers, Greeks and Romans, who gathered to watch the landing, then at her drab garment. She sensed she was about to enter another world.

Stephen held the railing, jumped up and down, then ran back to Antonius. "We will be in port soon." Antonius lifted him, then pointed to the sail and yard above and watched it turn.

"It won't be long before we stroll the streets of Corinth, the capital of Achaia." Jacob and Abigail stood by the railing next to Jerusha and Samuel. "Greece depends on Corinth. Its ports make trade easier than going overland." He took her Abigail's hand. "I warn you. There are many temples to the gods. The temple of Aphrodite or Venus, as the Romans call her, is located at Acrocorinth, high on the hill surrounded by a wall. It houses hundreds of harlots. The temples of Apollo and Octavia are in the main city on the plateau below it. I only mention them because I want to prepare you. This is not like any city you have seen."

Jerusha cared nothing about their gods. She came only to free her husband.

"Where will we stay?"

"With Priscilla and Aquila, followers of the Way. Aquila is a tentmaker, like Saul. Here they would call him Paul. They make their tents out of cilicium, black goat's hair from Tarsus, like my workshop tent." He chuckled. "Looks like Samuel's more interested in Antonius's sword, than the shoreline." Samuel and Stephen examined the sword as Antonius held it.

Jerusha gasped. "A slingshot is good enough for them. It's all David needed to kill the giant."

"Don't forget, my daughter, David cut his head off with a sword."

Jerusha groaned and looked at Miriam who had come up from below deck.

"I am finished feeding Joshua. Do you want him back?"

"Yes, thank you." Jerusha took him in her arms and smiled down at him. "You will meet your Father soon, my smiley boy."

"I do believe you are right about his smile." Her mother looked over her shoulder. "I am sorry I suggested it was gas. He most certainly has the joy of the Lord."

"Have you noticed how much time Moses and Miriam have spent together?" Jerusha watched Moses's grin broaden as Miriam came near.

"Yes. They remind me of you and Timon, after you finally decided to trust him."

"I didn't trust any man, but I am so glad I came to my senses. Timon has been my rock and strength." She touched her father's arm. Jerusha felt an urgency growing within her as the shoreline came into focus.

"How long before I can see him?"

"I am not sure. As soon as we get you and the others settled at Priscilla and Aquila's, Antonius and I will see what we can find out. Aquila may know something, too."

***

"May I?" Antonious walked beside Jerusha and extended his arms to take Joshua. She had adjusted the sling that held him numerous times on the walk inland. It was several miles to their destination. The weary travelers had just turned inland to Corinth. Not much further, she hoped. She glanced at this tall muscular soldier.

Is he serious? She stopped and started to lift Joshua out of the sling, but then shook her head no. She would not have another man hold her son before Timon.

"As you wish." He dropped his arms and quickened his pace to catch Moses, who walked ahead with Miriam. She tipped her ear to hear their conversation. She hadn't meant to hurt him. If he endured the games, he would have hardened his heart against feeling anything. How else could you kill? She convinced herself it didn't matter.

Ima, I am getting tired." Stephen pulled on her cloak. Antonius glanced back, stepped to the side, and extended his arms. Stephen ran straight into his arms. Antonius swooped him up and placed him on his shoulders. Jerusha looked back at her mother and father and shook her head.

Samuel gawked as he walked past one of many Roman statues that lined the roadside. Jerusha felt the same way. She wondered why she brought her children to this lascivious city. She raised her eyebrows when she came upon a column with the words inscribed, Andronicus is my hero and I long for his powerful love. Daphne. She steered Samuel away from it.

They entered a long stoa, the marble columned walkway to the agora with more rows of shops than Jerusha thought necessary. Hundreds of people, most dressed in silk with golden jeweled clasps, talked with merchants. The others wore colorful togas. Some slaves, who followed behind their masters, were dressed in clean white togas, others in dark ones. Many stared at Jerusha in disgust. After their long journey, she felt dirty and smelly and couldn't blame them for staring.

"Jacob, my friend," A merchant stepped out of his shop. "What are you doing here? I saw this bearded Hebrew and wondered who he was. After careful scrutiny I discerned it was you. Not Rome's soldier any longer, eh?"

Jerusha and the others gathered around. "Aquila, my family." Jacob pointed to Jerusha first. "Jerusha my daughter. My wife, Abigail. Jerusha's sons Samuel, Stephen, and Joshua. Miriam, her wet nurse. Moses, a dear friend, and you know Antonius."

"Antonius, so good to see you. Looks like you fare well." Aquila clasped arms with Antonius.

"Aquila, we need lodging for a short while."

"You know my house is your house any time you need it." Aquila shut the heavy door to his shop and locked it.

"Thank you, my friend. I think we all could use a good bath in your bathhouse. I do not think my family would appreciate the openness of the public bathhouse." Jacob laughed and slapped Aquila's back. "It is good to be with you. Are you reaching any for Yeshua?" He took Abigail's arm and walked beside Aquila, Antonius on his other side.

"It is hard ground. Our house church is growing, though, even amidst the persecution."

Jerusha and the others followed under the long portico past the public bathhouse and garden of Apollo, then beneath an immense arch decorated with a colorful mosaic. They entered Lechaiaon Way and headed west toward the other port. At the second mile marker, they turned onto a path lined with olive trees on both sides. A woman dressed in a well-stitched, dark blue toga waited at a gate. An obvious patrician woman of high status.

"Priscilla." Aquila broke from the other two men and met the woman with a kiss. "I have brought home Jacob and Antonius."

"And who are these?"

"Abagail, Jacob's wife. Jerusha, his daughter, and her three sons. Miriam, her wet nurse, and their friend Moses. They are in great need of a bath and a place to stay."

"Welcome."

***

Jerusha left Joshua with Miriam and followed Priscilla to the bathhouse. She dropped her dirty tunic and cloak in the first room and stepped into a steam-filled room and walked down the tiled steps into warm waters. Ah. It felt wonderful to her achy muscles. She scrubbed her body with the perfumed waters, then dipped below the water surface and let her hair float behind as she swam the short distance across the steaming pool.

She had heard about the bathhouses and spurned them. However, she found that it felt absolutely divine. She raised up and leaned against the wall on her elbows. Timon would love this. She imagined his teasing smile and twinkling eyes. She could not stand there any longer in luxury while he suffered in a prison cell. She swam to the steps, rose up out of the water, and grabbed the towel Priscilla had provided. At that moment, the fog cleared, and Antonius stood before her with a towel around his waist.

"Oh! What are you doing in here?" She was glad the large towel hung down and covered her body.

"I was told the bathhouse was empty." A slight grin parted his lips. "I can see I was told wrong."

"Then leave." Jerusha felt a warm flush creep up her neck and face.

"If you had no husband, I would pursue knowing you better."

Jerusha glared. "Get out! I cannot imagine why my father sees you as a friend."

He retreated backwards, keeping his eye on her, then chuckled, turned, and left.

"That man is despicable." Jerusha chatted to herself, dried off, and peeked around the corner of the doorway to the other room. "Father needs to know what kind of man he has for a friend." She slipped the silk tunic overhead and struggled with the long piece of material called a toga. "What do they do with this thing?"

"Do you need some help in there?" Antonius stood outside the door and waited.

"No! Go away! If my father finds out what you did, he will, he will—"

"He will understand it was an accident, one that I enjoyed, but an accident none-the-less."

She wrapped the toga around the best she could and stomped out the door and circled around him off the path, making sure she didn't fall like she had done with Timon when she first met him.

"If you had any decency, you would be long gone."

"I like your hair down like that."

"When Timon is released, he will make sure you are sorry you said that. Only he can talk to me that way."

She scampered barefooted, down the path into the villa.

"Jerusha, I am sorry for your discomfort," he yelled, and then chuckled.

"Not stoic tonight. He had plenty of emotion," she mumbled as she rounded the corner.

"What are you saying?" Her mother stood in the doorway to her room.

"Nothing. I am exasperated with that stoic soldier, who pretends to be father's friend."

"Antonius? What has he done to you?"

"Nothing. Absolutely nothing."

"Jerusha, without him, your father will not be able to get to Timon."

"Well—" Jerusha could not tell her mother what happened. If her father knew, he might punch him. She would wait until after Timon is released, then her father and Timon could both punch him.

Her slammed door echoed in the hallway. She fell on the silk-covered bed and wept, thankful she was alone. She felt so humiliated. "Timon. I need you." She sobbed. "Yehsua, I need you. Do not abandon me."

I will never leave you or forsake you.

Chapter 41

"Jerusha, wake up," Abigail shook her shoulder. "Your father and Antonius are waiting for you and the boys. They found Timon. He fights tomorrow in the amphitheater."

A sick sensation drained the strength from Jerusha's body. "Father must stop it!"

"Hurry." Her mother ignored her statement. "Get dressed. Wear these Roman garments Priscilla provided. You will be less conspicuous. Your father and Antonius are in the courtyard. Moses is readying Samuel and Stephen. Miriam will bring Joshua to the courtyard." Mother's troubled expression scared Jerusha. She had not seen that look since being at Herod's palace. Her strength returned and she jumped up.

"Is Timon well?" Jerusha slipped the tunic overhead.

"You will have to ask your father and Antonius about that. They had no time to fill me in on the specifics. Just to get you and the boys ready as soon as possible. Let me help you with the toga. Getting that

273

thing wrapped the right way is a bit tricky." Jerusha smiled as mother struggled with it, like she had the night before, but she finally won the battle with one final tuck at the shoulder. When finished, she pulled up the hood from the tunic. "Keep your head covered and tuck your hair inside." She gave her a quick hug. "I am praying. Do not forget that you are not alone. Yeshua is with you."

Jerusha's heart raced as she walked the path to the courtyard. Her hands shook. Her father was shaved and dressed in his red Roman toga with his armor over it, his helmet under his arm. Antonius stood next to him in his soldier attire as well. His stoic expression had returned. Miriam waited at the gate and placed Joshua in her arms. Samuel stood tall and straight next to Jacob, wearing a toga, trying to look grown up. Stephen stood next to Antonius in a toga, his bright eyes bigger than ever. Her whole family was dressed in Roman attire. Well, if that's what it took to get Timon released, it would be worth it. Then they could dress however they wanted and go someplace where no one could find them.

"Is Timon well?" Jerusha searched Father's eyes.

"He is well. They are holding him under house arrest with the other men who will fight tomorrow. It is their last night, so they provided them with women, wine, and food.

"Women?" Jeruha's eyes widened.

"Do not worry about Timon. He would have nothing to do with their delicacies." Jerusha felt remorse for going to the bathhouse.

"They want to see a good fight tomorrow." Her father placed his helmet on his head. "We have orders to bring you to see Timon, but it must be right away."

"But father, will he be released?"

"Only if he accepts Antonius's offer." Her father laid his hand on Antonius's shoulder. "He has offered to fight in Timon's place."

"What?" Jerusha's eyes met Anonius's. His expression had not changed. "Why would you do this?"

"I owe my life to your father. I would do anything for him or his family." Antonius stared straight ahead.

"Since Antonius was a respected gladiator in the past, they would like to see him fight again." Jerusha had never seen her father so troubled. "The procurator has agreed. If Timon accepts, then he leaves with you and the boys tonight." Her father's eyes glassed over. "It was not my idea. Antonius is like a son. He insisted."

"We must go now." Antonius placed his helmet on and exited the gate so quietly Jerusha barely noticed he had left. He held the reigns to his horse outside the gate and lifted Stephen up, then mounted. Jacob took Joshua, helped her mount, and then handed him back.

"Will you be able to hold him and ride?" He asked.

"Yes, Father." She slipped him into a makeshift sling her mother made and held him close with one hand and took the reigns with the other. "We will be fine."

"Samuel climbed on behind Jacob. Abigail and Miriam watched from the gate with Aquila and Priscilla.

"We will be praying." Aquila spoke with authority. "Go under the shadow of his wings my friends."

The crescent moon gave little light in the cloudless sky. The constellations overhead twinkled in the blackness like diamonds. Jerusha looked over her shoulder at her mother. There were tears in her eyes. When would she see her again? The clip-clop of the horses' hooves against the stone pavement mesmerized Joshua, and he fell asleep.

The paved road ended, and they continued up a dirt path lined with walls on both sides. She heard the waves crashing against the shoreline below. Even in the darkness, the harbor bustled with activity, the sailors' voices echoing off the canyon. She urged her horse on up the steep slope. Antonius and Stephen rode in front of her, Jacob and Samuel behind. Antonius reined his horse to a stop on the side of the path.

"We leave our horses here." He helped Stephen slide to the ground before he dismounted, then tried to take Joshua so Jerusha could dismount. She glared and turned away. She didn't trust him. What was his angle? Why would he fight instead of Timon? No Roman would do that for a Hebrew, especially him. There must be another way. If not, then better his death than Timon's. She knew that was a cold-hearted thing to think.

"Jerusha." Her father motioned with his head toward Antonius. "He only wants to help." He took Joshua so she could dismount. His eyes begged her to be kind. When she dismounted, her eyes caught

276 A Royal Family

Antonius starring off into the horizon. For the second time, she wondered if she hurt him. She looked away. All that mattered was getting Timon and leaving this godforsaken place.

The wind howled in the canyon, and the horses whinnied as they tied them to the lowest branch of an olive tree. Jerusha's hair flew out from under the hooded toga as she staggered up the steep incline. She was glad father carried Joshua. At the top, a sentry of soldiers, who guarded the small stone building, came to attention when Antonius came into their view, admiration in their eyes. They did the same when they saw Jacob.

Through the iron crossbars, in a square window at the top of the door, Jerusha could see a faint light flickering on the wall. Even the whistling wind could not drown out the low murmurs inside. The guard unlocked the door and opened it.

Timon knelt in the corner with three men, shackles on their hands. They were praying. Another man sat in the opposite corner shackled to the wall and glowered.

"Aba, Aba," Stephen and Samuel ran to greet him. The chains jingled and grew taut as he lifted Stephen. He held him on his hip and hugged Samuel with his other arm, then looked at Jerusha.

His smile widened into that endearing lopsided grin.

"Welcome to my humble abode." His eyes twinkled. The bruises and wounds on his face had diminished and were healing. She remembered what the soldier said at her villa about being sure he'd be treated well, in honor of her father. YHWH had blessed him with great favor with these Roman soldiers. For that she was thankful. She glanced at Antonius. She was also grateful for him.

Antonius left the room and came back with a guard, who unshackled Timon and opened the door to an adjacent room.

"For you and your family." He motioned them to enter.

"Let your mother and father have a few minutes alone," Jacob instructed Stephen and Samuel.

Timon took Jerusha's hand and led her into the lamp-lit room. "My little butterfly." He pulled her close and tried to kiss her, not waiting for the door to close.

"Timon, the boys." She pushed away and looked back.

"Let them see." He kissed her on the lips. "It is good for a son to know how much his father loves his mother." His joy in these circumstances overwhelmed Jerusha.

"Timon, be serious."

"I am serious." He kissed her again. This time she let herself be immersed in his love and snuggled against his chest.

"I can't live without you." She gazed into his eyes. "Antonius said he arranged it so he could fight in your place. Is he telling the truth?" She enjoyed his arm around her shoulder as they took a seat on a wool pallet.

"He is a good man. I am honored." He squeezed her hand.

"Then we need to go before he changes his mind." She felt Timon's fingertips on her lips.

"I refused his offer."

"What? Why?"

"I fight against the man who sits in the corner of the other room. He has not yet accepted Yeshua's love and entered the kingdom. If Antonius fights, he will kill him. If I fight, he lives another day to receive YHWY's gift of eternal life. The others in the room, like me, have decided to die rather than kill someone who has not yet entered Yeshua's kingdom."

"Did you tell Antonius this?"

"He knows."

"Jerusha," Jacob interrupted. "The boys want time with Timon." He glanced at Timon as he laid Joshua in her arms. Stephen bumped her shoulder as he ran past. She cuddled Joshua and stroked his chin with her finger. Samuel's shadow moved across the wall as he walked up.

"You have a new son." Her voice quivered. She bit her lip and put him in his arms. "This is Joshua, a warrior for YHWH's kingdom."

"He has a big smile." Stephen held his hands far apart. "Aba, are you coming home with us?" He crawled up on Timon's lap. "I miss you."

"No. I am not coming with you." He tipped his chin up and looked into his eyes. "I need you to be big and take care of your mother. I am not coming home. I am going to live in Yeshua's heavenly kingdom."

"Why?"

"Because if I don't go to live with him, another man, who doesn't know Yeshua, will die, and he will live forever without him."

"Aba, I will take care of mother." Samuel ran to his father and jumped onto his lap, tears running down his cheek.

Timon held Joshua close to his chest and pulled the other two boys into a tighter hug.

"Samuel, teach Stephen everything I have taught you in the Torah and in the workshop. Moses will teach you the things I have taught him. No matter what happens, remember I love you."

"Timon, I don't accept this." Jerusha stood and turned away. "You will live and not die and declare the works of the Lord."

"Yes, Aba, you will live and not die and declare the works of the Lord."

"I will live in his kingdom, and by dying I will declare the works of the Lord to the one I let live."

"I don't understand." Stephen rubbed his eyes.

"Mother." Samuel came to Jerusha and pulled on her hand. "Light is on Father." He looked into the other room. "And on the other three men. That is what my vision meant. Yeshua touched Father with the light of his scepter, and Father touched these men."

Jerusha ignored Samuel. "This cannot be happening. Timon, I cannot live without you." She slid down the wall, held her knees, and sobbed.

"Boys, come with me." Antonius spoke softly. In a blurry haze, she watched as Timon kissed each boy, then Antonius pulled Stephen away, holding the crying boy against his shoulder and walked out of the room. Jacob started to take Joshua from Timon, when Samuel grabbed his arm.

"I will take him, Grandfather. I am the man of the house now." He looked at Timon.

"Don't worry, Father. I will take care of him, too."

"Remember, Samuel, you are not alone. Your heavenly Father will never leave you or forsake you." Timon's lip trembled as he watched his sons follow their grandfather out the door.

He came to Jerusha, took her hands and raised her. She fell into his arms.

"I cannot live without you." She wept into his chest. "I can't accept this. You will not die but live and declare the works of the Lord." She poked her finger in his chest.

"Yeshua is your husband now." He held her head against his chest and stroked her hair.

"I want you. Timon, do not do this. Take Antonius's offer. You cannot die."

"Jerusha. Do not be afraid to love again." He lifted her chin and looked into her eyes for a long time. "You have my blessing to marry another man, if YHWH wills."

"No! I want you." She turned her back to him.

"You always wanted your own way. Jerusha, YHWH's ways are not our ways."

Antonius opened the door. "We need to go now." He took Timon's arm. "I am sorry. I have to put the shackles back on." He led him into the other room. Jerusha slumped to the floor.

"I give you one more chance to take my offer." Antonius spoke as he locked the shackles.

Jerusha heard Timon's words between sobs. "You are a good man, Antonius. I am honored. I hope to see you one day in Yeshua's kingdom."

Jacob lifted Jerusha to her feet. She walked in a stupor into the other room. At the threshold of the outside entrance she looked back at Timon.

"See you in His kingdom," he hesitated, then added, "Jerusha, later." He smiled that infuriating lopsided grin, a twinkle in his eyes.

"No." She stomped her foot. "You will not die, but live and declare the works of the Lord."

Chapter 42

Jerusha walked into the courtyard. The sun shone bright off the marble columns and reflected in her eyes. Dressed in her Roman garment, her hair braided and covered with the royal blue hood of the toga, she hesitated at the gate and looked through the bronze bars at the tree-lined path.

"Jerusha." Abigail called as she and Jacob walked up the tiled path, a deep concern in their eyes.

"You cannot stop me." Jerusha wiped a single tear from her face. "Timon will not die but live and declare the works of the Lord. I cannot desert him now. If YHWH saved Daniel in the lion's den, he can save Timon in the arena." She opened the gate and looked back. She wanted to hug each one. If she did, she might not go. She had to be strong.

"If you insist on going, your father is going with you." Her mother spoke with an authority not used with Jerusha since she was a child.

"Antonius goes with us. He knows ways to get inside the amphitheater that will be safer." Jerusha groaned. Her father took her hand and placed it in the crook of his arm. "You will not go it alone." He glanced up at Antonius, who stepped out from under an olive tree, horses' reins in hand and leading three horses. So intent on convincing her mother and father that she was going, Jerusha had not seen him earlier. She nodded and mounted the horse, her thoughts on Timon and her mission to get to the arena before he fought. *If Father and Antonius must come, then so be it.* She galloped up the path without looking back.

She remembered passing the amphitheater the night before and knew her way without them. Antonius caught up, grabbed her reins, and pulled her horse to a stop as Jacob reined in on the other side.

"Follow me. I know a better way." Anontius waited for her answer. She eyed him for a moment. Prudence said to go with him. Her emotions said to go it alone. She looked at father, who nodded.

"Show the way." She yanked on her reins.

As they approached the arena, they could hear the crowd cheering in the distance. Her stomach churned. "He will not die, but live and declare the works of the Lord." She kept repeating the words over and over.

Antonius led them into a dark tunnel in the side of the amphitheater, where they left their horses. Jerusha breathed heavy as they climbed up a long stairway. The crowd roared again. Her heart thumped like a hammer against her chest. "He will not die, but live and declare the works of the Lord."

Finally, she stepped out of the darkness. She squinted and cupped her hand over her eyes eyes. "Timon." He wore his Hebrew tunic, his muscular body apparent to all. "He will not die, but live and declare the works of the Lord," she decreed.

The crowd, mostly men, jeered and mocked. She glanced around at their faces, contorted by a sick hunger for blood. They reminded her of the starving dogs in the dark alcoves in Jerusalem, ready to pounce. *What's wrong with these people?*

"Death! Death! Death!" The crowd screamed in unison, their thumbs pointed down.

"He will not die, but live and declare the works of the Lord."
She spoke louder and louder, her words drowned by the thousands of voices around her. Timon looked up, arms extended, and smiled. "He will not die, but live and declare the works of the Lord."

"Death! Death! Death!"

Stunned, the other gladiator froze, his sword in hand.

"He will not die, but live and declare the works of the Lord."

"Death! Death! Death!"

The gladiator struck Timon's gut. Timon fell to his knees.

"No!" Jerusha covered her face.

The crowd's chant stopped. Silence.

"Yeshua, my King!" Timon cried.

"Look!" A man in the crowd yelled.

Jerusha looked up. A shaft of light shone from heaven and encompassed Timon.

The hushed crowd stared in wonder.

"It's his God," a man whispered.

"Yeshua! Yeshua! Yehsua!" The crowd yelled. Timon slumped over. "Yeshua! Yeshua! Yeshua!"

"Yeshua, my God and my King." Antonius saluted, his fist on his chest.

"Timon, my love." Jerusha stared at the glowing light around him, then buried her face in her father's chest and sobbed. When she looked up again, the gladiator kneeled beside Timon's lifeless body. A man ran out and lifted it onto a stretched. The other gladiator saluted him as they carried him away. Jerusha whispered, "Later, my love."

***

Jerusha waved at Aquila and Priscilla on the wharf as the ship disembarked.

"We are going home, little Joshua." She whispered and looked down at his smiling face. Samuel and Stephen stood next to her, one on each side. "Our family is going home."

She pulled her radiyd over her head, the cool breeze blowing against her face. "A new beginning."

"Ima, tell me again how Father died." Stephen asked.

"Your father did not die but lived and declared the works of the Lord. Yeshua's light shined for all to see."

"How bright was it?"

"Bright as the light I see in your eyes." She hugged him to her side. "What Samuel saw in his vision was true." She smiled at her little prophet, almost a grown man. "I am sorry I didn't listen to you when we were with your father before he died. The light you saw on him and the others was Yeshua. I was too concerned with what I wanted that I ignored what Yeshua was showing you. Forgive me?"

"I forgive you." He snuggled against her chest.

"Yeshua touched your father with his shining scepter, just like you saw in your vision, and in his death Yeshua's light was released for all to see. A miracle. Your father died a hero of Yeshua's kingdom."

"He touched my life with that light, too." Antonius lifted Stephen in his arms and patted Samuel on the head.

Jerusha smiled. That man. He never goes away, no matter how much I shun him.

"Years ago, your grandfather told me about Yeshua—" Antonius looked first at Stephen, then Samuel, "—but it was when your father died that I saw the truth. I had never seen anyone love their God like him. He gave his life that another may live to know him. That was Yeshua, the One who died for us, living in Him." His eyes sparkled. He looked at Jerusha, and a grin spread across his face. It was the first time she had seen him smile, besides the time in the bathhouse. "May I talk to your mother alone?"

Stephen and Samuel nodded. "May I?" He reached for her hand. Jerusha looked at the boys, who grinned.

"Well, I suppose." She placed her hand in his, and he placed it in the crook of his arm and walked a few feet away.

"I want to apologize for my behavior at the bathhouse. I was completely out of order. Will you forgive me?" Flustered at his mention of her most embarrassing moment, she pulled her hand away and grabbed the deck railing with both hands, then glanced back. His wavy blond hair blew in the breeze. He waited for a response. She cocked her head and peered into his deep blue eyes and saw another man.

"Yes, I forgive you." She turned and stared at the waves. When she looked back, he was gone.

***

Jerusha, her sea legs under her, stood on the deck and listened to the waves. She peered into the night sky, admiring the beauty of the constellations, and thought of Timon. She missed him terribly and wondered if the ache would ever go away. The door hinge creaked, and Jacob stepped onto the deck. She smiled at her father, and would rely on him more than ever. She leaned back against his chest as he wrapped his arms around her.

"Father, I understand better what you and Grandfather said about YHWH's ways are not like our ways. I declared His word over both Grandfather and Timon. One lived. The other died." Her voice cracked. He hugged a little tighter.

"One thing to remember." He rubbed his hand on her arm. "Yeshua said what His Father said, and did what He saw His Father doing. Always seek what your Heavenly Father is saying and doing. He tried to show you through Samuel, what He was doing, and because it wasn't what you wanted, you couldn't see it. Sometimes our own desires get in the way. The scriptures are not a sorcerer's amulet to control YHWH." He paused and then continued, "Not only are His ways not our ways. They are better than our ways."

"Better for who? How can leaving three sons without a father be better?"

"YHWH has not left them as orphans. As their heavenly Father, he has them in the palm of his hand. You will see, as time goes on, the royal inheritance He has left them."

Antonius stepped from the shadows and leaned against the railing across from her. He was wrapped in his Roman cloak, the scarlet garment a striking contrast against his blond hair. Snug in her father's arms, Jerusha stared for a moment at the man who would have fought in Timon's place had he allowed him. What kind of man would do that for someone who he only met once?

"You said Antonius had suffered much pain. What happened?"

286 A Royal Family

"I think that is something only he can tell you." Her father's tone was somber. "He shares his life with those he trusts. Like you, trust does not come easy. Maybe now that he knows Yeshua, he will be ready to peel back that hard, outer covering, and be vulnerable enough to receive healing."

Jerusha thought she saw Antonius wipe a tear away with his fist. How could a seasoned Roman soldier be so tender? She would leave that to YHWH. She had three sons to raise in Jerusalem. Would they be safe there? Only Yeshua knew. Like Timon said, their lives were in His hands.

Many daughters waited in darkness, hidden from the world. There were others, like Devorah, Inez, Cassia, and Helena. After what Jerusha saw in Caesarea and Corinth, she grieved even more for those who received their worth in pleasing men. She had thought about it a lot. As long as YHWH's provision lasted, she would provide a refuge to hopeless young women, both Jew and Gentile.

She smiled thinking about how many times she begged Timon to leave Jerusalem. Her call to nurse daughters at her side would begin in Jerusalem and then spread to the uttermost parts of the earth. Timon would be pleased. She rubbed her finger around the purple butterfly jewel in Father's pendant that still hung around her neck. "Timon, your little butterfly will flutter from destination to destination, until I see you again in His kingdom," she whispered. A single tear escaped and ran down her face.

Her father squeezed tight and whispered in her ear. "My little lioness, never forget who you are. You are royalty. You will dance again before the King." When she turned to embrace her father, she noticed Antonius was gone. How did he do it? He appeared and then disappeared like a ghost.

"Father, what will happen to Antonius?"

"When we dock, he leaves for Rome. His assignment in Germania will be dangerous. I fear for his life and will be praying for him daily. In his own way, he reminds me a lot of Timon."

"Maybe." Jerusha sighed. "There is only one Timon." She envisioned that lopsided grin and smiled.

Chapter 43

The gate to the villa creaked as Jerusha opened it. Total darkness. No one there to greet her and the family. The only sound was Moses mumbling to the horses as he took them around the outside wall to the stable. Miriam carried Joshua. Samuel and Stephen stared into the dark courtyard and held Father's hand.

"Is someone there?" Jerusha called, her voice swallowed by the darkness. "The gate's unlocked. Where are the servants?" Thunder rumbled in the distance. After their long journey, a cloak of weariness weighed heavily on Jerusha's shoulders, especially now that she carried the load without Timon. Jacob let go of the boys' hands and swished past.

"Stay here." He gripped the hilt of the sword strapped beneath his cloak. Its blade gleamed in the darkness as he removed it from the scabbard. "Moses, come with me, but stay behind me." Jerusha corralled the boys and waited beneath the jujube tree, being careful not to catch her radiyd on its thorny branches. Abigail comforted

Miriam. Jacob and Moses crept like thieves into their own villa, quiet and alert. A bright flash of lightening lit up the courtyard. The boom of thunder made Stephen jump.

"Mother, I hear something." Stephen clung to her cloak.

"It's thunder."

"No. It's sounds like someone crying."

"I hear it, too." Samuel added.

"Shh," Jerusha put her finger to her lips.

"There it is again. Did you hear it?" Samuel crept forward and cupped his ear. "It's coming from the garden."

Jerusha grabbed his arm. "You stay with Stephen. I'll see what it is."

"I'm coming with you." Abigail stepped next to Jerusha. "Miriam, stay with the boys."

Jerusha slipped through the gate and held it for her mother, trying not to let it squeak. It thundered again. The crying became louder. She glanced back at her mother.

"It did come from the garden." She tiptoed along the tile path and peaked around the pomegranate bush at the end. It was too dark to see, so she crept through the open garden gate and around the corner. Lightening flashed and she saw a figure hunkered down on the other side of her father's bench. Jerusha's heart thumped in her chest. Another crash of thunder. The muffled cries continued. Jerusha came closer. It was a child. Jerusha reached down, and the child gasped.

"Don't hurt me anymore," the high-pitched voice screamed, followed by heavy sobbing.

"I won't hurt you." Jerusha lifted the trembling child. It was a young girl, perhaps a little older than Sarah when she died. The girl backed away.

"Why are you here?" Jerusha's heart ached for the little one.

"I ran away. I needed a place to go. The gate was open." The girl had bruises on her face and arms.

"Ran away from your parents?" Abigail asked.

"No. From my master. He—" She crumpled to the ground, her face in her hands. "He made me let him touch me." She broke into tears. Jerusha understood the helplessness and shame the girl felt. "I thought you were the soldiers. They came once."

"Someone touched me like that once." Jerusha bent over. "May I come closer? We could talk about it."

The girl nodded. Jerusha lifted her up and sat on her father's bench. She remembered how her father had tried to get her to open up about her secret.

"Come sit with me." She patted the bench. "What's your name?" Jerusha smiled.

"Hannah." The girl fiddled with her fingers. Jerusha looked at her mother, who had tears in her eyes.

"I will leave you two alone." She backed out the gate.

"A soldier is here!" Stephen peered around the corner bush into the garden. Jerusha jumped up.

"Don't be afraid," she told Hannah. "Go with him." She watched the girl run to Stephen, and the two ran with Samuel toward the kitchen. Jerusha hurried to the entrance gate. Six Roman soldiers marched toward her and stopped at the fountain.

"We are looking for a woman named Jerusha."

"I am her." She felt bolder than in the past. Confident.

"You are to meet our centurion at the garden by the market. Now. Come alone."

Jerusha looked behind her at the children gathered under the portico. She could not let them see a skirmish.

"Tell him I am on my way." She ran back for her cloak.

"Pray." She looked at her parents and hugged each one. As she turned to leave, her father touched her arm.

"I will be all right, Father. The children need your presence."

She hurried down the terraced steps into the lower city and wound through the narrow street. She kept going until she came to the same garden in which she had spent many hours with her father and grandfather. It was their favorite meeting place outside of the villa. The centurion knelt on one knee by the spring, his helmet under his arm and slurped water with his hand to his mouth.

"Why did you send for me?" she asked as she drew near.

He turned his head. "Antonius. What are you doing here?" She stepped back as he stood.

"You must warn your father to leave immediately. Soldiers come in the morning to force him to serve again in the legion that goes to

Germania. Tell him to hide for a week. After that, it will no longer matter. They will give up their search."

"Why didn't you tell him yourself? Why tell me?"

"Because I cannot be seen at the villa until morning. I am the centurion with the orders to enlist him. I could not do that to him, or you. You will need him." He stared at the ground. "Jerusha, the high priest conspires with Rome to take the villa from you. I have learned through my sources that you have an authority with Rome to keep it, if you use what has been given."

"What are you talking about? I am a woman. I have no authority, especially with Rome."

"You have more authority than you know." He sounded like her grandfather. "Write a decree and seal it with your father's signet ring. For now, Rome will honor it. The high priest can do nothing about it. I have heard you have a scepter."

Jerusha's eyes widened. How could he know that?

"If he challenges you, present the scepter. The priest will know what that means."

"How do you know these things?"

"I have connections, both in Rome and Judea." He placed his helmet on his head and strapped it under his chin. Jerusha stared at her feet, and her heart raced.

"What kind of connections?"

"I don't have time to explain." He stared into her eyes. "Trust me, or you will lose your father again, as well as your villa."

A storm raged in Jerusha's stomach. Could she trust this man? What other choice did she have? She could not risk father's life. She stared deep into his blue eyes and again saw a different man than the one in the bathhouse. She saw a man she not only trusted but cared about. He offered to save her husband and now her father.

"Antonius, thank you." She shifted on her feet and fiddled with her fingers, and then looked up into those deep blue eyes. "Be careful."

A slight smile parted his lips. "I am honored you care. I will have my soldiers escort you back to the villa. Remember, your father must be gone by tomorrow morning." He motioned to his soldiers, and they stood ready by her side. She looked over her shoulder as she walked away. He was gone.

***

"Unlock the gate!" Antonius called, his voice familiar now. The sun rose in the distance behind his back, shedding a rosy glow across the city. His cohort stood shoulder to shoulder down the hill. The temple guard and the high priest shook the gate. "Why is this gate locked?"

"What can I do for you? We just arrived back yesterday." Jerusha acted casual and undisturbed. She hoped they could not see the thumping in her chest. "We were surprised to have found our gate was unlocked and open."

"Get out! This villa belongs to the priests now. Your father leaves with them today," The priest pointed to the soldiers. "He goes to fight in Germania. May he never return!"

Jerusha clenched her jaw. *Be calm.* Her eyes looked past the priest to Antonius.

"My father is not here." She opened the gate. "Search for yourselves if you don't believe me"

The temple guards burst through and began their search along with the Roman soldiers. Jerusha followed.

"Check the stable for his horse," the high priest commanded his guards. "Show them the way." He glared at Jerusha.

Jerusha led them through the kitchen, out the back door, and through the herb garden to the stable. She rubbed Boaz's nose and watched as they checked the stalls one by one. Jerusha prayed her father's horse, hidden in the secret hiding place with him, remained silent while the soldiers stood in the barn. She barely breathed.

"He is not here." The guards reported to the high priest. "Nor his horse."

"We found no sign of him," the soldiers reported to Antonius.

"He will be back. I know this man. He wouldn't leave his daughter alone again." His stern, stoic look scared Jerusha. Was it an act? She searched his face for the man she saw in the garden. Not a sign of emotion. Had he deceived her? Had her father ever told him about the secret hiding place? Her distrust of the man, who appeared and disappeared at a blink of an eye, churned in her belly.

"Get those half-breed sons of yours out of this villa. Your mother and any other followers of the Way." The high priest glowered. "This property belongs to us," he cackled.

Jerusha looked at Antonius. A slight nod of his chin. She reached into her cloak and pulled out the parchment sealed with her father's signet ring. A slight smile curved her lips as she rubbed her finger over the wax. The lion and the butterfly. *My little lioness.* Her father's words. *My little butterfly.* Timon's words. She handed it to the priest. As he unrolled it, she caught Antonius's slight wink and breathed a sigh. He could be trusted after all.

"This is preposterous! This means nothing! Guards, escort them out now!" The priest threw the parchment to the ground. His black robe swooshed as he turned to leave. Jerusha nodded at Samuel, who removed the scepter.

"Wait!" She stood tall and straight. "My son holds a scepter that gives credence to the parchment and its seal." She stared at the priest's back.

He turned slowly and peered through narrow slits, his face turned dark red. His eyes darted back and forth between the scepter and Jerusha. He clenched his fists and jaw.

"This villa belongs to my family, and you have no authority over us. I am not asking. I am telling you to leave my property." The authority in her voice surprised her.

The priest waved at the guards. The sun had risen in the sky. A new day. She watched as he descended the terraced steps to the Temple, his black robe blowing in the wind. She moved outside the gate to the vine-covered wall that looked over the city. The soldiers marched away, the aquila high in the air. Once again, Antoinius disappeared without a word.

"Thank you," Jerusha whispered, "Be safe."

Chapter 44

One Year Later

"Look, Jerusha, he's walking." Joshua held Hannah's fingers and tottered past. The lamp-lit courtyard buzzed with activity as everyone prepared for Moses and Miriam's marriage feast. Jerusha finished with preparations in the room her father had made for the couple and sat on a bench. Their chuppah awaited. She clapped for Joshua, watching as he wobbled along free of Hannah's help.

Moses and Miriam had jumped in delight that Floriana and Devorah had made the seventy-mile trip from Caesarea. Devorah chatted with Floriana as she served a platter of roasted lamb next to the bread and wine. Figs, grapes, dates, and, of course, pomegranates filled the rest of the table. Cassia and Helena talked with Samuel, who acted more mature than his age, especially while talking to older girls.

Stephen's eyes widened as Joseph pulled back the slingshot and aimed at the target on the rock. She felt someone tap on her shoulder, and looked up at Timon's mother. She had a few more gray hairs sprinkled in with her dark hair but still had the countenance of an angel. The two widows had bonded even more since Timon's death. Jerusha grinned and made room on the tiled bench for her.

"I remember when you and Timon were married," Chaya spoke, a tenderness in her voice. "His love for you reminded me of King Soloman's Song of Songs. He was so nervous that night when he came for you."

Jerusha chuckled. "Not any more than me. When I looked out the window and saw his jubilant dance, my hands trembled so much Mother had to finish putting the flowers in my hair." She started to laugh again, and noticed that faraway look in Chaya's eyes. Jerusha took her hand. "He loved you too. Raising him as your own son without a father, in a world that rejects orphans, took courage. He honored your love by loving other orphans."

"Thank you, Jerusha." She wiped a tear away. "Look as those two lovers." Chaya nodded toward her mother and father.

Jerusha laid her head on Chaya's shoulder. "All this marital love in the air makes me miss Timon, even more."

"I promise, even now, his eyes are on you." She patted her hand.

"He's coming. He's coming. The groom is coming." Stephen pulled on Jerusha's hand. A shofar blew in the distance. As Jerusha arose, those waiting in the courtyard rushed past to greet the groom. Miriam stepped into the lamplight wearing the bejeweled garment Jerusha had worn on her wedding day. Her hair had the same red and white flowers woven in it. Moses entered the courtyard, his eyes on Miriam. Her eyes were fixed on him. Jacob pronounced the wedding blessing.

"My sister, may you increase to thousands upon thousands; may your offspring possess the gates of their enemies." Jerusha felt a tear run down her cheek and wiped it away. Stephen jumped up and down at her side. The tambourines, flutes, and stringed instruments played their high praises. The women formed a circle around the couple.

"Come, Jerusha," Helena urged. "You are a dancer."

She shook her head and stood under the olive tree. It warmed her heart to see Chaya laughing with the other women as she joined in the merriment, placing her hands on the shoulders of Helena and Cassia. The men formed a circle on the outside of the women. Even little Stephen gave it a try. The circles moved in different directions. Moses held Miriam's hand up, his gaze on her.

Timon. Jerusha slipped away unnoticed by the others and sat on her father's bench, her hands in her lap. The lamp-lit garden had become her hideaway when overcome with grief.

"My sister, may you increase to thousands upon thousands; may your offspring possess the gates of their enemies."

"Jerusha." The stranger with a long gray beard stood at the gate. "Do not be dismayed by your loss. YHWH's plans for your life are for good, not evil."

"Who are you?"

"Ask your grandfather."

"Grandfather's here?"

He nodded.

"Where?"

"I am here, Jerusha." He stepped out of the darkened corner.

"Grandfather!" She ran and threw her arms around his waist, then looked back at the stranger. He was gone.

"Where did he go?" She ran back to the gate. "He was standing right here. The man with the long white beard. He came to Shiloh. He came to my betrothal. Who is he?" She scratched her head. "And why weren't you at the wedding celebration? Why are you hiding in the garden?"

Her grandfather chuckled. "My little lioness, always full of questions. I could ask you why you are in this garden? But I knew you would come. That's why I waited here for you. The giant sat and motioned for her to sit next to him.

"Oh, Grandfather, I am so glad to see you." She sat and leaned her head into his chest.

"The man with the white beard is my father." He stroked her hair.

"Your father?" She straightened up and looked at him.

"The scepter you received at Shiloh came from his royal lineage, all the way back to Melchizedek. He has kept it all these years, until he gave it to you."

"Your father has a way of appearing and then disappearing. Reminds me of Antonius."

Her grandfather raised an eyebrow. "Antonius?" How often do you think of Antonius?"

Flustered, Jerusha quipped. "Never! Well, hardly ever. Well, I pray for him."

"Well, since you are praying for him, you might want to know he was wounded in Germania." He watched her eyes.

"Wounded? Jerusha tried to act nonchalant. "Is he all right?"

"My father has been nursing him back to health in Perea. They met when Antonius was a procurator there. Good man."

"Why was your father in Perea?" Jerusha was glad to get the subject off Antonius. She felt guilty. Her thoughts had been on Timon when she came to the garden.

"As a Judean prince, he accepted Yeshua as his King. When the religious leaders had Yeshua crucified, he left Jerusalem. He believes what Yeshua said—that when we see the armies surrounding the city, we should flee. He has been preparing a place for us."

"Grandfather, I have wanted to ask you this for a long time. Why do you have blond hair and blue eyes, like Antonius?"

"You hardly ever think of him, huh? He chuckled.

Jerusha felt a flush rise in her cheeks and looked away.

"Anonius is a Roman Gaul. The truth is I do not know why I have these traits. I was mocked by my Jewish friends growing up. They called me a half-breed. I ran away and was captured by the Roman army, I became their slave, and then fought my way into Roman citizenship. It was then that I was given the Roman cognomen Regulus, little prince. The Romans honored me more than my own people."

"That's why Father told me not to forget that I was royalty from the tribe of Judah."

"You are royal because you are YHWH's daughter, bought by the blood of Yeshua."

"It's been a long journey, but I know that now."

"Come to the gate." He stood and pulled her to her feet. "Remember when I gave you that word from YHWH, 'the children you shall have, after you lost the other, shall say in your ear, make place for me to dwell?' Look, Jerusha." He pointed to the celebration. "Many have come. YHWH's sons and daughters, a royal family. You are not cursed. You're a mother of nations."

"What good is a mother without a father?" She walked back to the bench. "I miss Timon."

"The only father Timon knew was YHWH, until your father apprenticed him. YHWH will send another man for your sons at the right time."

"Timon gave his blessing to marry again, but no man can take his place."

"Antonius, maybe?" He grinned.

"Yeshua is my husband now." She looked at the twinkle in his eyes and crossed her arms under her chest. "His love is enough." She lifted her chin and up and down for emphasis, but wondered if she spoke to convince herself more than him. His grin spread wider.

"Neither death, nor life, nor principalities, nor powers, nor things present, nor things to come, can separate you from Yeshua's love." He cupped her chin and lifted her face. "But don't be afraid to love another man. Your eye has not seen, your ear has not heard, nor has entered into your heart what YHWH has prepared for you." He stood and pulled her up. "I must go. I will be in Perea with my father if you need me." He kissed her cheek and hugged her. "Do not tell anyone I have come. When the time is right, I will be back to Jerusalem and reveal that I am alive." He stepped away and peered into her eyes, then turned and disappeared in the darkness.

She grasped her lion and butterfly pendant. "Timon, my love. Would it be all right for your little butterfly to fly to another man?" she whispered. "Oh, this is foolishness." She began to pace the garden walk. "Though the fig tree should not blossom, and there be no fruit on the vines, though the yield of the olive should fail, and the fields produce no food, and the flocks should be cut off from the fold, and there be no cattle in the stalls." She stopped pacing. "And I have no husband, except Yeshua." She smiled. "Yet I will exult in YHWH." She extended her hands to heaven. "I will rejoice in the God of my salvation." She twirled around. "The Lord God is my strength. He has made my feet like hinds' feet, and makes me walk on my high places." Her feet kept time to the music in the courtyard and she twirled around and around, her hands lifted to Yeshua.

Breathless, she stopped and looked into the night sky at Regulus. It shone brighter and brighter until its light encompassed her. She fell on her knees. A golden door opened before her eyes. Children laughed and ran from flower to flower, chasing butterflies. Sarah held her hand up to Timon. A beautiful purple butterfly fluttered and landed on it. She giggled and laughed. He turned his head, and looked at Jerusha, a twinkle in his eye and that endearing lopsided grin. Jerusha reached for him. "Timon." Tears ran down her cheeks as the image faded into the black sky.

"Ima," Stephen came running from the gate. "Why are you on your knees?" He came close and put his face in hers. "Don't cry, Ima." He wiped her tears with his hand. "Antonius is here."

Epilogue

"Though the fig tree should not blossom." The words vibrated from earth and pierced the darkness.

"She is doing it again." The reptilian creatures shrunk back into the blackness. "Her love is stronger."

"And there be no fruit on the vines." Vibrations rumbled beneath her feet, like thunder.

"Though the yield of the olive should fail. And the fields produce no food." The sound increased in volume and vibration.

"Agh! Clawed fingers covered their ears.

"Though the flock should be cut off from the fold and there be no cattle in the stalls."

"Stop! Stop!" Black-hooded imps screamed.

"I will exult in the Lord." The thundering decree shook the darkness.

Yellow globes blinked. "We killed her husband, and still she worships."

"I will rejoice in the God of my salvation. The Lord God is my strength." Diamond-like sparkles scattered into the atmosphere with every twirl and dip she made and exploded into the second heaven blackness.

"He heard." The serpent leader's chest expanded. "His warriors are coming!" He rose up. "Attack! Attack!"

Glittering swords slashed the darkness with light and pressed back the black warriors.

"He has made my feet like hinds' feet." With every twirl she advanced toward the open portal above, each step guided to the light landings provided.

"He makes me walk on my high places." His glory cloud exploded through an open portal and surrounded her with a protective covering as she ascended to His throne.

"Your kingdom come. Your will be done. On earth as it is in heaven."

"No! This earth belongs to me." The serpent screamed as he looked up through the portal and groaned. The King touched her head with the scepter. "Mother of nations rule." Light vibrations exploded out of her belly. The portal closed as she descended to earth.

Galatians 4:21–27

Tell me, you who want to be under the law, do you listen to the law? For it is written that Abraham has two sons, one by the bondwoman and one by the free woman. But the son by the bondwoman was born according to the flesh, and the son by the free woman through the promise. **For this is allegorically speaking***: for these women are two covenants, one proceeding from mount Sinai in Arabia and corresponds to the present Jerusalem, for she is in slavery with her children.* **But the Jerusalem above is free, she is our mother.** *For it is written, Rejoice, barren woman who does not bear; Break forth and shout, you who are not in labor; For more are the children of the desolate than of the one who has a husband.*

Sons and Daughters

My greatest desire is to walk with you on your journey here on earth as you accomplish everything written in your book of destiny. (Psalm 139:16). I AM the one who goes before you to prepare the way and walks behind you as your rear guard. I will never leave you or forsake you. I gave my Son's life to make a way back into my family. I have always loved you and always will. There is nothing you have done, or will ever do, that will block my love for you. I wait only for you to turn to me and embrace my love. My love never fails. Even when you are groping in darkness, I am there and will show you the way.

Your loving Father, the One who created you and who has plans to prosper you and not harm you.

About the Author

L inda Fergerson, a gifted storyteller and dancer, has a passion to see the Father's sons and daughters enter into their royal destiny. Dancing in initimacy with Yeshua helped break many of the chains of worthlessness, anger, and rejection that accompanied the sexual abuse she experienced as a child from a neighbor boy.

For several years she held "A Night with the King" meetings for women in her basement. After the women partook of a meal at the King's table, they stepped into His royal presence and listened as His sweet voice whispered love songs to their hearts.

Later, she ministered in Israel with Warring Dove International. She walked the shores of the Sea of Galilee, danced in Jerusalem, and had a divine encounter with Yeshua at Shiloh.

As vice president of Women's Aglow in her hometown of Dodge City, Kansas, she gained a desire to see Holy Spirit–led worship and prayer overtake the city.

She founded His Writers, a writers' group that prayed and interceded for editors, writers, and publishers to hear the Father's voice and bring forth the "child of promise" given to them that only they could birth.

Her greatest ministry is to her husband, Steve, and her three adopted sons, Samuel, Stephen, and Joshua.

She's available to speak. Some of the topics she speaks on are the following: Hebrew Dance, Intimacy with the King, and I Will Not Leave You Orphans.

To contact Linda Fergerson for prayer or speaking engagements email her at lfergerson1950@hotmail.com.